W9-AHK-444

THE TIN HAT

Other books by Kevin Bartelme

O'Rourke: another slopsink Chronicle

The Great Wall of New York

The Great Redstone

Ain't Life Swell

upcoming:
Let them Eat Rubbish
(short stories 2020)

THE TIN HAT

THE TIN HAT

a novel by
KEVIN BARTELME

Coolgrove Press, NY

Copyright © 2020 Kevin Bartelme

Coolgrove Press, an imprint of
Cool Grove Publishing, Inc. New York.
512 Argyle Road, Brooklyn, NY 11218
All rights reserved under the International and
Pan-American Copyright Conventions.
www. coolgrove. com
For permissions and other inquiries
write to info@coolgrove. com

ISBN 13: 978-1-887276-86-3 • ISBN-10: 1-887276-86-6
Library of Congress Control Number: 2018956651

Book design: coolgrovearts

Coolgrove Press is a past recipient of
Community of Literary Magazines and Presses [CLMP]'s
Face Out Re-grant funded by
the Jerome Foundation.

This book is distributed to the trade by SPDBooks

Media alchemy by Kiku

Coolgrove Press NY

THE TIN HAT

For all the spirits of the departed who just won't leave us alone.

In the beginning was the Word and the bird, bird, bird, the bird is a word! The real Word, however, it's secret... You didn't know it in the beginning, and you won't know it in the end!
  —The Grand Poobah Zofar

THE TIN HAT

1

"I am not a paranoid. Not in the normal sense anyway. Even if I were, just remember even paranoids have enemies. Just remember that. So take a moment and let me tell you what's going on. It's not an opinion, it's a fact. Number one, you don't have any control over your own mind. Everything you think, everything you feel, everything you do has been organized by someone else since the day you were born. You are immersed in propaganda so deep and pervasive that you don't even recognize it. After all, it's your natural environment. You do what it tells you to do, you feel what it tells you to feel, and, above all, you think what it tells you to think. You don't really exist at all. You are just a figment of someone else's imagination. Now things get really interesting. If you are a figment of someone's imagination, is that someone a figment of someone else's imagination? You can see where this is going, can't you? Frankly, I can't. But I'm trying. At least I'm trying, which is more than I can say about all the zombies standing in line with me at the check out line in the grocery store.

"Speaking of groceries, I eat gluten. In fact, I eat all the gluten I can get. Within reasonable limits, of course. Bread is and always has been the staff of life. For tens of thousands of years. So who are all these freaks babbling about how it's poisonous or something. And one more thing. Their gluten free dough is completely unworkable without adding sugar. Sugar!"

"So what do we have here?" Professor Gershem looked up from the note he was reading aloud and threw the question open to the five Ph.D candidates in his graduate seminar on abnormal psychology. "What sort of person wrote this?"

"A nut," the fat class comic wisecracked.

"Thanks for your perceptive diagnosis, David, but what sort of nut is this guy?"

"I think he's a paranoid schizophrenic," Rhoda Memberman suggested.

"Why is that?"

"Well, the first thing he claims is that he's not paranoid. Then he goes on to say we are all being controlled by propaganda. Everyone but him, that is. That's sort of the same thing as voices in his head that no one else can hear."

"Okay," said Professor Gershem, "now we're getting somewhere, but paranoid schizophrenia is a really strong term. How about someone just walking down the street listening to their iPod? They're hearing voices too."

"But those voices are real," Akisha Lumumba objected. "If you put on the iPod you can hear them too."

"So if everybody was listening to the same iPod tune, this guy would be perfectly fine," said Barry Breen. "That's just monotheism. One voice, one word."

"You're not just talking about monotheism," Akisha objected. "You're talking about patriarchalism, the white man with the long white beard who looks like Santa Claus coming down the mountain like Charlton Heston with the Ten Commandments."

"No one shall pry my stones from these arthritic old hands!" David Kogan erupted theatrically.

"I think Akisha might have a point," said Breen. "Actually, Moses was the very last person in the Bible to talk to God so that makes him the final authority on God's wishes."

"Why are we talking theology?" Rhoda Memberman complained. "The guy who wrote what Professor Gershem just read doesn't even mention religion. He seems more concerned about his digestive system than God. Don't do it," she warned David Kogan. "You're going to say the guy must be Jewish. Ha, ha, ha."

"You said it, not me," said Kogan.

"I think we're all missing the point here," Professor Gershem tried to get the discussion back on track. "This guy is talking about propaganda, not voices in his head. He is talking about human, not divine, agency. He is talking about people manipulating, or attempting to manipulate, other people. By the way, I know nothing about gluten. I'm not a nutritionist. but this guy thinks that the people in the supermarket check-out line are zombies created by some sort of malign conspiracy."

"Apophenia?" said shy Rino Matsui who very rarely spoke at all but, in the Professor's estimation, was the sharpest student in the room.

"Please, elaborate."

"He thinks that the world revolves around him and he's the only one who can read the messages it's sending."

"So he's a solipsist," said the Professor.

"I'm sorry…" said Rino.

"A solipsist is someone who thinks the world, as you just said, revolves around himself alone. Does anyone here ever read their horoscope in the newspaper or wherever? Have any of you ever read a fortune cookie?"

Everyone, of course, murmured in assent.

"Did you ever, even for a tiny split second, think that it actually applied to you?"

"Do you mean the horoscope in the Post isn't true?" David Kogan wailed. "You've ruined my whole day."

Gershem actually had a good heckler put-down to shoot back, which started, "Well, in your case…" but he decided to ignore Kogan.

"What I mean to say is that we all suffer from apophenia, if only in a very mild way. As individuals, we all are occasional victims of self-referential delusions. But that doesn't seem to apply in this case. This guy thinks that everybody is getting the same message but he's the only one that can see through this 'natural environment' as he calls it."

"He's hardly the only one," Breen objected. "There are whole books written on the subject of propaganda. Maybe you should just send him a reading list."

"So when we talk about propaganda, when we talk about a system of indoctrination orchestrated by those in power, what are we really talking about?" Gershem asked his class.

"Government," said Rhoda. "In order to rule, the government has to manipulate the governed. But there's nothing new about that. It's been around through all recorded history and probably well before that."

"As I said before, I don't know much about gluten," said Gershem, "but is this guy a nut? Is he wrong about a deliberate attempt by a small group of people to manipulate everyone else? Is he a tinfoil hat conspiracy theorist or a highly perceptive observer of society as a whole?"

"We can't really analyze him," Breen objected, "without a whole lot more information. Is he one of those guys who think the reptilian shapeshifting Queen of England rules the world through the Satanic Bilderbergers? Is he a big alien invasion enthusiast?"

"You're right, Barry," said Gershem. "We shouldn't draw conclusions based on a single piece of paper but I think this guy's attitude is becoming more and more prevalent in our society. People are reflexively questioning the legitimacy of any sort of official narrative."

"Well, look, we know we're being spied on and we're being lied to about it," said Akisha. "I think that creates a lot of anxiety and the result of all that anxiety is a lot of people think someone is conspiring against them as individuals."

"It makes them feel more important than they really are," said Rhoda. "It simultaneously makes them feel in the know and, because of that, dangerous to the powers that be."

"It's sort of like 'Invasion of the Body Snatchers'," said Kogan. "The iPod People are closing in on him."

"Zombies," Breen corrected him.

"So how to treat this guy?" Gershem asked. "He's going to look at any attempt to disabuse him of his notions as proof of a wider conspiracy, that the therapist is trying to turn him into a zombie."

"And if some shrink tries to put him on some psychoactive drug he'd be right," Akisha observed.

"We don't have to disparage our more pharmaceutically inclined colleagues in the mental health field," said Gershem. "I'm sure a tiny fraction of them are well intentioned."

He got his laugh.

"So that's the problem," said Gershem. "I want to hear your suggestions next time we meet." The professor looked at his watch. "Sorry, I've got to run but I've got meeting in ten minutes. See you all on Tuesday."

The seminar dispersed as usual with everyone going their own ways. The tenuous camaraderie of the classroom seemed to evaporate as soon as they were out the door. But not this time with Barry Breen attempting to converse with exceedingly polite and seemingly unattainable Rino Matsui. "I thought what you said was very interesting. Do you have time for a coffee?"

His spirits soared when she said rather offhandedly, "I think I have a few minutes."

They found a little coffee bar right across and down the street from the main university entrance, and Breen paid for her latte, a most forward thing to do indeed from her point of view.

"You don't have to do that," she said almost petulantly. Actually she was secretly thrilled.

"I just wanted to break this fifty," he explained. "The next one's on you. Just kidding. It's my pleasure. Kanpai," he said lightly bumping his paper coffee cup against hers,

"You speak Japanese?" she said.

"Yes I do. I can count; ichi, ni, uni…"

She giggled. She couldn't help herself.

"I can say thank you very much; *Arigato gozaimasen..*"

This time she squealed with laughter. "Who taught you Japanese? It's so bad."

"You really think so? It's that… yabai?"

She suddenly looked at him with reluctant respect. He was teasing her. He knew what he was saying.

"Perhaps you could teach me more?" he pressed.

"Perhaps. When I've got time."

"Why don't you give me your phone number?"

"Give me your phone number. I'll call you." She looked at her watch. "Now, really, I have to go. Thank you for the coffee."

As she walked off down the street, it was impossible not to notice that little extra swing in her hips.

"What do they want anyway?" Breen mumbled with no extra swing in his hips at all.

Professor Gershem, who had been summoned by the head of the department, along with two other senior faculty members, to discuss a matter as yet to be disclosed, was the last person to enter the room, and the meeting commenced on his arrival.

"Sorry I'm late," he apologized. "My students just wouldn't stop asking questions."

"I thought you were a clinician, Ted," his colleague Alan Garret needled him. "You're supposed to ask the questions, not answer them."

"You have a point there."

"Well, now that we're all here," said Alvin Spurtz, "I can tell you what this is all about and I don't want this discussion to leave the room. The department has been offered a rather substantial amount of money for research purposes. Actually, it's a government contract but we're not supposed to know that. The funding will be provided by a private foundation right here in New York, the Spuyten Duyvil Trust. They want us to do a study on the psychological aspects of the notions of good and evil. What do people think is good? What do they think is evil? And why?"

"Isn't it all relative?" Alan Garret asked. "I mean we think eating other people is horrifying but a cannibal has an entirely different opinion."

"Exactly," said Spurtz. "The question is how do people acquire and maintain these conceptions, these perspectives."

"This sounds like anthropology," said Conrad Boardman.

"That may be, "said Spurtz, "but we don't want the anthropology department to get the grant, do we?"

They all laughed.

"But seriously," Spurtz continued, " I think, with the aid of our many grad students, we can put together a report by the deadline."

"What's the deadline?" Gershem asked.

"It's the government," said Spurtz. "We could spend the rest of our lives working on this and even pass it on to our grandchildren."

"In other words," said Boardman, "the deadline is when they bury us in the cold, cold ground."

"Well, that's one way to put it," Spurtz agreed enthusiastically.

"Talk about a sinecure," Garret agreed. "Where to even begin?"

And so, under no particular pressure, they outlined a plan for their inquiry into the psychological origins of the nature of good and evil and left Spurtz's office on collegial terms with the assurance they would be equally rewarded for their efforts and might possibly aspire to some sort of award or other.

As they walked down the hall together toward the exit, Gershem and Garret considered the nuts and bolts of such a study.

"You must have had a few patients with strong opinions on the subject, I mean paranoids and the like," said Garret.

"Not nearly enough for a survey study. I think we're going to have to go to Bellevue or Pilgrim State or something like that for the kind of numbers we need. But then, why not just average people? You don't have to be nuts to have a take on good and evil."

"You may have a point," said Garret equivocally. "What's your take?"

"Are you calling me average?"

Gershem walked out the door of the building thinking of his much younger Israeli wife who had deserted him as soon as she got her green card. He wondered what poor sap she was hustling now as he walked down the street to his apartment on West End Avenue. The large space, some six rooms, presented him with something he could never fill again so he only went into the kitchen and his bedroom. Even the study with all his books had been abandoned to the maid's occasional feather dusting. It was too early to go to his favorite Chinese restaurant on Broadway so he sat down at the kitchen table and began writing notes on possible groups of people to interview for the new project. Religious people, of course, the more hardcore fundamentalist the better. Political extremists were definitely another fertile hotbed of material on the subject. And, of then again, there were conspiracy theorists who abounded on all sides of the political and religious spectra. As a psychologist he was not much interested in religion, though he had read quite a few books on its expression of unconscious forces, but it certainly was central to the notions of good and evil to which large numbers of people subscribed. Politics was more about economics with a healthy dollop of jingoism, war-making technology, and unparalleled corruption to spice up the stew. Good and evil sat in the back of a shiny bus being driven by greed and the lust for power. Conspiracy theorists such as the patient who'd written the note he'd just read in class, on the other hand, came from the left, the right, the fervently religious, the atheists, and the completely deranged. There was no clear agenda and there were tens of millions of them lurking out there, flooding the Internet with their opinions and proofs. This wildly disparate group was the one Gershem decided to study. In retrospect, it might not have been the wisest choice.

The first thing he would do was have his students scour the Internet for every conspiracy theory they could find. Then they would categorize and cross-reference them, since many seemed to overlap. After that, they would try and set up interviews with the various theorists. It all seemed so simple and logical at the time. What was in store, however, would not be so simple or logical at all. But innocent abroad Gershem did not know that yet and happily went off for supper at the appropriate time to King Wok Szechuan where the staff knew better than to serve him anything with monosodium glutamate which made him break out in a rash. Or so he claimed. No doctor had confirmed this allergy and one had even implied it was psychosomatic.

While he was sitting eating his moo goo gai pan, he wondered what the Chinese conception of good and evil was, but he didn't know how to broach the subject with the professionally obsequious waiter. It was early and there were very few customers in the restaurant so Gershem decided to give it a shot.

"Wo Chung, what do you think the difference between bad and good is?"

The waiter reacted with alarm. "Moo goo gai pan no good?" he asked.

"No, no," Gershem reassured him. "It's very good. That's not really my question."

"No? What you want?"

"Forget it."

"Yes, I will," Wo Chung nodded and smiled.

Gershem decided the Chinese were too inscrutable to seriously discuss good and evil. Or too smart to think about good and evil at all.

At loose ends after he'd dined, he decided to walk south down Broadway to a local bar that he knew, the Stay Put Club, where the crowd was more or less his age and it was highly unlikely that he would run into any of his students. Wouldn't do to get caught quaffing a scotch and soda with a bunch of semi-inebriated regulars, most of whom knew him by name. It was, however, as good a place as any to poll the clientele on the nature of good and evil.

Gershem went into the bar, took an available seat, was brought his drink without even ordering, and immediately confronted with an old acquaintance, John Connelly, asking him, "Say there, Ted, how about those Mets?"

The question, of course, was just a joke. Gershem decided to dig right in.

"John, are you Catholic?"

"Does the Pope shit in the woods? But I haven't confessed since I had a whole lot of things to confess about. I mean, would you go tell some silly old faggot sitting in a phone booth that you'd just had a three-way with two teenage girls? Would you?"

"I don't think you're being compassionate," Al Griffin butted in. "That guy would be jerking off like crazy if you told him the story."

"So the priest would consider it evil and you didn't?" Gershem pressed on.

"Whaddaya, kidding?" Connelly retorted. "It was one of the best times I ever had in my life."

"You didn't feel guilty or anything?"

"Guilty? Why should I? It was their idea."

Everyone laughed and Griffin said, "Well, you've confessed already so just drink three Bloody Marys and take a cold shower."

The irony laden sense of humor peculiar to New York City was a fortress against the intrusion of philosophical questions, which would always be met with derision, Gershem realized. He had to find people brimming with romantic prejudice who considered anything humorous or satiric as frivolous and lacking any serious intent, the people who meditated on the woes of the world and simply did not get the joke.

Just at that moment, Anna Bunch came into the bar in all her not quite over the hill floozy glory and was greeted by the congregation.

"Anna," said Connelly as she took the seat right next to Gershem, "Ted here has brought up a question on the nature of good and evil."

"He has? What do you want to know, Ted?" she vamped. "Have I been naughty or nice?"

"I'm not Santa Claus," Gershem pointed out.

"Oh," said Anna despondently, " Just when I thought I could sit on your lap and tell you what I want for Christmas."

"Okay, then I am Santa Claus," he quickly rejoined. "Come, sit." He'd wanted to fuck Anna Bunch since he'd first met her but they'd never got around to it. Maybe tonight was the night.

Anna seemed to be of the same mind. She turned toward him and pressed her knee against his leg. "So what's with this good and evil stuff? You mean like the Devil?" she asked as the bartender set down her Margarita.

"Some people look at it that way, I guess."

"The scary devil or cute Li'l Hot Stuff? I'm a big fan of a little hot stuff every now and then." The sexual innuendo was too blatant to ignore.

"So you didn't tell me if you've been naughty or nice," said Gershem.

"I didn't, did I?" Then she leaned close and whispered in his ear. "When we've finished our drinks, you leave first. I'll meet you on the corner." She didn't want to stir up any more gossip than she usually did.

Two drinks later, after some convivial bar banter, Gershem said good night to all, walked down to the corner and took a seat on a convenient bus bench. Five minutes later, Anna Bunch joined him and they took the short walk to her apartment on 106th Street. He had never been there before and was surprised by its sleek, minimal appearance. He'd expected something more cluttered. She sat him down on the black leather couch and adjourned to another room down the hall. When she returned in stiletto heels, she was stark naked, thrusting forth her magnificently pelted mons pubis and holding a fly swatter in her hand. Needless to say, Gershem was startled by this sudden transition and even more befuddled when she handed him the fly swatter and knelt down on the floor with her Rubenesque ass in the air.

"Give me an A, professor," she moaned. "Give me an A plus."

"What are you doing?" he demanded.

"Don't worry," she smiled up at him. "Just do it. Spank me. I like it."

Now, Gershem was neither a prude nor a complete naif. Many years ago he'd once tied a girl's hands together with her own panties before he had his way with her. At her own request, of course. So…

He lightly swatted Anna on her raised behind.

"Harder, harder," she moaned. "Punish me!"

Suddenly, the clinician in Gershem came out. "Why do you want to be punished?"

"I've been naughty, Santa. So naughty," she panted. "Spank me!"

He swatted her harder.

"Oh yeah," she moaned. "Swat those flies!"

Later, after he fucked her doggy style, they lay sweating on the floor in each other's arms.

"That was so good it was evil!" she gasped.

"Hmm," was all Gershem could manage. Was feeling good evil? The Puritans thought so. It was certainly distracting.

Their little party was rudely interrupted by an insistent knocking on her door.

"Who is it?!" Anna yelled.

"Ricardo!" came back the muffled answer

"Just a minute!"

As Gershem quickly dressed Anna retrieved a robe from her bedroom and opened the door a crack.

"The people downstairs complaining dampness coming through the ceiling," Ricardo, a short Puerto Rican in a T-shirt and sweats explained. "You got any leaks?"

"Not that I know of," she said evasively.

"You know what I mean," he leered.

"Not tonight, Ricardo," said Anna and closed the door in his face.

"The super," Anna blithely informed Gershem. "I think he's got a thing for me."

"I can't say I blame him."

"You're so sweet, Ted," she purred.

"Well, I guess I should be running along. Busy day tomorrow," he said and kissed her on the cheek.

She saw him to the door. "Thanks for the fun. Let's do it again sometime."

"Let's."

Safely back in his own kitchen, Gershem called his students and invited them in for a special meeting where he intended to exploit their talents and time for no pay for his own benefit, something like a plantation owner. "Way down upon the Suwannee River." he hummed before retiring to his bedroom.

❖

2

The next day, Professor Gershem and his students once again convened, this time in the much smaller confines of his office, and he strongly suggested that they reconsider their thesis subjects in light of the new project. To say strongly suggested is a collegial term implying they could mull things other and take his suggestion or not. In reality, it was a flat out order to anyone who wanted to have the grand title of Doctor of Philosophy conferred upon them.

"The specific area I want you all to address is very much like the note I read to you yesterday, I want you to comb any sort of information you can come up with on conspiracy theories, no matter how seemingly reasonable or completely insane. We will meet on a weekly basis and compare notes as we refine the inquiry with special emphasis on the various theorists' conceptions of good and evil, which will assuredly differ wildly. You should all exchange phone numbers, if you haven't already, and keep your fellow researchers abreast of any discoveries that your colleagues might find of immediate interest."

Music to Barry Breen's ears. He was certainly going to report any "discoveries" he made straight to Rino Matsui.

"What we're trying to do here," Gershem justified himself, "is get to the root of how people look at the world in terms of their hopes and fears. We're up to nothing less than defining the cognitive imperative vis a vis good and evil through the motive forces we see all around us."

"That's a pretty tall short order," said Breen. "I mean people have been working on this for centuries."

"You're absolutely right," said Gershem, "but yours is not to reason why; yours is to do and get your Ph.D."

"I wanted to write my thesis on how the feminine subconscious responds to male domination," Rhoda Memberman complained.

"What's the title?" said David Kogan, "What Do I Want Anyway?"

"I think that might be pretty fertile ground for this study, Rhoda," said Gershem. "The whole Mars versus Venus thing. A lot of feminists think the whole structure of society is a male conspiracy to subjugate women."

"It's not a conspiracy," said Rhoda sourly. "It's a well-known, very much out in the open fact."

The point of this rebuke did not escape Gershem. "I'm not forcing anyone to participate in this project. It's just a suggestion. Write your thesis on anything you like."

"Okay," she said, "what if I go along with you? Am I free to investigate any kind of conspiracy theory out there?"

'Absolutely," said Gershem. "I mean that. Just so long as the conspiracy theorists think they are good and those conspiring against them are evil. I've put together a syllabus of books on the topic that you can reference but the idea is really to come up with completely original research and draw our own conclusions independent of what anyone has said before."

"So you want us to read the books and then just forget about them?" Kogan asked.

"Not exactly. I want you to be aware of the literature on conspiracy theory precisely so you can take a fresh point of view. Then, of course there is the evidence you will be gathering on your own."

"How about slavery? Is that a conspiracy?" Akisha asked.

"Hmm, interesting question," said Gershem who, if he had a pipe, would have taken a thoughtful tug. "Actually slavery was a quite openly conducted business. There was no hidden agenda. Certain people were regarded as property and that was that," Gershem responded. "It was the abolition of slavery that involved a number of conspiracies such as John Brown's raid and the Underground Railroad. The very complexity of that system would fit right into this study."

"So conspiracies don't have to be evil?"

"Point taken. Conspiracies might not be evil, but from the point of view of the slaveholders they were definitely an affront to their entire society and that's what this study is all about. What did the slaveholders think was good and evil? There are a number of people that believe that space aliens are trying to save the earth from itself," said Gershem. "They just haven't been doing a very good job of it."

The class chuckled.

"You're making fun of my question, " said Akisha. "There are conspiracies that can be called good."

"I'm not making fun. I completely agree. The conspiracy to assassinate Hitler, for example."

"That didn't work out very well," said Breen.

"That's not the point. To serve Hitler in the first place was evil. But did the conspirators try to assassinate him based on a sudden repentant epiphany or out of pure expedience?"

"You're talking about moral relativism," said Rhoda Memberman.

"Call it whatever you want. Doesn't everybody, every day of their lives face some moral dilemma, no matter how minor?"

"Kenneth Burke said that morality is all based on the situation we're in, that we define what's good and what's bad within certain specific circumstances," said Rino Matsui.

"Exactly," said Gershem. How did this little Japanese girl know about Kenneth Burke anyway? "And that's that we're going to investigate, the very formation of the concept of good and evil in the minds of individuals and groups of individuals. Now I suggest we all get on our computers and collect every conspiracy theory out there, no matter how ludicrous or insane. After that, we'll cross check them, divide them into categories and each one of you can choose your particular area of interest."

"I've already made my choice," said David Kogan. "I only want to deal with the ludicrous and insane ones."

"Who would've guessed?" said Rhoda Memberman.

"This is an abnormal psychology seminar, isn't it?" Kogan shot back.

Gershem shook his head "Okay, all of you get out of here and get to work."

Leaving the classroom, he ran into Conrad Boardman in the hallway. "Ted, you're doing conspiracy theory, right? I think I've got a hot lead for you."

"Really? What's that?" said Gershem, half expecting a joke.

"There's this group that meets downtown every Thursday night in St. Marks Church basement to discuss 9/11. Anyone can join in so it must be a real wacko carnival."

"Thanks. Maybe I'll check it out."

It just happened to be Thursday and Gershem wondered if it was worth the effort to haul his ass downtown to listen to a bunch of people obsessed with an event that had taken place seventeen years ago. Well, he had nothing else to do. Why not?

So, that very evening, Gershem betook himself to the East Village and entered into a meeting of the believers with one troll so obvious the rest of the assembled disparaged him right to his face. His defense was passive aggression: "There was no conspiracy. Just read Popular Mechanics. You're picking on me because you know I'm right!" Gershem had seen this type many times in treatment and immediately recognized the most egregious symptoms; total identification with authority, lack of logical coherence, and stubborn resilience in the face of attack, which they actually seemed to welcome.

One of the wits in the crowd of mostly middle-aged men spoke to this troll. "Bernie, I understand you're mother is sick in Las Vegas."

"How did you know that?" was Bernie's suspicious reply.

"Let's just say word gets around. Are you going to visit her? I guess it's expensive."

"I don't see that's any of your business," Bernie muttered.

"No, of course not," he man agreed, "and I know we've had our differences, but I think you should be able to see her if you want and I'm willing to buy you the ticket."

Bernie was clearly startled by the offer. "That's very kind..." he stammered.

"One way," the other punched the line.

The rest of the people in the room all snickered and guffawed making Gershem respond with completely uncalled for sympathy, but isn't that what passive aggression was all about? Bernie was calling the tune here and he knew it.

"I see we have a new member here with us tonight," the jokester surprised Gershem. "I'm Baxter Allen. Welcome to the congregation."

"Ted Gershem," Gershem replied simply.

Everyone murmured their welcome and Gershem wondered whether the whole thing was going to devolve down to some sort of twelve step meeting.

"Okay," said Allen, "Walter's got something from the flat-earthers."

"I know you're just joking, Baxter," Walter, a portly gent with long grey hair wearing a poncho, protested, "but you can't just pigeonhole people whose beliefs differ from the norm as cranks and loonies. There is some evidence that suggests the earth really is flat."

"And that's why everybody calls us cranks and loonies."

Oddly enough, at least to Gershem, the conversation carried along in this vein for another hour and a half without the subject of 9/11 coming up at all. It was as if the years had depleted the event of any significance except as a touchstone for paranoia in general, a central reference point in the cosmogony of conspiracy theory that no longer existed in any kind of tangible, viceral way. The cry, "Remember 9/11!" was now just another slogan echoing down the hall, like "Remember the Alamo!", completely devoid of meaning and context.

As the meeting drew to a close and the theorists dispersed, Baxter Allen called after them. "Donations accepted! This coffee doesn't grow on trees, you know!"

"Bushes!" someone called back. "The Bushes are responsible for everything!"

Outside, Gershem was approached by a man in a black velveteen cape, the Grand Poobah Zofar actually, though he didn't introduce himself as such. "Please allow me introduce myself," he said, "Edward Smith. What on earth brings you to our little, long forgotten conclave?"

Gershem decided to be blunt. "I'm doing a study on the nature of good and evil and I thought 9/11 theorists might give me some perspective on the way perceptions of good and bad, right and wrong, are formed."

"Talk about biting off more than you can chew!" Smith guffawed.

"I know it sounds like a rather broad subject…"

"Rather broad! What say you and I have a drink? I know a place right down the street."

Before Gershem could either accept or decline the man's invitation, Smith took him by the arm and propelled him across the street to the east. In short order, they entered a small dive where Gershem was content to sit at the bar but his companion insisted on a small table in a dark corner. "I'm a regular. This table is my spot, my regular spot," he explained.

Once Smith had procured them drinks he proposed a toast: "To friends both old and new! So it's good and evil you're after. You certainly won't find them with that sorry lot at the meeting. They're just looking for the Wizard of Oz."

Gershem decided to play along with his new acquaintance as one might humor an interesting nut. He was usually paid for this service but this one was obviously on the house.

"But they must see the conspirators behind 9/11 as malign, as evil."

"Who cares what they see?"

"Well, for professional reasons I guess I do."

"I guess you would," Smith pooh-poohed him. "But you don't know anything yet. You don't have the slightest idea."

"You said 'yet'," Gershem pressed him. "Perhaps you'd care to enlighten me."

"Well, I'm going to give it a shot. Not my best shot, mind you. I'm saving that for later, but just enough to let you to know that I know that you understand I'm not talking through my hat. What do you say?"

"You're not wearing a hat." Gershem was beginning to regret his own promiscuous amiability. "So give it a shot."

"Not my best, not my best," Smith cautioned him. "Just a little something for now. Are you ready?"

Vaguely bemused Gershem was ready. "Go for it."

"The Devil is a myth. Satan is a myth."

Gershem chuckled. "Gee, Edward, next you'll be telling me there's no Santa Claus. Don't spoil all my illusions." He looked at his watch, slugged down his drink, and started to get up. "Listen, it's been nice…"

"You don't understand what I'm saying. Mythology is far more powerful than reality."

The Grand Poobah had caught Gershem's attention. He sat back down.

"It's much easier to fool people than it is to convince them they've been fooled, even if the evidence is overwhelming. They believe what they're told to believe, no matter how silly or insane."

"I'll go along with that, but what's it got to do with formation of concepts?"

Smith seemed puzzled by Gershem's response. "Don't you see? Everything! Good and evil are part of a belief system. It's not necessary that they actually exist. What's necessary is that people subscribe to a set of definitions."

"I think you're missing my point. I'm not interested in the putative existence of any given concept; I'm interested in how it's formed, how it's passed on, and how people react when it's challenged."

"Wooo, heavy stuff," Smith mocked him. "Okay, let's look at the belief that when a plane crashes into a building it leaves a perfect contour of itself as it passes cleanly through the outer wall instead of being smashed to pieces. Where did people acquire this belief? Blind acceptance of the televised image? Certainly not from an elementary school science book which contradicts the notion on every level with its pesky laws of motion, thermodynamics, and conservation of energy. I put it to you that they got it from watching Road Runner cartoons."

Gershem laughed. "The funny thing is you're probably right."

"They have been conditioned since they were very young to simply accept this physical impossibility and even vehemently defend it. Wile E. Coyote's numerous silhouetted disasters prove it! Besides, who paid any attention to their sixth grade science book anyway?"

"I can't say I remember much of it," Gershem agreed.

"But you remember the Road Runner! You remember Wile E. Coyote!"

"I do indeed."

"Well, so did the people who made the mockumentary epic, "The Planes Crash into the WTC."

"Tell me something, Edward. Why didn't anyone discuss the World Trade Center tonight?"

"They're tired of it. It's not sexy anymore."

After some more chatting, the Grand Poobah noted that his harridan wife would be waiting up for him – "The love of my life, fire of my loins, the bane of my existence!" – and they took their leave with an agreement to reconvene at the 9/11 meeting the following week. It wasn't until Gershem got home that he noticed his wallet was missing.

He had always thought of himself as nobody's fool but Edward Smith had apparently proven otherwise and all he could do now was gnash his teeth and look forward with dread to reconstituting all the documents that lent credence to his existence and to his position in the society as a whole - his driver's license, his faculty card, his medical I.D., not to mention his Visa and Mastercards, which he stopped immediately.

Faith in one's fellow man is often misplaced, especially in a city like New York, and Gershem kicked himself repeatedly for allowing himself to be conned by a man who had himself had said it was easier to fool someone than convince them they'd been taken to the cleaners. The man had said it right to his face as he deftly picked his pocket and Gershem had ignored this obvious red flag much like an ingénue being offered a role by a seducer producer. He'd gotten the part all right– Mr. John Q. Sucker.

As he quietly fulminated, the phone rang. Barely able to control his sore vexation, he picked up the receiver and snapped, "Hello?"

"Ted? This is Edward Smith. You left your wallet behind at the bar. I've got it right here and I can get it back to you anytime that's convenient."

Gershem's spirits took a one hundred eighty degree turn, soaring aloft from the black pits of dejection as he tried to contain his relief and glee. "Edward! That's great! I noticed it was missing just a moment ago."

"All's well that ends well," said the Grand Poobah. "Losing your wallet isn't the end of the world but it's close. Now what can we do about getting it back to you?"

They agreed to meet the very next day at a coffee shop on Second Avenue near Fourteenth Street. After that, Gershem would proceed to his bank and get his credit cards reinstated. Not for a second did he reflect on his snap judgment of Smith as a thief. The painfully complicated had turned into a mere nuisance and, as he brushed his teeth, he found himself humming, "Oops, there goes another rubber tree plant," which made him feel a little foolish when he noticed what he was doing.

❖

3

The next morning, Gershem took the train to Times Square and caught the shuttle to Grand Central, but the shuttle wasn't going anywhere. After waiting fifteen minutes in the station, the passengers were informed by the public address system that service had been suspended and that they should seek other transportation across town. Gershem looked at his watch, realized he was going to be late for his appointment, and pulled out his cell phone to give Smith a call. He then realized he could not give Smith a call because he didn't know his number. He looked at his call history and found that Smith's return number was blocked. What to do? Get a cab, of course.

When he got outside on the street, the sidewalks were bustling with the rush hour crowd and unoccupied taxis were scarce. He decided to walk down Broadway where all the rag trade people would be arriving for work and there was bound to be a cab dropping off a fare. Still, it took another ten minutes to find one and he had to fight for it at that.

"That's my cab!" an imperious woman barked at him.

"Sorry, lady," said Gershem as he slammed the door behind him and gave the driver instructions.

"Fuck you!" she shrieked after him.

As traffic crawled down the avenue at a snail's pace, Gershem kept looking at his watch and getting more and more agitated. Then his phone rang.

"Hello?"

"Hey there," said Edward Smith. "I just wanted to be sure you were going to make it what with all that mess in midtown."

"I'm in a cab right now. What mess in midtown?"

"You haven't heard? Terrible accident at Grand Central. A young woman got caught between a train and the platform and got sucked right down. Not much left of her, I guess."

"That is terrible," Gershem agreed.

"A twister. I believe that's what they call that sort of accident. That's because the victim goes down spinning like a top, blood and gristle flying everywhere."

"Is that so? Pretty gruesome. Well, anyway, I'll be there as soon as traffic allows." After he hung up, Gershem realized he still didn't have Smith's number.

The cab arrived at his destination a half hour late and Gershem found the coffee shop where Edward Smith was waiting.

"Sorry I'm late. Couldn't be helped."

Smith chuckled as he pushed Gershem's wallet across the table. "In these troubled times, even getting from uptown to downtown becomes an unwelcome adventure."

"Thanks so much for doing this," said Gershem. "Now I just have to get these bank cards reinstated and I'm all set."

"You stopped your cards?" This news seemed to disturb Smith.

"Of course I stopped the cards."

"You don't trust me?"

"I stopped them before you called. Of course I trust you."

Smith seemed relieved. "Wouldn't do for new friends not to trust each other, would it? Oh, I think I've got something for you, someone you should interview."

"One of the 9/11 people?

"No, no. Argyle is on the cosmic plane, an astrophysicist of the illusory universe."

"Well, okay," said Gershem as the waitress set down a cup of coffee and a roll in front of him. "How do I get in touch with him?"

"You don't. He gets in touch with you."

"You're making this sound very mysterious," Gershem humored him.

"There's nothing mysterious about him. He simply likes to initiate things himself rather than be petitioned. I'll talk to him and he'll call."

"Fair enough. When do you think this might happen?"

"Right now," said Smith and got on his phone. "Argyle? It's

Edward. I have someone who'd like to meet you. His number is 212 637-4713... Right."

Almost immediately, Gershem's phone rang. "Hello?"

"Hello, this is Argyle. I understand you want to meet me."

"Yes, well, Edward..."

"Is right now okay with you?"

"Right now?"

"I mean would you like to meet right now? I'm sitting here in the corner booth to your left."

Gershem looked to his left and there was a man on a cell phone staring at him. "Well, since we're both here..."

The man waved. "Come join me. Tell Edward to get lost," he said and hung up.

"He wants me to join him," Gershem informed Smith. "He said..."

"Well, that's all set," said Smith. "I'll be on my way."

As the Grand Poobah took his leave, Gershem picked up his coffee and roll and made his way to the corner table where he noted that Argyle was a very thin, almost dissipate, middle-aged man with Appaloosa eyes, the kind you can see the sclera all the way around the pupil.

"Please sit down, Mr...ah..."

"Gershem. Ted Gershem."

"Just call me Argyle. I misplaced my last name some time ago. So I understand you're interested in the origins of good and evil. Is that so?"

"Well, actually the individual perceptions of good and evil that people hold."

"Their perceptions don't much matter. Besides, there is no such thing as good in the universe, but there is evil aplenty. Have you heard of the Demiurge?"

"No, I can't say I have."

"The Demiurge created the universe. He degraded spirit by turning it into matter. The only question is whether he is malevolent or merely incompetent. Whatever people's perceptions are, they are automatically skewed by the deeply flawed world around them."

"But you just said there is no good and plenty of evil," Gershem objected. "Dialectically, evil needs good to define it."

"Just so," Argyle agreed, "but that good must necessarily exist outside of this universe. The Demiurge and his mother conspired against the true God to put good aside and bring this dreary, barren cosmos of ours into existence."

"The Demiurge has a mother?"

"Everyone has a mother. Even you and me."

"So the universe itself is a conspiracy. Tell me, how did you come by this information?"

"What do you mean 'come by'? Isn't it perfectly obvious?"

If there was one thing these conspiracy theorists shared, Gershem thought, it was their certainty and their surprise that other people didn't see things exactly the way they saw them. He wondered if he should bring up Burke's terministic screens with Argyle and decided against it. There was no point in antagonizing the man.

"It's not perfectly obvious to me," he said, "but then this is the first time I ever heard of it. Definitely food for thought."

"Please don't patronize me. Your terministic screen is not functioning properly at the moment, but we can put that right."

To say Gershem was startled would be quite the understatement. Was Argyle reading his mind?

Argyle continued. "And I'm not reading your mind. You think I'm nuts, a real 'character', don't you?"

As a good clinician, Gershem was quite prepared to answer a question with a question of his own. "Why do you say that?"

"I say it because it's true. And you can take your cheap psychoanalysis and shove it up your ass." With that, Argyle abruptly got up. "We'll meet again. By the way, I wouldn't eat that thing if I were you." He pointed at the roll. "Gluten." Then he was gone.

Gershem simply sat there in a mild daze. One person in a million even knew what a terministic screen was. But he had other things to do other then contemplate this weird encounter as the waitress reminded him by handing him the check. He was low on cash and he had to go to the bank and get his cards reinstated.

At the closest Citibank (not his own branch), Gershem asked to speak to an officer and after a fifteen minute wait was ushered into the open cubicle office of one Elijah Jones. Gershem explained his situation and showed Jones his old cards and his identification. Jones mulled over the problem and asked:

"How do I know you're not the thief? You tried to use the cards and found out they were stopped. Now you're trying to impersonate the real Theodore Gershem."

"But I am the real Theodore Gershem," Gershem protested. "Look at the pictures on my driver's license and faculty card."

Jones stared hard at the pictures and squinted up at Gershem. "I don't know," he said. "All white people look the same to me."

"Now see here..." Gershem sputtered before he noticed Jones' broad smile.

"I'm sorry, Mr. Gershem," said Jones. "I get so bored sometimes I like to have a little fun with the customers. I'll get your new cards right away."

"Oh, heh, heh," Gershem managed. "Thanks."

In a bit of a funk after the good-natured ribbing by the bank officer (it was good-natured, wasn't it?) and flush with cash, he left the bank and impulsively decided, as long as he was downtown, to walk over to the West Village and revisit some of the haunts of his youth. He soon found himself at the Waverly Place entrance to Washington Square and walked into the park, which was decidedly uncrowded and quiet. In fact, as he walked down the path towards the fountain, the place reminded him more of a cemetery than the festive gathering place he remembered. There were no conga drums, no street performers, there were no hustlers selling weed, there were no more young transients with backpacks, only a sparse crowd of old people idling away on the benches. This was gentrification with a vengeance, as if all the life had been sucked out of the place by real estate vampires disposing of the riff raff. Perhaps they would next put a fence around it like Gramercy Park, making the grounds available only to the chosen few with keys. Now there was a conspiracy he could relate to — the creeping takeover of Manhattan by a cabal of evil realtors intent on throwing him out of his own rent stabilized apartment. He had kept them at bay so far but their insatiable dispossession lust had not abated and required him to remain alert to all their continuing behind-the-scenes machinations to put him out on the street. Such were Gershem's dour thoughts as he passed out of the square at the corner where all the chess players used to congregate and decided to head south. As he walked, he had no idea why someone he didn't know and had never seen before might take an interest in his activities, so he never even bothered to glance over his shoulder as the Happy Shadow followed him down the street at a discreet distance. Not that the distance mattered much. The Happy Shadow was so exquisitely ordinary that he had been rendered nearly invisible by his singular lack of identifying characteristics. Gershem wouldn't have noticed his presence if he were standing right next to him, much less twenty-five feet away. He was, quite literally, indescribable.

Now, you may wonder why the Happy Shadow was following Gershem. The first reason was simple. He had nothing else to do. The second was more complicated. The Happy Shadow had been at the 9/11 meeting and, along with everyone else, duly noted the newcomer. Since Gershem had not spoken except to give his name, most of the regular attendees had assumed he was some sort of police agent. Not that they cared. In fact, it made them feel more important, more of a threat to the long accepted official narrative. The Happy Shadow agreed with their assessment and put the newcomer out of his mind until Gershem just happened to walk by the park bench where the Happy Shadow was eating his morning corn muffin. Needless to say, Gershem had not recognized him and the Happy Shadow, with no particular goal in mind, had decided to follow him on his way. What the Happy Shadow didn't know was that someone else was already following the professor.

Happily unaware of all this attention, Gershem proceeded down MacDougal. It was still morning and almost all of the shops, restaurants, and clubs were shuttered. It looked more or less the same as it had twenty years ago but something had changed. It wasn't a neighborhood anymore. It was "MacDougal Street" floating in formaldehyde like a specimen in a lab jar. It was history and, as Gershem well knew, history was bunk. He stopped in front of the Minetta Tavern, formerly a saloon with caricatures of the patrons all over the walls, now a semi-private club presided over by a celebrity restaurateur who specialized in bar rehab where he sucked out all the flavor of an older establishment and left a husk to be filled with the glitterati of the city, at least until these privileged few moved on to the next watering hole of the moment. All this was of no interest to Gershem who disdained "scenes" of any kind and did his best to avoid them. He wondered if the celebrity restaurateur would one day take over the Stay Put Club and send the regulars packing.

The Happy Shadow, on the other hand, who dwelt in a sort of extroverted solitude since no one ever noticed him, favored the warmth of crowded gatherings, which made him feel less alone than he knew he was. Since he was functionally invisible he could circulate without being noticed and absorb the warmth of the herd, something like a heat favoring reptile. Now the Happy Shadow, who had stopped when Gershem spent a moment looking at the Minetta Tavern, continued along with the object of his attention down to Prince Street.

On that corner, Gershem had an inspiration. He looked straight south where the twin towers used to be and decided to walk down and see what they'd done with the site. There was, of course, the Freedom Tower, which no one ever referred to by that name. In fact, nobody ever mentioned it all as if it were a shameful relative that no one wanted to acknowledge or have anything to do with. Gershem, immersed in a rather morbid state of mind, decided to walk the mile or so downtown and look upon this ersatz resurrection and the adjacent memorial. As he walked down Sixth Avenue, he couldn't help but note all the new high-rises that seemed to have gone up overnight. He had thought the whole area was landmarked but that was apparently not the case. Would the ghost of Robert Moses soon realize his dream of building a freeway straight across the island over Canal Street?

So Gershem walked south on Sixth to its juncture with West Broadway where he continued downtown to "Ground Zero", which the press had labeled an event that had nothing to do with either Hiroshima or Nagasaki, a phrase which had, in fact, been coined by crisis actor Nick Pugh (aka Mark Walsh) on Fox News immediately after the second tower collapsed. But what did

Gershem know about that? He'd only attended one meeting of 9/11 conspiracy theorists and had not yet been exposed to their volumes of evidence.

Upon his arrival at the site, he was greeted by a New Jersey high school marching band in full mufti playing the Star Spangled Banner at the edge of one of the two "reflection pools" which looked like nothing so much as gigantic versions of Michael Heizer's negative space sculptures with water running over them. Gershem didn't know anything about art and had never heard of Michael Heizer but he could feel the emptiness, that very subtle whoosh in the air, as if everything was just about to be flushed down the toilet. The Memorial Museum itself was a slanted roof structure that was dwarfed by everything around it. Gershem didn't know that most of it was underground.

The Happy Shadow was intrigued by Gershem's choice of destination, which seemed to be the museum. What was he doing at this completely fraudulent spectacle built to wow the rubes? Was he looking for clues? The Happy Shadow followed him to the ticket office and watched him vainly try to gain admission.

"You mean it's sold out for the whole day?" Gershem reacted incredulously to the woman behind the window.

"Yes, sir," she replied. "You can make a reservation for tomorrow if you like."

Gershem did not like. He was already appalled by the twenty-four dollar entry fee these ghouls were charging. It was, however, not public property and he guessed the house of horrors proprietors could charge anything they wanted. As he walked away from the box office past the people waiting in line for their tour to be called, he was approached by a short, swarthy man wearing a red hoodie.

"Hey, man, you want to go in? I got a ticket. Sixty dollars."

"Sorry, that's a little steep for me."

"Whassamaddawidyou?," the scalper called him out indignantly. "Support the troops, man."

Gershem hurried away with the Happy Shadow in leisurely pursuit. Well, he thought sourly, Auschwitz was a tourist trap too. He wondered what they sold at the 9/11 memorial gift shop. Firemen's hats, twin towers keychains, Osama bin Laden wanted dead or alive posters? Had

Kevin Bartelme

27

America really become such a tawdry pastiche of itself, devoid of anything but the mercantile impulse? It was time to go back uptown.

The Happy Shadow left off his stalking when Gershem disappeared into the subway but the professor's other tail did not.

❖

4

Back uptown, Gershem was obliged to get together with his class that afternoon just to make sure they had all chosen a group to study and that there weren't too many overlaps.

"Okay, what's everyone decided?" he threw the question open.

"I want to do religious fanatics," said Breen.

"I'm going to do people with power," said Akisha, "people who have a concept of good and evil that's pretty much the opposite of everyone else's."

"Interesting," said Gershem. "Rhoda?"

" I'm going to do the realpolitik people, the government people who believe the end justifies the means no matter how cruel or horrendous they are. I also want to look into large groups who conspire against much smaller, weaker groups, who create scapegoats."

"You already know what I'm doing," said David Kogan. "Nuts and lunatics."

"Yes, of course. Rino?"

"I want to do comparative cultural norms on the definitions of good and evil."

"Very good. That sounds like it might dovetail nicely with Mr. Breen's study of religion."

Breen leaped at this opportunity so fast his pants almost fell off. "I'd be glad to share any of my notes with Miss Matsui."

"Thank you," Rino said with her pants still very much in place.

"As you know," Gershem continued, "I'm going to focus on

reasonable conspiracy theorists who might easily stray into a few of your own choices, politics and religion for example, so I suggest that we all keep each other informed about what we're investigating. Let's meet on a weekly basis and share what we're doing just to make sure we stay on the same page. Agreed?"

His students murmured their assent and that was that. As Gershem left the building, he was immediately accosted by balding young man in a trench coat wearing wire-rimmed glasses. The man flashed a wallet with some sort of identification.

"Professor Gershem? F.B.I. I'd like to have a word with you."

Startled Gershem could only ask, "About what?"

"About your associates."

"What associates? What are you talking about?" Gershem demanded.

"I think you know who I'm talking about."

"No I don't. Could I see your identification again?"

"No you can't. Stop wasting my time."

"Look, unless you're going to arrest me, I'll be on my way."

"I don't have to arrest you. I can detain you. Don't you know anything about the Patriot Act?"

At this point, Gershem realized he was dealing with a nut. "Okay. Detain me." He pulled out his cell phone.

"What are you doing?" the man said with concern.

"Calling the police," said Gershem.

"Please don't do that," the man whined. He hung his head and started sobbing. "All I wanted to do was have a conversation."

"Maybe some other time," said Gershem and walked off down the street. The man followed him.

"Wait! Please don't go! There are things I know! Important things!"

Gershem turned. "If you don't leave me alone I really will call the police," he threatened.

"Don't do that! You don't know Edward Smith! You have no idea how evil he is!"

This peculiar news brought Gershem up short. "Who are you anyway?"

"My name is Arthur, Arthur Sachs."

"Okay, Arthur, what do you know about Edward Smith?"

"Almost everything. Really," said Sachs excitedly. He had an audience now.

"So what's with the F.B.I. routine, Arthur?"

"I don't know. It's just something I always wanted to do."

"I see. So tell me about Edward Smith."

"Right here on the street? No way. We need a little privacy. If anybody overhears this…well…"

"How about that coffee shop down the street?"

And so they wound up at a back table at Kaffeeklatsch, a franchise operation that promised a taste of "Olde Vienna" with two Mit Schlags.

"You said that Edward Smith was evil," Gershem got right to the point. "What do you mean by that?"

"He is the Grand Poobah Zofar of the downtown Manhattan Illuminati." Sachs said no more as if title or whatever it was explained everything.

"I'm sorry, I'm a bit new to this sort of thing…"

"I'll say. Don't you see? It was the Grand Poobah and his minions who brought down the twin towers, not some Arabs in caves."

"Let me get this straight," said Gershem. "Edward Smith was responsible for 9/11."

"Not entirely. The uptown Manhattan Illuminati were the ones who originated the plot."

"I see. What was their motive? What exactly did they have in mind?"

"They don't need a motive. They are the spawn of pure evil."

"So you're saying that evil is its own reward."

"Well, if you want to be flippant about it…"

"No, no," Gershem protested, "I'm really interested in what you're saying." Arthur Sachs was definitely a fish he wanted to keep on the line. "Tell me more about Edward Smith. Why did he single me out after the meeting?"

"Oh, he's always looking for new acolytes. He just sized you up as simple enough to buy into his nonsense."

"Should I take that as a compliment? Just where do you fit into all this, Arthur?"

Sachs hesitated. "I don't know if I should tell you this…"

"I don't mean to pry," Gershem hurriedly backed off. He didn't know what Sachs was about to reveal and it was possible he didn't want to know. He was certainly right about that.

"I was the Grand Poobah's… lover," said Sachs shyly. "I'm not gay, I'm not," he almost begged Gershem to believe him. "He just has such charisma. He swept me away into his world of lewd, forbidden pleasures. I was putty in his hands, a slave to passions I'd never known before. Surely you must have felt his magnetic power?"

"Uh, listen, Arthur…"

"You're judging me. I know you are. You're judging me."

"No, no, nothing like that," said weirded out Gershem as non-judgmentally as he could.

"Next you're going to tell me you're very broad minded, Ha, ha, ha," said Sachs bitterly.

"Is all this why you think Edward Smith is evil?" was the only thing Gershem could think of to say.

"Oh, there's so much more, so much more."

"Like 9/11, right? How exactly did Smith pull that off?"

"You're just patronizing me."

"But you're the one who said it," Gershem protested.

"Did I? I don't remember saying anything like that."

Gershem was sorely tempted to get up and walk out but he had one last question. "But you did say Smith was evil. Are you good?"

"I try to be."

So Edward Smith was just an old catamite. But why was Sachs so willing to confide this to a complete stranger?

"Why are you telling me this?" he prodded.

"I didn't want to see another poor innocent get seduced by the Grand Poobah's Satanic charms."

"Well, thank you for your concern, Arthur," said Gershem with no little irony. "You've really opened my eyes."

"I have?" said Sachs batting his own.

Oh Jesus, thought Gershem. "Listen, Arthur, thanks for the tip. Maybe I'll see you around." With that, he left as abruptly as his legs would allow.

"But wait!" Sachs beseeched him. "There's so much more…"

Gershem did not stay his leaving. Only a few minutes later when he walked in the door of his apartment, the phone rang.

"Hello Ted, this is Edward Smith. I understand Arthur Sachs has been bothering you."

Thoroughly exasperated Gershem could only sputter: "How would you know that? What's going on here anyway?"

"Arthur called me up to tell me what a bad boy he's been, stalking you and all that."

"Listen, Edward, how does Arthur Sachs even know who I am?"

"He's a stalker, Ted. He likes to follow people around. That's what stalkers do. What did he say to you?"

"Well, let's see," said pissed-off Gershem. " He told me that he was your former lover, that you are the leader of something called the downtown Manhattan Illuminati, that you are responsible for the collapse of World Trade Center, and that your real name is the Grand Poobah Zofar. He also warned me that I too might fall in love with you."

Smith was delighted. "That's our Arthur!" he exulted. "Sometimes he lets his creative side get the better of him."

"No, that's your Arthur, Edward," said Gershem acidly.

"Well, you might say that. No reason to get bent out of shape though. He's really quite harmless."

"I'm sure he is. Just tell him to go be harmless someplace else."

"Tell him? It's not like I control him or anything. He does pretty much what he pleases. Are you coming to the meeting on Thursday?"

"No, Edward, I'm not. Goodbye," said Gershem and hung up.

Of course, the next Thursday he found himself sitting in the St. Mark's basement with the rest of the other "truth enablers" as Baxter Allen referred to his fellows. Conrad Boardman had dissuaded Gershem from giving up on the 9/11 crowd by making fun of him.

"I didn't realize that you subscribed to the notion that insanity is contagious, Ted. Next time, just show up in your Hazmat suit. Keeps the cooties off."

"Ironic detachment doesn't work on these nuts. They want to

get an angle on me. They want to 'understand' me."

"I see," said Boardman. "They've turned the tables on you."

"They're damn well trying."

"You mustn't let them get the upper hand. Soldier on. Show them the stuff you're made of, crack the whip and cow them with unassailable rationality. Let them know they're not your friends; they're just lab rats."

His students had been equally supportive of his return to the meeting.

"They're conspiracy freaks," said Barry Breen. "They're bound to be eccentric."

"Barry's right," Akisha Lumumba agreed. "They're also bound to be suspicious of strangers."

"All right, all right," Gershem threw up his hands in surrender. "I'll give it another shot."

The first thing that Gershem noticed after he took a seat in the back of the room was that neither Edward Smith nor Arthur Sachs was there. He actually experienced a pang of disappointment though he really didn't want to see either one of them anyway. The Happy Shadow's presence would probably not have cheered him, but then he didn't even know that the Happy Shadow existed.

"All right," said Baxter Allen holding up his hand, "anyone with any new information?"

"My *sciatica* is feeling better," someone in the front row cracked wise.

"I'm sure we're all happy to hear that, Clarence," said Allen. "Doesn't anybody do their homework anymore? Where's the new stuff? We used to come up with new stuff all the time."

"We've already heard everything over and over again," someone else piped up. "We have our disagreements but we all know 9/11 was a put-up job. It's just that no one else is listening."

"No one?" said Allen. "How about you, new guy?" he pointed at Gershem, who certainly didn't want to say anything at all. He played for time.

"The name is Ted."

"Hi Ted!" everyone responded and erupted in cynical laughter, as if they were intentionally doing a parody of an A.A. meeting.

Gershem acknowledged their greeting with a nervous nod and tried to explain. "I really don't know much about 9/11..."

"Why not?!" someone catcalled.

"Well, that's why I'm here. I thought I might learn something."

"What have you learned so far?" Allen not unkindly asked him.

"Well, I learned that the official story about the plane contours in both buildings was based more on Road Runner cartoons than elementary physics."

The crowd laughed and cheered. Gershem felt like he'd successfully passed through a ceremonial hazing.

"Listen, Baxter," said Clarence, "even if Ted here comes around to our way of thinking, so what? We're just a bunch of old farts – my apologies to the younger farts here – sitting around scratching and jabbering and doing absolutely nothing about the defining act of the twenty-first century."

"The defining act of the century was the assassination of JFK. It was a CIA coup and they've been in power ever since," someone objected.

"That's the twentieth century," Clarence pointed out. "Look, we've been over the same territory a million times and where has it gotten us? Nowhere, that's where."

"Okay, Clarence, if you've got a suggestion, let's hear it," said Allen.

Clarence looked around the room. "Okay, you know I can't say it, but you all know what I'm thinking."

"I am *Sciatica*!" someone mocked him.

"No, I am *Sciatica*!" someone else chimed in with more mockery.

"Conan the Veterinarian!" a third muttered.

"Go fuck yourselves," Clarence said calmly. "You're just cowards."

Now we're getting somewhere, thought Gershem.

"I don't care what you think," someone stood up, "but I lost a lot of my buddies on 9/11."

The crowd groaned as one as "Joe the Fireman" took the floor. Opinion was more or less equally divided among the congregants as to whether Joe was a whizzed out fantast or a completely incompetent agent provocateur.

"And those buddies of mine, their souls cry out for justice, for revenge! How can they find peace until the perpetrators of this vile act are punished?! If the so-called justice system won't do it, we got to stop being such wusses and take matters into our own hands!"

The room was strangely silent. They'd heard it all before.

"You know what the rules are, Joe," said Baxter Allen. "No advocating violence on the premises."

"Fuck the rules!" Joe protested. "The tree of liberty must periodically be watered with the blood of patriots!"

Everyone just looked at him in silence until he sat down muttering to himself. Then he stood up again. "If we don't do something about this, it will just be forgotten. Maybe it already has."

"What do you think about that, new guy," Allen pointed at Gershem.

"Ted," Gershem reminded him again. "Well, I think Joe here is worried about relevance. Since he thinks he's not, he feels alienated."

"Edward Smith tells me you're a shrink. Is that so?"

"I'm a psychology professor." Sensing an advantage, Gershem pressed on. "What do you do for work?"

"I'm a pimp. I take delivery of toothsome young women, sometimes boys, from Eastern Europe and the Middle East and sell them to rich people uptown."

The whole room hooted and laughed. Gershem ignored the clamor.

"Business must be booming. Do you enjoy your work?"

"Wouldn't you?"

More hoots and laughter.

"Don't answer a question with a question."

"All right, I'm not a pimp. I'm retired. I used to work for Benton & Bowles."

Gershem threw caution to the air conditioned wind. "Well, there's not much difference between a pimp and an ad man anyway."

"Oh yes there is. With a pimp you actually get something for your money."

Even Gershem had to laugh. Out of the corner of his eye, he noticed someone he hadn't seen before, a woman with short black hair and lots of bangles. She was the only woman in the room and she was staring straight at him with her preternaturally huge eyes. He looked away at Baxter Allen for a decent interval and then snuck a peek back at the woman. She was still staring at him.

The conversation turned to yet another false flag school shooting, which did not interest Gershem much. He was more preoccupied with the women and tempted to go over and ask her why she was staring at him. But that could end badly, couldn't it? She could simply deny it and possibly make an embarrassing scene. Anyway, his temptation was rendered moot when he turned again and she was gone.

When the meeting broke up, Gershem tossed a dollar into the coffee fund and walked out into the churchyard with a slight sense of disappointment. Were the concepts of good and evil simply rooted in loneliness and alienation? Wasn't the very first example of alienation when Adam and Eve were kicked out of the garden?

"Hi," the woman he thought had left the meeting startled him. "Got a light?"

"I'm sorry," he phumphed, "I don't smoke."

"I don't either. I was going to light you on fire."

Taken aback Gershem could barely manage, "What?"

"Joke." she said. "I haven't seen you here before. I was just curious."

"This is only the second time I've been. I guess you weren't here last week."

"No, I wasn't. I'm sorry, I'm Sylvia. I already know your name. Ted, right?"

"Yes, glad to meet you." Gershem looked her over more carefully. Even in the dark, he could make out the contours of a woman shaped much like Anna Bunch.

"What are you looking at?"

"You look like someone I know."

"Hmm. Are you busy? Would you like to have a drink or something?"

"Well…sure." What now? he thought.

She took his arm and guided him in the opposite direction of Edward Smith's hangout to a much fancier, sleekly designed establishment of the pansexual persuasion where they seated themselves at a bar that reminded Gershem of the old TV show, The Jetsons, a sort of bar of the future set in the all too mundane present. The perilously thin bartender with a dyed blonde fender cut appeared in a puff of blue smoke to take their orders.

"Two chocolate mojitos," said Sylvia. "It's the house specialty," she explained.

Gershem, who had no idea what a chocolate mojito could possibly be, acquiesced easily. He wasn't in a drinking mood anyway.

"So you're a friend of Edward's," said Sylvia.

"Not exactly a friend. I met him at the last meeting and we had a drink together."

"And he stole your wallet and then called to tell you you'd left it at the bar."

"How do you..?" Gershem looked up sharply.

"He does it all the time. It's a weird kind of kleptomania."

"So, what else so you know about Edward?"

"Just about everything. I'm his wife. You don't have a wife, do you?"

"Well, I used to. Why are you asking?" Gershem felt dizzy. He had lost his theoretical compass and was now bobbing afloat in a very uncertain sea.

"I'm not asking. You just want to know how I know. You don't know anything, do you."

"No I don't," Gershem shot back. "Who is Arthur Sachs? What is the downtown Manhattan Illuminati, what does..?"

Sylvia interrupted Gershem with a peal of laughter. "Oh my," she gasped. "You really don't know. Edward didn't tell you."

"What's so funny? No, he didn't tell me anything."

"The Downtown Manhattan Illuminati is a theatre club. Edward's a playwright and director. Arthur Sachs is an actor. So am I."

"So what's that got to do with me?"

"Nothing, really. Edward's always looking for new talent."

"I'm not an actor. I teach college."

'So that's the difference?" Sylvia shrugged. "You stand up in front of a group of people and try to be convincing."

Gershem was confounded. After all, she was right.

"You should drop by our workshop. How's that chocolate mojito?"

"A little sweet for my taste."

"About the workshop…?"

"Well, I don't know…"

"It's going on right now. Why don't we just drop in?" Her wide eyes went all iridium and Gershem would have followed her anywhere. In this case, anywhere turned out to be a storefront theatre space a short walking distance from the bar. They quietly walked in the door where there was a rehearsal in progress. Edward Smith was directing Arthur Sachs and two pretty young women who sat in folding chairs on the miniscule stage. Gershem and Sylvia discreetly took seats in the back.

"Okay, let's take it from the top," said Smith. "Arthur, I want you to be more assertive, more manly."

The two young women snickered.

"What's so funny?" Arthur whined.

"You're such a fag, Arthur," one of them drawled and the other giggled.

"That's enough of that," Smith snapped. "Let's do it. One, two, three go."

"Of course, as the century's foremost intellectual, Ayn Rand's legacy will live on in the universities and think tanks where other great minds who were influenced by her philosophy will carry on with the core of her teachings," quothe Arthur Sachs like the last drag queen in Omaha. It was so bad that Gershem turned his head away from the stage in embarrassment.

"That's good, Arthur," Smith interrupted. "Much better. Much more… humanistic. One more time."

"Look," said one of the annoyed young women, "am I ever going to get to read my line? Just because Arthur is completely wrong for the part, I mean, I could play Nate better than he does."

"Calm down, Amalia. Who's the director here anyway?"

"As far as I can see, nobody," she said.

Gershem could not stifle a chuckle.

Smith whirled around and peered into the dark theatre seats. "Who's there?" he demanded. "This is a closed rehearsal."

"It's me," said Sylvia. "I brought along Ted Gershem."

Smith was suddenly all good cheer. "So you did go to the meeting, Ted. I knew you would. Please join us."

So Gershem and Sylvia moved down to the third row.

"Hello, Arthur," Gershem waved.

"Don't speak to Arthur," said Smith. "He's trying to stay in part. Okay, let's take it from, 'As everyone knows.' Ready? Go."

"As everyone knows, *The Fountainhead* and *Atlas Shrugged* are works of genius," Arthur read, "unquestionably the finest literature ever produced in the English language or any other for that matter. I was stoned..."

"That's 'stunned'. Arthur," Smith corrected him as the young women giggled.

"I was stunned," sheepish Arthur continued, "and overcome with a sense of exhilaration when I first read them. A whole new world where the possibility of human perfection was revealed as a given, a world where the slackers and parasites would be banished and Superman could come into his own."

"Superman?" Amalia camped out on the line.

Gershem laughed along with the two young women. Edward Smith was not amused. "This is not a comedy," he scolded. "I can see this just isn't going anywhere tonight."

"Let me just finish the scene," Arthur whined.

"Okay, okay," said Smith impatiently.

"Not the cartoon character, of course," Sachs went on, "though he does embody many fine qualities – strength, high morals, and a willingness to defend free trade from its enemies. No, I'm talking about a world where we can all aspire to be Supermen."

"And Superwomen!" the other girl chimed in brightly.

"That's right, Devers. We all have within us the potential to rise to heights we can only yet imagine, to ascend to the stars and take our rightful place as Masters of the Universe, to go where no man has gone before, to dream the impossible..."

"That's enough, Arthur," Smith groaned with his head cupped in his hands. "That was very, uh… very much improved."

Arthur hung his head in shame. "I'm so sorry I disappointed everyone again."

"God, Arthur," Amalia scolded, "if there's anything worse than listening to you read, it's listening to you whine. Go ahead, sulk. It's about the only thing you do well."

"So, Ted, what do you think?" said Smith cheerfully.

"I – I really don't know what to say."

"You would like to join us though. I think you'd make fine addition to the group. What do you think, Sylvia?"

"It's fine with me," she said with smirking enthusiasm.

"Look, I'm not an actor and I'm not really familiar with this play…" Gershem tried to ease himself out.

"Of course you're not," said Smith. "I wrote it myself." He pointed at his chest. "Me. I wrote it. I'll give you a copy. You can read it tonight." He put his arm around Gershem's shoulder. "You say you're not an actor but I can feel this tremendous potential. You've got what it takes, Ted. Really. Don't waste that talent."

This bizarre pep talk did not dampen Gershem's spirits as much as you might think. In fact, he very much looked forward to reading the ravings of this lunatic for entirely different reasons than Smith had in mind. "Okay, I'll just take a copy and run along," he said agreeably.

"Not without me, you won't," Sylvia hissed.

Her unexpected urgency startled Gershem, but then everything startled him lately.

"I'm taking Ted to the train," she explained. Amalia and "Devers" exchanged a knowing glance, which made Gershem even more nervous.

"You do that, my wayward darling," said Smith, the sinister impresario.

As they left the makeshift theatre, Sylvia hooked her arm through Ted's and pulled him close. "Well?" she asked.

"Well what?"

"Do you like what you see?"

"Well, I didn't see much," Gershem allowed.

"Then you'd probably like to see more."

"Well, I'll have to read..."

"More of me, I mean. Kiss me, you fool."

And what did the fool do? He stepped over the edge into the downward gyre as she clutched him in a hot lingering embrace and pressed up against his crotch.

"Oh look, we woke up Uncle Willie," she purred. "What will it take you to join the club, Ted? I'll suck you off anytime you feel like it. I'll let you tie me up and get all creative on me. What so you say?" she asked as she continued rubbing his cock. "Come here," she ordered and pulled him between two parked trucks. She quickly opened his fly and was swirling her tongue around the head of his tumescent member before he knew it. "Oh, baby, give me that fountainhead." she moaned and gagged.

He ejaculated almost immediately but she wouldn't let go. Whimpering and puling, she didn't stop sucking until she'd drained the very last drop of male essence from his shriveled blue balls. Only two witnesses, a dazed old bum who chanted in a mumbled cadence: "Fuckerfaster, fuckerfaster, fuckerfaster..." and the Happy Shadow were privy to this coupling. The latter, of course, went entirely unnoticed.

Quite equally dazed Gershem pushed Sylvia away and pulled up his zipper. "I've really got to go," he pleaded.

"Go, go," she said, "and read your lines. Practice in the mirror if you can't get someone to read with you."

"What lines? I don't even know who the characters are."

"But you will. You will."

Without further ado, she headed back in the direction of the storefront theatre and somewhat rattled Gershem made his way to the subway to contemplate this peculiar evening as the train clattered uptown. His car was shaking too much to permit a perusal of the script but he resolved to read it as soon as he got home.

Two hours later, as he lay in bed studying the last few pages of "Ayn and Nate", written in the form of a screenplay actually (did Smith have Hollywood aspirations?), this is part of what he read:

AYN

I want you all to know that however we
have been taken in by these traitorous
swine that the ideals of Objectivism -
my ideals! - live on! There is nothing on
the face of the earth that can stop the
power of an idea! Not even a brazen,
little minx with hot pants for her boss!
I propelled Nathaniel Branden to the
heights where he could look out over the
land and see clearly for miles and miles
and miles! From the top of that mountain I showed him things he would
never have seen otherwise! How does
he thank me? He stabs me in the back
and runs off with a little slut. Now I'm
going to push him off that damn cliff.
Anyone in the Objectivist movement
who ever associates with that man will
be banished on the spot. In these dark
times, absolute loyalty to my principles,
absolute loyalty to me is required if we
are going to emerge triumphant on the
other side of midnight! I thank you all
for coming to see me tonight and I hope
Nathaniel Branden's balls shrivel up and
his cock falls off!

The stunned audience doesn't know what to do.
ALAN GREENSPAN applauds as if he is leading a cheering
section and slowly the audience joins in.

AYN
Thank you, thank you.

She leaves the stage with Greenspan.

INT. NBI OFFICE - NIGHT

NATE and PATRECIA are sitting dejectedly in the office.

                    NATE
          I knew this would happen.

                  PATRECIA
          The woman is insane.

                    NATE
          Of course she's not. I mean if she's in-
          sane then we're insane. I can assure you,
          Patrecia, as a psychotherapist licensed to
          practice in the state of New York, that
          no Objectivist could possibly be insane.

                  PATRECIA
          Then how would you describe her
          behavior?

                  NATE (VO)
          How would I describe her behavior
          indeed? As time went on, I realized the
          full extent of Ayn's hatred. She even
          made my so-called friends, Leonard
          Peikoff and Alan Greenspan, sign a
          statement publicly denouncing me.

INT. NATE'S LIVING ROOM – NIGHT

Older Nate is still talking to the reporter.

                    NATE
        She turned my life into such a living
        hell, I was forced to leave town and live
        happily ever after in California where
        Patrecia died of cancer shortly after our
        arrival. If I could blame Ayn for that,
        I would, but I still remain a confirmed
        Objectivist with some minor variations
        that I've introduced to the philosophy
        as a whole. You can read all about it in
        my new book, *How To Raise Your Self
        Esteem.*

Nate stands up.

                    NATE
        Now, if you'll excuse me, it's time for
        Devers and I to do a little brain
        breathing.

                    REPORTER
        Brain breathing?

                    NATE
        Old Aztec thing. Does wonders for the
        synapses. I'll see you out.

        After Gershem had finished the whole opus, clearly a sex farce
about Ayn Rand and her much younger lover Nathaniel Branden
(nee Nathan Blumenthal) and even laughed out loud at several
convoluted punch lines, Smith's assertion that the play wasn't a comedy was disingenuous at best. What part could Sylvia possibly have
in mind for him? Alan Greenspan? Ayn's drunken husband, Frank
O'Conner? Since it was a period piece, Greenspan's part was probably too
young for him though he would have really liked to dig into that loath

some serial destroyer of economies. What interested Gershem most about the play was the intention of Rand's cabal, or "collective" as she wryly called it, to not only demolish the government and install some sort of uninhibited meritocracy, which they of course would lead, but to smash the very foundations of Western philosophy and bring paranoid schizophrenic Abrahamic dogma to the fore. Gershem had never read her books. He had made it through the first few pages of *Atlas Shrugged* which a female student had left behind in the classroom and been defeated almost immediately by the sheer fatuousness of the prose. Yet the sort of nonsense Rand spewed had found a home with the Milton Friedmans of the world with their "Invisible Hand" of the unrestrained market. Even after the 2008 fiasco, their acolytes could still be found baying through the television set about "supply side" and "deregulation" as if these holy of holy doctrines were the answers to rather then the causes of our collective economic woes.

It came to Gershem in a flash that the Russian Rand was probably a Stalinist mole sent to bring down capitalism by rubbing its nose in its most egregious contradictions. Now there was a conspiracy theory! And where did that place Ayn in the spectrum of good and evil? Who cared?

As he turned off the light, he found himself humming, "It's A Long Way To Tipperary", one of Ayn Rand's favorite dance tunes. I mean, how lame can you get?

❖

5

When he woke, who should be hovering over him but his ex-wife Tsipora. At first he thought he was hallucinating.

"Tsipa?"

"Yes?" Tsipora was a dark eyed, dark haired, very Sephardic

beauty.

"What are you doing here?" said Gershem sitting bolt upright. "How did you get in?"

"I have keys. I came to check on the rest of my stuff."

"Stuff? What stuff?"

"Personal stuff." She picked up the script. "What have we here?"

Gershem leapt out of bed and grabbed the script away from her. "I think you've taken quite enough stuff already, Tsipa."

"It's not that kind of stuff, Ted. I came to tell you that you're hanging around with some very dangerous people. The Downtown Manhattan Illuminati theatre club."

Gershem broke into laughter. "Oh no, don't tell me you're...!

"There's nothing funny about it. I studied acting with Edward."

"Jesus, Tsipa," he snorted. "Talking about dangerous people, aren't you hooked up with some Wall Street hedge fund crook now? That's what I heard."

"That's my business and it has nothing to do with anything." She grabbed him by the collar of his pajamas. "I gave you those pajamas," she said apropos of nothing.

"You want them back too?"

"Don't be absurd. You have to listen to me. Stay away from Edward Smith."

"And his mesmerizing charisma? Don't tell me you're porking him too."

"I don't do pork. I'm kosher."

"Ha ha. Now would you kindly get out of here? And give me back those keys!"

Gershem woke in a shaken and slightly confused state as the dream evaporated. It seemed so immediate, so real. But what did it mean? As a psychotherapist licensed to practice in the state of New York he ought to be able to figure that out, he chuckled, very much relieved that Tsipora had not actually graced him with her presence but only appeared as some sort of omen.

He got up and went into the kitchen to make himself a cup of tea. He had nothing to do that day but he felt restless. He felt like going out, maybe even going out of town. He did have a car, which he rarely used anymore, parked in an increasingly expensive garage. Maybe he would take a drive upstate where he had friends. Well, sort of friends. He didn't see them much anymore. Maybe it would be his last drive because he had already decided to stop paying for the rental space and sell the car. But then who was going to buy an old Volvo? The junkyard was probably the next stop. He decided to go. He went to the garage, wiped the accumulated dust on the car body and windows off, and he was on his way

Driving up the thruway was a little unnerving. When he was younger he had liked to drive fast himself, weaving in and out of traffic that was too slow for his speed demon instincts, but now everyone seemed to be going too fast. Even hunkered down in the slow lane, he felt as if the little old lady from Pasadena had a point. As he left the haul ass, double trailer semi-rigs thundering north behind at the Kingston exit he cast a palpable sigh of relief and resolved to take the slower more picturesque back roads when he returned to the city. Halfway between Woodstock and Kingston he turned off to the right toward the reservoir and curved this way and that to Spillway Road, a road of historic importance where even George Washington may have slept. Not on the road, of course, but perhaps in an adjoining house. But enough about roads. Where can they possibly lead anyway?

In this case, right to Coriolanus Cheezowitz's derelict dairy farm, where the formerly famous artist had converted the barn into a vast studio so long abandoned there were cobwebs weaving themselves everywhere. Cheezowitz had decamped back to city some time ago to resume his former career as a commodities trader, gotten busted for running a Ponzi scheme and sent away to prison for a year and a half. His present tenants were Gershem's old friends, Bob and Marta Applewhite who quietly grew a dispersed acre of marijuana back in the woods. Gershem had known Bob since college when the world was young and the Gipper was still president. That had been enough for Bob who talked about leaving the country and wound up moving to the country where he and his wife had lived ever since. Gershem found their house and pulled into the gravel driveway where he was greeted by two bounding Labrador retrievers along with Bob carrying a shotgun.

"Ted! Long time no see!"

"Hey there, Bob. What's with the shotgun?"

"Oh, this. I carry it all the time now. Sort of like a crutch. You never know what's going to come down that driveway," he laughed and slapped Gershem on the back he ushered him into the house more or less at gunpoint and called out, "Look who's here, Marta! It's Ted!"

Marta, the perfect old hippie with her Mendocino beano, appeared from out of the kitchen and greeted Gershem rather too effusively. For a brief moment, he felt as if he were in the arms of Sylvia Smith. "Ted, it's been so, so long since we've seen you."

"Hey there, you two," said Bob jovially leveling the shotgun, "I just might have to blow you away in a love triangle!"

"Bob's just so funny," Marta giggled as she gently but firmly guided Gershem into the living room

"So, what can I get you, Ted?" said Bob, laying down his firearm and moving over to the open island kitchen in the spacious farmhouse. "White wine, whiskey, perhaps some fine homegrown?"

"Wine is fine," said Ted uncomfortably. Marta had still not let go of his arm. What did he have to do? Shake her off?

"So what brings you up to the boonies, Ted?" Bob asked, handing a glass to Gershem who took it with his free hand.

"I don't know. I just wanted to get out of town."

"I know the feeling," Bob chuckled, lighting up a joint. "In fact, I've felt it every day for the past twenty years."

"Has it really been that long?" Gershem shook his head as Marta continued clinging to his arm.

"Time goes by. Are you still practicing psychoanalysis? Maybe you could help us out. You notice how Marta won't let go of you?"

"Well, now that you mention it..." But that didn't stop her. She just kept clutching his arm and smiling up at him.

"It's this thing she's developed over the last year. She'll grab onto just about anybody and hold on for dear life. Is there a name for that?"

"Uhm, maybe she's feeling insecure."

"Well, what can I do about that?"

"Let me try something," said Gershem. "Marta, let go of my arm." Much to his relief, she did so instantly.

The Applewhites broke into uproarious laughter and Gershem somewhat reluctantly joined in. Were they making him the butt of some kind of practical joke?

"Don't bogart that joint, Bob," said Marta merrily. "So what do you think of our new digs?" she asked as Ted surveyed the impressive appointed space with an eclectic mix of Catskill furniture, many potted plants and a giant flat screen TV dominating one wall.

"Very nice. I was here once before you redecorated."

"So you were, so you were," Marta recalled through the marijuana haze wafting around her in a beam from the skylight. "Coriolanus said we could keep it for a while, even when he gets out of jail. For a commission on the crop, of course."

"I thought pot was legal these days," Gershem kidded them.

"That's almost so," said Bob, "and I've given the prospect of legalization some thought. If, or should I say when it happens, we're going to go into opium. More bang for the buck anyway!"

"And such pretty flowers!" Marta chimed in enthusiastically.

"So, what have you been up to, Ted?" Bob asked as he took a liberal swig from a whiskey bottle.

"Conspiracy theory."

Bob was nonplussed. "What do you mean?"

"The department got a grant to do a study on how people develop and maintain their perceptions of good and evil."

"What's to develop and maintain? The world is a conspiracy and it's against you," said grinning Bob. "It's obvious."

"I don't think so," Marta objected. "It's people who conspire against the world. Look what we're doing to the planet."

Gershem couldn't resist being reasonable, which was pretty silly under the circumstances. "So, Bob, you think the world is evil and Marta thinks that people are evil."

"Let's put it this way," said Bob. "It's all just one big, goddam practical joke perpetrated by the dualistic nature of things. Good and evil are just two sides of the same coin and no matter what we do, as long as that coin keeps spinning, we can't escape the ironies of existence."

Gershem had a thought. "Do you mean actual existence or your consciousness of existence?"

"What's the difference?"

"The difference is that every living thing has a different consciousness of the world. What we're looking at in this study is how human beings form perceptions of specific desirable and undesirable behaviors, namely doing good and doing evil."

"Maybe they don't. Maybe the perceptions are imposed on them. Take a toke. It'll clear your head."

"No thanks," Gershem begged off. "If there's one thing pot doesn't do for me, it's clear my head. I will have another glass of wine though."

"So let's forget about good and evil for the moment," said Bob, pouring Gershem another glass. "Which conspiracy theory are you interested in?"

"Well, all of them."

"All of them? How long is this study supposed to take?"

"Forever. Or at least what's left of forever."

"I see. Ted jumps on the Holy Grail of the academic gravy train and its perpetual dividends," Bob chuckled.

"That's not fair," Marta chided him. "Most people would just call it job security. It's like that Japanese guy physics professor on TV who promotes whatever nonsense the government tells him to."

"Otherwise they'd put him back in an internment camp." Bob laughed again. "Wasn't he born there or something?"

"Not so funny," said Gershem. "That childhood experience might have scarred him for life."

"So, anyway, you evaded the question," said Bob. "Which particular conspiracy theory are you looking into?"

"Well, it started with this 9/11 crowd. They meet every week in the East Village. That's where I met up with this guy Edward Smith and… what?" The Applewhites were gaping at him in open mouthed astonishment. "What did I say?" he demanded.

"Nothing, nothing," Bob phumphed. "This, ah, Edward Smith,

what do you know about him?"

"Not so much. He seems to know everyone else who goes to these meetings. Some pretty strange characters."

"Anything else?"

"Why are you interested? Do you know this guy?"

"Maybe," said Marta vaguely, "but Edward Smith's a pretty common name, isn't it?"

"This Edward Smith is involved with something called the Downtown Illuminati theatre club."

Bob and Marta looked at each other then back at Gershem. "This is pretty complicated, Ted, but we may have a business association with Edward Smith. Does he have wife called Sylvia?"

"Yes he does."

"Oh my," Marta sighed. "Has she given you a blowjob yet? She gave Bob one. More than one. I almost threw him out of the house'"

"You know you sucked off Edward," Bob complained. "Can't we just put that in the past? "I didn't just suck him off. I let him do anything he wanted to with me. It was scary and hot, just like Edward, but I did it and now I'm an initiate of the Illuminati. I've even been in one of the shows, Dr. Faustus. I was Helen of Troy. I never participated in the work they do outside the theatre though."

Thoroughly uncomfortable Gershem was reduced to, "So you act with the group?"

"Not really," she said. "Bob?"

"It's a complicated situation, Ted," said Bob. "One of those things you just fall into and it's comfortable enough so that you wind up hanging out for a while. But after that…"

"Edward Smith is our biggest customer in the city," said Marta.

Gershem could barely believe his ears. "Edward Smith is a weed dealer?!"

"Well, how else do you think he finances that theatre group?"

"I had no idea. Well, I'm no actor but he wants me to be in one of his plays, something called 'Ayn and Nate'."

"I'd pay money to see that," Bob chuckled. "What do you play?"

"I'm not doing it so don't hold your breath."

"Why not?" Marta pressed him. "You've got real presence, Ted. I think you'd hold the stage very well."

"Thank you but I don't think so. So you know Edward Smith. What's his involvement with the 9/11 group?"

"You really don't know anything, do you?" said Marta.

"People keep telling me that lately," Gershem groused.

"I could say let's change the subject," said Bob, "but we really don't have anything else to talk about, do we? More wine, Ted?"

"Edward has a lot more to do with 9/11 than you might imagine," said Marta.

"That's what Arthur Sachs told me."

"Oh. You've met Arthur."

"Look, I've met all sorts of people," said Gershem as if he were issuing an ultimatum. "Why don't you just tell me what's going on here."

Bob laughed. "We wish we knew."

"Well, you seem to know him better than I do."

"He's like religion. Puritan religion," said Bob. "It's all about the Elect, those chosen for special treatment during their brief stay on earth. The Chosen. You're a Jew. You can relate to that."

"I'm not religious," said Gershem defensively.

"But you take it seriously. Edward Smith really takes it seriously."

Gershem got irritated. "Stop talking in circles. What is Edward Smith up to?"

"Take the part, Ted," Marta soothed him. "You'll find out more than we know."

"Hey," said Bob, "you haven't seen my new canoe."

"Canoe?"

"My Adirondack cargo canoe. It's really a beauty."

"And I thought you were going to show me a little man in a boat," Gershem joked. Bob laughed and Marta practically blushed through her giggles.

"No, nothing like that. It's my new cargo. I keep it right down the road in a trench, Come on, you can help me throw it on the back of the truck."

So Gershem followed Bob down the driveway to where the craft, an antique Adirondack wooden canoe was wrapped up in tarps in a hole in the ground.

"Keeps out the riff raff. If this were up on a rack it would be half eaten by termites not to mention all the other little varmints around here."

"I see."

"Just give me a hand and we'll have it up on the truck in no time."

Gershem acquiesced and it turned out much easier than he had anticipated,

"Ain't she a beauty," said Bob prompting a similar compliment from Gershem. "There have been moments when I wanted to drag her back in the boat shed and have my way with her. Never have, of course. Just a fantasy."

"Typical barcophile," Ted pointed out. "It's a condition associated with a twisted, perverted lust for light watercraft."

"Have you ever fucked a boat?"

"Not in a while, " Gershem played along, "but then there are so few opportunities in the city."

They drove for a few miles with the dogs yammering in the back and Bob's shotgun properly racked in the rear window. They parked at a small landing and put the boat in the water. Then they paddled down the river until they reached the Rondout, the last tributary into the Hudson. The water was somewhat rougher on the other wide of a small weir which Bob and Ted transversed with no problem,

"Okay, all we've to do is ease this baby over the dam into the river," and, knee deep in water, they did as required. However, having crossed the Rubicon, it was now on to the Hudson, which loomed before them. Bob had a small outboard motor, which he attached aft and they were off. Surrounded by substantial powerboats, they were quite the object of curiosity.

"You guys got any life vests?" one of these onlookers called from his own boat. "Here!" and he tossed two orange ones into the canoe.

"I assure you that's unnecessary, "Bob called back, "but God bless!"

Gershem wasn't sure such measures were unnecessary at all and strapped on his life jacket as soon as they hit the light chop of the virtually deserted river and puttered across to a series of small islands the local teenagers used for parties. They beached the canoe on one of them where they found all manner of campfire remnants, beer cans, used condoms, and other Dionysian detritus. The dogs took off into the cover of the trees and Bob, cradling the shotgun, turned to Gershem. "You don't mind if I give you a little pat down. Just a precaution."

"What?!" said Gershem.

"No joke. I've just got to make sure you're not wearing a wire. After that talk about Edward Smith and all, well… Just humor me."

And so Gershem did. What would you do with a man holding a shotgun?

"Okay, cool," Applewhite concluded from his body search. "Now I can speak freely."

Slightly miffed Gershem said, "Okay, speak. I really can't imagine…"

"It's a dirty business, Ted. Get used to it."

"Jesus, Bob, you make it sound like something out of a cheap spy movie."

"It is. Only worse."

Exasperated Gershem asked, "You were going to tell me something?"

"Right. I just can't remember what it was." He seemed genuinely puzzled. "Weed, short term memory," he apologized. "Oh yeah, about the Downtown Illuminati, that Sylvia Smith could suck the chrome off a tailpipe, don't you think?"

"You didn't really haul me off to this island to talk about blowjobs, did you?"

"Oh, no, no. I just don't want to be overheard if you catch my drift. There's a few things I have to tell you. In the strictest confidence, of course."

"Of course."

"The Smiths are nice enough people – a bit strange, a bit eccentric I'll grant you – but nice enough. The problem is they're Reptilians."

THE TIN HAT

"Reptilians." Gershem echoed.

"Thousands of years ago when humanoids were broken up into different evolutionary groups by a planetary catastrophe, homo sapiens managed to overcome the Neanderthals and such but they never completely got rid of he reptilian strain that walks side by side with us to this day. Reptilians need warmth so they are always trying to recruit human beings to rub up against them, It's how they maintain their energy level."

"I see. Why don't they just go out and bask in the sun?"

"They do. Just look at Hollywood."

"You," said Gershem, "are mocking me."

"I'm afraid not. I just don't know whether to tell you to give the Smiths a wide berth or get as much information out of them as you can. Me, I'm staying hunkered down with Old Betsy and the dogs till the whole thing blows over."

"You call Marta Old Betsy?"

"No, the shotgun, Can you think of something better?" He pulled a pint from his down vest and offered Ted the bottle. He took a slug.

"Just assuming I go after this mysterious information you seem interested in what would I be looking for?"

"You recall Marta said she's never worked on any of their outside projects. I'd like to find out a helluva lot more about that."

"You want me to infiltrate the group and spy on them."

"Something like that. You're interested, aren't you?"

"Frankly no."

"Then how did you think your were going to get any information out of these people? A standardized test? It's raining oil, Hallelujah," he sing-songed, "we're drinking lead, Amen, now what we gonna do is chug a few down, drink it all up and, and, AND... wind up in bed!" He blew off his shotgun a couple a couple times in the air in concert with the imagined backbeat of the song. Then he blew his head off and reloaded. Ted was astonished for a lot of reasons, one being that that the body seemed to still possess perfect dexterity with no head at all, as if the action were reflexive.. "Arrwhu abar!," were the last sounds that burbled out his neck hole before he collapsed in a contorted heap,

He was not dead at all, of course. Gershem was hallucinating. "So," said Bob, "what do you think? It's called HOG. I put a little in the whiskey."

Ted, reeling from the effects of the drug, was in an amorphous world of such overwhelming complexity that trying to make sense of anything was futile.

"Don't worry. The initial rush only lasts about ten minutes," said Bob. "Just lie down here on the grass and take everything in."

Gershem did as he was told. In his twisted state he really didn't have much choice. Besides, it's hard to stand when one leg is three feet longer than the other. What he saw as he lay there was a universe of such unbearable complexity that its own tangled wiring could only result only in an ultimate massive short circuit of the cosmos. No theory, no model could possibly encompass, much less explain, the zillions of transactions taking place every second in his lone, completely insignificant body. What was going on in his immediate surroundings, this little island on the Hudson, was unfathomable. Even God could never figure it out.

Such were his reeling perceptions as the effects of the drug began to moderate into a simpler vision of so-called reality. In order to keep people from running off screaming into the night at the sheer disorder of things, an illusory order had to be constructed, a religion, a political or economic theory, a dogmatic fundamental worldview that broaches no question of its absurd validity. And so it had. It didn't matter what you called it. It didn't matter that its principles were contradictory or even insane. What mattered was its general acceptance. And just who engineered these imposed cognitive constructs? Usually a priestly caste who manipulated their subjects through constant fear-mongering, cruel punishments, and periodic rewards for obedience. It was simple. It was a formula that had existed from the beginning of recorded history. The only things that changed were the tools and the superficial aspects of this conspiracy to govern. There, he'd said it. Conspiracy.

"So how do you like that?" Bob, he himself slowly emerging from the primordial soup, asked Gershem,

"You ought to tell me before you spike my drunk," Gershem scolded. "Very interesting though. Seems to make suicide a well considered option."

"Hey, look at the bright side. You couldn't even consider suicide unless you were alive."

"I didn't say I was."

"Alive or considering suicide?"

"What's the difference?" Gershem laughed it off.

"It's interesting stuff, though, don't you think?"

"I don't know if I'd take it again."

"Ted the Psychedelic Ranger retires!"

"At my age, I'm more interested in your opium farm."

Back at the ranch, they unloaded the canoe and joined Marta in the kitchen.

"Welcome back!" she enthused. "I'm making fondue!"

❖

6

The next day on his way back to the city after a late night of good cheer at the Applewhite's, Ted did not realize that there was an emergency shutdown and possible leakage at the Indian Point nuclear power plant, and, since he wasn't listening to the radio, did not understand the number of cars pulling off onto the median strip of the thruway and trying to turn around to head back north. So, oblivious to the thousands of Becquerels he might have been absorbing by the second, he motored on down to the George Washington Bridge and was soon back at his apartment. He only realized something was amiss when he turned on his answering machine and got a terse recorded message that the college was closed until further notice. He decided to call Conrad Boardman to find out what was up.

"Haven't you heard?" said surprised Boardman. "Turn on the TV."

So Gershem did and was presented with a field reporter standing some distance down river from the two domed reactor containment buildings.

"State authorities and representatives from the operator of the plant, Entergy, have assured us that there was no release of radioactive material and the reactor is in cold shutdown." Blah, blah, blah.

Ted wasn't sure what to make of this bland reassurance. If there had been a leak the reporter would not risk going anywhere near the plant but there he was. Or maybe he wasn't. Maybe he was standing in front of a green screen in an underground shelter. Wouldn't do to panic everybody, would it? The very impossibility of evacuating New York City was obvious. You didn't even have to be a conspiracy theorist to know that. The phone rang and he rather reluctantly answered.

"Ted, it's Anna. Isn't it awful? I'm so scared."

"I was just watching the news and they said there's been no leakage."

"What are you talking about? A woman in my building just got murdered. I can't stop shaking. Can I come see you?"

This not so welcome intrusion put Gershem in a state of two minds. He would like to fuck Anna but how long did she plan to stay? He immediately chided himself for his lack of empathy.

"Of course. You know my building. Come on over."

At the very same moment, Barry Breen and Rino Matsui were lying in the warm drench induced by a considerable amount of physical exertion in her bedroom.

"Baby, I love you," he murmured.

"You're a liar. You just want to fuck me," she rebuked him playfully.

"Well, there's that too. You don't like?"

She took his penis in her hand and started to rub. "Not so

much," she giggled, "but we can try again."

Barry didn't yet realize that he had been "captured" (a direct translation from the Japanese) by Matsui-chan and was now her subject. It certainly wasn't bad at the moment but the future is always murky at best.

Breen responded to the stimulation with admirable aplomb and they once again locked together as the beast with two backs.

"Oh, YEAH!" she shrieked as he came again. Lathered in sweat and panting like someone who just ran a marathon, Rino gasped, "You're so healthy!"

He looked down her moist brown body and gasped back, "You're so beautiful," which was certainly enough for Rino or any other female of the species.

"Maybe I love you too."

A few minutes later, she was making him green tea in her tiny kitchen and practically glowing in the dim light with the delicious sensation she was feeling.

"I have a joke," Breen called out from bed. "Ni gaijin walk into a bar…"

"Stop your bad Japanese," she ordered.

"But you're going to be my teacher now…"

"Don't learn from me. Then you sound like a girl. You have to learn from a man." Rino was absolutely right. If he learned how to speak Japanese from a woman, he'd wind up cooing like a pigeon all the time. She brought him a cup of tea and they snuggled up.

"So, what have you worked up for Gershem?" he asked her.

At the moment, Gershem was getting worked up by Anna Bunch over a couple of glasses of gin and tonic water.

"How well did you know this woman?" he gently prodded her.

"I didn't know her at all," said shaken Anna. "I mean to nod at in the hall but that's all. That's what makes it so upsetting."

Gershem wondered if she were just faking all this anxiety, inserting herself into a drama which was actually none of her business. He wondered if he'd be upset if someone he didn't know in his building, and there were plenty of them, got bumped off.

"Do the police have a suspect? Someone in custody?"

"I have no idea. I certainly hope so. It's all so awful," she puled right on cue and Ted was obliged to put his arm around her shoulder. She immediately pulled him close and started to sob. Ted remembered something his ex-wife had taught him. The most manipulative thing a woman can do is cry. But what exactly did she want? It didn't take long to find out.

"Can I stay with you a day or two? I'm so afraid to go back right now."

"Ah, sure, there's plenty of room. You've never been here, have you?"

"No I haven't. Why don't you show me around?" Her mood was suddenly upbeat. No more tears. There hadn't been any in the first place. As she walked through one dusty room after another, her manner was authoritative, "This place needs a good cleaning. Then we really get to work on it. Such possibilities. A respected college professor needs a place to entertain, don't you think?"

Not much respected college professor Ted Gershem thought no such thing. The very idea of "entertaining" was anathema to him. And who was this "we" getting to work? "Uh, you may have something there," he allowed.

She looked in the bedroom. "Well, it looks like someone's been in here at least," she said, flopping on the bed. "Oooh, not hard enough. I need support for my lower back. How about you?" He now looked so befuddled she knew it was time to move in for the kill. "So what say we have another gin and tonic?"

"That sounds fine to me," he agreed.

But she didn't move from the bed.

"Come here," she purred. "Come to mama."

"So you want me to spank you again?" he wondered.

"I don't think that's necessary. Let's just cuddle up and have some fun."

He was startled how quickly she got out of her clothes.

"Need some help?" she offered.

"I'll be right with you," he assured her and so he was, pumping away with her legs up over his shoulders.

"Don't stop," she whimpered, "Come in my mouth."

He pulled out and knelt over her head where she sucked his cock in a frenzied symphony of slurping and gagging. Then he came, spurting again and again, pulled deeper and deeper into the vortex of lust.

"So yummy!" she gasped. "So perfect with a gin and tonic back!"

The phone rang, Gershem did not answer, and the machine took the call: "Ted, it's Edward. Are you coming to rehearsal this afternoon? Five o'clock sharp. Give me a call. And give that little cutie you've got in bed with you my best regards."

"What was that?" Anna demanded.

"Just somebody. He was joking. He has no idea you're here." Or did he?

"No, no, what's this about 'rehearsal'?" she pushed.

"It's a theatre group. They want me to be an actor."

"Really," said Anna petulantly, "I actually am an actress and no one calls me anymore."

"Is that so?" said Gershem. "You never told me."

"It's true. I even used to do character parts on Broadway. I never got the lead though," she grumped with a fine blind of rue and bitters, something like a very dry Campari and soda. "How about those gin things?"

"Oh yeah," said Ted, "coming right up." He went to the kitchen, made the two drinks, and returned to the bedroom. If orgasm was the "little death" then he had been reborn as someone perfectly willing to amuse himself by exploiting Anna Bunch's vanity.

"What say you come along with me to the rehearsal?" he asked her. "They're looking for someone with your background."

"Really? Just who are these people anyway?

"The Downtown Manhattan Illuminati theatre club. The have a space in the East Village."

"Oh, I've heard of them. Very contemporary."

"Right on the cutting edge," said Gershem with no little irony.

"You're serious? You want to take me along?"

"Absolutely. I've even got a script for you to read." He handed her his copy of "Ayn and Nate".

"This is written like a movie," she pointed out. "Are they going to film it?"

"Couldn't say."

"Hmm," murmured said and started reading. After a while, she started giggling. "This is funny," she said. "Not what I expected."

"What did you expect?"

"I don't know. Something more artsy fartsy."

"Who do you see yourself playing?"

"I'm not in my twenties anymore. Ayn Rand, of course. Didn't she have some sort of accent?"

"Russian."

Anna's voice descended to the guttural. "Let me lick your greasy little *piroshki*," she growled.

"Very good," Gershem applauded. "I think you should try out."

"Love to."

And so, later that afternoon they cabbed down to the theatre club and walked into a circular firing squad in progress.

"No, you listen to me!" Amalia scolded the little group sitting facing each other in folding chairs. "Is there one person here who really thinks Arthur can play Nate?"

"Don't you think I can bring out the real animal in Arthur?" Sylvia Smith retorted.

Amalia and "Devers" (her real name was Deirdre) laughed scornfully.

"With those saggy old tits…" Amalia started.

"That's enough of that," Edward snapped. "Look what you've done to Arthur. Now I want everyone to take ten deep breaths."

Arthur, sitting dejectedly with his hands between his legs, whined. "I know I'm terrible for the part. I should be Alan Greenspan or Leonard Peikoff or something, but I know someone from the gym I go to, the weatherman Studs Zenith. He says he's interested in acting."

Everyone was suddenly impressed. "The Studs Zenith?" Amalia demanded. "Not some guy in chaps with no pants?"

"It's not that kind of gym," Arthur protested weakly.

At this point, Gershem was on the verge of making a hasty,

quiet exit.

"No, stay," Anna hissed. "Don't you understand? They're theatre people."

But it was too late to understand anything.

"Ted! There you are!" said Edward Smith. "And I see you've brought a friend, Come, come, please join us!"

It was not an entirely welcome development for Gershem but Anna Bunch was a little more than enthusiastic.

"Hi everybody!" she said brightly. Then in her Russian accent, "I'm Anna! Do you know I once gave Studs Zenith a blowjob right on TV? All he had to say was the barometer went way up!"

Sylvia Smith scowled while everyone else laughed nervously. Just who was this brazen hussy who looked and sounded more like Ayn Rand than she did?

Edward was considerably more cordial. "That was great! Let's see where we can fit you in!"

Anna continued with the accent, "Don't you mean let's see where I can fit you in?"

That was enough for Sylvia. "Can't you see we're working?" she snapped. "What are you doing here anyway?"

"Oh, I'm sorry," said Anna. "Ted told me that the Ayn Rand part was open."

"This is what I get for sucking your cock?!" Sylvia howled at Gershem. "Stabbed in the back?!"

"Well, I sucked his cock too, you know," said Anna.

Edward Smith clutched his face between his clenched hands. "Stop! Stop! Stop!" he wailed. It was not the sort of behavior his acolytes expected of the Grand Poobah and they buzzed with consternation.

Gershem, who had certainly not anticipated this sort of brouhaha, grabbed Anna by the arm and hustled her out of the theatre.

"Ouch, you're hurting me," she complained. "You didn't really let that woman suck your cock, did you?"

"Of course not. She's just very melodramatic."

"Oh, I see. So 'suck your cock' is some kind of metaphor," Anna said with playful sarcasm.

"For God's sake, Anna, that was her husband sitting right there. He wrote the play. He's the director. You were coming on pretty strong yourself."

"When you're auditioning, it's always good to make a strong impression."

"Well, you certainly did that."

"Oh, Ted, what are you doing with that pathetic crowd anyway? Even at my very worst, I could blow them all off stage."

"Do you really want to hear the story? Let's get a drink."

"It sounds like I'm going to need one. Let's go someplace nice."

So they walked over to a hotel bar on the Bowery and Gershem told her the whole saga - with some strategic omissions, of course.

She looked at him with concern. "I don't know if these people are completely nuts or perversely interesting."

"What makes you think those two categories are mutually exclusive?"

"Well, you got yourself into it…"

"Indeed I did. What do you think I should do?"

Before she could answer, his phone went off. "Hello?"

"Ted, it's Edward. I'm afraid there's been a dreadful misunderstanding. We'd love to have you and your friend back to the club."

"Look, Edward…"

"Never mind what Sylvia said. She was just staying in part. Didn't she do exactly what Ayn Rand would have done?"

"I have no idea what Ayn Rand would have done…"

"But I thought you read the script. You know the part where she hopes Nate's balls fall off. Please, Ted, you and your friend have to join us."

"As I recall, she hopes Nate's cock falls off."

"You did read it! Oh, Ted…"

"Not tonight, Edward." And he hung up.

"What was that all about?" Anna demanded.

"He wants us back."

"Us?"

"Especially you."

"Ooooh! I got a call back!"

"You think this is funny?"

"Well... yes," she giggled.

At that very same moment, Rino Matsui and Barry Breen were having coffee in a small café on Amsterdam Avenue discussing the concepts of good and evil in Shinto, formerly the Japanese state religion.

"In western religion suicide is a sin. In Shinto it is the opposite, a positive even."

"Like the Kamikazes?"

"Kamikaze means wind of the gods. It was the storm that destroyed the invading Chinese fleet back in the fifteenth century. Did you know that most kamikazes didn't even try to do their missions?"

"What do you mean? I thought that once they took off they couldn't land."

"That's not true. If you didn't crash your plane in five tries, they kicked you out. My great uncle was a kamikaze. He just died two years ago."

"Didn't he feel bad that he didn't go through with it? Like a coward or something?"

"Are you kidding?"

Just then, a young man approached them. "Hey, aren't you guys in the psych department?"

"Yeah, are you?" said Breen.

"I'm an adjunct instructor, Calvin Card," he said and they introduced themselves all around. "Mind if I sit down?" He didn't wait for an answer. "So you're working on the big project with Ted Gershem."

The couple looked at each other. "Well, I don't know how big it is," Breen allowed.

"Interesting subject though, don't you think?" said Card. "Good and evil, conspiracy, all that stuff. What are you two working on?"

"Er, we were just discussing relative perceptions of good and evil in different cultures," said Breen.

"Fascinating," said Card. "Really, fascinating." He didn't seem to realize he was beginning to give Barry and Rino the creeps.

"What do you teach?" Breen ventured.

"Boring stuff. Psych 101, undergrad stuff like that. Not like Ted. I'm pretty low on the totem pole." He paused. "I wish I were doing something interesting like you. Maybe you could just kind of keep me informed about what's going on with your research. I'd love to look it over." He looked at his watch. "Well, I've got to run. Inquiring young minds await. Here's my card." He handed them both a card with his name and email address. Nothing more. No title, no college affiliation. "Be in touch." Then he was gone.

"What was that all about?" slightly annoyed Breen wondered.

" Maybe he's lonely."

"Everybody's lonely."

"Not me," said Rino, lightly touching his knee.

Gershem and Anna did not go back to the theatre club but took a cab back uptown to King Wok Szechwan where they shared a large deep fried fish perched on a bed of vegetables which the waiter Wo Chung highly recommended.

"This is very good," awkwardly wielding chopsticks Gershem, who had never tasted this particular dish, informed him.

"No evil?" said Wo Chung with a very broad wink and a little nod toward Anna Bunch, who was digging into the fish herself. Gershem had never brought a woman to King Wok since his wife left him.

"Don't you have something else to do?" Gershem muttered to the waiter.

"Yes, of course. Many things to do," and he was off.

"Listen, I'm sorry…

Anna wasn't having it. "About what? I had a good time and an invitation to once again demonstrate my instrument."

"Your what?

"My acting ability. It's not as easy as it looks."

"I'm sure it isn't. But you just called those people pathetic. You said you could blow them off the stage."

"Don't you see it's exactly what they need? Someone to educate them in the finer points of presentation, someone to look up to, someone to adulate."

"Don't you mean emulate?"

"Well, both," she giggled. "Isn't this fish good?"

So let us leave our two romantic couples for the moment and take a closer look at Calvin Card, which, of course, was not his real name nor was he an adjunct anything. He was simply a depraved degenerate and the Grand Poobah's principal investigator and recruiter. His current assignment was to develop contacts and find out anything he could about the Columbia project. To this end, he had obtained a list of the students attending Gershem's abnormal psychology seminar and was now tracking them down. His earlier run-in with Rhoda Memberman had been quite a revelation. Her dusky Mediterranean complexion, her frizzy black hair, her zaftig contours, her sneering dismissal, "I don't care who you are. I don't talk to strangers about what goes on in class," all of these had enchanted him. How he longed for her to dress in skintight black rubber and walk him around naked on a leash through the park.

❖

7

When the seminar convened the next day, the subject of Calvin Card was immediately introduced by Rhoda Memberman. "There's this creepy guy who claims he's an adjunct in the department who was asking me questions about the project. His name is Calvin Card. I think he's stalking me. I might actually call the police. Have you ever heard of him?"

"No I haven't," said Gershem, "but I don't know most of the adjuncts."

"He hit on me too," said Akisha Lumumba. "Real nosy."

"Ah," said Barry Breen, "he introduced himself to Rino and me in a coffee shop. He was sort of weird."

"Am I the only one he hasn't bothered with?" David Kogan

mock complained. "What do you all have that I don't?"

Gershem immediately thought of Arthur Sachs. "What did this guy look like?"

Their descriptions did not fit the bill.

"Well, if he comes snooping around again, send him to me. Now let's get down to business." And so they did with each reporting on his or her particular area of inquiry. It was all pro forma with each of them assuring Gershem that they were "making progress" with vague promises of future troves of information. The absent minded Professor Gershem's thoughts wandered out of the classroom dialogue to Anna Bunch and how to get her out of his apartment. But did he really want to? It was nice to get laid every day but her calculating insinuation into his life was still instinctively disquieting.

Later that afternoon, Smith called again to reiterate his invitation to Anna. "Bring your whole class if you want. We're always looking for young talent."

"Anna is not in my class and my students aren't actors," Gershem said tersely. "Tell me something, Edward, do you know someone called Calvin Card?"

"Never heard of him," said Smith a bit too quickly.

Gershem paused before he spoke. "Leave my students alone, Edward."

"Oh my, aren't we paranoid. I just thought they might enjoy a little theatre. Broaden their horizons and all that."

"That's not what you said. You said you were always looking for young talent."

"Ted! Really! All I meant was that it might be a good idea for them to get a behind-the-scenes experience, to see how things are put together before the curtain goes up. What's wrong with that?"

"Edward, what do you want?"

"Well, at least your friend Anna could join us. She was very good, you know."

"She told me she can't work unless she smokes marijuana."

There was a pause at the other end of the line. "Uhm, I really wish you wouldn't say that on the phone. But this is the East Village. I suppose anything can be arranged."

"I've got to talk to Anna. I'll call you back."

When Anna came back from her secretarial job at a white shoes law firm, Gershem told her about Edward's call.

"It sounds like I've already got the part. I know I'm better than that old hag."

"She's Smith's wife," Gershem pointed out. "Don't count on anything from these people."

"I'm going to do it, Ted. It makes me feel young again. You make me feel young again."

"How young is that? I'm supposed to be an authority figure."

"Can't you just stop thinking about it and fuck me?"

That evening they arrived at the theatre club where Sylvia was nowhere to be seen.

"Ted and Ted's friend!" Smith enthused. "Please, Anna, take that chair next to Arthur."

"Who's Arthur?"

"Can't you see? Your Nate, of course."

Amalie and Deirdre snickered.

"Arthur," said Anna, "you're madly in love with me. Show it."

"Uhh…"

Anna didn't waste any time. "I love you, Nate, I love you," she crooned as she pulled Arthur's penis out of his pants and turned to Gershem. "You don't mind, do you, Ted? It's method."

He shrugged as Anna began to rub Arthur's cock.

"Uhm, nice one," she said as she quickly massaged him into a spurt after spurt ejaculation that she purposely aimed at Amalie and Deirdre.

"Eww!" they squealed in chorus as Arthur vainly tried to squirm away from Anna's iron grip. "He's probably got AIDS!"

"Ahh," said Anna in her thick Russian accent, "my rearing wild stallion! My throbbing hammer drill! My towering skyscraper soaring into the spermament!"

Actually none of this happened except in the form of a Ted Gershem waking dream as they entered the theatre.

"Ted and Ted's friend!" said Edward Smith. "Come join us." Except there was no us. Smith was the only one there. Well, not the only one. The Happy Shadow went unnoticed in the dark back row. "I was just about to roll a joint. You two smoke?"

"Oh my yes," said Anna.

"No thanks," said Gershem.

"The others will be along any minute now," said Smith, lighting up and inhaling deeply. He handed the joint to Anna who followed suit. "So I'm so glad to see you again, Anna. Sylvia didn't really want the part anyway."

"Really? She seemed pretty angry with me. She's your wife, isn't she?"

"Well, that's just it. She was doing me a favor by sitting in until we found someone more appropriate. By the way, Ted, Argyle's dropping in to read for Frank O'Conner and Arthur claims he's bringing along Studs Zenith. Isn't that something? You, of course, are perfect for the mature Nate."

Gershem laughed warily. "I'll just warm up with little Aztec brain breathing."

"This stuff is really good," said Anna taking another toke.

"Isn't it? I can get you all you want," said Smith.

They were interrupted by the arrival of Argyle padding in on little cat feet. "I'm drunk," he announced. "It will keep me in character."

Gershem went on high alert, so to speak. This was getting even weirder than the 9/11 meetings.

"Oh, it's you again," Argyle noticed him. "How's the old terministic screen working?"

"The what?" Anna giggled.

"Private joke," Gershem muttered.

"I don't care how drunk you are, Argyle," said Smith handing him a script. "You've still got to study your lines. The pages are marked."

"Oh, I will, I will," said Argyle, who took a seat in back and promptly went to sleep.

"This is all such fun," Anna gushed. "I'm so glad I came."

And just at that moment plenty more fun walked in the door in the form of Arthur Sachs and Studs Zenith. The famous TV weatherman was all gleaming teeth as Sachs introduced him to Smith. "Glad to meet you. I've always wanted to do theatre."

"So wonderful of you to grace us with your talent," Smith shamelessly brown-nosed. "Such an honor. And you bring all that credibility with you."

"What credibility?" Zenith said with a perfectly straight face. "I'm wrong about the weather sixty percent of the time."

It took Smith a full puzzled second to realize Zenith was joking. "Oh, you're having me on!" he laughed. "Well, check your sense of humor at the door. This is a serious part."

"I'm sure it is," Zenith agreed amiably. "Arthur showed me the script and I think I need one myself."

"If course," Smith handed him a copy as Amalia and Deirdre walked in the door together. "Ah, your two love interests in the play."

"What about me?" Anna said indignantly.

"Oh, Anna, I'm so sorry," Smith nervously apologized. "Studs, this is Anna, our Ayn Rand."

"Charmed, I'm sure," she said in her Russian accent.

The two younger women were not nearly so forward. In fact, they gaped in open-mouthed astonishment at the weatherman.

"Are you...?" Amalia managed.

"Look who Arthur's brought us," said Smith with pride. "Your new Nate. And Anna and Ted here have agreed to play Ayn and old Nate."

Gershem was surprised at his own vanity. He did not like being referred to as "old Nate".

"Okay, what say we get to work," Smith took charge. "Start at page nine. Ted, you read the television announcer and you read the stage directions, Deirdre. Wake up, Argyle!"

The ensemble sat down in the folding chairs on the stage and leafed through their pages.

"Okay, everybody ready?" Smith called out. "Let's do it."

Deirdre started out: "Nate and Barbara get out of his car in front of the house. Barbara wears a powder blue suit and white gloves."

Amalia: "Gosh, it's so modern."

"Ayn comes out the door dressed in an embroidered Mexican blouse and an elaborate woven skirt. She has clearly dressed for the occasion," Deirdre read.

Anna: "Mr. Branden – or should I call you Nathaniel? – introduce me to your pretty friend."

The cast stifled their chuckles at her over the top accent.

Zenith: "This is Barbara Weidman."

Anna: "I am so glad to meet you, Barbara. Please, come in."

Deirdre: "As she walks in ahead of the young couple Barbara whispers to Nate – "

Amalia: "Branden? Nathaniel? What's going on here?"

Zenith: "She's recreating me. She'll probably do the same for you."

Deirdre: "Frank O'Conner is sitting on the couch with a drink in his hand watching an antique television. He waves to the new arrivals but doesn't get up."

Anna: "I'm sure you'd like to see the house, Barbara. It was designed by Richard Neutra, a student of Frank Lloyd Wright. Marlene Dietrich used to live here."

Amalia: "A real movie star's house!"

Anna: "Mine now. Come along."

Deirdre: "Ayn conducts Barbara into the spacious, mirror-lined bathroom."

Amalia: "Gosh, this is fantastic!"

Deirdre: "Ayn points at the bidet."

Anna: "Marlene's idea."

Amalia: "What is it?"

Anna: "A bidet. To wash your puss puss."

Amalia: "Oooh."

The cast cracked up. They couldn't help it.

"Stop laughing," Smith admonished them. "That's the audience's job. Continue."

Deirdre: "Nate and O'Conner are watching a television newscast."

Gershem: "Reporters are still trying to pin down Senator Joe McCarthy on the exact number of Communists who have infiltrated the State Department. Last month, McCarthy made the bombshell announcement that there were 215 Communists but since then he's scaled the number down to eighty-one."

There was silence. "Argyle, that's your line," Smith reminded him.

"Oh yes, sorry. Now that's one hell of an Irishman! Need a drink, Nate?"

Deirdre: "Ayn and Barbara re-enter the room."

Argyle: "Look, Fluff, McCarthy's on TV."

Anna: "One of the only politicians with the courage to tell the truth. Barbara, let me show you the kitchen."

Deirdre: "Ayn and Barbara enter the kitchen."

Amalia: "May I ask you a question, Miss Rand?"

Anna: "Of course. And please call me Ayn."

Amalia: "Why do you call Nathan 'Nathaniel Branden'?"

Anna: "Because it suits him. You're a very lucky girl, Barbara. One day Nathaniel Branden will be famous and powerful. Do you think Nathan Blumenthal could aspire to anything beyond a dental practice? You must let me guide him for his own good and yours as well. Now let me show you something you've never seen before. It's called a Radar Range. Personally, I hate cooking and this machine has been my savior."

Deirdre: "In the living room, Nate is trying to engage O'Conner in a conversation."

Zenith: "Where did you meet your wife, Frank?"

Argyle: "Which one? Oh, you mean Ayn. We met on the lot."

Zenith: "The lot?"

Argyle: "The studio. I had some bit part and we kind of walked into each other."

Zenith: "Was it love at first sight?"

Argyle: "What? Are you kidding? Look at her. No, Nate, as I got to know her better, it was her mind that attracted me. She took over mine, so to speak, and here I am today."

Zenith: "I think she's taking over mine as well. I've never met such a brilliant woman. She's so modern, so ahead of her time. I only hope the rest of the world can catch up to her."

Argyle: "I've been trying for years myself."

Deirdre: "Ayn and Barbara rejoin them in the living room."

Anna: "I hope Frank hasn't been boring you to death, Nathaniel."

Zenith: "No, no, not at all.

Anna: "Really? That would be unusual. Why don't we have

Kevin Bartelme

73

some music?"

"All right! Let's stop and take a break!" Smith called out. "That was wonderful, just wonderful! Really fantastic! I feel so lucky to have such a brilliant group of players!"

"What are you talking about?!" Sylvia startled him by shouting from the back of the theatre. "It was awful and you know it!"

"I thought you weren't going to be here today," Smith protested apropos to nothing.

Sylvia strode down the center aisle like a woman possessed. "Well, it's a damn good thing I changed my mind. Just what do you think you're doing toadying to these completely inept amateurs?"

Gershem immediately smelled a rat. This was no spontaneous display of disaffection. Smith and his wife had planned it in advance. But why? And then the Grand Poobah emerged from his Edward Smith cocoon.

"Sylvia, how can you say such a thing?!" he declaimed. "We are all of us embarked on a great adventure! An adventure that will not only transform us as individuals but transform the whole world! You act as if people should just spring full bloom as professionals with no direction or encouragement whatsoever!"

Sylvia buried her head in her hands and sobbed. Gershem noted that there were no tears. Then she suddenly looked up brightly. "I'm so sorry. I didn't mean to discourage anyone."

"It was a test! That's all!" the Grand Poobah backed her up. "We had to see if you could take rejection, wallow in your despair, and stand your ground! Still maintain your integrity, your ambition. That is, after all, the life of the actor. All Sylvia is saying is that you have to bring everything to your art and if you don't it's not enough!"

The rest of the cast cheered. Not Gershem. He was thoroughly familiar with the "good guy/bad guy" routine and knew exactly what he was watching. The urge to get up and walk out of this sales pitch was getting the better of him but Anna had him clamped in place.

"Look, that's enough for me," he whispered. "You can stay if you want."

"I do want. I'm still fine tuning my instrument."

"I think I popped a string." With that, Gershem stood up. "I'm sorry," he said to all, "but I've got to go. I will leave Anna to your tender

THE TIN HAT

mercies though,"

"Bye, bye, Ted, don't be a stranger," said Edward. "We've got more work to do, you know."

"I understand. See you soon," he waved as he walked out closely followed by Sylvia.

"I meant what I told you," she purred as she took his arm. "As long as you're here you can do anything you want with me. Would you like a blow job right here, right now? If we could find someplace private you could fuck me in the ass. Would you like that?"

"Maybe some other time. I'm a little distracted right now."

"Do you really do it with that Anna woman? I can see what she sees in you but I don't understand what you see in her."

"She's just a friend, Sylvia."

"Whatever. *Chacun a son gout.*"

"Why don't you tell me what was going on there tonight? That fake argument with Edward and all."

"Aren't you the clever one," she batted her eyelashes. "Nothing. It's an exercise. You didn't understand because you're not familiar with acting technique."

"True enough, but if you're going to cry, you might try squeezing out a tear or two."

"In a rehearsal? What for?" Her logic was unassailable.

"So you take teaching people to act seriously."

"Very seriously. What do you think the Downtown Manhattan Illuminati is all about? Some hick town little theatre group doing 'The Fantasticks'?"

"Maybe you should. Wasn't it the longest running play of all time?"

"Don't patronize me. When I say seriously I mean it. There are things you don't know."

Gershem was sick and tired of this pseudo-mysterious aura the Smiths worked do hard to maintain. But then marijuana dealers wouldn't be very forthcoming about their activities, would they? What was he supposed to do? Tell her he knew all about it? Not a good idea.

"Yes, I'm quite sure there's much more to it than meets the eye," he conceded. "I don't really know anything about the theatre."

"No you don't. But one thing you should know. The world

really is a stage."

"Thank you for that tidbit of received wisdom," he verged on scoffing.

"You don't understand, do you? The stage is just where the perceived action takes place. It's what goes on backstage that's important. The lighting, the set, the rehearsals, wardrobe, props, and especially the direction."

"Of course I understand that."

"Do you?"

"Look, I've really got to go. I've got a lot to do tomorrow."

"You're coming back, aren't you?"

"I don't know."

"You will. That woman will make you."

"You never know." With that he turned and headed for the train.

He went to bed early and when he woke Anna wasn't there. He didn't know whether to be disappointed, worried, or relieved. The latter seemed the most attractive but he couldn't help but wonder what might have happened to her at the hands of Smith and his wife. And then, perhaps unable to withstand to the throes of celebrity worship, she had succumbed to the charms of Mr. Zenith and bedded the studly weatherman . This thought actually cheered him and he laughed out loud. But, as Brecht pointed out, those who laugh have not been told the terrible news. The phone rang and Gershem picked it up.

"Ted, I'm so sorry."

"Anna. What do you mean?"

"After the rehearsal, well, everyone was feeling so… connected. I went home with Argyle and here I am."

Suddenly Argyle was on the phone. "That's right, you twit! And I fucked her! In fact, I'm fucking her right now! Listen!"

Gershem could hear Anna moaning, "Oh yeah, oh yeah, OH YEAH!"

"Did you hear that, you twit! I'm fucking her right now!"

"Excuse me, could you put Anna back on the phone?" said thoroughly annoyed Gershem.

"Are you joking? I'm just about to shoot my wad!"

After a rather long pause, punctuated by grunts and squeals, Anna came back on the phone.

"Oh Ted," she panted, "I'm so sorry."

"I'll bet. Would you just lay off this ridiculous practical joke? Is this one of Edward's acting exercises?"

"Well, sort of," she admitted. "but he really is fucking me."

"With what? A dildo?"

"What's wrong with that? Sometimes it's better than the real thing."

"Good. Then you can forget about the real thing!" Gershem surprised himself with his own vehemence.

"Sylvia told me you'd say that. Don't lie to me, Ted. I know you fucked her."

Gershem immediately went into analytic mode. "What business is it of yours who I fuck?"

"Ted," Anna sobbed. "How can you say such a thing after all we've had together?"

"Go fuck Argyle!" he fumed as he slammed down the receiver.

Needless to say, this unwanted intrusion or whatever it was, put Gershem in a sour frame of mind. He kicked himself for ever allowing Anna to stay at his apartment, realizing it had all been a damsel-in-distress ruse to prove that her female charms had not faded away entirely. Now she was trying to make him jealous! With Argyle, of all people! It was nothing but a childish insult to his intelligence and he was having none of it. He made himself an English muffin and a cup of tea. When he's finished with these, he decided to take a walk to cool off but no sooner had he left his building than he ran smack into Anna breezily walking down the street with a bag of groceries.

"Hey there, Ted. What are you doing? Running away from home? God, I can't believe you actually thought I was doing it with that old coot," she turned the tables on him, making him feel childish and ridiculous. "It was a joke, Ted, a joke. I was acting. Lighten up."

"I know you weren't doing it with Argyle," he snapped. "But you were out all night, Anna. What was I supposed to think?"

"It was a fantastic rehearsal. You should have been there.

We worked till dawn and then I went out to coffee with Argyle."

In the not so distant past, when Gershem had practiced privately, there had been clever patients who over the course of a few sessions had learned how to push his buttons. Now, he was once again confronted such a "case" and he responded as he would have done then.

"Why are you trying to manipulate me?"

"What do you mean? It was a joke, Ted."

"It was a practical joke. Aren't all practical jokes manipulative? They wouldn't be practical if they weren't, would they?"

The tables firmly turned back on her, Anna was now on the defensive.

"I didn't mean any harm," she protested. "I just couldn't stop... stop acting."

"So you're one of those actors who can't leave it on the stage? One of those actors who's always 'on'. Is that it?" he asked neutrally with no vehemence at all but not without a silent chuckle. Who was acting now?

"I didn't mean to upset you," she whinged. "Really. I'm sorry."

"Forget it," he dismissed her contrition. "What's in the bag?"

Now, for many young people, college students specifically, it's difficult to understand that those in authority, their professors, have any lives at all beyond their scholarly demeanor and the classroom so when their lives intersect outside the hallowed groves of academe it is often an embarrassing situation for both parties, much as a psychiatrist running into one of his patients at a dinner party. Rhoda Memberman, who was wearing a skin tight, black rubber ensemble walking naked Calvin Card on a leash, saw her professor. That's not true but she was walking her small dog and had watched the whole interchange between Gershem and Anna from across the street. She had two choices: say hello or keep walking. Her curiosity got the better of her.

"Professor Gershem!" she called out and waved.

Startled Gershem looked across the street in dull horror as Rhoda approached. Then he quickly pulled himself together and was all nervous collegiality.

"Well, hello there, Rhoda. I didn't know you had a dog."

"Why would you?" said Rhoda.

Gershem ignored this pointed question. "Anna, this is Rhoda. She's in my graduate seminar on abnormal psychology."

"Really? I've always been interested in abnormal psychology myself," said Anna extending her hand. "Pleased to meet you."

"Anna's an old friend," said Gershem and then lamely caught himself. "Well, young friend actually."

Anna batted her eyelashes. "Really, Ted."

"Nice meeting you," Rhoda all but winked. "I'll see you in class, Professor Gershem." She pulled on the dog's leash. "Let's go, Petunia," and off they went.

"Who was that?" Anna demanded.

"A student. Rhoda Memberman."

"Rhoda what?"

"It's her name for chrissake."

❖

8

Calvin Card, who was apparently no longer among the living, had apparently fallen out the window of his apartment building and been pronounced dead on arrival at the Beth Israel emergency room. Edward Smith had just learned this because Card had Smith's phone number in his pocket. He blandly told the hospital that he didn't know anyone called Calvin Card and had no idea why the deceased would have his phone number. After hanging up, Smith went into panic mode. Card hadn't "fallen" out a window. He'd been pushed. Smith was sure of it. The only question was why and by whom.

He immediately called Sylvia.

"Listen, my dear, Calvin has just been murdered."

"What!!"

"They tried to make it look like an accident but we know better. You have to get in touch with your connection at Retalitron right away."

"But what if it was them?"

"Then we're in a world of shit."

Now, given their backgrounds, it shouldn't come as any surprise that Edward and Sylvia had a tendency to dramatize just about everything so it was hard tell if they were just drinking their own Kool-Aid. However, making a call to someone at Retalitron, the largest private security agency in the world, was problematic at best.

"I'm not going to do it," said Sylvia. "I'm not going to do anything until I know why they threw Calvin out the window."

In point of police report facts, Card actually had fallen out the window in a HOG induced epiphany when he thought he could fly. He'd spread his wings and soared into a resounding splat on the street. At least, that was the official story. It might, perhaps, be incumbent to take a closer look at Calvin Card's background, especially since he was so recently introduced to the fray and so quickly discarded. Card was a typical East Village whizhead, who had introduced himself to the Smiths as a sort of soldier of fortune engaged in a variety of secret operations for Retalitron. He had even once introduced Sylvia to one Gunner Black, his immediate superior at the security firm. Sylvia still maintained contact with Gunner, well, more of a sexual liaison actually. Black was a submission freak like Card and took the opportunity every now and then to dress up in women's lingerie and be chastised at the end of a chain by Sylvia, dressed as a Nazi storm trooper. Edward Smith very much approved of this relationship, at least up until this particular moment. Card and Black had been useful sources of very low level information about Retalitron, particularly regarding the company's involvement in various false flag operations, such as the Newtown school shooting, the Boston bombing, and the rap group "Niggas For Hillary" as well as their sister group "Miss Anne". Black had also procured both of them jobs as "demonstrators" at a few political functions and paid them slightly above SAG minimum. Smith wanted to work himself into a position as a sort of casting director for such events and Card's "murder" had thrown a monkey wrench in the gears of such ambitions.

"I think you should reconsider," Smith sharply rebuked his wife. "Gunner has been invaluable to us in the past. Just get him on the phone and call him a worm or cockroach or whatever you do. Then get him to a session."

"Fine for you to say," Sylvia retorted. "You're not the one holding the noose."

After much cajoling, he finally convinced her they had no choice. Gunner Black probably wouldn't even know that she was aware of Card's sudden demise and speak more freely after a good tongue-lashing. So Sylvia called Black.

"You vermin, this is your mistress calling! Where have you been?! If you don't see me right now, you are DISMISSED!!"

"No, no, please," Black whined, "I'll be at the dungeon right away."

"You better be!" Sylvia snarled.

With her appointment confirmed, Sylvia headed for the theatre where she and Edward had built a little soundproof set in the basement complete with whips, chains, and all sorts of other recreational gear. Gunner Black had so quickly responded to her command that he was waiting outside when she got there.

"Mistress, I'm so sorry…"

She slapped him across the face. "Shut up, you insect!"

Now, Black was a big, fat, mucho macho guy and little Sylvia really had to reach to clock him on the snout, but all he could do was pule, "Please, please, mistress…"

"Did I give you permission to speak?! Did I?!" she demanded as she opened the door. Sylvia was not a sadist. Well, sort of not a sadist, but she very much enjoyed playing one as an acting exercise. Once downstairs she dressed in her black leather S.S. uniform, complete with riding crop, he in his panties and D cups. After she had chained him to the wall, they got down to business.

"Eww!" she held her nose. "Don't you ever wash those panties?"

"I…"

"Shut up! You'll speak when I tell you to speak!"

Chastised Black held his tongue as she continued.

"What about Calvin Card? Tell me what you know about Calvin Card. You may speak."

Befuddled Black, who actually knew nothing about Card's recent defenestration, could only mutter, "What about Calvin?"

"You know very well what I'm talking about!!" Sylvia shrieked.

But Black didn't. "I, uh…" For that, he got a hard tap on his forehead with the riding crop.

"You don't know that someone threw Calvin out a window just a few hours ago?! You think you can lie to me, you WORM?! If I put you on the rack and broke you in half, there'd be two of you! How disgusting would that be?!"

"Not the rack, Mistress!" Black wailed.

"Then talk! Tell me what I want to hear!"

Black quickly tried to figure out what she did want to hear, as torture victims often do, and came up with the following:

"All right! All right! Calvin knew too much! They had to get rid of him."

"What did he know?!"

"If I knew I'd be dead too," he whimpered.

"Who is they?!"

"I don't know! The government!"

Sylvia whacked him with her riding crop and hissed, "Listen, you loathsome piece of shit, you find out what's going on and report directly back to me. Do you understand, Mr. Turd?"

"Yes, Mistress," he groveled before her.

"Good, now get out of my sight before I change my mind and put you in the Iron Maiden!"

Black scurried to do her bidding and quickly departed feeling quite refreshed. Sylvia called Smith.

"He doesn't know any more than we do. I ordered him to find out whatever he could."

"Hmm. Well I guess we have to just sit back and wait for the next shoe to drop."

"Don't speak that way. It sounds like squishing a bug."

Ted Gershem, happily unaware of many things, was listening to the end of an audiotape made by super star philosopher, the late

Alistair Couch:

"The ideal of progress could not exist without the language inherent in social hierarchy since it implies a superior future form of being. The concept of superiority, of course, relies on its opposite, inferiority, for definition and is therefore entirely dialectic in nature. The social constructs of custom dictate what is good and what is bad and serve as inviolable guidelines within any civilization be they derived from either religious texts or secular constitutions. The illusion of civilization could not exist without one or the other."

So the secular and the divine were so intertwined as to be practically indistinguishable from each other. They served the same purpose and aspired to the same goal; power and dominion. They also mutually reinforced notions of good and evil in any given culture. But Gershem knew all this already. He turned off the tape and realized he was already bored with the whole project. Maybe Rhoda Memberman was right. People needed to feel more important than they really were, to be "in the know", to be on the "right side". But then, Rhoda Memberman called her dog "Petunia". Gershem didn't feel important at all. In fact, he felt mildly ridiculous. All this simian nattering and jabbering, not to mention fucking and fighting, what did it all amount to? Nothing but a way to pass the time one was arbitrarily allotted on the planet. Such were his sour thoughts when the phone rang.

"Ted, it's Alvin Spurtz! How are you? I'm not catching you at an inconvenient moment, am I?"

"No, no. I'm just fine, Alvin. What's up?"

"Just checking in. Making any progress with your conspiracy buffs?"

"Actually, there are so many of them coming out of the wood-work I can barely keep up."

"Wonderful," Spurtz enthused, "that's just wonderful." There was a pause. "Have you ever heard of a guy called Calvin Card? He called me up and told me he was a friend of yours."

"Did he? That's bullshit. I've never met him but he's been bothering my students. What did he want from you?"

"I'm not sure but I just heard on the news that someone with the same name jumped out a window downtown. Killed himself."

"Really?" This news was somewhat unnerving. "What do you

want me to do?"

"Nothing. You're quite sure you never had anything to do with this guy? That is if he's the same guy."

"Quite sure."

"Well, that's good. Wouldn't want to stir up a hornets' nest, would we? Just, ah, keep up the good work, Ted."

"I'll try, Alvin, I will."

Even though he'd never even met Calvin Card, this news left Gershem in a brown study. If Card were connected with Edward Smith, and Gershem assumed he was, what did it means in terms of his own association with the Grand Poobah? Was he in line to be tossed out the window himself?

Let's put this in perspective. As a clinician, Gershem had been threatened with physical harm by his own patients a number of times. He had taken their anger seriously but for entirely different reasons than his own safety. Actually, he'd seen it as a positive sign in their therapy. He'd hit a subconscious nerve that so disturbed them they'd reacted with furious denial. It was that point of recognition that was important and occasionally led to positive outcomes in the therapeutic process. But he couldn't quite conjoin the ideas of a painful personal breakthrough ("I can't believe it! All along it was my mother I wanted to kill!") with actually acting out murderous impulses. The stakes on abnormal psychology had just been raised. But maybe he was just conflating the incident to mythic proportions. Perhaps Calvin Card had committed suicide or even simply fallen out the window. He was sorely tempted to call Edward Smith but decided against it, a decision which was rendered moot anyway when Smith called him minutes later.

"Ted! How are you?"

"I was doing fine until just this moment."

"Oh my. Who got out of the wrong side of bed this morning?"

"Edward, who is Calvin Card? And please don't bullshit me. By the way, I know he's dead."

"Who? Dead?"

But Gershem could hear in his voice that Smith was clearly shaken. "Didn't I just politely ask you not to lie to me?" he pressed.

"Well, if I don't know what you're talking about, then... I don't know what you're talking about."

Gershem hung up and the phone rang a few seconds later.

"Okay, okay," Smith said petulantly. "I saw something about it in the papers. Poor devil."

Gershem hung up and this time the phone didn't ring again for a full five minutes. Now Smith was dissembling irritation.

"You don't have to get all bent out of shape, Ted," he said petulantly. "It's not like I know everyone in the East Village. I mean, I might have run into this guy. I just don't recall. Why do you care anyway?"

"Actually, I don't. He's been bugging my students, my department head. Good riddance."

"What are you saying? You're not quitting the play, are you?"

"I don't know. I've got to talk to Anna."

"Oh please, Ted, don't do anything rash. She's so perfect for the part," Smith sounded a little desperate.

"Believe me, Edward, I won't do anything rash," he said and hung up. This time Smith did not call back.

❖

9

"Hey, look at this," said Rino to Barry Breen. There was picture in the Post of Calvin Card. "It's the guy who talked to us."

Breen glanced at the paper. "So it is. It doesn't say anything about him teaching here."

"I knew he was lying," she said emphatically. "So creepy, so kimoi."

"I thought I was the only kimoi one around here?" Through Rino's good offices, Breen had learned how to say "weird" and two variations on pervert in Japanese, *hentai* and *chikan*.

"You only be chikan with me or I call the police," Rino giggled and got a good tickling in response. She tried to wriggle away but she didn't really want to and they were soon at it again. But enough about their fun and games. They had, through their disparate investigations, stumbled both accidentally and academically into much more interesting terrain than they'd expected, the world of the Devil. While Breen had concentrated on the Abrahamic tradition, Judaism and its two depressing schismatic spin-offs, Christianity and Islam, where the Devil rode in tandem with all three of them, the eastern religions (non-Islamic) either discarded the Devil entirely or tepidly embraced him in the form of demons, evil spirits, etc. but not as a single entity aligned against "God." In fact, if the eastern religions (Islam excluded once again) either subscribed to no God whatsoever or a polytheon of antagonistic gods which rendered "God works in mysterious ways," absolutely ridiculous, much as the Greeks and Romans had assigned different gods different roles in the basic lie called civilization. It was the monotheists who were forced to embrace the concept of the Devil. What other explanation could there be for all the torments people suffered under God's supposedly benign supervision? Of course, monotheist absolutism describes anyone who doesn't go along with the program as heretics, to be banished, tortured and murdered by the true believers, The Chosen, The Elect, the Exceptional, the Jihadis, who routinely visit havoc on their neighbors, which a Roman historian so succinctly described as, "To ravage, to slaughter, to usurp under false titles, and call it peace."

When they weren't otherwise engaged, they actually sat down and discussed this dichotomy. Although Breen was initially not much interested, it was a Japanese thing to take education seriously and Rino had set off a few circuits in his brain that ordinarily went unused.

They had quite by chance wandered out of the Garden of Academia into a world fraught with all sorts of sinister implications, not that they minded being naked together. Their assignment was to delve into the concepts of good and evil and they agreed that they had to move out of the library and hit the streets. They had to meet with the priests, the rabbis, the imams, the lamas, the shamans, the Zen masters, and, of course, the Satanists. They researched and wrote up a list of people who might deign to see them and got on the phone. Being a grad student at Columbia turned out to be a sort of magic key so it was the first thing they mentioned to their prospects. The first to eagerly bite was the Magus of the Tabernacle of Lucifer, which had been formed in an acrimonious split with Satan's Synod, and they set up an appointment for the very next day at his Gramercy Park apartment where Margaret Hamilton used to live.

Ted Gershem, who had through sheer boredom almost given up on the nature of good and evil, was wrestling with his own demons, specifically Anna Bunch and Edward Smith.

When Anna came "home" that evening, Ted told her everything he knew for sure about Calvin Card along with a few things that were pure conjecture. Anna objected:

"How many people know about your project? It could have been anyone. Why are you blaming Edward?"

"I just know he's got something to do with it. I don't think we should have anything more to do with him."

"Who's we? Oh, come on, Ted. You're just making a mountain out of a molehill. Lots of people commit suicide. What's so special about this Calvin Card?"

"You mean you're going on with the theatre thing?"

"What do I need? Your blessing?"

Gershem reluctantly reconsidered. "Maybe I am overreacting. Do whatever you want."

"Shall I tell Edward he needs a new old Nate?"

"No, I'll do the part. Just to keep and eye on you."

"Oooh, I like that. But I'd also like a little hot stuff in my puss puss. It's the one trick to a great performance. Always get laid before you go on. That golden feeling lasts for hours." She didn't have to work too hard to get him into bed where one of the preliminaries to a fine turn on stage was consummated. All that remained was hair and make-up.

And so at the appointed time, Ted and Anna showed up for

rehearsal.

"Oh, thank God you both came back!" Edward gushed. "There are just so many things going on this week. Important things! Studs Zenith called and said he'd be a little late because he was on Hurricane Watch! Isn't that exciting?! All this climate change thing has just got everyone running around in a tizzy. So dramatic, don't you think?!"

"Earthshaking." said Anna in her thickest Ayn accent. "I'm just sorry that studly Mr. Zenith isn't here to shake my world."

Deirdre and Amalia weren't quite sure what to make of Anna's antics but they were just as eager to get into Mr. Zenith's pants themselves. Just imagine! A real celebrity!

Of course, the locale, at least for the beginning of the play, was Los Angeles where a not so secret, underground currency circulated freely called the "media sighting." It had denominations like any other currency but they were determined on a peculiar scale invented by the advertising industry called the "Q" rating. The more people who recognized your name or face, the richer you were. This was not so very different from its Sugar Daddy, Capitalism, where your wealth depended on another abstract concept called "credit." Just like actors desperately seek prominence in the beginning and end rolls of a movie.

"Well, you'll just have to put a cork in it for the time being, Anna," Edward teased.

"Oh, I need something more than a cork. Perhaps Argyle could oblige."

"My whole head wouldn't fill that flabby old pussy," Argyle snorted.

"Please, Argyle," Edward admonished him. "Well, enough with the fun and games. Where were we?"

"Well, there's not much we can do without young Nate," Deirdre pointed out.

Ted had an idea. "I could read for Studs until he gets off Hurricane Watch."

"Now there's an idea!" said Edward enthusiastically. "What scene should we do?"

"How about the part where Ayn announces to Barbara and

Frank that she and Nate are going to have an affair?" said Amalia.

"Excellent!" said Smith. "Okay, Anna, Amalia, Argyle and Ted, find your parts and get ready."

"I can't even remember this scene," Argyle complained. Amalia found it on his script.

Deirdre read: "Interior, Rand apartment, next day. Ayn, nervous Nate, O'Conner and Barbara are gathered in the Rand living room."

Anna: "Well, here we all are together again."

Argyle: "We're always together, Fluff."

Anna: "I know, Cubbyhole, I know. Do you love me?"

Argyle: "Of course I do. What kind of question is that?"

Anna: "A silly one, I suppose. And Barbara, do you love Nathaniel?"

Amalia: "Yes I do."

Anna: "How could you not love the man who launched the Objectivist movement last night with such notable success? You're a lucky woman, Barbara, but you do understand you're going to have to share Nathaniel with the world now just as Frank has shared me with all my many fans."

Amalia: "I suppose I'll get used to it."

Anna: "I'm sure you will. There's another thing though. You're also going to have to share him with me."

Amalia: "I don't understand."

Anna: "Tell her, Nathaniel."

Ted: "I, uh – "

Amalia: "Yes, tell me, Nathan."

Ted: "Well, it's like this. After working together all these years to further the cause of Objectivism, Ayn and I thought it was only right to adhere to our principles at any cost."

Anna: "Stop pussyfooting around. What Nathaniel wants to tell you, Barbara, is that he and I have fallen in love."

Deirdre: "O'Conner's jaw drops and Barbara stares at Ayn as if she's lost her mind. Then she laughs."

Amalia: "This is a joke, right. You're old enough to be his mother.

Anna: "I don't see what age has to do with it. I love Nathaniel and he loves me. That doesn't mean he doesn't love you and I don't love Frank. Neither you nor Frank has anything to fear. Nathaniel and I just need a little time together alone, say once or twice a week. If we all agree, everything will be just fine."

Amalia: "And if we don't?"

Anna: "We must. For the sake of everything we stand for."

Amalia: "For the sake of everything you stand for!"

Anna: "You could put it that way. I'm not one of the greatest thinkers of this or any other century for nothing, you know. I certainly deserve a man like Nathaniel as much as you do."

Amalia: "Why don't you say something, Nathan?"

Ted: "Barbara, what's happened between myself and Ayn was as inevitable as the morning sunrise, as inescapable as destiny itself – "

Anna: "Save the poetics for the seminars, Nathaniel. What he means is that we've got the hots for each other and nothing can stop that."

Amalia: "Do you really need a hard young cock up your pussy that badly?!"

Anna: "Don't you?"

Argyle: "I think I need a drink. I mean that, by the way."

"Just wonderful!" Smith clapped his hands. And just at that moment, Studs Zenith walked in.

"Sorry. I'm late. Hurricane Watch and all that."

"Well, is there going to be a hurricane?" Deirdre demanded.

Zenith looked puzzled. "I don't think so, but then I just read what they tell me. By the way, I got them to name it after me if it ever does show up. Hurricane Studs. Did I miss anything?"

"Just the scene where Ayn announces she going to have an affair with Nate."

"Well, that's sort of obvious. I mean, look at me, look at Argyle. What would you do?"

"You seem to be forgetting something, Studs," said Edward, "your wife Barbara."

"Right, I get it. It's awkward."

"You cheeseball asshole," Argyle muttered.

"I'm going to pretend I didn't hear that," said Zenith magnanimously. "We have to work together as a team. Like Team Nine at my station."

Ted, just relieved to be out of the fray, only had to contain his laughter.

"Well, let's do it!" said Studs enthusiastically.

Gershem took the opportunity to go outside and get some air. Of course, the Smith woman and the Happy Shadow were both waiting for him, though he was unaware of the latter.

"So," said Sylvia, "how does it feel to be upstaged by a weatherman?"

Gershem broke into laughter, which she did not understand. "I guess that all depends on which way the wind is blowing," he chuckled.

"He's just a silly fop. You were much more of a young Nate than he is."

"I don't know whether to thank you or take that as an insult. Both the characters seem to be idiots."

"Oh really, Ted, how many times do actors play the fool?"

"I'm sorry, you're right. Every drama needs a villain."

"I'm willing to play the part. I know you're all hung up on Anna but – well, maybe you want to go downstairs. You know she's fucking Studs Zenith anyway."

"No, I don't know she's fucking Studs Zenith and what do you mean downstairs?"

"Let me show you."

A sidewalk elevator suddenly popped up and she ushered him into "my real world." Down they went, down to the nether world of painful pleasures.

"I don't do this for just anyone," she cooed as she opened the locked door of the dungeon. "Behold!"

Gershem was flabbergasted. "Jesus Christ, Sylvia…"

"I could crucify you if you want."

"What are you talking about?!" he spluttered.

"Just joking, darling. I want you to do me."

"You want me to crucify you?!"

"Whatever you want, Ted, whatever you want."

"Sylvia, get a grip on yourself. Anna's right upstairs rehearsing."

"You think I don't know that! I want her to smell your odor

right through the floor! The odor of you with another woman!"

"Is this another acting exercise?"

"Life is an acting exercise!"

Gershem had had enough but his curiosity was piqued by all the bizarre instruments of torture in this cloistered cellar. "What is this place for? What do you do here?"

"So you do want to play," she said seductively.

" Not necessarily. Why don't you tell me what this is all about?"

"It's all about torture, Ted. It's all about those split seconds between every other second when you have no idea what's going to happen next! That's why I want you to chain me to the wall and deee-grade me! Don't think about it, Ted! Just do it!"

Gershem laughed. "How much more can I do?" Even the Happy Shadow who had joined them on the sidewalk elevator unobserved, had to stifle a chuckle.

Sylvia, of course, broke into tears.

"Look, I'm sick of this routine. Why don't you tell me about Calvin Card?" said Gershem.

The waterworks dried up instantly and Sylvia suddenly became as hard and cold as an iceberg. "I don't know any Calvin Card."

"Sorry, I must have been thinking about someone else."

That was not a satisfactory answer as far as Sylvia was concerned. She picked out a riding crop from her collection and tried to lash Gershem across the face. He caught her by the arm and took the whip away from her.

"Go ahead! Beat me!" she yowled. "But I'm not telling you one more thing!"

Gershem walked out of the dungeon back to the elevator, figured it out, and ascended to the sidewalk. With the Happy Shadow along for the ride, of course. When he walked through the door into the theatre, Sylvia was already there.

"That man sexually assaulted me!" she shrieked.

Gershem was at a loss. Sexual misbehavior was serious business in college as opposed to the real world. Then the whole room cracked up. Even Anna. "I hope your balls shrivel up and your cock falls off!" she vamped in her Ayn Rand voice and really brought down the house.

"We can all go downstairs after the rehearsal and let our

imaginations run wild!" Edward Smith exulted. "Well, maybe that's a more advanced exercise than we're ready for."

Gershem felt dizzy. Was the Downtown Manhattan Illuminati some sort of S & M club? He should have known it all along. What could be more kinky than a little theatre group?! No wonder Anna with her "Spank me!" routine was so attracted to the whole thing.

"All right, Studs is here. You don't need me tonight. I'm going home," Gershem announced.

"Well, we all gotta do what we gotta do." Edward shrugged good-naturedly.

As soon as Gershem walked out the door, banks of rain shimmered up and down the street in some sort of complex dance pattern. And the wind! He could barely keep his footing as he staggered toward the subway with all kinds of garbage swirling around him. He made it just as a flying stop sign smashed the large green bulb just there at the subway entrance. Hurricane Studs wasn't messing around. Gershem rushed down the stairs and was soon standing on the uptown platform. It was warm, it was dry and he just hoped the whole thing would blow over by the time he got to his station. That wasn't happening. As he stood there, a shallow flood of water came rushing down the tracks, inundating the third rail and sending sparks flying everywhere. Then a second surge raised the water level another foot and it didn't stop rising. Gershem quite logically assumed that if the water flow rose above the platform level he would not only get his feet wet, he'd be electrocuted. It was time to move to higher ground. So he did. But it turned out things weren't that easy. Water was pouring down the stairs from the subway entrance and making it back to the street impossible. Ted had this horrible Hollywood vision of a monstrous tsunami crashing down on Yul Brynner's charioteers as Charlton Heston unparted the Red Sea. At least he could swim. He heard a tremendous crashing sound downstairs and assumed it must be a derailing train. The several people standing on the relatively safe mid-level glanced nervously at one another. No one moved to investigate the crash and one young man gave voice to their general anxiety. "I ain't getting fried for nobody!"

And then they began arriving from below, the survivors of the crash, soaking wet but with no apparent sign of electrocution. Hell had opened and released these drooling, spluttering, hacking and coughing zombies from the netherworld and they showed no sign of stopping. They took the cascading stairways to the street like salmon climbing a fish ladder to spawn up and down the highways and byways of the East Village, a longstanding tradition in the breeding pool of Manhattan, although other creatures lurked around the pool; crab lice, intestinal worms and all manner of bacteria, who were quite happy to abound for their happily short lives and also provided young doctors with an opportunity to treat any symptom that might arise and require closer consultations with the patients.

For his own part, Gershem stayed put. His options were limited. It was obviously flooded both up and downstairs but relatively dry where he was stuck. And then Anna Bunch came sliding down the fish ladder. He rushed to her assistance but she didn't need all that much.

"Ted!" she gasped. "You can't believe what's going on out there! The whole street is under water!"

"Not just out there. The subway is flooded."

"Oh my, what are we going to do?"

Strangely, the flooded street drained into the subway's own storm drains leaving the entrance level pretty dry while the water filled the tracks. Of course, all the rodents who lived down there fled the deluge and were soon swarming all over Ted and Anna's refuge. She was surprisingly nonchalant about this invasion.

"Oh, poor babies," she sighed. "You know I used to keep rats as pets. Lab rats, not like these ones. I got them from the college."

"Really?" said Gershem, who was completely creeped out by these fellow refugees.

"They're no different from hamsters or guinea pigs. People just hate their tails."

Gershem was not much interested in discussing the merits of rodent pets. "What happened to everyone else?"

"They just took off whichever way the wind blew them. The theatre was taking on water and there was nothing else to do."

"Speaking of water," said Gershem, pointing at the staircase to the street. The cascade had stopped. "What do you think? We can't just stay here."

So with rats and mice scurrying about all around them, they

cautiously made their way to the entrance and with some trepidation ascended to the street where the wind and rain had abated and there were all sorts of emergency vehicles speeding by with lights flashing and sirens blaring.

"So now what?" Anna wondered.

"We walk?" Gershem suggested. It was, after all, the only choice they had.

"Walk?" Anna snorted. "You sound like a defendant who just got the charges dismissed."

Gershem laughed. "I wouldn't know."

"My shoes are ruined," she complained but walk they did all the way to the Upper West Side.

The aftermath of the storm caused all kind of wrack and ruin from power outages to wide swathes of fallen trees to total destruction of shoreline homes, but what did Ted and Anna care? They simply spent the next three days in a sort of quarantine where sustenance was delivered by beleaguered Chinese delivery guys and the sex was free and frequent. But then they were interrupted by Edward Smith.

"I've got a job! For all of us. We simply appear down the Jersey Shore and read scripts about how our houses were destroyed. It's for a good cause! And, of course, we get part of the contributions."

"What's this all about?" Ted demanded.

"It's easy. You just do an interview in front of a ruined house on the Jersey Shore. A lot of boohooing and hand wringing. You get the picture."

"What about the real owners?"

"Who cares? They've been evacuated. It's just a pile of rubble. Could be anywhere. A thousand dollars cash apiece for you plus SAG cards."

Anna had commandeered the phone. "So how do we get to the Jersey Shore?"

"We don't. It's just a set in Queens. Don't worry, I'll get you there."

"You said cash plus the card. I already have the card. I think I deserve more."

"All right, all right, twelve for you. But I want to see a manly man comforting his grieving wife."

Kevin Bartelme

"Of course, I'll coach him myself."

"What..?" said Ted

"Well, come on. It's broadcast news! Up to the minute! Right on time! Just hold me on your arms while I sob and wail, 'We lost everything!' That's all there is to it. One thousand dollars for five minutes!"

And so there they were on the five 'o'clock news, Gershem suitably disguised in a mustache, a baseball hat, and a Jets jacket with his arm around Anna, in the frumpiest dress wardrobe could find, while she sobbed her way through a stack of sodden family snapshots.

Imagine what Gershem was thinking when he saw this performance later. Did he feel guilty? Was he ashamed of himself for participating in this sham? He tried parroting back Anna's rationale. The purpose was to raise money for the real victims who were probably too traumatized to make a proper telegenic appearance on the tube. Anna had carried the whole show as he just stood there mutely and he had no doubt that she had jerked a few tears and loosened up some wallets. But this sort of reasoning didn't work. He was a fraud, a con man. Yet he still felt no shame. For the first time, he realized what acting was all about, dissembling to create a desired response. It was seductive, it was, psychologically speaking, the craving for the periodic reward, where, much like compulsive gamblers, the actor puts everything on the line for the adulation of total strangers. It was sick, even depraved, but it was addictive.

"Wasn't I great?" Anna enthused as she watched herself on television and rubbed her pussy to distraction. She fairly basked in the glow of her own image, looking very much like a woman who has just been nicely laid. Who was Gershem to rain on her parade? But she was looking for rain of a different sort.

"Yes, you were," he agreed, "but I think I'll take a pass if any more of these events pop up."

"Really?" she purred. "What about that thousand dollars in your pocket. Or is that something else popping up? God, I make myself so horny! Come on my face! Come in my hair! Come all over me! I'm ready for my close-up, Mr. Ted!"

At this point, Gershem thought it was time to tell Anna to go home. But he didn't. Can you guess why? Frankly, I can't. In retrospect, it would have certainly been the best option. Instead he freely distributed his sperm wither the way it squirted and spurted after an expert blowjob and let the streams of sticky jism dribble from her chin, her bangs, and finally course down the riverine gorge between her breasts.

"Oh God," she moaned, "I feel like I've just been over Niagara Falls in a barrel!"

Gershem didn't want to spoil the fun. "But you, survived, my dear, you survived, And the camera is still rolling."

"The camera, the camera!" she gasped. "What more do they want? Fuck me, Ted! Do it for my fans!"

Well, there's no point in dwelling upon what happened next, except that by the dawn's early light, Anna had convinced him that so-called crisis acting wasn't such a bad deal after all. Then she left for work and he went back to sleep where he had a dream. He was in a crowded house, a sort of party really, where everybody's identity kept changing every time he turned his head. It didn't bother him that the person he'd just been talking to had turned into someone else and they just kept conversing as if nothing had happened, a sort of weird variation on speed dating, an activity with which Gershem was not familiar.

He woke to the ringing phone. It was Edward Smith of course.

"Ted! Did you see yourself on the news? Great job!"

"Well, thank you, Edward."

"The perfect blend of shock and brave resignation, all without saying a word! Really, just fabulous. And for what a good cause! You should be very proud of yourself."

"Pride goeth before a fall, Edward."

"Well, you know what I mean. By the way, I've got your SAG card. You're one of us now."

"You make it sound like the zombies at the supermarket."

"What?"

"Nothing. Private joke."

Meanwhile, just at that moment, Barry Breen and Rino Matsui were being ushered by a butler into the Tabernacle of Lucifer to meet the Magus in his aerie high above Gramercy Park, an art nouveau apartment decorated with all manner of occult esoterica. There was a bronze statue of a goat having his way with a woman from behind, a satyr engaged in much the same activity, and a giant Sigil of Baphomet done in red enamel hanging over the mantle of the room where the bright daylight was shut out by thick red velveteen drapes. All in all, it looked like a rather flamboyant fortune telling parlor, which, of course, was exactly what it was.

"Please sit," said the butler. "The Magus is on the phone. He will be with you in a moment."

A few seconds later, the Magus appeared in full mufti, a devil mask, which concealed his face and a flowing black robe.

"Sorry to keep you waiting," he said graciously. "I am the Magus of the Tabernacle of Satan. So I understand you're working on a research project at your university with the renowned professor Theodore Gershem. That's splendid. I'm all yours. Ask me what you want to know. I assume there's some sort of honorarium for my interview."

"Well, no, actually..." said Breen uncomfortably.

"No matter," said the Magus waving him off. Would you like some refreshments? Igor! Three Glades please! Okay, what do you want to know?"

"What exactly is Satanism?"

"Satan rules the world," said the Magus. "Isn't it obvious? All the other namby pamby religions know this and they feebly try to oppose him with all manner of resist temptation dogmas, especially persecution of the followers of the Master!"

Igor returned with a tray of three green drinks in martini glasses and a plate of tiny beignets. He handed them each a drink and left the plate on the coffee table.

"What is this?" Rino asked timidly.

"A Glade," said the Magus, "a very fine cocktail indeed. Down the hatch!" And he drank his without coming up for air.

Breen and Rino looked at each other, shrugged and followed suit. The drinks were tropical without all the sugar, leaving the fetid taste of swamp water and chaya on the palate, strange but not unpleasant.

"But who always has the last word?" the Magus went on. "Satan, that's who! Who rode the tank in the General's rank when

Blitzkrieg raged and the bodies stank? Who said, 'Pleased to meet you. I hope you guessed my name!' Satan, that's who!"

"So," Breen ventured, "Satan is just defending himself against the people conspiring against him?"

"Exactly."

This idea of Satan being the victim of a conspiracy rather than the perpetrator was so bizarre that the two researchers had to follow it up.

Rino spoke up, "So what is Satan doing about all this plotting against him?"

"Watching them destroy each other. My advice was to drop video players and porno tapes on Afghanistan to enrage the ragheads, but the Master was against it. He said it might stop the war and the spread of heroin addiction. In retrospect I have to agree."

"You speak to the Devil?" Breen asked.

"But of course," the Magus said dismissively. "So can you," he leaned forward and leered. "For a fee." He could see the Glades he'd served them going to work. "Devil his due and all that."

"Uh, like I said, we don't pay for interviews," said Breen, who was feeling pleasantly dizzy.

"Not even with Satan himself?" the Magus leaned even further forward. "He doesn't require anything so crass as money, you understand. He simply wants to see you two fornicate right here on the carpet,"

Rino, Gladed up as she was, laughed. "You tell Satan that will cost him a crass three hundred dollars."

"Ah, a little businesswoman I see. Let me talk to the boss." He muttered some gibberish and announced, "The Master says that will be quite all right."

"Up front," she said.

"What are you doing?" Barry demanded.

"I'm negotiating," Rino purred.

"Well, I'm not," said Barry indignantly, "and I'm not fucking you in front of some dirty old man."

"Oh, come on, Mr. Breen," said the Magus. "Don't be such a prude. Satan doesn't like prudes. Just think of it as an unrecorded porno movie."

"Go fuck yourself," said Barry grabbing Rino's hand and pulling her along out of the Tabernacle to the elevator.

"What on earth's gotten into you?" he demanded.

"I don't know, but it sure feels good." It was, of course, the Glade working its own black magic. Breen weighed quite a bit more than Rino and he had only been slightly affected but he could plainly see she was highly intoxicated. One thing was for sure. They were not going to mention this peculiar encounter to Professor Gershem.

As you might have guessed already, Edward Smith was not only the Grand Poobah Zofar but the Magus of the Tabernacle of Lucifer as well. Arthur Sachs played Igor. The reason Smith maintained these different identities was pretty simple. He was peeper. He liked to watch other people do it, though he had no desire to participate himself except as a spectator. The real thing was sticky and complicated. He never even fucked Sylvia and let her go about her carnal activities as she pleased. Except, of course, for splitting the take on the dungeon. But that was business. Better to just sit on the sidelines and jerk off. So, it must be said, that the Magus was somewhat disappointed at the young couple's abrupt departure since he had always wanted to see whether Oriental women's' lady parts were indeed slanted.

Somewhat let down Smith asked Sachs, "Was it something I said?"

"I don't know," said Arthur. "Would you like me to give you a hand job?"

"Really, Arthur, contain yourself."

The Happy Shadow had, of course, been privy to all these goings on and very quietly took his leave to audit Professor Gershem's abnormal psychology seminar where he would, of course, go unnoticed.

Rhoda Memberman was speaking about the importance of identity politics in the formation of conspiracies and logically from there to the formation of concepts of good and evil.

"It's tribal, in a way," she said. "Any kind of 'ism', capitalism, communism, Catholicism, atheism, defines itself as good and the opposite point of view as evil."

"The dialectic at work," Gershem agreed.

"How about jismism?" David Kogan asked. "Sorry, seriously, how about nudism? We've had a Black president, a circus clown president. How about a nudist president? I can just hear the inaugural address: 'I stand naked before you. If ever I have to wear clothes, I assure you they will be transparent. I have nothing to hide!'"

The whole room cracked up, if a bit grudgingly in Rhoda's case.

Gershem quickly moved to regain control of the situation. "Just take off your clothes and you've got my vote, David. Can we get this back on track? Okay, what I think Rhoda is saying is that in order to even have a concept of good we have to formulate a concept of not good, that is, evil. If we examine…"

Akisha interrupted him, "What I think this whole good and evil scam is just an excuse to be cruel to other people."

"That's what I said," said Rhoda. "It's all tribalism."

"That's not exactly true," Akisha shot back. "People are cruel to each to each other right here in this room. And we're supposed to be some sort of tribe ourselves, the educated, the rational, but let's face it, Rhoda, you're Jew and I'm a nigger."

"What exactly do you mean by that?" Rhoda reared up.

"You know what I mean, girl," said Akisha with a scowl.

"Okay, that's it for today," said Gershem who knew that saying anything at all would be like throwing gasoline on a fire. And please note that Barry Breen and Rino Matsui had not uttered a word during this discussion.

On his way out of the building, Gershem ran into Conrad Boardman.

"Hey there, Ted. Did you make peace with your downtown kooks?"

"They're not my kooks, Conrad, but yes, I've reached out to them again."

"Reached out?" Boardman mocked him. "How very millennial of you. Are you feeling them up?"

"Rather the opposite."

"Most interesting. Maybe you could introduce me to some of these reacher outers."

"Tend your own garden, Conrad."

"Mara claims she saw you on TV last night. Did your New

Jersey beach house get destroyed by the storm?"

"Conrad, I don't have a beach house, and, if I did, it certainly wouldn't be in New Jersey."

"Well, everyone who's not French looks the same to her."

Boardman was referring to his hot little wife whom he'd met in Mexico at the world renowned artists' and scholars' retreat, the Instituto del Pacifico some years ago. Gershem had heard a rumor that Mara was fucking everyone in town (not him of course) and that Boardman endured his cuckoldry with the dry aplomb with which anyone with a live wire wife has to put up and shut up. Collegially of course.

"It wasn't me," Gershem chuckled, "But give your wife my regards."

"You've been fucking her too, haven't you?" Boardman challenged him. "After all, she's been fucking everyone else"

"What, are you kidding? And get a grip on yourself. You're fantasizing."

"Quite right, I'm sorry," said Boardman coolly when they parted ways at the exit with the Happy Shadow wondering which one to follow. Boardman, of course.

So Gershem went on his way, happily unshadowed and wondered what Anna was making for dinner, The slow, but inexorable slide into domesticity, tended to annoy him occasionally, but the benefits were manifest. Food and pussy. What more did he really need? He would soon find out.

❖

10

A good lawyer is hard to find since the subject itself is an oxymoron, but Edward Smith had just been preliminarily offered a single event contract with Retalitron to provide them with crisis actors, which might very well turn into something more long term and he needed someone to go over the paperwork before he signed on the dotted line. Enter contract specialist Tootie Wookums LLD. Wookums was a curious looking fellow with an orange face, presumably from cheap tanning spray, but his fee was not outlandish and his references seemed passable.

"So," said Wookums as he pawed through the sheaf of papers Smith had presented him in his small office in the Woolworth Building, "Retalitron. No finer company. Impeccable reputation. You must be proud to be associated with them."

Smith was a bit puzzled by this pitch. He was the client, not Retalitron. "Er, yes, of course, Mr. Wookums. Proud. That's the word."

"Well, I see these papers are all in order," said the lawyer, though he'd barely glanced at them. "I'd suggest you just sign and be done with it."

"But you haven't even looked at them," Smith protested.

"No need," said Wookums, "As I said, Retalitron is rock solid, but if you insist." He looked annoyed as he began to actually read the document. When he'd finished he looked up and said, "I see a win-win situation, a strategic partnership with real solutions. Get on board before the train leaves the station!"

"Well, of course," said Smith uncertainly, "but…"

"No ifs, ands, or buts," said Wookums. "He who hesitates is lost. Now, about my fee. Cash would be nice."

"It would, I suppose, but I don't have it on me." Smith had no intention of paying this two-bit shyster. "I'll just go downstairs to the cash machine and be right back." With that he fled the building vowing to give Argyle a good tongue-lashing for recommending this guy. But Smith had bigger fish to fry at the moment. His wife was going to perform in the dungeon with a real Wall Street mover and shaker in half an hour and he had to be there to clandestinely videotape the show for the archives. Later, he had to pick up a package from Bob and Marta Applewhite who were in town for the afternoon. Such a busy day ahead!

Sylvia Smith, in full black leather regalia, welcomed her investment banker client, who shall remain anonymous, – let's just call him Mr. X – to the dungeon with a snarling, "Off with those clothes, you piece of human filth!"

"Yes, Mistress," he puled as he hurriedly undressed.

Then she shackled him to the Big Wheel and gave it a good spin while she reviled him. "How much money did you cheat people out if today, you insect?! How much?!"

"I don't know!" he wailed. "A lot!"

As the Big Wheel slowed, Sylvia stopped it so Mr. X was hanging upside down.

" Widows and orphans?" she spat out and shocked him with a cattle prod.

"Yow!" he gasped. "Yes! Widows and orphans!"

"How many, you loathsome parasite?!" she roared.

"I don't know," he gasped. "Many!"

She shocked him again. "You vile piece of shit! And how about old retired people?!"

And so it went on for the better part of an hour until a very well satisfied Mt. X put his clothes back on, paid up, and left.

"Did you get all that?" Sylvia called out to Edward behind the one-way mirror.

He emerged holding the camera in his hand. "Of course. You want me to play it back? You were really quite superb."

"Thank you, Edward," she mock simpered. "I've got to get out of this outfit first."

Anna Bunch had plans for the evening. She had acquired two tickets to a Broadway musical called "Devil Moon" and she expected Ted to accompany her. Gershem loathed Broadway shows with all their exuberant, saccharine, mawkish singing and dancing specially designed for blue heads with homosexual sons, so it was a hard sell.

"But it's going to be fun!" she pouted. "They call it, 'The Disco Dr. Faustus',"

"Really? How could I resist," Gershem said drily, "but I'm going to. What are you doing buying me a ticket without telling me?"

"I told you days ago. You just never listen to me. You have to go."

"No I don't."

"If you don't go, I'll never suck your cock again."

And that is how Gershem found himself in a front row balcony seat in the Belasco Theatre. What followed was too painful for Gershem to even remember afterwards but some ordeals have their rewards, in this case the final falling of the curtain.

"Wasn't it great!" Anna gushed. "All those demons on roller skates!"

"Did you pick this show because it has the Devil in it?" Gershem said stiffly as if he were a Brit about to deliver a "crusher". "Some sort of commentary on my current subject of interest, the various concepts of good and evil?"

Anna laughed." But of course, I do it for you, Ted, I do it for you."

Gershem was just happy it was over and they could leave.

"Where to now?" he asked her.

"Nowhere around here. It's like Disneyland. Maybe further up the west side, say Columbus Avenue."

"So they took a cab to 68th St. and walked uptown. There were lots of crowded little restaurants with outdoor service so they just picked one at random and sat down. The toothsome, obvious acting (yet to be working) class waitress cheerfully took their orders and they settled in for a little people watching.

"Did you know," said Gershem, "that silly all singing, all dancing piece of trash we just saw is based on a Christopher Marlowe play?"

"You mean the one who actually wrote Shakespeare's plays?"

"The very same, but he didn't write all of Shakespeare's stuff. There were several others."

"I can see this conspiracy thing is getting to you, Ted. Who were the others?"

"Well, let's see," he searched his memory, "besides Marlowe there was Thomas Kyd, Edward DeVere, Robert Greene, William Stanley, and, of course, Ben Jonson who put together the folios and pinned them on the recently deceased Shakespeare."

"What do you mean pinned them on?"

"Shakespeare was their alibi. After Queen Elizabeth died, the Puritans, who were just as nasty then as they are today, took over and banned the theatre. These killjoys even made putting on plays a capital crime. Not such a bad idea in retrospect, but a terrifying prospect for the real authors who just blamed it all on Shakespeare and beat the rap."

"How do you know all this?" Anna demanded.

"I read it in somebody's graduate dissertation. The main thesis was pretty simple. The Globe Theatre put on a new show every week, sort of like a television series. One person could not possibly write that fast or that much so it was done by committee, a pool of writers much like the people who write today's sitcoms."

"Really, Ted," Anna said indignantly. "Are you comparing Shakespeare to Eight is Enough?"

"Well, it is a different sensibility, isn't it?"

"It's sure makes a good conspiracy theory."

The waitress arrived with their drinks and a basket of French fries.

"Cheers," Gershem held his glass up. "To anonymous plotters everywhere. The nightmare landscape of history is littered with well-known pathological monsters. Better to lay no claim to fame and quietly disappear!"

"Quiet down," said Anna softly. "You'll discourage all these ambitious actors sitting around us."

"You're right. Who am I to judge? God, these fries are greasy. You know I was thinking about another conspiracy theory today. My very own, by the way."

"How original of you. Tell me about it."

"I call it my grand unified Ayn Rand theory. You know, I didn't know anything about the woman until we got involved in this play so I did a little research."

"I'm all ears," said Anna in her guttural Ayn Rand accent.

"I don't agree. As far as I can see, you're mostly tits and ass." For this, he got rapped on the knuckles with a spoon. "As I was saying," he resumed, "I did a little digging and found out a few things. The woman was supposedly a refugee from Stalinist Russia who somehow magically winds up in Hollywood writing screenplays. In her spare time, she writes an epic bestseller. The prose may be awful and the plot may be ludicrous, but copies of the book, a hokey paean to laissez faire capitalism, are snapped up like hotcakes and she continues on as a far right cult figure to this day."

"So?" said Anna. "Look at L. Ron Hubbard, look at Ronald Reagan."

"My contention is that she was a deep mole Soviet agent right from the beginning. She was sent to push capitalism to its absurd conclusion, to heighten the contradictions, as they say. The Russians wrote the book and then bought all the copies to make it look like a bestseller and lure the suckers into the tent. And it worked! Her acolyte Greenspan, acting on her insane theories, brought the economy to its knees in 2008. She just wasn't around to witness her triumph."

"Speaking for my late self," Anna continued in character, "your theory is absurd. My sole motivation was my raging, uncontrollable lust for Nathaniel Branden."

"Well, it was just a thought," Gershem conceded. "You want another drink?

❖

11

Undeterred by their meeting with the Magus of the Tabernacle of Lucifer, Barry and Rino were on their way to meet another prospective opinionator of the spiritualist persuasion. Mary Eddy McPherson presided over a small flock of adherents who made regular contact with the dead through ritual ceremonies involving telephones and she was most eager to talk with her two investigators. Having made an appointment, Barry and Rino took the train under the river to Sunnyside in Queens, then walked down a pleasant, tree-lined street to their destination, a modest frame house which served as the nerve center of Senders International.

Mrs. McPherson, an old bluehead in a dowdy black dress with piercing, flinty eyes, greeted them at the door and ushered them into her antique filled parlor where hundreds of snapshots lined the walls.

"Would you like some lemonade?" she offered. She fetched a tray with a pitcher and three glasses. "I make it myself. Now what was it you wanted to talk about?"

"We're doing a project…" Breen started.

"I'm sorry," she interrupted, picking up an ear trumpet off the sideboard. "Can't hear a thing without it." She inserted it in her ear and leaned forward. "Go ahead."

Breen started again. "We're involved in…"

"You know my husband left me for a younger woman," she said loudly. "Said he couldn't stand any more of the spirit world. Said that I was just a crazy old biddy prone to hallucinating. But you're real, aren't you?"

"I think so," said Barry.

"There! That man was just no darn good. And that woman he ran off with, well, she was positively evil! That's what you want to discuss, isn't it? Good and evil? Well there you have it."

"Yes we do," Breen cautiously humored her. "Can you tell us

about Senders & Receivers International?"

"What for? Do you want to sign up? There's a membership fee, you know."

"We'll certainly consider it but we'd like to learn more about the organization."

"Well, of course you would. Just follow me." She got up and led them into another room dominated by an old-fashioned telephone switchboard, the kind you might see in an old movie with operators frantically plugging in calls. "This is Drusilla," Mrs. McPherson explained, "She keeps us in touch with the beyond. Do you have the number of a departed loved one you'd like to talk to?"

Baffled Rino and Barry looked at each other.

"Well, that's all right. Who carries around the phone numbers of dead people anyway? Why don't we see if Ayn Rand is in? You know who that is? She's one of my favorites."

Had the two of them known about Professor Gershem's extra-curricular activities, they would have been stunned, but they didn't and Breen could only reply, "I've heard of her."

"Well, you're in for a real treat." The old lady sat down at the switchboard and plugged in a cable.

"Hello Ayn? Are you here?"

"I most certainly am," a guttural, heavily accented, female voice from which Anna Bunch could have taken some cues, boomed from a loudspeaker overhead.

"I have two young people with me."

"I can see that. Very hot, very juicy."

"Now don't be naughty, Ayn."

"But I like being naughty," the voice purred.

"They want to talk with you about good and evil, Ayn."

"They've certainly come to the right place then. As an objectivist I want to make myself perfectly clear. Good and evil are not mere constructs with relative worth. They exist in nature and the evidence is abundant. Nature is not benevolent, it is not empathetic, it is not altruistic. In nature, to the victor go the spoils! That is the good! The evil lies in the weak and feeble, the moochers begging for a handout from the real movers and shakers! The good men who create giant corporations for their own profit! The entrepreneurs who wrestle wealth from the earth and turn it to their own ends!"

"So you think..." Breen started.

"Shut up! I haven't finished yet! Let's be honest, Barry. Here you are doing it with a little hotty from an inferior species. I won't even call them a race. That would imply that they are human beings, which they most certainly are not. More like monkeys really. What you need, Barry, is an experienced woman, a woman like me! God, I'd like to suck you into a magnificent..."

"Ayn!" Mrs. McPherson snapped. "If you don't stop that, I'm going to pull your plug!"

"It's Barry's plug I'd like to pull," were Ayn's last words before Mrs. McPherson cut her off.

"I'd like to apologize. Ayn hasn't been the same since she banished Nathaniel Branden," the old woman explained to the astonished couple. "I can't say that I blame her, though. Some men are just no darn good. Would you like to talk to another spirit?"

Barry and Rino demurred and were on their way as fast as they could politely leave.

"Stay in touch!" Mrs. McPherson called after them as they hurried off down the street.

"How did she do that? Is she some sort of ventriloquist?" Breen wondered.

"I don't know," said Rino, "but she sure had the hots for you."

"She called you a monkey."

"I've been called worse. At least monkey's are cute."

"I don't think she meant it that way."

"Who cares? She's just jealous."

Mrs. McPherson was not the only one raising the spirit of Ayn Rand from the great beyond that day. Edward Smith was walking down the street when he was approached by a furtive, swarthy man who slapped him with an envelope that fluttered to the sidewalk and said, "You're served," before scurrying off down the avenue. In his checkered career as entrepreneur and artiste, Smith had been slapped with subpoenas a number of times, so. As he picked up the envelope, his trepidation was tempered by a sense of déjà vu. He'd been there before.

He looked over the court order requiring him to defend

himself from a cease and desist order for the production of "Ayn and Nate" on both copyright infringement and libel grounds. Since the script had not been published nor shown to anyone outside the small group of Downtown Illuminati, Smith wondered who had spilled the beans to the plaintiff, the Objectivist Institute, an organization that had staggered on after Rand's death to mere oblivion, reduced to filing nuisance suits against all and sundry attempts to discredit their late Shamanette.

For Smith, this was not as an unwelcome development as you might think. The free (minus lawyers' fees) publicity it was bound to generate was potential box office magic!

Whatever, the court date was two weeks away so he had time to find suitable representation if there even were such a thing. Tootie Wookums had pretty much soured him on the law.

When he got back to his apartment, he showed the summons to Sylvia and she went wild. "How dare they!" she huffed. "Once again persecution of the arts rears its ugly head! I want to play your lawyer!"

"This is not theatre, my love. I think I need a real one."

"Nonsense, I can do a lawyer better than any cheap mouthpiece can. All I'm going to do is ask for a postponement anyway."

Smith mulled it over. "I'll consider it. You can't be worse than Tootie Wookums."

"With a name like that?" she snorted. "I'll shine in court, Edward. I really will." She looked at her watch. "I've got a date. Nobody important. Just a Hassid diamond dealer."

"Give him a smack upside his rabbi hat for me, darling."

"I'll do that," she purred.

"When I was a lad, I served a term as an office boy in an attorney's firm," he sang as she took her leave.

Then it was time to get down to real business. Retalitron business. There was job coming up that required a little more rehearsal time than the storm coverage. A fire department upstate needed extras for a drill after a nuclear power plant accident. It was all hands on deck for the theatre club. They would play the walking wounded staggering around in a daze with elaborately fake injuries. Another group of actors, actual amputees, would play the most severely injured. It wasn't being filmed for public consumption but the acting had to be good enough for the first responders to take it somewhat seriously. Maybe he could recruit some of Sylvia's clients. They were certainly into pain.

These musings were interrupted by his vibrating cell phone. He noted the number and answered, "Hello, Arthur, What do you want?"

"You have all new friends now, Edward," Sachs whined. "Why don't you pay any attention to me anymore?"

"I'm sorry, Arthur, I've just been so busy lately. Do you know I'm getting sued?"

As soon as it was out of his mouth, Smith regretted his lack of discretion.

"Really?!" Sachs was all agog. "By who?"

"Whom, Arthur," Smith corrected him. "The leftover Ayn Rand crowd."

"No! How exciting!"

"I think so. I feel all persecuted and censored like James Joyce or William Burroughs or something."

"Who?"

"Forget it. What else do you want except to whine and complain?"

"Don't be that way, Edward."

"I have an acting job for you next week where you'll really get to be a victim."

"A job? That's great!"

Anna Bunch was not nearly as enthusiastic about this job as Sachs seemed to be. "We don't have any lines and no one will even see us," she complained.

"But think of all the good you'll be doing!" Smith pointed out. "There are nearly five hundred nuclear plants across the country and any one of them could have an accident at any time! Local fire departments have to be prepared and this film will show them how!"

Anna had to concede the point but she still wasn't happy about it. "Will we even be recognizable?"

"You'll be bleeding! You'll be maimed! Like a zombie in a horror movie! You'll also be getting two thousand dollars for one day on the set."

Suddenly the offer sounded a whole lot better. "Ted too?" she asked.

"Of course," he reassured her.

Later, when she broached the offer to Gershem, he unexpectedly showed very little reluctance at all. In fact, he very much liked the idea that he would be unrecognizable. "It sounds like fun," he said.

"Doesn't it?" she hastily agreed before he changed his mind as she had already spent the imaginary money on a week long idyll in Cancun, a possible prelude to the ceremony at City Hall she had in mind.

Gershem, living comfortably in male oblivion, still thought of Anna as a guile free friendly fuck. He was, in that respect, a bit of a fool and only peripherally aware that he was being led around by the nose, a tenured university professor reduced to a rutting beast! What a representative anecdotal paradigm. Which in vulgar common discourse translates as horse's ass.

And speaking of horse's asses, even Studs Zenith wanted in on the action. "It's in violation of my contract, but I could really get into playing a hideously mangled accident victim. Of course, I can't accept any money…" he dribbled off.

"Not to worry," said Smith. "It's cold, hard cash on the barrelhead. Just a little pocket change between men of the world like you and me."

"Well, if you put it that way," Zenith cordially allowed.

"I do. I do," said Smith.

The Happy Shadow, who had not been invited to particpate, was nonetheless well pleased that things were proceeding and convening along lines quite similar to his original expectations. After all, nothing is certain and choreography is never perfect, but the symmetry of his vision was loosely holding together at the moment. By the way, the Happy Shadow had fucked minxy little Mara Boardman while she bent over the cheese section at the organic grocery store on Broadway and she hadn't even noticed. Such were the subtleties of his shadow motions. His next target was Anna Bunch whose instrument might be more finely attuned to the rhythm of his gyrating, love making, soul shaking, sex machine! And then there was that Japanese girl. Like the Grand Magus, the Happy Shadow was also curious about the placement of Asian lady parts. He would get around to it one of these days. So much to do and so little time! And one thing the Happy Shadow knew for sure – there wasn't a whole lot of time left.

❖

12

The object of the Happy Shadow's predatory speculation, Rino Matsui, had stumbled on a particularly wacko little group while perusing Asahi Shimbun on the Internet, the Japanese Nazi Party or Zaitokukai, which had just staged a ceremony at the site in Tokyo where General Tojo was hanged, She translated the article for Barry Breen who explained to her that there were neo Nazis all over the world.

"But this is Japan," she said. "Hitler thought that Asian people were inferior."

"Well, he probably did, but the Japanese were also a major military power. I mean, he signed a nonaggression pact with Stalin and then he attacked Russia. I'm pretty sure the German Nazis would have frowned on our relationship. Why don't you call these Japanese Nazis up and ask them about their program. They sound a little confused."

So Rino did and found out that the Zaitokukai hated everyone except a very select few equally insane Japanese. The rest of the island nation was just a bunch of pussies controlled by the Koreans. Rino did the best she could to be polite but the addled party "official" was so crazy, he demanded to know, much as the Happy Shadow would like to know, if her vagina was aligned with the Japanese magnetic field. Also, the rest of the world was conspiring to do away with these brave few who would disembowel themselves rather than submit. He promised her she would soon be seeing Zaitokukai committing seppuku on YouTube. "Banzai!!" he shrieked and the line went dead.

"I don't think they're a very good subject for the study," she informed Breen. "They don't have any clear dogma on good and evil."

"Well," said Breen, "neither do we. What are we doing anyway? What's the real purpose of this project?"

She chuckled.

"What's so funny?"

"As far as I'm concerned the purpose is we get to spend a lot of time together."

"So we do, so we do," Breen agreed. "Who's next on the interview list? Can't we dig up someone a little more respectable than these fruitcakes we've been talking to?"

"How about the president of the New York Flat Earth Society?"

"The what?"

"I'm not kidding. He was quite enthusiastic about talking to anybody."

"What's a Flat Earther got to do with good and evil?"

"Everything apparently. The people who are perpetuating the myth that the earth is a globe are the epitome of evil trying to conceal the truth that we are the center of the universe."

"I see. Well, let's make an appointment. What's this guy's name?"

"Walter something. He lives downtown." So she made the call and they arranged to meet that very afternoon.

Walter Birmingham, the poncho wearing man with long grey hair whom you may remember from the first 9/11 meeting Gershem attended, greeted Rino and Barry at the entrance to the former Con Edison substation where he made his home and graciously invited them in. "So glad to know you. Would you like something to drink?"

"Just water," said Breen warily. "Or maybe Rino would like

a Glade," he gave her a sidelong glance and she pursed her lips.

"A what?"

"Nothing. Private joke."

After Walter fetched them two glasses of water it was time to get down to business. "So, what do you two young people want to know?"

"Well, we're doing a study for a project on various conceptions of the nature of good and evil..."

"No such thing."

"No such thing as what?"

"Good."

"But, dialectically speaking..."

"Fuck the dialectic. The whole idea comes from the ridiculous notion that a person can stand upside down on the other side of a non-existent globe."

"Uh," Rino ventured, "what happens when I fly to Japan?"

"You fly to Japan,"

"But..."

"Listen, have you ever looked out the window of a plane and seen the so-called curvature of the earth? Have you? This so-called globe we live on supposedly has a circumference of more than 24,000 miles. That means it's spinning at more than a thousand miles and hour. Don't you think you'd notice?"

"But..." Breen tried to object.

"I know what you're going to say. That we can observe the speed by the movement of the planets and stars. What if there is no moon, no planets and stars? What if it's all an illusion created to make us think that we're puny and insignificant?"

"Created by whom?" Breen got three words in edgewise.

"Beats me, but whoever it is has a pretty nasty sense of humor."

"But we landed on the moon."

"Nonsense. Who's 'we' anyway. Have you been to the moon? Talk about creating an illusion," Birmingham snorted. Do you know this little ditty? 'There's a place on Mars where the ladies smoke cigars and the men go bare because they have no underwear'? That's NASA for you. Just another fairy tale. Who did you say was running your project?"

"Ted Gershem."

"You know, I think I've seen him before at the 9/11 meeting at St. Mark's. He hangs out with Edward Smith and that theatre crowd."

Breen and Rino looked at each other. "So he mentioned," said Breen cautiously.

"Bad sorts, theatre people."

"I wouldn't know…"

"I mean bad sorts in general. All theatre people. They'll do anything to get in the limelight. Sick, really, that craving for the adulation of total strangers."

"Uh, maybe we could get back to the source of this illusory planet, the people who created it?"

"Who said they were people? Could be anything. Aliens, beasts, what have you."

"I don't understand their motive," said Rino. "What's in it for them?"

"How should I know? Schadenfreude. Reveling in the misfortunes of this inferior species. How evil can you get?"

"Inferior species?"

"People monkeys. Human beings. Maybe they're like cruel children pulling the wings off flies. Who knows? I can't prove anything except the earth is flat."

Rino giggled.

"What's so funny?" Birmingham demanded.

"I think you're right. That's the way I experience it anyway."

"Now there's a young lady with some brains! A cause to celebrate! Let me get you a Glade! Whatever that is!"

"It's secret," said giggling Rino. "Only the Magus of the Tabernacle of Lucifer knows how to make it."

Birmingham gaped at them. "So you do know Edward Smith!"

"The theatre group guy?" thoroughly puzzled Breen wondered.

"Oh, he goes by a lot of different names. Have you ever heard of the Grand Poobah?"

"The what?"

"Nothing. Private joke. Glade anyone?"

Breen laughed. "Are you telling me that this Edward Smith is the Magus? He's playing two people?"

"Three actually. He's the Grand Poobah Zofar as well. When he was just a child he saw a television program called, 'I Led Three Lives,' and he's been doing it ever since. He's the one you should talk to. Most of the people at the 9/11 meeting think he's a double agent. And his wife! Watch out, young man. She tries to seduce anything in pants."

"How about you, Walter?" Rino teased him. "Did she seduce you?"

"You mean have I ever done it with Sylvia? Who hasn't? I heard your Professor Ted's been having at her like a rutting bull moose."

All this and more was discussed at some length and when Barry and Rino left they had a clearer picture of their mentor Ted Gershem, but a much murkier take on the conceptual nature of good and evil.

"I think we better keep this to ourselves," said Breen as they walked down the street.

"I know what you mean," Rino agreed. "This is getting weird. What is Professor Gershem up to with these people?"

"We don't know and maybe we don't want to know." Which was true, but whatever their intentions, they were going to find out anyway.

Walter Birmingham didn't much care about their quandary. He'd already efficiently stirred the shit enough to set off waves of gossip about Edward Smith and he would just wait until all those muttered words washed up on the sand.

❖

13

Anna Bunch had a job at a law firm where she did nothing but keep track of the client's accounts on paper ledgers. It was so easy she couldn't even understand why they still employed her. A cell phone would be more efficient. On the other hand, she did understand why she still had a job. The less information on the computers the better the partners liked it. So much for paper trails. All you had to do was run the ledger through the shredder and it was a whole new day.

Her boss, five years her junior, was so terror stricken by her competence that they never spoke except to say hello and goodbye. She enjoyed her star turn as de facto office manager but was not much more enamored of her tedious job than that and yearned for the wherewithal to quit. In her mind's eye, Edward Smith represented a potential way out, a return to the dim limelight of a character actor with a paycheck. Ted Gershem was not only the bridge to this new future but a very good catch for a woman her age. What a lucky girl she was! she thought as she basked in the warm glow of her good fortune.

Gershem, who had only the faintest inkling of what Anna had in mind, was content to humor her and get laid on a regular basis. To his own surprise, he actually enjoyed this acting business. Maybe Sylvia Smith was right. There wasn't much difference between an actor and a teacher after all. In fact, this acting training might lead to the lucrative lecture circuit where projecting oneself as a bit of a clown, a bit of a blowhard was highly valued. "Your genial emcee and Toastmaster General, Ted Gershem," he chuckled and hummed a few bars of "Miss America" a la Bert Parks. He didn't remember the lyrics.

So now these two, conjoined by their mutual interest in acting and fucking, were about to embark on the steady, if not all that well paying, temp jobs that the industrial and training film businesses offered.

"I hope they don't make me look too awful," Anna worried.

"Really?" Ted needled her. "Get into the spirit of the thing. I want to look like I've just been on the outskirts of an atomic blast with my charred flesh falling off in chunks."

"Ew, that is so disgusting." Anna whinged theatrically. "Maybe I don't want to be in this thing after all." She was not being entirely candid, of course, and would probably appear as the Incredible Singing, Dancing, Oozing Mutant Pussy for the right money. You could almost hear the carny barker barking, "Step right up, ladies and gents…"

"You know I have three weeks vacation saved up," she said. "How about you?"

"One of the privileges of working at the university is almost unlimited days off. Why? What did you have in mind?"

"I just thought that after this film shoot we could go away somewhere."

"I see. We take the money and run. Not a bad idea."

Anna hadn't thought it would be so easy to pry Gershem out of his territory into hers. Once she had him away from all things familiar, he would be at her conditional tender mercy, the ac-credited deep thinker reduced to "marriage material". But that was in the future and this was now. In what seemed like no time at all, she and Ted were on a charter bus with the rest of the actors headed for a small town on the Hudson River. The whole gang from the Downtown Manhattan Illuminati was there along with others and Edward Smith was leading them all in a stirring rendition of "One Hundred Bottles of Beer on the Wall" as they passed through bucolic village after village at five in the morning.

"Singing is the key to spontaneity, the key to your instrument!" he called out and cupped his hand to his ear. "I can't hear you! Come on, let's really belt it!"

Gershem, if only for the morning, had graduated from ironic detachment to a sort of team player and enthusiastically matched baritones with Studs Zenith while the ladies stretched for soprano high notes. "Sixty-nine bottles of beer on the wall, sixty-nine bottles of beer! You take one down and pass it around and sixty-eight bottles of beer on the wall!"

They soon arrived at their destination, a defunct Walmart parking lot in Putnam County, and were herded into the make-up and wardrobe tent where a team of specialists was applying very realistic latex "wounds" to the victims of the accident. The amputees, who had arrived on another bus, were being fitted with appropriately shredded clothing covered with fake blood. Many people apparently knew each other and a rather festive mood reigned as they chatted and drank coffee, many reminiscing about other jobs where they'd worked together. Relatively inexperienced Gershem was left in the dark as they enthusiastically remembered "that Boston thing" or "the school shoot", telling knee-slapping stories about blowing their lines or getting a chance to mingle with real, live celebrities. "I thought Anderson Cooper was a nice guy until he tried to grab my cock," was greeted by uproarious laughter.

A production assistant came around and handed out release forms, which, if anyone had bothered to read them, were actually confidentiality agreements with all sorts of onerous penalties attached if any stipulations were violated. Ted and Anna were soon called to make-up and wardrobe where she turned down a facial burn for a leg wound and a crutch. Gershem, who was only too happy to remain anonymous, opted for a severely singed hair wig and a grotesque gash across his cheek. They were given blood-spattered outfits – Ted got to be a fireman – and then they were all herded out into the parking lot where a massive green screen had been erected. The director, in his Federico Fellini hat, strode around with a bullhorn positioning the actors as the crew, dissembling television news teams, moved in with their cameras. All Ted and Anna had to do was look stunned and walk by as a few of the "survivors", all seasoned professionals, were interviewed in the foreground. They did about twenty takes and that was that.

After the wrap, the Downtown Manhattan Illuminati gathered together and congratulated each other on their costumes and performances. Edward Smith was ecstatic. "You were just all so fabulous!" he gushed as he handed out envelopes filled with crisp, one hundred dollar bills. "If there were awards for this kind of thing, you should all be nominated!"

Studs Zenith, with his horribly disfigured face and his arm in a sling, suggested they all go out and have a drink together when they got back to the city, a proposal that was endorsed with giddy acclamation.

On the bus, Anna and Ted, stripped of their bloody vestments and suppurating wounds, cuddled up and discussed the future.

"Edward says there will be a lot more of these jobs."

"You're the actress," said Gershem. "Run with it. I already have a job."

"But you were so good, Ted."

"Flattery will get you nowhere. Besides, playing a zombie firefighter is a hard act to follow."

"So where do we take the money and run to?"

"I don't know. Anywhere you like."

"How about nowhere?"

"What do you mean?"

"One of those Carnival cruises to nowhere. You just go out on the ocean and come back a week later."

"Well, I don't know. I've never been to nowhere. Why not?"

Back in Manhattan, Gershem was not enthusiastic about socializing with his fellow actors over a few drinks, but allowed himself to be dragged along to a fancy bar on lower Fifth Avenue for the "wrap party." Edward Smith was beside himself with puffed up pride as he proposed toast after toast to his fellow thespians.

"We're in the carny now," he sang, "we're not behind the plow, you'll never get rich by digging a ditch, we're in the carny now! With it and for it!" he raised his glass and the rest of them cheered.

Gershem complained to Anna that he was tired but she wanted to stay. "I won't let you go," she said in her Ayn Rand accent. "Not on the night of our triumph!"

Where's Studs?" Arthur Sachs wondered.

"And where's Deirdre?" Amalia asked.

Had she known her friend was getting fucked by Studs Zenith in a bathroom stall, she would have hurried to join in.

The revelry eventually wound down to the point that one could beg off and leave without being a party pooper and Gershem took full advantage of the lull.

"If you don't leave with me right now," he said to Anna, "I won't spank you."

"Well, if you put it that way…"

And off they went in their shiny hired yellow car in the night.

❖

14

The Happy Shadow had gone along with Smith's actors to the shoot and tried to have his way with Anna Bunch from the rear but her prop crutch made any sort of congress impossible and he was forced to sit unnoticed in a folding director's chair and watch the boring proceedings for the better part of the day. As he watched Ted and Anna drive off in their cab, he decided to turn his attention to Rino Matsui whom he knew to be at a party that evening for young moderns in Brooklyn with the Breen boy. He took the subway and got off at the station closest to a loft hard by the Gowanus Canal, rumored to be the next Venice by local real estate boosters. The rather sedate gathering was billed as a wine tasting and hosted by a local liquor store to drum up business for which the actual hosts, a graduate student couple in the creative writing program at Brooklyn College, received a fifty percent discount.

Rino was trying to describe exactly what she and Barry were working on but her words fell flat in this densely intellectual atmosphere where the talk generally turned on whom to brown nose for a grant. In one case, literally brown nose.

"I licked his hairy asshole and the next thing you know I got the MacArthur grant," a young writer of the female persuasion bragged to her peers. "And the publishing deal for Exurbandia he set up is, well, it's rather generous."

"You really are a genius," one the young men swarming around her gushed without any irony whatsoever, "and all at the age of twenty four."

"Twenty three," she corrected him. "Don't try to age me. Don't you think this red is a bit okay?"

The attentive liquor store representative immediately offered her another infusion of the grape. "Try this. In my opinion, it's got a much smoother nose."

Barry Breen was talking to a fey adjunct professor at the New School who taught an elective course in Social Knitworking.

"We do it all over the internet. People have no idea how important knitting is in the history of the species. I mean, where would we be without sweaters? We all get together socially sometimes. You'd be surprised who knits. Everyone from football players to drag queens. Some of them even formed a band that plays around here. The Nitpickers. Have you heard of them? Very Philip Glass or something."

Breen was at a loss since he knew very little about Brooklyn. He decided to rejoin Rino who was standing alone next to the wine bar.

"Having a good time?" he asked her.

"No, Stop that! Not here."

The Happy Shadow was trying to insert his penis into her vagina but was having a problem due to the peculiar alignment of her mons pubis. Peculiar to him anyway.

"What are you talking about?"

"Stop goosing me."

Breen held up his hands as the Happy Shadow quickly retired without honor. Puzzled Barry let it go. "Well, what say we take a walk around the neighborhood. Someone told me there are some good bars down the street."

"Sounds better than this," she agreed.

So they made a quiet exit and walked a few blocks before deciding to check out a small live music venue called Perp Walk. The band, the Latecomers, was on a break, so they ordered a couple of drinks and sat down at a table well away from the stage.

"Sometimes I wonder what I'm doing going to school," said Breen. "Do I stay in academia like those people at the party or set up a clinical practice or go to work for the CIA on psy-ops? I don't really want to do any of that. How about you?"

For Rino it was a novel idea to give up everything you worked for and do something else. So un-Japanese. "I want to help people. Maybe work with children. That sounds so corny, doesn't it," she said and giggled.

"If I went clinical I'd do therapy for nymphomaniacs."

"That's even cornier."

This banter was interrupted by the Latecomers return to the stage. As the four young men with shaved heads and did an ear splitting sound check, the sparse audience became very excited.

"Come later! Come later!" they shouted. It was hard to tell if this was some sort of chant or they actually wanted the band to go away. Whatever, the Latecomers remained on stage and launched into their first song, if you can call it that. It was so loud that Barry and Rino immediately fled the bar. Had they taken any interest and stayed, virtually impossible due to the painfully infernal din, they just might have been able to decipher the lyrics and this is what they would have heard:

I am corruption!
I am decay!
All I have to do is smile!
And you'll do what I say!
I'm not exactly evil!
I'm certainly not good!
But I will lead you by the nose!
Is that understood?

And so on. Outside on the sidewalk they cracked up.

"You don't want to stay for Jumpin' Jack Flush and the Water Closets?" Rino demanded. "They're up next!"

"These people will all be deaf by the time they're thirty!" said Breen.

"And blind from texting on their smartphones!"

They couldn't contain their good cheer and attracted many sidelong glances as they returned to the train station.

❖

15

The very next day the abnormal psychology seminar reconvened as something more than a conventional college course, something along the lines of total immersion.

"So, David, how are your nuts doing?"

"Is that a straight line or are you trying to pick me up, Dr. Gershem?"

Everyone laughed including Gershem.

"Couldn't run that one by you, could I. But seriously, any reports from the front."

"Plenty," said Kogan. "A friend of mine's brother who's a shrink got me a sit-down with a bunch of patients at Pilgrim State."

Gershem couldn't resist. "That's very interesting. That you have a friend, I mean. By the way, it's not called State anymore. It's Pilgrim Psychiatric Center."

"Whatever. I stand corrected. Anyway, I drive out to the middle of the island and there's this humongous building surrounded by acres of grounds. I'd never seen it before. They've even got their own police force and fire department. I meet the shrink and he takes me to this sort of conference room with a big oval table with all these nuts sitting there eating cake and candy."

"'That's their reward for talking to you,' he tells me. I ask him if anyone there is prone to violence. 'They're all on what we call a chemical restraint, trazodone.'"

"So I take a seat at the table and tell them what I'm there for, to get their opinions on the nature of good and evil. One of them raises his hand like he's in school and I give him a nod. Then he goes into this lengthy, rather eloquent philosophical discourse. I'm taping the meeting and I'll read you the transcription in a minute. But things went kind of downhill from there. One of them stands up and starts babbling about how he shouldn't be in the hospital, he should be in jail because the drugs are better. Then another one starts yelling, 'I killed Jon Benet Ramsey!' over and over again until he's red in the face and his keepers drag him out of the room. 'Get out of here, you fucking nut!' one of the nuts yells after him and everybody starts laughing. They don't stop laughing andthe shrink tells me that's about all I'm going to get.

"So anyway, this is what the first guy had to say." Kogan read from a piece of paper, "'Good and evil stem from the need for common community, which is good, and the need to destroy and do harm, which we call evil. Take this place, for example. It provides us with community, even if it is imposed against our will. The world looks upon this with some reason as good. The evil is the harm it does to the individual, the destruction of his soul. The world is squeamish about calling this evil and prefers to fall back on the strange rationale that they are preventing us from doing harm to ourselves or others and our incarceration is for our own benefit. Not so long ago, right at this very institution, giving people lobotomies and electroshock was not considered sadism but some sort of benign therapy. It could be said that exiling us from the larger community is ipso facto evil, but most people hold the view that it's necessary to divide people into categories of consciousness and persecute those least able to defend themselves. And there you have it. What we call good is quite often merely a sugar coating for evil.'

"There's more," said Kogan, "but that's all I transcribed. Pretty amazing for a nut, don't you think?"

"He doesn't sound like a nut at all," said Rhoda Memberman. "He certainly sounds saner than you."

"He sounds saner than all the rest of us put together," Kogan deflected the insult. "And we're the ones studying him."

"Okay," said Gershem, "this guy is defining community as good and banishment from that community as evil. If I were in his position I'd probably feel the same way. He mentions doing harm to himself or others. Why is he in the hospital anyway?"

"The shrink told me he killed his family and burned down the whole block."

Akisha gasped. "That man should..."

"Just kidding, just kidding," Kogan held up his hand. "Actually I didn't get a chance to ask after things heated up."

"Well, moving right along," said Gershem, " I understand that you and Rino are working together, Barry."

"If you can call what they're doing together working," Kogan cracked wise.

Breen ignored the comment. "Yeah, we've been talking to various religious and cult leaders who we found have very strong opinions on good and evil. Some think there is an epic struggle raging between them and others dismiss it altogether."

Rino interrupted him with a pointed look. "Most of them have an agenda which isn't principally concerned with good or evil."

"Any examples?" Gershem asked.

Breen looked at Rino for permission. "How about the spiritualists?"

"That was interesting," Rino agreed.

"We met this old woman in Queens," Breen continued, "who gets in touch with the dead through a telephone switchboard. She told us the only thing she could think of as evil was the woman who ran off with her husband."

Everyone chuckled.

"Seriously, she talks to the dead by simply plugging a line into the board. We got to talk to Ayn Rand."

Gershem was visibly startled. "Ayn Rand?" he echoed.

"You know, the Objectivist..."

"I know who Ayn Rand is," Gershem almost snapped. He didn't recall having mentioned his theatrical turn to anyone in the seminar.

"Well, anyway, we talked with her until the old lady cut her off."

"She was insulting me and putting the make on Barry."

"Who? The old lady or Ayn Rand?" said David Kogan.

"Ayn Rand," said Rino. "She was very aggressive. She also had an opinion on the nature of good and evil. Poor people were evil and big businessmen were good."

"You heard her say that?" said Gershem. "What did her voice sound like?"

"Sort of deep and husky."

Gershem didn't press it. Was Anna moonlighting for some spiritualist in Queens? What's the matter with me? he thought. Wacky paranoia.

"That sounds like the Protestant ethic.," said Rhoda.

"So it does," Gershem agreed.

"But Ayn Rand was dumpy little Jewish woman," Kogan pointed out.

"There you go again!" Rhoda exploded. "Body shaming women! If you weren't Jewish yourself I could get you kicked out of here for hate speech!"

"Just because I prefer tall blondes?" Kogan baited her.

"I appreciate your feelings for each other," said Gershem with no little irony, "but let's move on. Akisha? What's up with you?"

"I don't know. I had to take care of my grandmother last week and I had some time to rethink this whole thing. My grandmother thinks that "lizard people" run the world and we're all just sheep waiting to be slaughtered. Everyone thinks she's just senile and maybe she is, but how many people believe stuff like this?"

"A lot and they're probably right," said Rhoda.

"There's some guy in England who's been promoting this reptilian thing for years," said Kogan. "According to his theory anyone in this room could be a lizard in disguise."

"Well, I know I am," said Gershem, "so why don't we all just let down our hair and speak with forked tongues?"

Everyone laughed as he continued. "A lot of what goes on in our brains involves the so-called back brain, the medulla. That's what lizards have. In fact, that's all they have. No cerebellum or cerebrum. The medulla is purely reactive so if you want to look for lizards masquerading as people just find the most reactionary and ask them some tough questions. Like, 'Are you a lizard?'"

Kogan jumped in with, "Someone asked a silicon valley CEO that very question and his answer was that he'd already been checked out by a doctor and a veterinarian who both assured him that he wasn't a reptile."

"Well, it's always good he got a second opinion," said Gershem. "Now if lizards are conspiring against the human race, they are obviously evil. So that's a non-starter."

"Not from the lizard's point of view," Rino quite rightly pointed out.

"All right, Akisha," said Gershem. "Go back to your grandmother and have her identify one of these lizard people. Then try to get an interview."

"I know you're just making fun of me," said Akisha, "but that's exactly what I'm going to do."

"Okay, I think it's time…"

"What about me?" Rhoda protested.

"Oh, I'm sorry," said Gershem. "Go ahead."

"I've been hanging out with this transgender group who have all kinds of issues about good and evil. They're not homosexuals who might enjoy being a little evil now and then. They're just displaced, trapped in a kind of limbo where nothing makes any sense. As one of them said to me: 'I'm not a sissy. I'm a woman. I don't understand gay people at all.' They think the whole cosmos is a conspiracy against them, as if they were born into the wrong gender and no one will tell them where the complaint department is located."

"Okay," said Gershem, "they feel they're being persecuted and there's nothing they can do about it, that they're victims of an accident of birth."

"Anyone can feel that way," Akisha said.

"And what's this got to do with good and evil?" Kogan pressed. "Being transgender isn't the only accident of birth. How about deformed people? How about people with Downs Syndrome?"

"I didn't say I agree with them. That's just the way they look at the world," Rhoda defended herself.

"Rhoda's right," said Gershem. "We're not here to argue with people about their concepts of good and evil. On that note…"

"You didn't tell us anything about your 9/11 people," Breen interrupted.

Rino shot him a glare that burned into his skin like sunlight through a magnifying glass.

"They're still there and I'm still listening," said Gershem breezily, not bothering to mention that he'd stopped going to the meetings altogether. "Nothing new to report actually."

As Gershem walked down Broadway back to his apartment, he wondered if he were becoming slightly unhinged. People with *apophenia* thought all sorts of external stimuli applied directly to them. This business about Ayn Rand was surely just a coincidence but it nagged at him in a way that made it difficult to put out of his mind. And why had Barry Breen, who'd brought up Ayn Rand in the first place, pressed him about the 9/11 meetings? New York was the biggest city in the United States, but, in many ways, it was a small town with all the attendant small town gossip floating around. Just what did Breen know anyway? If he knew anything at all, Maybe he should come clean about doing the play. Not the freelancing of course. Just Ayn and Nate.

When Anna came home, Gershem asked her, much in the way someone might interrogate a billionaire computer geek about being a lizard, "Have you been working with a spiritualist in Queens?"

The question gave her pause. "What on earth are you talking about, Ted?"

"Nothing. Just a dream I had."

"In this dream, did I have a Ouija board? Were we at a séance?"

"Yes, and I was rubbing your pussy under the table."

"How exciting. Did any spirits show up?"

"Only a couple of martinis. Would you like one? I think I've got some gin around here."

Gershem decided not to mention Barry Breen's story.

And just at that moment Barry and Rino were wondering whether or not to push Gershem on this theatre association, which he clearly did not want to talk about.

"It's really none of our business," said Rino. "A lot of people have some sort of hobby like that."

"But how about the tie-in with the Magus? Walter said that Professor Gershem is having an affair with the Magus' wife."

"You're going to take a flat-earther's word for it?"

"Well, he did seem to know more than we do."

"We're all researching these conspiracy people. It's inevitable we'll cross paths."

"I don't care about that. I just want to meet the Magus' wife. Walter said she'll do anyone."

For that he got a hard punch in the shoulder.

❖

16

The Magus had other problems on his mind than his promiscuous wife. Well pleased with his work on the nuclear accident simulation, Retalitron wanted to contract him to provide actors for a number of other training films and industrials and he had to form some sort of front entity, a state registered company with a bank account. In order to do that, he had to come up with a name for his doing-business-as and submit it to City Hall to make sure it hadn't already been taken. The possibilities were, of course, endless. TALENT POOL, ROLES TO GO, PART TIME, THE EDWARD SMITH GROUP, TEAM THESPIAN, were just a few of the names turning over in his head as he tried to make a decision. He decided to consult his wife.

"Sylvia, what do you think we should call the talent company?"

"How should I know? Those people like corporate sounding names like Exxon or Enron or Viacom, catchy buzzwords that have very little to do with what the company actually does."

"Okay, how about something like Actnet?"

"That's good, but I bet it's already taken."

"Playertex."

"Vertex, Vortex," she suggested

"I'm sure those are taken."

"You'll think of something, sweetie. I've got a dungeon date."

"Anyone worth filming?"

"No, just a regular nobody client."

But that was not so. Deirdre wasn't the only one who was going to get it on with Studs Zenith. The weatherman had expressed interest in what went on "downstairs" and he was about to find out. For free, no less. Sylvia met him at the theatre and took him into the basement.

"Wow!" he said. "Is this for real?"

"You want me to chain you up?"

"Well, what if I chain you up?"

"You can if you want. Then you can fuck me in the ass and make me suck my shit off your cock."

Studs thought that was going a bit too far. "What if I just fuck you in the ass with a condom. Then you don't have to eat shit."

"Whatever. We're here to be creative."

"Okay, let's take off our clothes and I'll chain you up," he said looking over at the rack of branding irons on the wall and the coffee pot sitting next to them on a hot plate. By the time they got out of their clothes, he was already hard." Hey, there, you've got some bod for a woman your age. Where's the chains?"

She rubbed his cock. "Umm, nice one. Right here, lover," she purred, handing him some shackles.

"What say I chain you to this ring on the wall?"

"Why not?"

He attached one shackle to her wrist, turned her to the wall, and chained her up.

"Oh, you do want to do me in the ass," she teased, wiggling her rear end.

But then he did something unexpected. He examined the branding irons, picked one to his liking, put the coffee pot aside, and started to heat the iron on the hot plate.

"What are you doing?" she demanded.

"This is going to take a few minutes so what say we get to know each other a little better. How did you meet your husband?"

"What's meeting my husband got to with anything? I want you to do me like you did Deirdre."

"That was just a fling. I'm serious about you."

"What do you mean serious?" she said nervously. "This is all a game, you know. It's just for fun."

"And I am having fun. Aren't you?" He picked up the iron off the hot plate. "I want anyone who sees that luscious ass from now on to know it's mine all mine. I'm going to brand you, sweetie. I'm going to brand you to keep the rustlers away."

"Really, Studs, don't you think this is taking things a bit too far," she tried to reason with him.

"Not really far enough," he said. "Now I'm going to fuck you right up until that magic moment when I make you my bitch."

She squealed as he rammed his erection right up her pussy until she was moaning, "Yes, yes, don't stop, fuck me, fuck me, FUCK ME!!"

"Are you ready, bitch?! Are you ready to get burned?!"

"Don't do it, Studs! Please don't do it!"

"Are you ready to smell your own roasting flesh?! Burn, baby, burn!"

"Please, please," she begged.

He came with a great heaving grunt. Then it was all over. Zenith put the unapplied branding iron aside and unshackled Sylvia.

"That was just great!" he enthused.

"Gee whiz, Studs," she said adoringly, "you really know what you're doing, don't you? I almost wish you had branded me."

"Any time, babe, any time. If you want to suck my cock maybe I can get it up and we can do it again."

So she did. And get it up he did, this time opting to ejaculate in her mouth at the exact moment Edward Smith came up with the company name he would register – Player Station. Coincidence? Who knows?

❖

17

Rhoda Memberman was a force to be reckoned with. That's what she thought anyway. And at the moment, confronted with the jet engine decibel level of her Dominican neighbor's hip hop merengue party, she was forced, forced, mind you... what do you think? To complain? To call the police? Not quite. She knocked on the door where the hostess greeted her warmly – "Rho-o-o-dah! Pase!" – and ushered her into a swirl of dancers drinking rum out of a large bottle packed with fruit and small lizards. You could see this marinade right through the glass. Rhoda took a big swig herself and she was off to the races, dancing with awkward abandon to the pulsating Caribbean fusion beat with the several gentlemen willing to humor her. After about an hour of fevered carousing, the party wound down to a more civilized tempo. The men adjourned to another room to play a gambling game called banco and the women got down to the serious business of gossiping.

Marta, the hostess, started things off with a breathless, "Rhoda, you must tell me what is going on at your abnormal psychology seminar."

Rhoda, now a couple sheets to the wind, was glad to abandon her grouchy feminist act for a little girl talk. "Well, my professor has a new girlfriend. I saw them on the street together when I was walking Petunia."

"Oh my. What does she look like?"

"Short, brunette, a little chubby. Not so bad."

"Your professor, did he look happy to be with her?"

"Actually, he looked embarrassed. It's like students aren't supposed to know their professors have love lives."

Marta laughed. "Because he's too old, right? My son thinks I'm too old to have a boyfriend."

"But you've had three husbands."

"So? Two of them are here tonight. We're all friends."

Rhoda wondered at such a culture that allowed for this easy-going promiscuity. It was definitely matriarchal. The women were at the center of everything but the men did pretty much as they pleased and no one seemed the worse for it.

"Why don't you have a boyfriend, Rhoda? Look at those hips. You could make many children. Is that dog really enough?"

Rhoda was taken aback. "You don't really think..?", she started indignantly.

"Of course not!" Marta broke into laughter. "Petoonia is a girl! But wouldn't you like, you know, a little action?!"

What Marta didn't know was that Rhoda kept a bottle of gin and a Mitsubishi Apollo 13 vibrator under her bed that combined a small rubber tire affixed to the end of a single blade eggbeater and mixed her own pound cake batter, so to speak. The saleswoman at the erotic appliance store had assured her that the Samsung Orbital would really make her sam sing, but Rhoda had been dissuaded by all the lithium battery explosions in Samsung's other little machines and opted for Japanese assistance.

"I have help in that department," said Rhoda coyly.

"Does he have a big hard one?"

"You might say that but I prefer a slow hand myself."

"I like a man with a fast tongue!" Marta exploded in merry laughter and Rhoda was, more or less, forced to join in. But her mind wandered. There was a guy she'd had her eye on for a while but he wouldn't give her the time of day. Not that he was conceited, mind you. In fact, he suffered from borderline pathological shyness, so it was difficult to make an approach without sending him into a beet red fluster. His name was Hyman Ryman and he was a Senior Fellow at the Spuyten Duyvil Trust's think tank headquartered at the university, the An Idea Grows in

America Institute. Rhoda knew this because she had made a point of finding out. He was a suitable match; Jewish, obsessively career oriented, and a complete wimp, the three main qualities that Rhoda found attractive in a man, and one day he would be hers, all hers. Who else would want him anyway?

"Rhoda!" Marta was snapping her fingers and staring at her with concern.

"I'm sorry," said Rhoda, "I just drifted off."

"You're sleepy, girl. You should go to bed."

"That's just what I'm going to do." She got up a little unsteadily, gave Marta a hug, and took her leave.

Back in her own apartment, Rhoda snuggled with Petunia–"You're such a pretty girl! You're such a smart girl!" – and drifted off to sleep. She didn't usually have particularly vivid dreams, but the distilled reptile essence in the Dominican rum punch often leads to excessive back brain activity, which in turn sets off all kinds of fevered reactions while the inebriate sleeps. So was the case with Rhoda. She dreamed she was in a steaming tropical jungle full of brightly colored flowers and small monkeys swinging on vines. She was being pulled as if by some powerful magnetic force toward a rendezvous with her betrothed, the mighty warrior-god Hyman Ryman, otherwise known as Gonad the Librarian. She arrived at a clearing where the natives, all Hasids in black hats, were beating out a frantic tattoo on their hollow logs. Hyman, dressed only in a leopard skin loincloth, was standing with his back to her gyrating to the pulsating rhythm. As she timidly approached the warrior-god, he sensed her presence and whirled around in all his glory! But this was not Hyman Ryman! It was David Kogan, pointing and laughing at her! She woke in a cold sweat and was unable to drive this horrifying vision from her mind. She spent the next few hours fitfully tossing and turning and obtained no rest that night,

❖

18

The next day was Sunday so Anna and Ted decided to go to the park and drop Ecstasy. Really. Anna had a young friend from the office who organized raves on the side in Brooklyn and ran a virtual drugstore. Ted, who had taken practically every psychedelic in the book, had never taken X but he was certainly game. So off they went that morning to mingle with the masses in a slightly distorted way.

"I asked the girl who got me this stuff to take me to a rave but she told me it was too loud," said Anna. "I think she meant I was too old."

"Time to put childish things aside, you old bag," he teased her as they walked through the park entrance at 79th Street.

"You should talk, Old Nate."

Gershem felt the signature speedy rush of the MDMA kick in. "Whoa. Where's this going?" he wondered.

"Relax," said Anna. "In a few minutes you'll feel so good you won't believe it."

And it was true. The initial lift-off graded into a pleasantly alert languor where anxiety and paranoia were impossible and all was right with the world.

"Hmm, interesting," said Gershem as they walked toward the Belvedere Castle where they could look out over the greensward without being bothered by the crowd which was just beginning to course through the park. Families, bicyclists, sunbathers, musicians, assorted fruitcakes, tourists, what have you. It reminded Gershem of a French impressionist painting. When they got to the castle terrace, they were the only people there and he looked at Anna speculatively. "If you take our clothes off, we would look like a Manet painting."

"You want me to? We're not sitting on the grass and I didn't bring a picnic but I have a bottle of wine in my bag."

"I don't think we can get away with it."

"Why not? There's no one here yet." She handed him the wine and a corkscrew, then quickly took off her clothes. "There," she said as the cork popped. She sat in exactly the same position as the nude model in *Dejeuner sur l'herbe* and Gershem handed her a plastic cup of Merlot. "What do you think?"

"Perfect," he had to admit. "Now I think you better put on your clothes. The hordes are ascending."

And so they were. Soon the castle became quite crowded so Ted and Anna descended and found a large rock outcropping below to perch and watch the world go by. But they weren't much interested in the world per se; they simply felt like talking.

"Do you know how long I had a crush on you before we, you know, did it?" she asked him.

"I was pretty hot for you too. That's the funny thing about getting to know someone in the barroom atmosphere. Nobody takes anything seriously."

Anna couldn't believe her ears. He was using the word "seriously". Her juices began coursing through a sluice gate, releasing a riverine flow of unexpressed emotions and heretofore dammed up hormones. Was he going to propose? Could she finally adopt a Chinese orphan?

"This rock isn't as hard as it should be," Gershem observed.

"What do you mean?"

"Many other people have sat just where we're sitting and worn it smooth."

"That doesn't make it any less hard."

"Point taken, but it sure is easier on the old rear end."

"You've got a boney butt. I've got a built-in cushion. How's your good and evil seminar going?"

"Funny you should mention it. I was just thinking what a waste of time the whole thing is. Who cares how people perceive things that don't objectively exist?"

"Objectivity isn't everything. Objectively you're just another human being with a penis. Subjectively, you're a whole lot more than that. To me anyway,"

"Well, thank you, but I'm not sure if my penis knows how to take that."

"Take it hard, Mr. Penis, very hard."

Gershem chuckled. "I once asked you if you'd been naughty or nice, Since you're both, the question is irrelevant, isn't it?"

"Well, I don't give it much thought, if that's what you mean."

"I don't know what I mean anymore."

"Don't…" she started but he interrupted her.

"I didn't mean that in a bad way."

"I'm sure you didn't," she teased him. "Look. Down there." She was pointing at a middle-aged couple dressed in blue overalls wearing tin, pyramid shaped hats on their heads who were walking by just below. "Hey, you!" she called out. "Where did you get those hats?"

They stopped and looked up at Ted and Anna. "We made them," the woman said. "They keep off the bad rays."

"How would you like to sell them? You know how to make them. You can make some more," said Anna.

The man and the woman looked at each other with the glint of the shrewd Yankee trader in their rheumy eyes. The man looked up. "Why don't you make an offer? It's first class tin, not the foil stuff,"

"How about ten dollars?"

"Apiece?" the woman asked.

"Yeah."

"Twelve," said the man.

"Twelve fifty," Anna countered. The couple looked confused. "Just kidding." She rummaged through her bag and pulled out a twenty and a five, which she handed down to the couple who took off their hats and handed them up.

To Gershem, they looked a bit like American Gothic. The man was mostly bald and his wife, or whatever she was, had her blonde hair pulled back tight in a bun. All they needed was a pitchfork.

"Where's my change?" Anna demanded.

"You're the one who said twelve fifty," the woman pointed out.

"Keep it," she chuckled and modeled one of the hats for Gershem. "How do I look?"

"Magnetic."

"Here, try yours on."

Gershem did as he was told.

"How does it feel?"

"Much better. No bad rays."

When they left the park another half hour later, they wore their new hats without embarrassment and hailed an uptown cab. The Honduran taxi driver was curious.

"What's those hats?" he asked.

"They're tin hats. They keep out the bad rays," said Gershem.

"Oh, wow! Is you, like, those conspiracy freak weirdos?"

"Yes."

The driver was delighted. "Cool. I'm with you, man."

"Maybe," Ted allowed.

When they got out of the cab across the street from the Stay Put Club, the driver called after them, "Keep you heads screwed on straight!"

Gershem and Anna studied the exterior of the saloon.

"You don't really want to ..." she wondered.

"No," he said and the next thing they knew they were seated at the bar in their tin hats.

"What are you two doing in here?" the bartender challenged them. "You're night time." Which was true. The day and night time crowds were completely different, probably because the night time people had jobs. "And what are those things on your heads?"

"Welcome, space aliens!" an old drunk toasted them from his corner seat at the bar. "May your stay on earth be agreeable and when you go back wherever you came from, may your memories of our planet fill you with nostalgia!"

"Cheers," Anna drawled in her Ayn Rand voice. "What makes you think we're going back?"

"Ah, immigrants, the backbone of the nation! Are you illegal aliens?" he inquired sotto voce. "None of my business, of course..."

"That's right. It's none of your business," Anna cut him off imperiously and laughed, She turned to the bartender and purred. "Two vodka grapefruits, please. We don't have grapefruits on our planet."

"You don't got shit for brains on your planet," the bartender grumbled.

"You know," said Gershem to Anna, "I like this hat." And this was coming from a man who never wore hats and ordinarily would have been dissolving in embarrassment and shame if he'd looked in the mirror. In fact, he was looking in the mirror behind the bar and, in his Ecstasy addled pate, he looked very suave indeed.

Telepathic Anna put her hand on his knee and growled, " Did anyone ever tell you how sauve you look, Ted?"

"Never."

"Well, you do."

Then they broke into almost uncontrollable laughter.

The bartender set down their drinks in front of them. "Well, at least someone's having some fun today," he said sourly.

Which, of course, made them laugh even more.

When they left the Stay Put Club, they were still in high spirits, though the effects of the drug had pretty much dissipated, and they retired to Gershem's apartment where there was a message from Edward Smith on the answering machine.

❖

19

Unlike their mentor and his would-be consort, Barry Breen and Rino Matsui had not let the day go to waste idling in the park. They had paid a visit on famous criminal defense lawyer, Alden Dirth, whom they had contacted the preceding week and set up an appointment at his country place in Beacon, New York, a village principally known as the home of the DIA Foundation art museum. The ride up the Hudson was pleasantly picturesque and the crowd on the train was about as festive as museum goers get, that is quiet and subdued, as if they were already perambulating through those hallowed halls of the fine arts whispering of Michael Heizerlo. Dirth, an avuncular con man in his sixties whose talents had been channeled into the respectable practice of the law, was there to pick them up at the station and drive them up the hill to his place in the woods.

"So nice to see young people taking an interest in criminal justice," he commended them after introducing himself. "Most people don't understand the concept of adversary defense and tend to regard me as a sort of devil because of my unsavory clientele. Here we are," They pulled into his gravel driveway where a very modern "cabin", as he called it, blended into the landscape like a Frank Lloyd Wright. "My little home away from home. Let's go inside and get away from the bugs with their Zika, West Nile, Lyme's disease, what have you," he said cheerfully.

Closing the screen door behind them, he asked, "Would you like something to drink? A white wine spritzer, perhaps? I have a Chardonnay from the very finest vineyard in New Zealand. Very refreshing."

When they were all settled in the living room, which overlooked a small pond created by an 1890's bluestone quarry, Dirth started his cross-examination.

"So, you're at Columbia. No finer university. Except Harvard, of course, where I got my degree. Tough school. Probably the reason I'm the finest criminal attorney in the world."

It should be noted that Barry and Rino had barely spoken. It was difficult to get a word in edgewise with this blowhard.

"So you're doing this thing on good and evil. Well, you've come to the right place. According to prosecuting attorneys everywhere I'm the walking, talking Great Satan, protecting evil-doers from the long arthritic arm of the law." He laughed, then: "By the way, if you get busted for something, I do pro bono work for people I like. Especially young, juicy people I like." His words hung in the air like strands of sticky goo. "How's that white wine? Good, isn't it?"

They had to agree, though it wasn't.

"Let me tell you a little story," he said. Ominous words indeed. "I have a client. An important client. To me, at least. He's got a problem. He just can't keep his hands off under-age girls. I don't mean teenagers like you, Rino…"

"Why thank you, Mr. Dirth," Rino chuckled.

"Wha? What did I say? And call me Alden. We don't stand on ceremony here. Anyway, this guy, he likes them prepubescent, eight, nine years old. He's got them playing with Uncle Willie like it's some kind of doll and they love it when they can make it squirt. So he gets busted and that's where I come in. What am I going to do? The guy's got money so everybody hates him even more than some poor schlub hanging around the playground. I mean they want to burn this guy at the stake! So I take him to this doctor friend of mine and have him declared legally blind. I had him walk into court with a seeing-eye dog. Then I explained that someone told him these girls were tiny Burmese hookers. Then I spread a little good cheer around, if you take my meaning, and that was that. Now, I know you think I'm evil for getting this pervert off. You do, don't you?"

"Well, you are a lawyer…" Barry began before Dirth cut him off.

"So you see. It's my job to put up the best defense possible and let the jury decide. I think that makes me good. I mean where would our justice system be if people couldn't defend themselves?"

"But you said yourself that your client was a pervert," Rino pointed out.

"That's the beauty of the system. Even a depraved pervert can have his day in court. So how do you balance out this whole good versus evil thing when justice is blind? You have to ask yourself if you're willing to let a few evil guys go or throw a whole lot of innocent people behind bars because that's exactly what would happen without adversary justice."

"So you make a little deal with the Devil?" Breen pressed him.

"Life is a deal with the devil, kiddo. And believe me, I've seen him. One of my clients was Johnny Boy Risotto, the gang boss. I mean this guy would rip your head off and blow hellfire down your neckhole for looking at him the wrong way. Other than that, he was a real gentleman, always paid his legal fees right on time. I got him off twice before he went down for good. Died of colic in supermax solitary."

"I thought colic was a horse disease," said Barry.

"Believe me, Johnny Boy was a horse. Excuse my French, but this guy had such a schlong on him he had to be careful not to step on it."

This blathering went on for another hour, with numerous recollections of serial murderers, bank robbers, dope dealers, and Wall

Street swindlers, who certainly all fell into the category of evil but were nevertheless great sources of voyeuristic interest, the sort of stuff that keeps the tabloids in business. Rino decided to play with Dirth.

"Have you ever represented a lizard in court?"

Dirth was taken aback. "How do you know about that? Half my clients are lizards! Always shape-shifting right in front of me. At first it's disconcerting. Then you get used to it."

Barry and Rino chuckled, but Dirth wasn't kidding around. He seemed confused by their response. "What's so funny? You're not lizards, are you?" he demanded.

Barry and Rino cracked up. They couldn't help themselves.

Dirth shook his head. "What have you two been smoking? You're laughing now. Not for long. Now, I don't want to rush you, but I'm working on this big case. It's been a pleasure," he said with a tight smile.

"All ours," Breen assured him.

"You'll find the walk down is very pleasant, Not like climbing up the hill." With that he escorted them to the door. "Just one thing. Nobody ever laughs at me. Ever. No one is above the law! Are we not men! And women too, of course,"

"Wow," said Rino as they walked down the hill. "What a weirdo."

"They're all weirdos," said Breen sourly. "We're in Beacon. You want to go to the museum?"

"Sure."

When they got there and went to the box office, the ticket seller asked them if they lived there because it was Community Free day. Of course they did and gave her Dirth's address. So without parting with a penny to the big oil financed DIA Foundation they entered into precincts of the old industrial bakery that had been converted into an exhibition space and wandered happily through this monument to Minimalism until it was time to catch the train back to the city.

❖

20

If Edward Smith didn't have any problems, it was his imperative as a card-carrying member of the dramatic community to create them himself. With this barely concealed compulsion to churn the shit, he had decided to kill Arthur Sachs. Not that Arthur had lately been any more obsequious or obnoxious than usual. It just gave Smith something to do. But first he had to set things up. He wanted to lay the blame on Studs Zenith, whom he knew was having his twisted, perverted way with Sylvia, but he needed to create a motive and his own plausible denial of involvement in this impending capital felony. To this end, he had concocted a simple plan. All he had to do was fire Zenith as young Nate and replace him with Arthur. He was already imagining being interviewed on teevee: "I had no idea how serious Studs was about the part. Poor Arthur." He was also imagining all the publicity it would bring the show. Sachs was a small sacrifice for a full house every night! They'd run longer than the Fantasticks!

But now it was time to get down to business. The reason Smith had called Gershem was to plant a seed. He was going to tell him that Zenith was making impossible demands and that he was tearing out what little hair he had left to find a solution. Gershem, a university professor, could easily appear to be rational as an abnormal psychology expert on the tube, and that's all Smith really needed.

"Hello, Edward, I got your message," Gershem had returned his call.

"Oh, Ted. Thanks for getting back to me. I'm on the horns of a dilemma and I'm not quite sure what to do. I have to tell Studs Zenith he's out and Arthur is back in as young Nate."

"Uhm, why do you have to do that?"

Smith sighed. "It's a long story. Just take my word for it. It has to be done."

"You're the boss," said Gershem affably, still under the diminishing influence of the drug he'd taken earlier.

"So you approve?"

"I didn't say that. It's your decision."

"Well, you know, under that calm façade, Studs is a real hothead. He might do anything,"

"Like what?"

"Well. I just don't know."

"This is all a joke, isn't it, Edward? Arthur can't play young Nate."

"But he can, he can. He's been improving every day. People just don't notice."

"But they do, Edward. If you put Arthur back in as the lead, everyone will quit. Maybe even me."

"You're right," said Smith sadly, "but what am I going to do? Sylvia's fallen for Studs like a ton of bricks."

There was silence at the other end of the line.

"Well, she has!" Smith insisted. "And the things they get up to."

"Why are you telling me this, Edward?" Smith was beginning to impinge on Gershem's good mood. "It's been nice talking to you, but I've got to go."

"Ted, wait," but the line was dead. And he couldn't even kill Arthur Sachs now. Gershem would immediately know something was fishy.

"What did Edward want?" Anna wanted to know. "Does he have another job for us?"

"I don't know. I think he's been drinking. He was talking about firing Studs Zenith and replacing him with Arthur Sachs. Something to do with Sylvia and Studs."

"I knew it!" Anna crowed. "I bet that weatherman's showing her which way the wind blows!"

"I don't think Edward was serious. Like I said, he sounded drunk. Who cares anyway?"

"I do. I'm not doing the play with Arthur Sachs as my love interest," Anna did Ayn Rand. "That's just… creepy."

Poor, lonely Arthur, consigned since early childhood to humanity's sub-realm of the creep. Disparagement and contempt were the only fodder he was allowed and he didn't much like chewing on either one. So why did this harmless schnud inspire homicidal loathing? Was it just social Darwinism with the strong targeting the weak? Was the species so lacking in compassion that Sachs had to be singled out for humiliation and even eradication? These were not questions that milled about in Edward Smith's fevered brain at that moment, but Sachs had been spared the assassin's cold embrace and the agency of his salvation was an email to Smith from Retalitron. As Smith eagerly read the invitation to meet with the security company brass to discuss the terms of their contract with Player Station LLC, he had full expectation of an advance payment that would finance the production of an Ayn and Nate showcase where the critics would swoon and launch him into the pantheon of celebrated theatrical directors, "princes of the blood" as the show business world knew them.

When Sylvia came home after another secret session with Studs Zenith, Smith projected nothing but serene confidence.

"I've done it, Sylvia. Nothing can stop the Downtown Manhattan Illuminati now."

"What are you talking about, sweetie?"

"Is that what you call Studs? Sweetie?"

The question put Sylvia on the hackles-up defensive. How did Edward even know about Studs? "Oh please, Edward. I'm sorry I didn't mention it to you. I didn't want to cause any trouble for the production. He wanted to be degraded and I treated him like any of my other clients. There, now you know. I stretched him on the rack and gave him a taste of the whip. I called him an insect, a worm, a slug, the usual."

"That's all?"

"It's what I do, Edward," she said patiently as if she were soothing a cranky child. "You're not jealous, are you?"

"Of course I am," he groused.

"She held him around the shoulders and cooed, "You're my sweetie, Edward. You know that. So what's this about the Illuminati?"

"Retalitron is offering a contract to Player Station. I'll have the money to mount Ayn and Nate."

"Wow!" Sylvia exulted. "You need a lawyer, Edward. And not Tootie Wookums."

"Are you joking? Do you think I would even consider that

freak? I was thinking of someone like Alden Dirst."

"Edward!" she reeled in disbelief. "Are you crazy? He's famous! He's super expensive. This is a contract, not a murder case."

"You have any better ideas?"

"I already told you. Me. What's to it anyway? I just put on my school marm suit from the dungeon, sit down and reject their offer. Then I make a counter-offer. A monkey could do it."

"Are you comparing lawyers to monkeys?"

"Well, maybe not Alden Dirst. He's more like a porcupine."

❖

21

Rino and Barry were at it again. He was pumping away from behind while she paged through Proust. I guess you know that's not true. Literally, anyway. In reality, whatever that is these days, they were going over the notes they'd made about their several encounters and Breen was not pleased.

"We've been letting these nuts control the parameters of the conversation. We should be asking tougher questions."

"We're their guests, Barry. You don't insult your hosts."

"Stop being so Japanese. We're not getting anywhere by being polite."

"If I weren't Japanese, I'd call you an asshole for saying that."

"Okay, how about this 'Radiation is Good for You' woman?"

"She wants to talk, of course. She thinks there is a conspiracy by the oil and gas companies to get rid of clean nuclear energy."

"Uh, well I guess after Hiroshima, Nagasaki, and Fukushima, you could probably cook up some questions. I mean, being Japanese and all if I'm not risking being called an asshole."

"Asshole," she said.

"So you've spoken to her and she wants to meet? Where?"

"This restaurant downtown."

"She wants to meet in public? Maybe she thinks we're some kind of Exxon assassins and she has to be surrounded by witnesses."

And so they wound up meeting with Winthrop "Winnie" Palmer Addison at the Odeon in the late afternoon. Without any prompting whatsoever this lacquered society dowager gone Buddhist bohemian in her twilight years immediately provided an answer to a question they hadn't asked.

"You must be wondering about my name. I'm a Winthrop, a Palmer, and an Addison, you see, and that's how we do things." It wasn't clear who "we" were. "I have a Buddhist name as well – Mayuhana – but I prefer to be called Winnie. It's a silly name but I'm used to it. Shall we order? I'm famished."

The Odeon is not an expensive restaurant but it's not cheap either and the two students looked over the menu with simmering fear and trepidation.

"Well, what would you like?" Winnie pressed them. "The cassoulet is very good here. The most perfect marriage of beans and organ meats I've ever tasted. None for me though. Not anymore. I'm a gluten free vegan since I found my dharma."

"I'm not really hungry…" Breen started to beg off.

"Nonsense. Order whatever you like. I'm paying. And how about a bottle of champagne? I always drink champagne in the afternoon."

She didn't have to twist their arms. The waiter took their orders and Winnie got right down to business.

"I just got back from the Marshall Islands. Fabulous beaches and practically deserted. I was there for hormesis therapy at this very exclusive resort. So much radiation from all those atomic tests and waste dumps. It's just the best. Oh, I know what you're going to say." She twirled her finger next to her ear. "She must be crazy. That's what you're thinking, isn't it? I mean, atomic bombs?"

Just at that moment the waiter popped the champagne cork with a loud bang and poured all around. Winnie held her up her glass.

"Cheers. I'm not crazy, by the way. My evil family made their fortune in the oil and coal businesses. They're the ones poisoning the world and trying to stop clean nuclear energy. No one understands that radiation is good for you. You just have to get used to it, to acclimate. It's like getting a tan. You don't do it all in one day."

Barry sensed the only opening he was likely to get. "So you define evil as the fossil fuel industry."

"Well, isn't it obvious? Do you know that oil is actually useful? It's the basis of our medicine, our agriculture, our construction materials industry, the list goes on and on. To burn it is completely insane. Especially when all the energy we need is right here in every atom."

Winnie reached into her purse and pulled out her Geiger counter. "Just look at me, not one surgical nip or tuck, the very picture of health." She turned on the Geiger counter, which pinned the needle on the gauge and made this terrible clicking racket. "I'm hot as a pistol and I'm doing just fine!"

Barry and Rino did not stay their leaving and raced out of the restaurant with their pants on fire. Well, smoldering anyway.

"That woman is a public menace!" said Barry as they hurried away up West Broadway. "Where did you find her anyway?"

"On Craigslist."

"Well, that makes sense."

Not so very far away, Sylvia Smith was servicing a particularly twisted and perverted hedge fund operator with particularly twisted and perverted tastes. What Mr. Hedge liked was to be chained naked on his back underneath a glass coffee table upon which his squatting mistress evacuated while she sang:

"These bowels were made for moving! And that's just what they'll do! One of these days these bowels are going to move all over you!"

Edward was, of course, recording all this from his hidden vantage point and marveling at the sort of degradation favored by the rich. It was as if they were doing penance for degrading everyone else with their grotesque depredations. In a way, Edward admired them for their contrition. Seeking redemption in the restorative power of coprophilia, learning to meditate on the subtle nuances of excreta, was an important step on the road to salvation for these movers and shakers. But what followed was even a bit much for Edward. Sylvia attached a leash to her client before she unchained him and yanked him to his hands and knees.

"Look at the mess I've made!" she snarled. "And all because of you! Clean it up! Now!"

Mr. Hedge immediately set to lapping up her poop off the table while she crooned: "Good doggy, that's my good doggy."

When the session was over and Mr. Hedge was putting back on his suit and tie he noted, "You've been eating a lot of whole grains lately."

"You could tell?"

"Of course. Just lay off the gluten for twenty-four hours before our next appointment. It gives me hives."

A real no nonsense kind of guy, thought Edward from his hiding place. No wonder he was such a success. Which reminded him of a movie he'd seen a long time ago, "The Sweet Smell of Success". Why that came to mind he had no idea

❖

22

Gershem woke from an unpleasant dream, not quite a nightmare, but disquieting enough to leave him with a slightly uncomfortable feeling even as he adjusted to the mundane reality of his bedroom and the woman gently snoring next to him. As the fog in his head dispersed he had difficulty remembering any details of the dream at all. Something to do with Anna being carried off by a bunch of pirates.. He got up to take a pee and when he got back to the bedroom Anna had wakened.

"I just had the most lovely dream, she purred. "I don't know if I should tell you."

"Why not?"

"Well, you weren't there. I mean you weren't in it."

"No I wasn't. I'm here."

"You are, aren't you? I dreamed that these pirates dragged me off into the jungle right off the beach where they were burying their treasure and had their way with me. That's why I wish you were there."

"What do you mean? To watch?"

"No! To join in. You have to stop talking in your sleep. But it's not too late. I'm not quite awake yet."

Gershem took her up on her invitation. After they were done, Anna got up, showered, and she was off to work.

At loose ends, Gershem decided to go to the university library and read up on people who hallucinate, that is, who have imaginations, a condition which practicing psychotherapists everywhere endeavor to ruthlessly suppress. People who have even the slightest trace of this disorder are referred to as those with "a rich inner life", a condition verging on schizophrenia but not quite dangerous enough to threaten the established order. Gershem's curiosity was new to him. He had previously thought of schizophrenics as disordered personalities best treated with pharmaceuticals. But Ecstasy had opened a door not easily closed. The calm evaluation of what was occurring right at the moment led to a whole string of causal relationships that he had shunted aside for most of his career. In the whole of psychotherapy, states of mind were judged on their correspondence to the current bourgeois state of thinking. Psychoanalysis was nothing more than getting people to conform to a certain set of values that the patient had to "accept" as "reality". If the patient didn't, he or she was cast out into the purgatory of the "maladjusted", which was a perfect word, sounding like something to do with automobile repair. The brazen psychopaths who ran this show had nothing to offer to anybody but themselves. And there he was, Ted Gershem, taking his paycheck from these malefactors and basking in the glory of enough to eat and the occasional blowjob from Anna Bunch. And making nice didn't cost a cent.

So the first book off the shelf was *The Origins of Consciousness in the Breakdown of the Bicameral Mind* by Julian Jaynes.

The basic thesis was that all of humanity was schizoid up until about three thousand years ago. Consciousness as we know it did not exist at the time but rather quickly developed from the talent to dissemble, to play a part, to seem to hold an opinion that you actually didn't. The ability to look at oneself "objectively", that is as an object that "you" could manipulate and control like a puppeteer was a novel way of seeing things. As the author pointed out, prior to this awakening, people could have been walking around, eating, drinking, fucking and farting, doing all the things people have always done without being conscious of their actions at all.

The reason they could do all this was that they were in a state of constant auditory hallucination. They were hearing commands which originated in the right lobe of their brain that they ascribed to the gods. They were taking orders, much as schizophrenics today claim they are hearing voices that tell them what to do. Jaynes contended that schizophrenia is a vestige of this former, non-introspective, preconscious state.

Gershem had always rejected these claims because it would require all this to happen in a time frame that was far less than the blink of an eye in evolutionary history, but now he wasn't so sure. Perhaps the brain was far more plastic than he'd thought. If it were so, then good and evil were completely relative, having more to do with survival than "morality". And, if they were relative, they didn't exist at all outside of human cognition. Just phantasms of the bicameral brain trying to preserve itself.

All this and more Gershem pondered until he got bored and decided to take a walk, a decision he almost immediately regretted. Waiting in ambush right outside the library was Arthur Sachs.

"Ted! I've been looking for you all day. Edward's going to fire Studs Zenith!"

For some reason, Gershem could not get over the humor of the situation. "So I heard. Do you think it's a bad idea?"

"Ted!" Sachs wailed. "You're the Old Nate! You've got to talk some sense into Edward!"

"But wouldn't you personally benefit? You could be the Young Nate again."

"Oh please! You know I can't do that! And Studs is my friend!"

"I don't think Edward's serious. Why would he fire Studs anyway? He brings star power to the production."

"Don't you know? Studs and Sylvia, well…" Arthur trailed off.

"Tell me something, Arthur. Are you the only one who hasn't fucked Sylvia?"

"Only once! And that was a long time ago. She made me," he whined.

"I tell you what, Arthur. I'll give Edward a call and sort this thing out. How's that?"

"Oh, thank you, thank you so much!" Sachs practically groveled in gratitude.

As Gershem walked off down the street, he chuckled and wondered if he should call the Grand Poobah and plead Arthur's case. No way. And then, before he could take any evasive maneuvers, she was upon him, Rhoda Memberman walking her dog.

"Professor Gershem, how are you?"

"Very well, thank you," he lied as the little dog tried to climb his leg.

"Oooh, she likes you," Rhoda crooned. "Say hello to Petunia."

Gershem did not say hello to the dog. It was bad enough to run into a student outside of class without this added distraction. He was tempted to kick Petunia down the block like a football but he restrained himself.

"Everything all right?" he inquired, which could mean anything and didn't mean anything at all.

Rhoda took it to mean her class work. "I think I'm making some progress…"

"Good. That's great. Progress." He looked at his watch. "Good to see you. Got to run." With those parting words he did not stay his leaving but rushed off down the street like a man with things on his mind. Important things requiring his full attention.

Rhoda was a bit nonplussed by this brush-off. Maybe Gershem didn't like dogs. But then, what did she care? She had things on her mind as well. One thing anyway and that was a trap she was setting for Hyman Ryman, the so far nonreciprocal object of her connubial ambitions. She had discovered from the psychology department's website that the Spuyten Duyvil Trust had made a substantial grant to the graduate program and that she and Ryman therefore had something in common. Well, sort of in common. Her intention was to waylay him as he either entered or left the offices of the An Idea Grows in America Institute and bring up this happy coincidence. They were being sponsored by the same people so shouldn't they get to know each other better? It certainly made sense to her. She would have to rephrase it as a command rather than a question, however, so as not to leave him any escape route. Not, "Shouldn't we?" but rather, "We must." Now if she could just get Petunia to pee on his leg so she could apologize and insist on washing his pants, but, alas, Petunia was a girl and didn't raise her leg to do her business.

So, doing as she did every business day, she walked the dog over to the building where the Institute was located and played with her in front of the door for a few minutes. So far, she'd had no luck, but today was going to be different. No sooner had she let Petunia off her leash than Hyman Ryman appeared, walking out of the building with his briefcase. Rhoda was on him like a fly on... well, she didn't waste any time.

"Hyman! What a coincidence. I was just thinking about you."

Ryman, an earnest nebbish in a polo shirt, khaki trousers and penny loafers which he thought made him look like a WASP, but which didn't work for him at all, recoiled in terror but there was nothing he could do. It was as if the Medusa had turned him to stone. Rhoda did have that tendency, or talent, or whatever you want to call it.

"Unh, wh – why?" he stammered.

"I just found out that we're both working for the same people. Isn't that something?"

"I – I don't understand."

"The Spuyten Duyvil Trust. I have so many questions for you. Let's get a cup of coffee at the Klatch."

"I don't know…"

"I won't take no for answer," Rhoda said merrily, or at least what she thought was merrily. "It's such a nice day. We can sit outside." She collected Petunia and virtually frog marched the poor fellow off campus to the coffee shop.

"Two Mit Schlags," she ordered without even asking him what he wanted. "So tell me all about the work you do, Hyman,"

"I, well, I can't. It's mostly classified."

"Classified! That's so sexy! So hush hush! Why?"

"I can't tell you. It's defense stuff."

"Oh, my, I had no idea you were such an expert. You must have security clearance and all that."

"Well, yeah," he allowed.

"I can tell you a secret then." She leaned forward and smiled lasciviously.

Alarmed Hyman tried to stop her. "I don't think that's a…"

"I think you're cute. There. I said it."

Poor Hyman glowed like a human whorehouse light bulb and was forced to dunk his red hot nose in his glass of water, which sent up a small cloud of steam that coated his thick horned rim glasses and would simply not evaporate. He couldn't see a thing after that and, believe it or not, wound up in Rhoda Memberman's bed reenacting the old TV show, The Wide World of Spurts, as she sucked and fucked him into a distracted fountain of – dare I say it? – Love!. There. I said it, as Rhoda herself might say. Hyman Ryman was hers now and he better not forget it.

Later, when she discussed this coupling with her neighbor Marta, she was ecstatic. "He's mine, Marta, mine!"

"Good for you, girl. Men are like fish. First you got to catch them and then you got to clean them and then you got to decide how to cook them, maybe a gentle low simmer or maybe red hot on the grill. That's what my mother always said and she was good in the kitchen." She laughed merrily at this peculiar metaphor.

"I'm not a cannibal, Marta."

"Yes you are, sweetie, yes you are. So tell me more. What did his esperma taste like? I can always tell what a man's been drinking by the taste of his sperm."

"Really, Marta!" Rhoda pretended to be appalled. "I don't think he drinks alcohol."

"You kidding me. You fucking a square? That's so cool. You're lucky he doesn't drink. That's going to save you a lot of money."

❖

23

If there was one thing that Anna Bunch knew, it was that she was not fucking a square. Not a complete square anyway. As she stood naked, modeling her tin hat in front of his bedroom mirror, she said, "I think this hat rather suits me. Maybe I'll wear it all the time. What do you think, Teddums?"

"I don't know," said Gershem from his bed. "People might think you are an intellectual trying to hide your pointy head."

"Yes, I can see where they might get suspicious, especially with me being so erudite and all. Why do people think that intellectuals have pointy heads? I thought pinheads had pointy heads."

"What's the difference?"

"I don't think you're taking me seriously. I think I'm going to have to show you I mean business." With that she tossed her tin hat aside and jumped into bed where she successfully showed him just how serious she was. With a little help from the Happy Shadow, who, quite unnoticed, managed to slip it up her behind while she bounced up and down over her true love and managed simultaneous vaginal and anal orgasms.

After they were done, she asked him: "God, I love it when you stick your finger up my ass. Do you think I'm good in bed? For an intellectual, I mean."

Gershem, who had not stuck his finger anywhere, replied, "I didn't realize you were concerned about it. I thought it was all acting anyway."

"It's not. I don't know what just got into me, but it sure felt good. Then, there's no business like show business. Let's go to a movie."

Gershem was agreeable. "What do you want to see?"

"I want to see the new Johnson Barr film, "Dirty Dog 33".

Gershem was mildly appalled. "Are you joking?"

"I love Johnson Barr. He looks just like you. And you don't have to be arty all the time just because you're an... intellectual."

"All right, all right. I'll just eat some popcorn and go to sleep."

This very up-to-date propaganda piece set in ISIS controlled east Syria featured dashing Johnson Barr as a sort of Lawrence of Arabia, ex Navy Seal turned archeologist, operating covertly to save ancient ruins and overthrow the Caliphate. His love interest was a sultry al Jazeera reporter who was undercover as a man but still managed to look like a beauty contest winner. Who knew those Daesh guys wore so much lipstick and mascara? The story was somewhat intriguing if you have a particularly morbid sense of humor, which Gershem did and he very much enjoyed himself. In fact, the people around him were a little disturbed by his seemingly inappropriate laughter at scenes such as the beheading of a Syrian archeologist whose vicious executioner asks him to keep blinking after his decapitation so this sneering, leering villain can ascertain how long his head stays conscious after the heinous act he is about to perform. Not long, Gershem discovered. At the conclusion, after Johnson Barr saves the Palmyra ruins and vanquishes the bad guys with a little help from a swarm of attack helicopters and heroic commandos in blackface, virtue triumphs with a little hot sex on the side.

Anna berated Ted for being so unappreciative of dreamboat Barr's performance in a sort of, "How could you?" hissy fit.

"You don't really think I look like that guy, do you?" Gershem protested. "Anyway, I thought it was a pretty good comedy. Not exactly Dr. Strangelove, but a cut above Jackass IV."

"Don't be so cynical. Brave people are fighting and dying to preserve…"

"Oil," Gershem interrupted her.

"Well, you didn't have to ruin it for everybody else," was her feeble rejoinder.

"Really? If people had laughed at Hitler rather than 'ruin it for everybody else,' maybe…"

Anna was aghast. "You're not comparing Johnson Barr to Hitler, are you?"

"Oh, please."

The cab ride back uptown was sourly silent. Their pleasant post-Ecstasy enchantment had been shattered by a silly movie and could only be rekindled by, of all things, a phone message from Edward Smith.

"Ted! Anna! I've got the money to do they play! Call me!"

Of course, he didn't really have the money. Not yet. But a producer has to be a pathological liar. How else would any show get on?

"That's wonderful, Edward!" Anna gushed when she called him back. "I knew you'd do it!"

"Well, thank you, Anna. Isn't it wonderful? And this isn't going to be just another storefront production. We're going to do it in a real theatre!"

"That's fantastic. So, what now?"

"We have to all get together and fine tune this thing. Is Ted up for that?"

"Of course," she drawled in her Rand voice. "I'll make sure Ted's up for anything."

"I'm sure you will, Anna." Smith wasn't sure whether or not she was making a dirty joke, which she was. "Can we get together tonight? Is that convenient for you?"

"I'll ask Ted and get back to you."

And who couldn't stay away? All the members of the Downtown Manhattan Illuminati "collective", as Ayn Rand might call them, gathered that evening in eager anticipation of fame and glory and maybe even Equity minimum. Smith distributed the sides he wanted them to read, assigned Argyle to do Leonard Peikoff and Alan Greenspan and they were off. Without going into the mistakes,

director's remarks, etc., here is the exact text of what they read:
Ayn, Nate, BARBARA, O'CONNER, Greenspan, and PEIKOFF are
gathered in Ayn's living room.

AYN

There's something I'd like to read you
from the talk I'm giving next week
in Boston. "If a small minority were
always regarded as guilty in any clash
with the majority, would you call it
persecution? If this minority was made
to pay for the sins of the majority,
would you call it persecution? If this
minority had to live under a reign of
terror, under special laws imposed
by the majority, if this minority were
punished for their qualities rather
than their failings, would you call that
persecution? If your answer is "yes" ask
yourself what sort of monstrous injus-
tice you are condoning and supporting. What do you think?

BARBARA
Are you talking about Negroes?

AYN
Of course not. I'm talking about the
most persecuted minority in America -
Big Business!

PEIKOFF
Yes!

They all applaud her.

NATE

I think it's going to be wonderful,
Ayn. Can we print it in the Objectivist
Newsletter?

AYN

Of course. I think you should use it
in the book as well. It goes a long way
towards explaining just who I am.

PEIKOFF

It certainly does.

The doorbell rings.

AYN

Frank, would you see who that is?

O'Conner runs off to do her bidding.

GREENSPAN

I think you should send it to the Times.

AYN
(scoffing)
Really, Alan, do you think those Communists would even consider publishing the truth?

Frank returns with Patrecia Gullison. Ayn looks up
curiously.

NATE

Patrecia, I'm so glad you could make
it. Everybody, this is our new office
manager, Patrecia Gullison.

                    AYN
Really? Welcome, my dear. Such a
lovely girl. You must sit down and tell
us all about yourself.

Flustered Patrecia does as she is told.

                  PATRECIA
Well, there's really not much to tell.
I went to a lecture at the Institute and
I met Mr. Branden and Mr. Greenspan. I was so impressed that I offered
to do anything I could for the Objectivist movement. I've always been
a great admirer of your work, Miss
Rand.

                    NATE
Patrecia read *The Fountainhead* when
she was nine years old.

                    AYN
At the age of nine? That's wonderful.
It gives me hope. Frank, get Patrecia
a cup of coffee. How do you like it,
dear?

                  PATRECIA
Lots of cream and sugar.

                    AYN
Tell me, Patrecia, do you have a boyfriend?

PATRECIA
Yes, I'm engaged to Larry Scott. He's
the most rational man I know.

Nate is visibly taken aback by this unwelcome news
and goes into a brown study.

AYN
That's wonderful. I hope you'll invite
us to the wedding.

PATRECIA
(gushing)
I'd be so honored.

AYN
I'm very pleased to meet you, Patrecia.
You remind me of myself when I was
younger.
(to the rest)
Now where were we?
PEIKOFF
Your speech in Boston.

AYN
Yes, I'm a little worried. This Ford
Hall Forum where I'm talking may
have leftist tendencies. I happen to
know that they once invited Adlai
Stevenson to speak there.

The group reels in horror.

AS ONE

No!
Adlai Stevenson?!
How can you go there?!

Ayn holds up her hands to calm them.

> AYN
>
> I know, I know. I may be a stranger in
> a strange land but go I shall. I may just
> teach them a thing or two. Nathaniel,
> have you arranged my hotel accom-
> modations?

Nate is jolted out of his funk.

> NATE
>
> Pardon?

> PATRECIA
>
> I'll do that, Miss Rand. It's my job now.

> AYN
>
> Thank you, Patrecia, and please call
> me Ayn. We're very informal here.

> NATE (VO)
>
> I must admit that the news of Patre-
> cia's wedding was very disturbing. I
> couldn't focus, I felt as if I were plung-
> ing into an abyss. As a rational man,
> I knew I had to accept the world as it
> was but, you know, I just couldn't.

"Bravo!" Smith exulted as Gershem read the last line. "That was just super! All of you! You were all just great!" He turned to his wife. "What do you think, Sylvia?"

"I think,.." she paused. "I think we're ready for Broadway!"

The cast cheered and basked in their mentors' adulation, congratulating each other on a job well done without knowing that the Smiths had already calculated, without even consulting an accountant, that the Ayn Rand project was all a tax write-off for Player Station. They could quite literally put on the show for free. The actors would actually be financing their own labor with their own labor! Capitalism at its best!

Gershem suspected that there was more to all this hoopla than met the eye, but who was he to rain on Anna's star turn parade?

"Now listen up, all of you!" said Edward over the very modest din. "Not only are we going to put on "Ayn and Nate" but we'll all be working on a whole string of jobs like we did for the nuclear safety people. Paying jobs!"

Once again, the cast sent up a cheer.

"But, first things first! We really have to double down on this production and open with a bang!"

Gershem thought that this was an unfortunate metaphor since stage plays that fail are referred to as bombs, but he didn't say anything, even if a wisecrack was completely appropriate.

"So now what?" was his only question to Anna as they rode the subway back uptown.

"Well, I guess we have to put our cruise to nowhere on hold. I'm nervous, Ted. I've never had a lead like this."

"Don't worry. You're going to be great."

"You really think so?"

Why was it that members of the acting community needed constant reassurance? It was as if they didn't exist at all except through their various personae. Even Ted knew that word. Clinical psychologists use it all the time.

"Who cares what I think? The critics are the ones you have to watch out for," he said cheerfully.

"Would you mind if I did anything, I mean anything, Ted, anything to get a good review?"

"I thought they were all homosexuals. If you can find a straight one, you have my blessings. But only if I can watch."

"You're such a pervert."

"Maybe. An abnormal psychologist anyway."

❖

24

As all things inevitable ultimately come to pass, so did Edward Smith's appearance in civil court to defend himself against the Objectivist Institute's lawsuit. Acting (literally) for the defense, Sylvia donned her Hillary Clinton power pants suit from the dungeon wardrobe closet and argued before the bar that whatever evidence the Institute had was stolen since the copyrighted play had never been produced or published. But that was only after a conversation with the Institute's attorney, one Tootie Wookums, in the hallway of the Hall of Justice, that the Smith's decided to go before the judge.

"Hey there," said affable Tootie to Edward, "good to see you again. So, look, we'll drop the suit for one half the show's proceeds provided we have our own auditor."

"Go fuck yourself, you cheap shyster piece of shit," was Sylvia's immediate response.

"You can't speak to me that way," Wookums whined. "I'm just doing my job."

"You can take your job and shove it," Sylvia snarled. "We're going to court."

As Sylvia had predicted, the case was thrown out when Wookums refused to divulge where he'd obtained a copy of the play. Since it was the only evidence he had, it was disallowed. However, since

Sylvia was not familiar with legal jargon, when Wookums requested that the case be dismissed "without prejudice" she didn't object, leaving the door open for a second filing. So the Smiths left with the mistaken impression that they would hear no more from the Objectivist Institute.

"Wasn't I good?" Sylvia preened.

"The consummate actress. But I don't know," Edward backtracked. "On one hand, I'm glad to get them out of my hair. On the other, we won't get all the free publicity a lawsuit would have guaranteed."

"Don't be silly. One of my clients has an in at Page Six. The fact that these people even tried to sue us is good enough."

"Well, don't use it now. We want it right before the show opens."

"Yes, of course," she said with a certain ambivalence. Although Sylvia knew that Anna Bunch was a better Ayn Rand than she was, it was Sylvia who was going to miss her star turn when the play opened, when her only acting credit would be "Miss Bunch's understudy" and this sort of resentment has a way of burrowing under the skin where it festers and grows, where it swells into a painful boil badly in need of lancing. Such are the consequences of willfully throwing one's self into the fearsome pool of other peoples' adulation because, as we all know, other people are Hell.

But that was when and this was now. The past and future can be distorted since they don't actually exist, but the present makes real demands that don't broach any stammered explanations. And the present was at that very moment making real demands on Barry Breen and Rino Matsui.

"But you told me," Rino whined, "that you wanted to introduce me to your parents this Sunday."

"I did, I do. They're just out of town this weekend."

"I think you're ashamed of me," she pouted.

"I should be ashamed," Breen pointed out. "Here I am taking advantage of this sexy little minx. I wait until she's asleep and I get down on my knees and worship her…"

"What are you doing to me when I'm sleeping?" she said suspiciously.

"Everything you can think of. Everything. Because you are my everything, Rino. The cream in my coffee…"

"Please just shut up. We have another meeting this afternoon."

"Who's this one with?"

"Armand Vogg of the Anti-Reptilian Society."

"Well, that certainly sounds interesting. Isn't that what Alden Dirst was railing on about?"

And so it was. Armand Vogg, a squat man dressed in fur everything – or was that his hair? - greeted them at the door to his small office with a sort of Geiger counter that did not click louder when he held it close to them.

"Sorry, " he apologized, "just checking."

"Checking for what?" Breen asked him.

"Checking to see if you're reptiles. You're not."

"That's good to know."

"Don't patronize me," said Vogg. "A man in my position has to be careful. Please, sit down."

Breen and Rino took seats across from Vogg's desk chair, which was considerably elevated and made them feel as though they were in a courtroom before the bench.

"I guess you're wondering why my chair is higher than yours. It scares the hell out of the reptilians," Vogg explained confidentially. "Those lizards think they're clever but they've got nothing on old believe you me. So what can I do you for?"

Since Rino was the one who'd contacted Mr. Vogg, she did the explaining. "We're doing a project at Columbia on how people perceive of good and evil and we'd like to know what the Anti-Reptilian Society's position is on the subject."

"This is a joke, right? Position? Isn't it obvious? It's right in the name. Anti-Reptilian. Human good, reptile bad. Capisce?"

"I think so," said Rino. "Do you think you could elaborate?"

"Sure. That's what I do. Elaborate. So I guess you know about the Garden of Eden. There was a certain snake there who seduced Eve. Then she seduced Adam and that was it for the Garden of Eden. There are serpent myths from all over the world, Africa, China, Mexico, and they're all the same. It was the Reptilians who messed everything up for people monkeys."

"People monkeys?"

"Us. Human beings."

Rino looked at Barry. "Those are the words Walter Birmingham used."

"Walter Birmingham!" Vogg erupted. "That reptilian fraud with all his flat earth nonsense. And now he's stealing my phrasing! Pissant plagiarist! That's what he is! But that's neither here nor there for our purposes. Let me tell you about the reptilian invasion of the planet and its consequences. Are you ready?"

"We're ready," said Barry.

"Fasten your seat belts. It's like this, you see." Vogg's eyes turned up to blowtorch intensity. "The reptilians landed in a negative orgone powered flying saucer on the Pyramid of Cheops and drove the Jews out of Egypt. They decided to call themselves The Illuminati and they basked for a while in the desert sun before they got down to business–reptile business. The first thing they did was assume human form through holography. They made themselves as beautiful or charismatic as they wished, commanding the admiration of real people monkeys. That's why movie stars and most politicians are actually reptiles. But sometimes the hologram has a power shortage and reptilians briefly shapeshift back to their serpent selves. Are you still with me?"

Barry and Rino were at a loss for words.

"I know what you're thinking. It is a bit much, isn't it?" Vogg allowed. "But that's the way it is. Now the reptilians are planning to reveal themselves on Judgment Day and take over the planet. What do you think global warming is? Reptiles like it hot! People will be domesticated like cattle and the reptilians will eat them for breakfast, lunch, and dinner. Now is that evil or what?"

"But you intend to stop them," Barry managed. "How are you going to do that?"

"With courage! With brio! Are you ready to join my crusade? We will ferret out the reptiles wherever they are and show them a little people monkey justice! Tell me now! Are you ready to take The Oath?!"

"Uh, listen, Mr. Vogg, we're just researchers," Breen fended him off.

"There are no innocent bystanders in this crusade, young man!

Perhaps you can see your way to at least make a donation to the cause! Say, fifty dollars?"

"Mr. Vogg, we don't pay for interviews."

"How about twenty-five?" Vogg haggled.

"Look, Mr. Vogg, it's been very nice meeting you, but we've got to go."

"Cowards." Vogg muttered as they made a hasty retreat from his office.

Assessing this encounter might have been difficult had not Rino and Barry already been through so many bizarre interviews that they could only give this one a rating.

"Was that the craziest?" said Rino.

"I don't know. He asked for money. That's rational for a con artist."

"He didn't deserve any money. He didn't even offer us a Glade."

"I agree. I had no idea graduate studies could be so entertaining," Breen marveled.

They both cracked up and went on their merry way.

Before the Downtown Illuminati people, now employees of Player Station LLC, could even get accustomed to their new role as professionals, they were they were called on for another job, a school shooting drill or, as the authorities called it, an "active shooter response exercise." The scenario for this one was much more complicated than their last performance. Rather than play largely silent victims, there were all sorts of speaking roles – state and town officials, teachers, worried parents, journalists, and so on. They would have to memorize lines and rehearse scenes. It was pretty exciting.

"I hate to interrupt our Ayn Rand work," Smith apologized to his assembled actors, "but duty calls! Don't worry. Just think of it as a sort of day job we have to do to support our art."

No one was worried. In fact, they were very much looking forward to another fat paycheck. Studs Zenith was the only one with any reservations at all. He took Smith aside and made things clear.

"I can't do this job if there's any chance of anyone recognizing me. You understand that."

"Of course I do!" Smith soothed him. "The SWAT team all wear these sort of ninja costumes with masks, completely incognito. You can do that, can't you?"

"Perfect," Studs had to agree. "No speaking though. I have one of the most recognizable voices in television news."

Anna, of course, had no reservations at all. "I get to play the school principal. Do you think I should use my Ayn Rand voice?"

"By all means," Gershem agreed. "Smith wants me to play the coroner. I don't know if I can get away with that."

"Of course you can," Anna scoffed. "Just act like a knowledgeable professional and mumble. I have to look like I'm on the verge of tears bravely containing myself for the common good."

"A commendable interpretation of the part," he said.

"Don't make fun of me. This isn't a comedy. The audience has to feel my pain."

"They will. I do already."

For that he got a kick in the shin, which reminded him of his abnormal psychology seminar. As some professors are wont to do, he had pretty much lost interest in the semester's good versus evil project and was content to let his students do the heavy lifting. It was, however, necessary to keep up appearances and show concern for their progress. He wondered if Conrad Boardman and Alan Garret were of the same mind. He hadn't spoken with either one of them in some time and that was just fine, but his innate sense of responsibility nagged at him. He should at least pretend to be collegial about the whole thing and have a word or two about what general direction they were taking. He didn't actually care, but if Alvin Spurtz called a meeting he should be at least conversant with his colleague's work. To this end, he did absolutely nothing, but rather applied himself to learning his coroner lines making Anna act as the whole pool of clamoring reporters at his press conference.

"How many people were killed in the attack?"

"I can't tell you that until the families of the deceased have been notified but we'll keep you posted."

"Were they all children?"

"No, there were several school staff members among the casualties."

And so on.

"You know, you do a stodgy, middle-aged square very well, Ted," Anna complimented him after his performance.

"Thank you. Did you catch that tinge of perversity I was trying to give off, the vibration of someone who has chosen examining dead bodies as a career?"

"I'm not sure. Let's do it again."

A little later, it was Anna's turn to be interviewed by some sort of Anderson Cooper fop read by Gershem. She did not use her Ayn Rand voice but something more akin to a fake empathetic, oh so concerned Diane Sawyer.

"What did you do when you heard the first shots?"

"I immediately told my assistant to call 911 and I went out in the hallway to see what was going on."

"You weren't concerned for your own safety?"

"Of course I was concerned, but my first responsibility is the well-being of my staff and children."

"And what did you see?"

"There was a young man with a machine pistol shooting into a classroom. Then he saw me and turned. I was sure he was going to shoot."

"So what did you do?"

"I said, 'Put that gun down.'"

"Then what happened?"

"He hesitated, then…he put… he put the gun to his head and shot himself."

Anna read the last line as if she were delivering a just on the edge of tears funeral eulogy. Gershem cracked up and she joined in.

"Was I good?"

"Very well done. You're not only ready for Broadway but I can definitely see you in a juicy schoolmarm porno."

"Oh, Ted," she vamped, "you're too kind."

Truth be known, Gershem, following in the footsteps of so many without any apparent exhibitionist tendencies before they were thrust on stage, was falling into the sinister allure of the make believe. The simulation of another person, even with the binding constraints of technique and rote practice, was the most liberating thing he'd ever done. He was ready to play his part as the script dictated; he was ready for his close-up!

Anna, of course, had been in this fevered state for most of her life and she sensed that Gershem had caught the bug. His ironic detachment was slowly giving way to genuine enthusiasm, which she could feel in the way he read his lines. Now, joined together in their love for the theatrical, it was only a matter of time until they would be joined in the blessed bonds of matrimony. Or so she imagined the two of them standing naked before some sort of altar in their tin hats.

Clueless Gershem was of a different mind altogether. He saw his acting stint as a welcome diversion from the humdrum life of academia and, though his feelings toward Anna were highly affectionate, they were hardly matrimonial. In fact, the very word matrimonial, with its distinctly matriarchal origins, was a flashing sign warning him to avoid any such trap. What was all this female nonsense about husbands anyway? Must be something in the hormones.

Even though he'd put "Ayn and Nate" on hold for the duration of the new contract, Edward Smith was actively looking for a suitable venue for the future production that would establish his theatrical credibility. He certainly couldn't produce on Broadway and off-off was also out of the question if he wanted to get any attention outside of a few arty losers. He needed a medium size house somewhere on the outskirts of midtown, say the thirties, and he tasked Arthur Sachs with the search.

"But I don't know anything about real estate," Sachs whined.

"You don't have to know anything, Arthur, anything at all. That's why I asked you to do it."

Sachs sensed he was being ridiculed but that had always been par for the course in his association with the Smiths.

"Go, Arthur, do your job," he dismissed Sachs just before he got the shock of his life. Who should walk into the theatre but bearded, bespectacled, but still quite recognizable Calvin Card?

"Jesus Christ!" Edward gasped. "You're dead!"

"Don't get all excited," Card shushed him. "Retalitron made me do it. They made me disappear. They need people who don't exist anymore."

"What?!"

"To balance the books. It's complicated."

"What do you want with me?"

"I want my old job back. I want to be a talent scout for Player Station. Under an assumed name, of course."

"Ah, I see," said Smith. "Retalitron wants to keep an eye on me."

"Well," Card phumphed, "you'd have to ask them about that."

"So I have no choice."

"Something like that, I guess."

"You know there are people I'm managing who have seen you before."

"Don't worry about that. You and I only meet in private. They want kids for the school thing. Cute kids. Find some. Also, I need a pound of smoke. I've got to get my buyers back. Ciao." And he was gone, leaving Edward to wonder if he were hallucinating. The weed he could understand but what was this about kids? They wouldn't be any use in his Ayn Rand project and he didn't like brat actors and their stage mothers anyway. Deirdre worked in some sort of after school program. Maybe she could round up some useful children.

❖

25

Rhoda Memberman's budding romance was progressing right along the timeline she had engraved on the stone convolutions of her brain. Hyman Ryman was not accustomed to being treated as the sexy beast that Rhoda insisted he was and which she emphasized by making love to him in every possible venue you could imagine. She turned off the elevator in his building and sucked his cock, she forced him into a broom closet at the An Idea Grows in America Institute and sucked his cock, she put a jacket over her head in a taxicab and sucked his cock, well, the list goes on and on. Not that Ryman was complaining, mind you. The question of possibly getting caught in flagrante excited him to distraction and, almost overnight, he went from wimpy nebbish to bold sexual adventurer under Rhoda's lubricious tutelage. Talk about getting led around by his dick, for which she even had a pet name – The Tower of Power!

But enough about all this carnality. Rhoda Memberman was a rather exaggerated woman. Her ass was exaggerated, her tits were exaggerated, even her smile was too big for her face, something like an R. Crumb cartoon temptress. But her most exaggerated feature wasn't even visible and that was her curiosity. Rhoda wasn't just a snoop, she was a snoop to the nth power. She had to know. She just had to.

"Tell me one of your secrets, Hyman," was her purring pillow talk as they lay bathed in sweat after a particularly gymnastic session. "Tell me what you do at that institute of yours or I won't suck your cock anymore."

"Ah, come on, Rhoda. You know I can't talk about work," he whined. "Do you want me to wind up like Edward Snowden?"

"I wouldn't mind. I could keep you warm through the Russian winter. I could whip the horses as the wolves chase our troika across the frozen steppes. Come on, Hyman, just one little tidbit. Office gossip, anything."

"It's all about psy-ops. There. That's all I'm going to tell you."

"I already know that, Hyman," said Rhoda, which she didn't. "Why do you think the Spuyten Duyvil people are giving the psych department money too?"

"So why are you asking questions? I had to sign a non-disclosure agreement. Did you?"

"Maybe. You think I'd tell you? I think it's time for your pussy eating lesson."

Ryman, who had never had his head between a woman's legs before he met Rhoda, was fast becoming a cunnilingus enthusiast whose very first awkward tonguings had required some remedial instruction, who now looked out upon Rhoda's lush pubic hair, which reminded him of aerial photographs he'd seen of the vast Siberian forest stretching for miles and miles in the distance, with the confidence of a man who knows his way around the nooks and crannies of his immediate environs. He could now locate the little man in the boat blindfolded and set the small craft tossing on a tempestuous sea of moans and groans as the storm built to hurricane force and Rhoda burst forth with louder and louder shrieks of abandon. That's the way he thought about it anyway. Who would have guessed this nerd could dredge up such a poetic metaphor? But enough about Hyman Ryman's late sexual revelations.

For her own part, Rhoda was quite happy to have found the man of her dreams, the man who know how to take orders, the man who realized who was boss, but there was one thing that rankled her and that was his stubborn refusal to spill the beans on the An Idea Grows in America Institute. No matter how much she pried and prodded, no matter how many times she sucked his cock, he simply wouldn't budge. Why she even cared would be a fair question and the answer was pretty simple. Information was control. Therefore she had to know everything about her prospective mate. There could be no secrets between them. Well, none of his secrets anyway. Hers were strictly on a need to know basis.

You might think that nebbish Hyman Ryman was blissfully unaware of Rhoda's snooping tendencies, but that was not the case. In fact, he himself was quite curious about the Spuyten Duyvil funding of some graduate program at the university and had immediately started researching the psychology department grant. He had not only learned the names of the faculty involved but was busy constructing a biographical picture of each one of them. Rhoda's professor, Theodore Gershem, was naturally among those he was investigating. Ryman's security clearance at An Idea Grows in America allowed him access to data not otherwise available from public sources and his dossiers were, as dossiers tend to do, growing.

Among the things he had learned about Gershem was his association with the Downtown Illuminati theatre group. This factoid was of some interest to him as a psy-ops specialist. Members of the entertainment community often participated as needed in many exercises, taking on the parts of Navy Seals, rape victims, the terminally ill, and other sympathetic characters used to move the target audience in one direction or another. The rationale was that so-called real people would simply not conform to the image the producers wanted to project and that trained script readers were much more desirable as public fronts. This conviction had been borne out in numerous false flag events where actors were found to be far more convincing, than, say, actual eyewitnesses.

Rhoda, with all her blind spots was entirely unaware of Hyman's interest until he asked her a question about her professor's acting.

"How do you know about that?" she demanded. She only knew herself because Rino Matsui had let it slip during a short talk about the project. Rino didn't think it was a secret anyway.

"Uh, you told me," said Ryman, pretending to be ever so slightly exasperated.

"I don't remember that."

"You told me he had joined a theatre group as part of the project."

"Hmm." Rhoda was now not sure she hadn't. How else would Hyman know? "Well, that's true, but that's all I know. Why are you interested?"

"I'm not. Just making conversation. That's all," he sloughed it off.

His apparent disinterest, of course, set her bursting out of the gate, off and talking, telling him everything she knew about Gershem.

"I couldn't really see it myself at first. On stage, I mean. He's friendly but kind of reserved. I think his girlfriend got him into it. She looks like she'd be into that sort of thing. The way she dresses, the way she speaks. I forgot her name. I only met her once," and so on, making Hyman sorry he'd asked. But not so sorry that he wouldn't continue prying into Gershem's background. If you just kept digging, there was always something more interesting than met the eye. That was one thing he'd learned for sure.

At that very moment, the object of this speculation was coincidentally rehearsing his lines for the school shooting shoot in the mirror. He'd actually gone to YouTube and looked at real coroners delivering their reports to the press. They all seemed to have gone to acting class themselves, managing to combine somber detached competence and authoritative photogenic appeal with just a whiff of the weird that lurked within.

Anna was at work so, with no one to play off but his image in the mirror, he decided to pack it in and take a walk. At the corner newsstand on Broadway he learned from the headlines that terrorists had staged a suicide attack on a boy band concert in Liverpool, England. He wasn't curious enough to buy the paper and went on his way. He also didn't know that the Internet was all abuzz about the presence of known "crisis actors" at this catastrophe, underground stars quite possibly deserving their own clandestine awards ceremony. Actors liked to get awards. It made them feel appreciated.

As Gershem continued up Broadway, he quite unexpectedly ran into Bob and Marta Applewhite who were in town to make a delivery.

"Ted, how are you?!" Bob greeted him and Marta clamped onto his arm. "We've been meaning to look you up."

"Well, here I am."

"You are, aren't you? Don't you live around here?"

"Pretty close."

"Well, what say you invite us over? I've got something to show you."

"Sure. Why not? Marta, let go of my arm."

"Can't I hold it for just a little while longer? I feel so insecure in the big city."

Gershem thought it over. "Okay, but just until we get to the door of my building. Can you limp or something? I have a lady friend, you know, and I don't want it getting back to her that I was walking arm and arm with another woman."

Marta immediately let go and jumped back like she'd been stung. "Why didn't you tell me?!" she wailed. "That's just so wonderful that you have a girlfriend! The last thing I want to do is make her jealous!"

When they got to Gershem's apartment, he offered them a glass of wine but Applewhite turned him down. "Doesn't go with this stuff," he said pulling a plastic bag out of his pocket. "You remember last time we got together I told you we were getting out of growing weed and going into another line of agriculture?"

"Not that HOG stuff," Gershem ventured,

"No, no, that's not agricultural. That's all chemicals. I'm talking organic."

"Yes, I remember…"

"I knew you would! Well, I did it and here's the product, my first batch." He poured the little brown balls in the bag on the table. "Opium straight from the seed pod! You want some?"

Gershem was understandably reluctant but his curiosity got the better of him. He had never smoked opium but a whole bunch of famous writers had, even Graham Greene. Why not Ted Gershem?

"Well, how do you do it? Do you have a pipe?"

"Completely inefficient. A waste of good stuff. You have to shove it up your ass."

"This is a joke, right?" Gershem guffawed.

"It's not," said Marta. "It's the best way. Trust me."

Bearing in mind that pharmaceutical opium is dispensed in suppositories, Gershem took the plunge, if that's the proper term, and did as he was told. Within a very few minutes, he began to itch. That passed quickly and he felt slightly drowsy but very pleasant. He looked around. Everything was the same as it had been before. Nothing had changed but his perception of the way everything was. A chair was a chair. Not just a chair. A chair. It had a thereness he had never noticed before and it was good. It was not alive, it did not have a spirit, it was a chair and that was that.

"So, how are things going with Edward Smith and his theatre group? Are you still doing that Ayn Rand play?" Bob asked.

"Yeah, it's still in rehearsal. I don't really have much of a part. I'm sort of the narrator."

"That's a shaaame," Marta grunted as she pushed a ball of opium up into her rectum. "I can see you in a starring role, like King Lear or something."

"That very flattering, but I don't really think…"

"What's this?" said Bob who had just noticed Anna's tin hat on the side table and picked it up.

"It's a tin hat."

"You're kidding," Bob guffawed. "I've never seen one before."

"Try it on," Gershem advised. "It keeps off the bad rays."

"That is just so cool," said Marta. "Where can I get one?"

"I don't know," said Gershem. "That one was custom made."

Marta tried it on. "Wow! All the bad rays just disappeared." Actually that was the opium's doing, not the tin hat. But there did seem to be something bouncing off the thing in that light.

"I know this tin knocker right down the road from our house," Bob told his wife. "The air conditioner guy. I'll get one made for you."

"You'd do that for me?!" Marta squealed. "That's why I just love you so much, my Bobby Wobby!"

This one really needs a tin hat, was Gershem's bemused thought, but he was feeling too good to dwell on Marta's childish enthusiasm. "Is Edward Smith still, uh, doing business with you?"

"Yeah," said Bob. "Not our best customer, but he's steady. Has he ever sold you anything?"

"No, no. I guess we're not supposed to know. He's been keeping us busy with some outside work though."

"What do you mean?"

"Acting jobs. Instructional films for first responders. We're doing a school shooting drill this week. I play the coroner."

"No shit," Bob chuckled. "He asked us to do that sort of thing but I turned him down. I don't want to be on film surrounded by a bunch of cops. What would my buyers think?"

"Fake cops, Bob. Actors."

"The audience doesn't know that."

"They probably do," Gershem pointed out." The audience is cops."

"So are some of my customers. So where's this main squeeze of yours? Marta wants to meet her."

"I do," Marta agreed.

"She's at work. Are you going to be around this evening? We could have dinner together."

"I'm not sure. I'll call you." Which meant no thanks. "Keep

some of these," he said, pushing a bulging plastic bag full of opium balls across the table. "You know the first one's always free."

Later, when Anna came home, he didn't mention the Applewhite's visit. Nor, of course, mention that he was loaded on opium.

"Ted, I got tickets to the Enoch Santina thing at Lerner Hall tonight. Just for you. We should wear our tin hats."

Former CIA operative and all around government conspiracy gadfly, Enoch Santina was a well-known figure in the community of the severely disaffected and filled auditoriums wherever he spoke with like minded I'm-mad-as-hell-and-I'm-not-going-to-take-this-shit-anymore folks.

"How did you get tickets?" Gershem wondered.

"It wasn't easy. It's been sold out for weeks but I pulled a few strings. Working for a high powered law firm has its benefits."

"This should be interesting."

"Don't you think?" she said. "I thought it would fit right in with your seminar stuff. We have to get something to eat before we go. I'm famished."

Ted wasn't hungry at all but he was content to accompany Anna to King Wok for a bite.

Later, they walked up Broadway to the Roone Arledge Auditorium where the event was taking place and were confronted with a clamoring crowd of petitioners who had failed to buy tickets in advance but were still determined to get into Santina's talk. Gershem and Anna had to literally push and shove their way through these indignant fans to the lobby where their tickets were carefully scrutinized by the uniformed thugs at the entrance. Having finally gained admission they found their seats in the middle of a buzzing swarm of Santina acolytes. These people were not your usual lecture crowd. They were loud and boisterous, calling across the room to their friends and milling around as if they were at a union hall shape-up. They were in no hurry to sit down until grey-maned Enoch Santina walked out on stage in his trademark bullet-proof vest and admonished them:

"What do you think this is?! A cocktail party?! This ain't no disco! This ain't no fooling around! Take a seat!"

The crowd cheered and moved to do what they were told as Santina assumed the podium and adjusted the microphone. Gershem was heartened by the fact that Santina didn't seem to have a presenter, some university functionary who would shamelessly brown nose and babble on as long as indecency permits just to bask in the attention owed to the illustrious speaker.

"So, what's new?" Santina addressed his audience and held up the New York Times. "Let's see. What's the CIA/Mossad Daily Press Release going on about? 'Terrorist attack on the eve of British election.' I translate that as, 'Falling in the polls, douchebag prime minister tries to goose up her ratings with brazen MI5 orchestrated false flag.' There, I've fixed it."

The crowd roared its approval.

"I kind of like it myself," he said, putting the newspaper aside. "Whenever you read anything in the so-called news, you have to ask yourself one simple question. Cui bono? Who benefits? In this case, not the supposed terrorist. He just blew himself to smithereens. Not his supposed allies in the Muslim community. They just got themselves more oppressive restrictions and unfettered hatred. But the douchebag prime minister? How about that bump in the polls just as she was going down? She's just loving that finger licking good thang! Blammo! It's better than fireworks on the Thames! It's the real thing!"

The audience cackled along with every rhetorical flourish.

"Sorry for all those trademark infringements. If there are any representatives of MacDonald's, Kentucky Fried Chicken or Coca Cola in the house, I apologize. No wait. I take that back. I'll apologize when you sponsor me! I'll even wear your goddamn logo on my vest here!"

The crowd went absolutely wild, hooting and chanting, "It's the real thing!!"

"He certainly knows how to rouse the rabble," Anna shouted over the din into Gershem's ear.

Ted could not remember ever having attended a more raucous gathering. Hockey game and prize fight fans paled in comparison. The 9/11 crowd down at St. Marks was positively demure compared to this group. Enoch Santina held up his hands to quiet his fans.

"We live in an age of miracles, my friends! Suspending the laws of man was relatively easy! Any fascist scumbag can do that! But suspending the first, second and third laws of motion, both laws of the conservation of energy and momentum, the first law of thermodynamics, well, the list goes on and on and on… That, my friends, is nothing short of miraculous!!"

The crowd went into a mockery of a typical revival meeting, shouting out fervent Hallelujahs! and Praise the Lords!

Ted and Anna looked at each other in astonishment. It was almost inconceivable this event was taking place in the hallowed halls of academe. Ted half expected someone like Alvin Spurtz to emerge from the wings and shut the whole thing down, but it soon became clear there would be no intervention. The whooping, hollering congregants would most certainly riot and probably burn the place down if anyone interfered with the festivities.

"So what are we going to do about these motherfucking pieces of human filth running this 4-D hologram?!" Santina continued. "You know who I mean! The talking heads, the stage managers, and their servile, co-opted minions! I'd tell you what I'd do but I'd probably get arrested for saying it! Just use your imaginations! A bunch of bloodthirsty maniacs in three piece suits are trying burn down your house! Do you just stand by and nicely ask them to please pretty please stop what they're doing? I don't think so. I think you do something about it and you use any means necessary!"

The crowd went wild again and Gershem wondered if Santina were actually an agent provocateur with his purported CIA background and all. Were he and Anna being video recorded at that very moment, soon to be archived as potential terrorists and placed on the no fly list?

"I think we should get out of here!" he yelled to Anna.

"Why?! I love it!" she yelled back.

Well, he couldn't just leave her there, could he? And Santina was just warming up.

"It's all just a rich man's trick! These fat cat slimeballs don't have to work so they amuse themselves by taunting the masses with their theatrical productions, the more elaborate the better! What did Karlheinz Stockhausen say about 9/11? He called it the most fantastic conceptual art piece he'd ever seen! And he's right! Because that's exactly what it was! What are the ad guy scumbags from creative going to cook up next to relieve their masters' boredom? Krispy Kremes and monster truck shows just won't cut it anymore! The audience is pounding on the table demanding blood! Not false flag Hollywood squibs! The real thing!"

"There will be blood! There will be blood!" the crowd chanted.

"To cower not before your masters!" Santina roared. "That is the law! Are we not men! To eat the rich! That is the law! Are we not men!"

At this point, Gershem thought he was hallucinating. It was all a dream, an opium dream.

"Isn't he fabulous?!!" Anna shouted, but Ted couldn't hear her over the clamor. He wanted to put a bag over his head in a doomed, futile attempt to avoid the repercussions of his folly.

"What is this?! What on earth were you doing there?!" he could see Alvin Spurtz holding up his picture and demanding an explanation as he pushed a boilerplate letter of resignation across the desk. Unable to contain himself any longer, Gershem bolted and raced for the exit with Anna trying to follow him.

"Where are you going?!" she howled like a banshee.

Gershem did not stay his leaving until he reached the street where he bent over gasping for breath.

"Professor Gershem. What are you doing here?"

He looked up. It was Barry Breen with Rino Matsui.

"We couldn't get in," Breen explained.

Anna joined them. "What are you doing, Ted? Those tickets cost plenty."

"That's enough for me," said Gershem emphatically. "I'm not going back in there."

"You have tickets?" said Breen.

"Well, stubs," said Anna, digging them out of her purse. "You want them?"

"Yeah," said Breen and he and Rino rushed off into the auditorium lobby.

"Who are those kids?" said Anna.

"My seminar students."

"Really? How embarrassing for you. I mean chickening out right in front of them."

"Now you see here," Gershem started angrily, then abruptly backed off. "I really don't feel well." Actually, with the combined effect of his hasty escape and the opium, he'd never felt better.

"Oh, I'm sorry," Anna soothed. "Let's go home and put you to bed."

Rino and Barry got away with showing their stubs, telling the security guards they'd just stepped outside for a smoke, and joined the throng of Santina fans in the auditorium, curiously named after television sports promoter Roone Arledge who actually dropped out of Columbia graduate school to take a job in broadcasting. To give him an honorary diploma for a significant donation was one thing. Naming a lecture hall after him? Well, that donation must have been very significant indeed.

Santina was pacing back and forth across the stage delivering staccato bursts of invective as the audience brayed its approval.

"The joke is the perpetrators of this monstrous hoax live just a few blocks from here, up and down Fifth and Park Avenues where they store their looted treasures and think of what else to plunder!" he thundered. "Just a few blocks! Makes you wonder, doesn't it?! I mean, anybody here could walk right over there and just hang out! Just sit on a park bench and enjoy human nature! It's still public! You can still do it!"

In the pandemonium that ensued, this not so disguised incitement to riot was not lost of Rino and Barry.

"There is absolutely no chance of getting an interview with this guy!" Rino shouted.

"Zbigniewzbigniew, that's all folks!" Santina did a journeyman job of a Porky Pig impersonation and the crowd roared. "You've got the whole world in your hands! So do something about it!"

The audience stormed the exits, presumably to wreak havoc in the midtown precincts of the rich and Santina was left standing on the stage all by himself.

"Mr. Santina?" Barry ventured from his seat.

"I don't do Q and A," Santina snapped.

Barry persisted. "We're the ones who called you about an

interview earlier? Barry Breen and Rino Matsui. You remember?"

Suddenly Santina was all affability. "Of course I do. Come join me backstage," he waved them up and conducted back to a small dressing room where he opened a pair of folding chairs and told them to, "Sit, sit." They did as they were told as Santina wiped the sweat off his face with a damp towel.

"So, what did you think of the show?" he asked as if they were Broadway critics. "I really had them going, don't you think?"

"It was very interesting," Rino agreed, "very provocative."

"That's what I like to do," said Santina. "Stimulate! Provoke! Not like some crazed TED talk. Those people are such creepy fascists with their nuclear backyard barbecues and their contortionist sex positions, well, don't even get me started."

Rino once again took the initiative. "We're working on a project here at the university, an inquiry into peoples' perceptions of good and evil, and we…"

"It's all good!" he interrupted her. "If you're the Devil, that is!" He laughed at his own joke.

"You believe in the Devil?" Rino pressed him.

"Of course not. What do I look like? A religious kook? I mean that corruption is entirely out of control. Don't get me wrong. A little corruption greases the wheels, gets things done, but the kind of corruption we see now makes anything in the whole of human history look small time. Have you ever read Guy DeBord? Have you ever heard of the Spectacle? I guess not. Not at this training camp for budding vampires. The Spectacle is your home. You are completely surrounded by it 24/7. You think what it tell you to think, you do what it tells you to do."

Barry and Rino exchanged a sharp glance. This guy sounded like the letter Professor Gershem had read at the first seminar. Santina caught their momentary lapse in attention.

"What? You don't think that's true? Don't you think it's funny that the CIA/Mossad Daily Press Release now bills itself as bringing you The Truth? Don't they know what Pravda means?"

Barry tried to sort things out. "So you're saying that evil is the dominant force in the world?"

"Isn't it obvious?"

"So what is…?"

"Good is opposing evil," Santina anticipated him. "It's just that simple."

"By any means necessary?"

"Yes, and don't try to get me into that ends and means stuff, Necessary is the important word. So let's examine just one case. Edward Snowden was and still is a CIA agent. He works for Langley and I know that for a fact. His job is to misinform the public by pretending he's a brave truth teller. What truth has this piece of shit revealed?"

Barry immediately took umbrage and challenged Santina. "He told us that the NSA spies on everybody all the time. Now the whole world knows."

"What exactly do they know? That an agency whose motto is 'Collect It All' collects it all? Big news. And then Edward is kind enough to tell us that 9/11 and the Boston Marathon bombing could have been averted but for the incompetence of various intelligence agencies. Since both events were false flags, all Snowden is doing is reinforcing the official lie. Is that insidious or what?"

This analysis left Barry and Rino tongue-tied. It was outrageous, unbelievable, but it had its own interior logic. It was difficult to dispute in the context of conspiracy theory in general. In Santina's world nothing was what it seemed.

"Well," was all Breen could manage, "that's very interesting."

"Food for thought, isn't it?" Santina agreed, "Now maybe you can help me out. I don't know much, really nothing at all, about Asian girls, but is it true… you know, about… you know what I mean."

"Asshole," said Rino and left in a huff with Barry trailing in her wake.

"I've been called worse!" Santina's shout echoed down the corridor.

Once the young couple were outside, Barry teased her," Why did you just run off? I could have set him straight. Man to man."

"You are so disgusting," Rino made a face.

"Well, let's not get emotional. We're supposed to be dispassionate analysts. What do you think Professor Gershem and that woman were doing there?"

"The same thing we were."

"He didn't seem to like the show. Good thing for us."

"I suppose so," she reluctantly agreed. "If I didn't meet him I wouldn't know what a repulsive creep Enoch Santina is."

"Oh, come on. He's just curious. A little crude in his approach, I'll grant you…"

For that, Breen got a punch in the shoulder. Then Rino took his arm and snuggled up against him. "You pay for dinner," she said.

In the meantime, other fun couple Ted and Anna had made it back to his apartment and were discussing the events of the evening while they watched a motley rabble on television throw rocks at buildings along Fifth Avenue. The police quickly intervened and drove the small crowd into the park where they went to ground and were heard no more.

"Oh, this is just great," Gershem spluttered. "There we were right in the middle of the riot planning session. If this gets back to the administration…"

"Don't be such a wuss. You had a perfectly legitimate reason for being there. Even a particularly dense bureaucrat could understand it," she scolded him just as a panicked Ted appeared on the television screen running out of the auditorium with Anna in hot pursuit and Enoch Santina bellowing from the stage in the background. That was all. Just a flash of the two of them.

"Jeezus Christ!!" Gershem howled.

"Well, at least we were leaving," said Anna who really hadn't had time to absorb the possible implications. "We're not cheering or anything."

They didn't have to wait long for the first phone call. "Hello, it's Edward. Was that you and Anna on TV? What great publicity for the show."

Gershem was dumbstruck and Anna grabbed the phone. "Edward? How did you like it? We did it all for you."

The next call did not start out as well.

"Ted? This is Alvin Spurtz. I just saw you on the news…"

"Listen, Alvin, I can explain everything…"

"It's just too bad you didn't do an interview. You've done a world of good for the department. Out of the classroom and into the field! Our new motto! What a great image! It's better than what Toad Gatling did for the Communications program!"

Gershem couldn't believe that Spurtz wasn't being sarcastic. "Look, Alvin, I'm sorry…"

"Stop apologizing already! This is the best thing that ever happened. We all owe you big time. And who was that lovely woman chasing after you?"

"Uh, just one of my fans. I guess. No really, I have no idea. I was in a hurry."

"Well, I'm going to talk you up with the Spuyten Duyvil people. They might even give you a personal grant. Sort of a combat medal."

"I'd appreciate that," said Gershem carefully. "Thanks for calling." He hung up before Spurtz could respond.

"What on earth was that all about?" Anna demanded.

"The chairman of the department loved the clip on TV. I can't believe it."

"Didn't you tell me that he once made a joke about the grant for your project going to the anthropology department?"

"So?"

"Don't you see? There you were, out in the field like Margaret Mead or something, studying the natives in their own habitat. Of course he loves it."

"That's absurd." But maybe it wasn't. Ted Gershem, intrepid explorer of the hidden recesses of mass psychosis, forging bravely into the jungles of the human psyche where no desk bound psychoanalyst has ventured before. He should get himself a pith helmet and a swagger stick, but then he already had a tin hat.

"Well, at least you're not going to lose your job," Anna pointed out.

And that was a relief. With that load off his mind he decided to offer Anna some opium.

"What are you talking about?" she asked askance.

"A friend of mine gave it to me. He grows it himself. You have to take it anally, like a suppository."

"Are you just trying to fuck me in the ass? You can if you want."

"Well, maybe, but I've really got this opium. Would you like to try it?"

Anna, hesitant at first, but all in all a good sport, inserted one of the little opium balls in her anus and the two of them disconnected their phones before settling into the arms of Morpheus for the rest of the evening.

❖

26

Arthur Sachs, through sheer serendipity, had found a theatre to stage Ayn and Nate. A salutary accident had brought him to the former Herpetarium Hall of Wonders, once operated by P.T. Barnum as a reptile zoo. The space in the west thirties stood empty during the interlude between a storage company moving out and the next presently unsecured tenant moving in and was available for a short-term rental. This happy accident had occurred directly in front of the building housing the defunct theatre when Arthur was run over by a Chinese delivery boy on a bicycle and covered in sticky, piping hot, shrimp chow mein. Concerned passersby had simultaneously rifled through his pockets and rushed him into the empty theatre space where he was doused with a fire extinguisher.

The building manager was a paragon of empathy. "This didn't happen here, right? Outside, right? Just sign this. Sign it, you dopey schnook!"

But things suddenly took a turn for the better when Arthur realized he was lying in some sort of presentation space. There was a balcony and a seating area in front of a raised stage, except there were no seats. He got to his feet and the building manager was ecstatic : "You can walk!" she shouted as if Lazarus had just risen from the dead. "Now just go home and forget all about this."

"Is this a theatre?" Arthur wondered aloud.

"No, no, used to be," the manager pushed him toward the door.

"Is it for rent?"

This stopped the manager in his tracks and the rest is the very short history of the Downtown Illuminati Theatre Company's tenure in its new, temporary home.

"Isn't this marvelous!" Edward Smith exulted on his first viewing of the space. "And the manager says all the chairs are in the basement. All we have to do is install them!"

"Who's we?" Sylvia asked.

"Everybody! Well, not you and me, of course. Someone has to supervise."

So everybody pitched in but Ted Gershem and Argyle. Even Studs Zenith showed up in a carpenter's apron and work boots looking like someone from the Village People. They soon had all the seats secured in a more or less orderly fashion and it was time to clean up. This was no easy task. In fact, it was Herculean. No one had really given the place a thorough cleaning since the Barnum days and who knew how many ancient reptiles were lurking in the rubbish? Certain lizards and tortoises can live for centuries. But the fact was no one was willing to clean this particular Augean stable and Smith had to fork over several hundred dollars to a sanitation service to get the job done. When it was all over, even Gershem was impressed. It had the shabby genteel look of a theatre from the 19th century where someone might even shoot Abraham Lincoln,

"Quite a job you did here, Edward," Ted commented when Anna brought him over to see the place.

"No thanks to you," said Smith. "Just kidding, Ted. I know you have a bad back and all. From now on, we rehearse here. What a change that will be."

"I hope that Nathaniel Branden's cock falls off!!" Anna boomed from the stage as her voice echoed around the room. "Great acoustics, don't you think?"

"Better than Carnegie Hall!" Smith exulted. "And all thanks to Arthur."

Sachs, whose second degree chow mein burns had sufficiently healed for him to be put to work with the rest of the company, acknowledged the accolade with a little wave from across the room where he was dusting.

"All right, everybody! Listen up!" Smith gathered his flock. "We have a job to do and I don't mean this one. Is everybody ready for the school shooting show?"

The actors growled their assent.

"Bus leaves from downtown at nine in the morning the day after tomorrow. Don't be late."

"Isn't it great?" Anna gushed as they left the theatre. "And I thought we'd be playing in a storefront to an audience of ten!"

"Well, it's not a storefront, but the audience might still be ten."

"You're right," she agreed. "Edward just doesn't understand how it works. He needs a publicist, someone who can get the production in the papers."

"Nobody reads the papers anymore. It's all the internet."

"Well, whatever. I know someone but he's much too expensive."

"Uhm, you're not talking about…"

"Giving him a blow job? He's gay, Ted."

"You want me to do it? How about Arthur?" he deadpanned.

"I think Studs Zenith is more up his alley."

"Thanks for letting me off the hook." He looked at his watch. "I've got to go to work."

Which, in fact, he did. The abnormal psychology seminar was to convene in an hour giving Gershem scant time to collect his thoughts. He had so completely lost interest in good and evil that he could barely come up with a string of platitudes to reassure his students, somewhat like a politician at a pep rally trying to hack it through to the last absurd slogan. "Peace! Plenty! Hot sex! What do you fucking idiots want anyway?!" But he did manage to collect himself, if not his thoughts, before he walked into the classroom. Of course, the only subject of any interest, for the students anyway, was his television appearance.

"Professor Gershem," David Kogan immediately rushed in. "Why were you leaving the Enoch Santina thing in such a hurry?"

"Prostate problem," Gershem responded acidly. "Why don't you ask Rino and Barry. They got my tickets."

The two looked at each other and Rino spoke first. "We tried to get in but it was sold out. Professor Gershem kindly gave us his tickets."

Barry Breen wondered at her perfect Japanese politesse and joined in her appreciation. "Yeah, thanks, Professor Gershem."

"Did you go to the riot?" Kogan pressed.

It was time for Gershem to intervene. "Look, Enoch Santina is one of the most famous conspiracy theorists in the country. It's our job to observe these people no matter how ludicrous their theories are. No one is participating in any riots. At least, I hope not."

"My old hippy uncle told me rioting is fun," said Kogan. "He used to do it all the time in California."

"Well, each to his own," said Gershem. "Anarchy does have a certain allure."

"My boyfriend told me that riots are useful for the police because they can identify and make dossiers on the participants," said Rhoda Memberman. "It's sort of like Facebook. And all these radicals do it voluntarily."

"You … have a… boyfriend?" Kogan was all agog. "Whoa!"

Rhoda didn't know how to react to this schoolyard taunt. With anger or pride? She decided on the latter.

"Didn't I tell you?" she said. "By the way, you never had a chance."

"I wouldn't do you with his junk," Kogan snorted.

"Hey, that's enough of that," Gershem reprimanded them, then tried to move in another direction entirely. "Akisha, have you talked with your grandmother lately?"

"I saw her yesterday and I did ask her more about the lizard people. She told me that even though only five percent of people are lizards they hold all the important positions in the world. The bankers, the presidents, the movie stars, the Pope, all those people are lizards."

"That might be a sensible point of view because it relieves us of the onus of our own failings," said Gershem. "The lizards made me do it!"

"Well, didn't they?" Kogan asked. "I tend to blame it on the parents who were both lizards of course. Which brings up an important point. Can humans and reptilians crossbreed?"

"I didn't ask my grandmother that, but I will," Akisha promised.

And so, as they whiled away the next hour, it became more and more apparent the narratives of good and evil had been supplanted by sane versus crazy and it was even more difficult pinpointing the origins of these two than any Manichaean moral absolutes. Actually, the vast grey area that presented itself took the burden of precision off the study and they could all relax a little.

When the seminar broke up, they went their separate ways and Gershem met up with Anna at King Wok for dinner. She was very much excited by her school principal part and insisted on rehearsing her lines until the other patrons began to look at her funny.

"I think I'm making a spectacle of myself," she said.

"Yes you are, but that's exactly what you want to do," Gershem pointed out.

"I just get carried away," she apologized. "I really don't like actors who are 'on' all the time."

"Do you know my whole class saw me on television fleeing the Enoch Santina thing? They didn't want to talk about anything else."

"That's wonderful, Ted! Now you're a star. Did anyone mention me?"

"I knew you'd ask. They don't know who you are and I want to keep it that way. Unlike some of my colleagues, I don't socialize with my students."

"You mean the ones who take up the little co-ed's offer of a blowjob in exchange for an A?"

"Oh, I do that, of course," he chuckled. "That's not socializing. It's just quid pro quo."

"Does that one with the yappy little dog suck your cock?"

"Rhoda Memberman? Yes indeed. She's so hot she could suck the chrome off a trailer hitch."

"Well, that's a relief. At least I know you're lying."

"Don't be that way. She speaks very highly of you."

"Jerk. Speaking of blowjobs, you know what's on TV tonight? *The Fountainhead*."

"Oh, Jesus, I think I remember it. With Gary Cooper and Patricia Neal?"

"The very one. I never read the book, but Ayn Rand claimed she had final say on the script."

"I never read the book either," said Gershem. "It might behoove is to take a little opium and view the auteur at work."

And so they adjourned to Ted's apartment, supposited their meds, and lay back to enjoy this Warner Brothers magnum opus, which turned out to be more soft core porn than philosophy. With throbbing hammer drills, rearing stallions, skyscrapers ascending into the firmament, and Patricia Neal with ants in her pants for architect Gary Cooper, much as Ayn had been enamored of Frank Lloyd Wright, Cooper's stone faced portrayal of a homicidal maniac who actually blows up an entire housing project because the clients changed his design, is a crisp send-up of psychopathology in action; paranoid, truculent, violent, and. above all, completely self-centered. By the end of the movie, Gershem was appalled by the fact that lots of people took this weirdo character seriously as a role model. *American Psycho* indeed.

"I never realized how crazy Ayn Rand was," said Anna. "I think I've got to up the insanity ante in my performance."

"And I'm your Nate, urging you on. Go crazy, Ayn, go crazier!" Gershem teased her.

"I'm not joking. What a monster that woman was. I've got to go all Lady MacBeth on her ass."

"I liked the movie," said Gershem. "It's a real window into the unfortunate conjunction of Puritan sexual repression and the impulse to murder thy neighbor. And all that phallic imagery—well, from a psychoanalytic point of view…"

"Don't get all pointy-headed on me or I'll make you wear your tin hat," Anna scolded him. "Women have a visceral reaction to hard cocks. It's in the genes. I'm amazed they got away with this movie in what, the fifties?"

"Ah, the good old days when men were men, women were

women, and sex was dirty."

"Well, you have to admit, people do like their pleasures illicit. Wouldn't you like it better if we were both unhappily married doing each other on the side?"

"Hmm. Interesting question from the abnormal psychological point of view."

"You're such a square, Ted," she said drawing the shape in the air with her fingers.

Ted and Anna weren't the only ones viewing *The Fountainhead* that evening. Edward and Sylvia Smith had watched it closely enough to cause him to complain: "God, I wish I could get those kind of angles in the theatre. It makes everyone look so imposing."

"I always thought imposing on people was rude," said Sylvia, "but I see what you mean. Silly piffle though. Was Gary Cooper gay? He sure acts like it."

"Not at all. He was quite the ladies man from what I understand. And a staunch Republican who liked to be spanked every now and then."

"You're making that up."

"Can't you just see him strapped to the big wheel in the dungeon?"

"Actually, I can. Tasting the lash with the stoicism of a manly man."

They both laughed.

"He wasn't really an actor," Edward observed. "No range at all. He could only play one part and that's why he was a star. The audience wants icons, not chameleons. Acting talent is secondary, even undesirable. Which reminds me I've got to call Deirdre about the children she's supposed to deliver for the school thing." He had not told Sylvia about his visit from Calvin Card and didn't intend to.

"You're contracting for children too?" Sylvia wondered. "Aren't you worried about child labor laws and all that stuff?"

"Well, I'm not going to be a stage mother cheating the little ones out of their wages, if that's what you mean. Everyone gets paid, everybody's happy. How's your Diane Sawyer coming along?" Sylvia was playing the part of a television interviewer.

"Just fine. You want to see me do sympathetic concern?"

"Why not? I've certainly never seen you do it before."

"It must be awful living with someone like me," she projected her inner crisis counselor with a bit of boohoohoo thrown in. "I mean, I just can't imagine how you manage."

"Splendid!" Smith applauded her. "I couldn't have done it better myself."

Though they hadn't mentioned it at the abnormal psychology meeting, Barry and Rino had not let the rest of their evening after the Enoch Santina interview go to waste. A few of the audience who had not moved on to Fifth Avenue were standing around in small groups heatedly discussing what they'd just witnessed.

"Enoch Santina is full of shit!" one of these street debaters shouted. "He's just trying to co-opt the movement with his nonsense!"

"What movement?!" someone else called out.

"The bowel movement!" another rejoined.

A middle-aged Japanese man was standing on the fringes of this small gathering but he was not interested in the crude polemics. He was interested in Rino Matsui and Barry Breen, arm in arm right next to him.

"Excuse me," he said politely to Rino. "You are Japanese? You are a student here?"

"Yes," she said cautiously.

"I am Professor Takada from the Asian Studies program. I'm not sure what is happening here. Perhaps you and your friend could explain it to me. I would like to invite you to my home just around the corner," he offered with a broad smile. "It's not so noisy."

Rino and Barry looked at each other. He shrugged, she shrugged. Why not? Professor Takada certainly looked harmless enough.

When they got to the second floor door to his apartment in an old brownstone, he admonished them: "This is a Japanese home. Please remove your shoes." This they did and he ushered them into what looked like some sort of shrine. "Please sit," he motioned to a pair of cushions on the floor. "Would you like something to drink? I have special cocktails imported from Japan."

The supple couple was not about to be suckered into another

Glade induced fiasco. "O cha arimasuka?" Rino asked.

"Please," said Professor Takada, "the young man is probably unfamiliar with Japanese. Let us speak English." Ignoring her request for tea, he produced three cans of Suntory Highball, a whiskey based drink generally sold out of vending machines and convenience stores in Japan.

Rino recognized this product and signaled Barry it was okay to accept.

"Kanpai!" said Takata merrily as he lifted his can in a toast. "It is to you Barry Breen san I drink. It is very important that the American and Japanese people remember that we were friends before the unfortunate war in the Pacific, a friendship that honored Japanese culture."

Breen had no idea what to make of this toast but he was agreeable enough. "To Japanese-American friendship," he raised his can.

"Yes," said Takada, "I'm glad to see that young Americans appreciate the need to honor Japanese traditions."

Barry may have been agreeable but Rino began to get a sense of where this was going. "Professor Takada, we are doing a project in the psychology department..."

"I am very well aware of your project," Takada snapped, then immediately reverted to the congenial host. "People have many different opinions on good and evil. Some of those opinions are erroneous."

Breen, foolish enough to think he saw an opening, stepped into the trap, "So, what's your opinion?"

"What do you know about Shinto, Barry?"

"Well, not much."

"Shinto is Japan, Barry. The Emperor is a god. Now the United States, along with their associates in the LDP, the true monsters of the Showa era, have reduced him to an old man who rides around in limousines to ladies' lunches. What do you think about that?"

"Well, I don't think it's any worse than the Queen of England."

"Exactly. It is a conspiracy to depose true monarchy and replace it with Donald Trump."

"Donald Trump isn't English, but I see what you mean."

Nervous Rino realized it was time to intervene. "Professor Takada. You're Nihon Kaigi, aren't you?

"You be quiet, woman. Men are talking!"

"Hey there, Professor Takada…" Barry started.

"Shut up, gaijin!" Takada snarled. "Japanese women know their place! And you let this little whore run all over you! Under the emperor she would live in a brothel! Real Japanese men would have their way with her as they pleased! Kotei ni akushu!!" He threw his empty Highball can at Breen who took the harmless shot and decided it was time to go.

Rino was of the same mind but there was something she had to do before she left. She jumped to her feet and kicked Takada upside his head. "Fuck you, kuso jiji" she hissed. To Barry: "Let's get out of here."

"What the fuck was that?" Barry demanded when they got outside.

Very flustered Rino tried to explain. "You're gaijin. You'd ever understand."

"Well, try me," said baffled Barry.

"There are these people in Japan who want everything like it was before the war. The want to get rid of democracy, restore the divine emperor, and make me wear a sort of Japanese burkha."

"Well, the last part sounds okay," Breen shrugged. "I don't know about making you live in a whore house."

"Don't joke about it. These people are serious even though they're really just a bunch of smelly old men trying to bring back a fantasy out of the ashes of the past."

"Are they dangerous?"

"Nobody knows. It's easy to dismiss them as a bunch of cranks but they keep trying."

"Are they a conspiracy?"

"They have an agenda to bring down the government but they're not trying to hide it. They consider themselves the only true patriots."

"The last refuge of scoundrels as someone once said."

"What are you talking about?"

"Never mind. Nothing."

And that's why they didn't say anything at the seminar.

❖

27

The Happy Shadow was up bright and early for the school shooting drill shoot. He wasn't quite sure what to wear but blending in had never been a problem for him. He decided to go in crisis counselor drab since nobody knew who they were or what they did.

When he got to the parked bus there were several children milling around on the sidewalk under Deirdre and Sylvia's supervision. The other actors were standing in a semi-circle listening to Edward Smith's wardrobe and make-up scheduling instructions. Ignoring this dry pep talk, he took a seat in the back of the bus and waited for things to start happening. He didn't have to wait long. They were soon on their way to a suburb north of the city where the drill was to take place, Hook's Roost on the Hudson shore. The kids made a lot of noise and Sylvia managed to calm them down by leading a rousing chorus of, "A Hundred Bottles of Beer on the Wall." The Happy Shadow noted that Deirdre was pretending to snooze on Studs Zenith's lap with her jacket over her head to cut out the morning glare. Studs tried to keep a poker face but his shuddering ejaculation was writ all over.

"Forty-six bottles of beer on the wall! Forty-six bottles of beer! You take one down and pass it around and forty-five bottles of beer on the wall!"

Ted and Anna were seated together toward the front of the bus and did not participate in the revelry. They were more concerned about nailing their roles and Anna was relentless as a coach.

"As far as we know, there are twenty-four confirmed fatalities and many wounded..." Ted read his lines until Anna interrupted.

"Dryer, weirder, like you're reading a laundry list," she said. "You've seen hundreds of dead bodies in your time. No emotion."

"Just how weird do you want me to get?" said Gershem. "Maybe I could have a tic?"

"That's great idea! You should run it by Edward."

So Gershem tried doing his lines with little facial spasms every few seconds.

"I love it!" Anna applauded him. "It makes the character so much more memorable."

Gershem had second thoughts. He didn't know if he wanted to be more memorable.

"Don't worry," Anna reassured him. "Nobody's going to see it but a bunch of firemen and paramedics."

Not so much later, commuter time really, they arrived at a former school building, privatized then bankrupt, in the little village of Hook's Roost on the Hudson. There was already a fair sized contingent of movie vans parked along the road working over costumes and make-up with none other than Calvin Card in a white Santa Claus beard and a camouflage suit orchestrating.

"Edward!" he barked at Smith who didn't recognize him. "It's me, Calvin. Thanks for bringing along the kids. They're going to appreciate that upstairs."

"There is no upstairs here, Calvin," said Smith, pointing to the one story abandoned school.

"Ha, ha, you're right, but you know what I mean," Card chortled.

"What's with the Z Z Top look, Calvin?"

"I don't want to be recognized. Even you didn't recognize me."

"I just don't know how it goes with the military costume."

"Are you kidding? I'm the militant Santa. Can't you see? The war on Christmas and all that."

Edward didn't see, but it was none of his business anyway.

"Have all your people signed their non-disclosures?" Card asked.

"Sylvia's handling that."

And so she was.

"I'm not signing anything," Studs Zenith balked. "I'm not even supposed to be here."

"But, Studs…"

"This is the last thing I'd disclose but you've got to see it from my side. I'm going to get a cab and take the train back to the city. You don't want to see your Nate get fired from his job just before the play opens, do you? I'm just an extra here anyway."

Sylvia thought it over and said, "You're right. We can't endanger the play for some silly moonlighting."

"If you want I'll tie you up and fuck you before I call a cab," Studs offered as consolation.

"Too busy right now. Save it for the city. Ciao, baby." They parted with a lingering kiss.

This clinch did not go unobserved by Anna Bunch. Well, she said to herself, what a shameless hussy! Actually, she was just a wee bit jealous but she had other things to think about, namely her part as brave, slightly shell-shocked school principal. As she mulled over her lines, an albino man in a blue suit and red tie walked up and introduced himself. "Hi, I'm Anderson Cooper."

Startled Anna laughed. "And I'm Katie Couric. We've probably met before, You sure do look like him though,"

"That's probably because I am him," said Cooper. "I understand we're working together today. You're the school principal and I'm the interviewer."

"But…"

Cooper held up his hand. "I know what you're thinking. Why am I here for some training film? Isn't that right?"

"You might say that. What are you doing here?"

"I'm a volunteer. I'm here to support our first responders, the men and the women in the vanguard of the war on terror. They make me proud to be an American. They do. Really."

There was something oddly off about this little speech. At least to seasoned actress Anna. "So," she said, "you want to run through the scene?"

"Sure. Just one question. Is that lovely young man I saw walking around here Studs Zenith?"

"I believe so," coy Anna replied. "I hear he's doing a show in New York next month."

"Studs Zenith is a television weatherman. What do you mean 'show'?"

"He's doing an off-Broadway play called 'Ayn and Nate'. He plays Ayn Rand's lover, Nathaniel Branden."

"Really? I've always been a big fan of Ayn Rand. Her devotion to a moneyed meritocracy and all that sexy imagery just throbbing away, well… Who's playing her?"

"Me, myself, and I" Anna preened. Then in her Ayn Rand voice: "I'm so glad you appreciate my work, you sweetie, you."

Cooper, if Cooper he were, slapped his checks in marvel. "That's just so fabulous, you!" he gushed. "Please get me a ticket. And maybe you can introduce me to Studs."

"But of course, my dear," Anna vamped in an accent as thick as gruel.

Over at wardrobe, Gershem had been outfitted with a white, blood-spattered doctor's coat. He was also introduced to the bearded director who was looking over his cast list.

"Ted, right? I'm Robbie Parker. We can do your thing before everything else. It's just one camera and I think the reporters are ready. You okay with that?"

"Yeah, sure," said Gershem. "Should we go over the lines?"

"Nah. Too much rehearsal makes it look less spontaneous."

"Your call," Ted shrugged his shoulders and took a seat near the makeup trailer.

If there was one thing Arthur Sachs could really do well it was whine and schrei so he was completely in his element playing a neighbor down the street from the school.

"The children, the children!" he wailed to Amalia who was reading the reporter part. "The little children, slaughtered!!" He broke down in tears.

"Wow, Arthur," said Amalia, "that's the best acting work I've ever seen you do."

"Thank you, Amalia. Do you really think so?"

"Well, it's not like you could get any worse."

Sachs did not quite know how to take this compliment, so he took it with his usual aplomb and broke down in tears.

"If you're trying to stay in character, it's working," Amalia noted.

"Thank you," Arthur sobbed.

"So let's get down to business, Ned," said Robbie Parker to Ted Gershem. "Are you ready?" The director led his coroner over to an impromptu podium where he was flanked by two state troopers and a small crowd of soon to be clamoring reporters, one of whom was Amalia who would also double as a distraught mother later in the shoot.

"Okay, what I want to see is subdued yet shocked authority," said Parker. "I want to see a man in charge who hasn't quite come to terms with what he's just witnessed. Can you give me that, Ned?"

"I'll do my best," Gershem promised.

"Great! Reporters! Action!" Parker shouted over his bullhorn.

"How many victims are there?!" one of the reporters called out.

"We're not sure yet," Gershem responded, utilizing his tic to best effect. "I personally pronounced five dead and…"

"Cut!" Parker shouted. "What's with the face stuff?"

"Well," Gershem tried to explain, "coroners are a little weird, I mean working with dead bodies all day long and I was thinking…"

"Stop thinking!" Parker bellowed. "I work with dead bodies all day long! They're called actors! Just do the fucking lines!"

Chastened Ted dropped the tic and read his answers off so-called idiot cards held up by a production assistant. They did the whole press conference in one five minute take.

"That's a wrap," Parker shouted and everyone dispersed, some done for the day and others to put on costumes for different roles. Gershem walked over to the craft services buffet and got himself a cup of iced coffee.

"Hey there, stranger." It was Sylvia Smith all got up like a news show lady in a red power suit, perhaps the second ugliest fashion choice of the upper crust, right below polyester green slacks with little tiny embroidered whales worn by obscenely rich white men at the golf course and the Saratoga race track clubhouse.

"Hello, Sylvia. What part are you playing?"

"Diane Sawyer. I'm interviewing Deirdre who's playing one of the traumatized teachers when she's not busy giving Studs Zenith a blowjob on the bus."

"I noticed that myself. I'm sure you'll do just fine."

"I'm sure I will too. I just saw you do your coroner thing. Why don't I practice on you?"

"Go ahead."

Sylvia stood there for a moment and looked at him quizzically. "Well, pull down your pants. Can't you just see Diane sucking the coroner's cock?"

"Sylvia," said Gershem in his best psychoanalyst voice," are you really the nymphomaniac you pretend to be?"

Sylvia was delighted. "That's good, that's good! Okay," she went back into part, "what do you mean pretend? I am Diane! I can have any man I want. Even you, Mr. Coroner."

"I have a name," Gershem rejoined, "but what would that matter to you?"

Sylvia laughed. "I don't want to be identified with those ridiculous improv people but sometimes I do like to go off script."

"Don't expect any more out of me," said Gershem drily. "I'm wrapped."

"You're not playing any other parts today?"

"Not that I know of."

But he was just about to be drafted. Edward Smith came running over with the news that Studs Zenith would not be playing his SWAT team role and would Ted like to do it? For extra cash, of course. Gershem had to mull this one over.

"SWAT team? Do you think I can play a cop?"

"There's nothing to play," said Edward. "You just put on the cop mask and walk by the camera. No lines, no sweat."

"How much?" said Gershem bluntly.

"Well, it's not a speaking role…"

"I want whatever Studs was going to get."

"But Studs is a star!" Smith whinged and then backed down. "Okay, okay, let's split the difference."

Just for laughs, Gershem decided to be a hardnose. "Sixty to me, forty for you."

"Right," said Edward. "Get over to wardrobe."

And so Gershem found himself in a camouflage suit with a bulletproof vest and an automatic rifle. Not loaded, of course.

Meanwhile, Anna, in a matronly chignon wig, was doing her interview with Anderson Cooper in a trailer fitted out like a suburban living room. Cooper was all concern troll.

"I just can't imagine how you must have felt at the moment you confronted the gunman."

"I didn't think of him as a homicidal maniac. I thought of him as a young lost soul with a gun. I thought, what if he couldn't get his hands on such a weapon?"

"I think that everyone agrees that mentally unstable teenagers and guns are not a good mix," said Cooper sententiously.

"Cut!" the director shouted. "Let's take five and pick it up from the reaction shot."

Cooper leaned close to Anna. "You know, you're good, You're really good."

"Thank you," Anna simpered.

"I mean, like, there are plenty of other jobs like this. I could set you up with an agency."

"I'm already signed with an agency. Player Station."

Cooper was impressed. "They're hooked up with Retalitron. Sure, stick with them."

The director called out, "Places, everyone! Let's do it again!"

"I simply did what anyone in my position would do," said Anna.

Cooper generated a gaze suitable for the adoration of the Virgin Mary. "I don't think most school principals could face down a madman with a gun. You are truly America's hero tonight."

"Heroine," she corrected him.

"Cut!!" the director yelled. "Heroin is an illegal drug! You are a hero! Pick it up from, 'You are truly'!"

Cooper read the line again and Anna responded, "I just did what I had to do. I don't think of myself as a hero."

"Well, I'm sure the people watching would disagree. Coming to you from Hook's Roost, New York, this is Anderson Cooper."

"Wrap it!" the director shouted. He also knew whose ass to kiss. "Anderson, that was just fantastic. Great working with you." He completely ignored Anna.

"Thank you, but I really owe it all to this lady here," said Cooper gallantly.

"Oh right. Good job. What's your name again?"

"Anna Bunch."

"Anna. I'll remember that."

But Anna wasn't thinking about the director. She was thinking there was something "off" about Anderson Cooper, something distinctly mechanical.

Meanwhile, Gershem had walked by the cameras a couple if times in his SWAT drag, and then been relieved of all responsibility for the rest of the day. He wondered where to go to shove another ball of opium up his ass.

Right at that moment, Sylvia was interviewing "Rebecka" in another living room set.

"So," said Sylvia, dripping with the ickiest kind of false empathy in a perfect Diane impersonation, "what did you do when you heard the first shots?"

Deirdre was all nervous apprehension. "I made all the children get inside the utility closet. We were packed in the there like sardines. Then I heard him come into the room. It's a miracle he didn't open that closet door." She broke down in tears, except there were no actual tears.

"Oh my," said Sylvia handing Deirdre a handkerchief. "I just can't imagine…"

"Cut!" the director yelled. "What's going on here? Where are the spray-on tears? Get her an onion or something!"

Deirdre, who thought she had done a good job, leaned close to Sylvia and asked, "Why are they trying to make a training film look so realistic?"

Sylvia shrugged. "I don't know. Maybe the director wants to make it look like a movie movie."

"I heard that," said Edward Smith who joined them for the break. "Of course he wants to make it look real. For his audition reel," he chuckled. "The man has ambition. He wants to be in pictures!"

A girl P.A. showed up with a little bottle and an eye-dropper. "This is going to sting a little bit."

"What is it?" Deirdre demanded.

"Onion juice. Strictly vegan"

"Go ahead."

Smith skittered off as Deirdre's eyes teared up and the director shouted, "Okay, take it from 'closet door'!" It was almost time for the Grand Poobah to put on the dog as the town mayor.

As the bus wound its way back to the city after the shoot, Smith broke out the champagne and plastic cups with a toast to his charges. "Today was an exemplary day for the Downtown Manhattan Illuminati, yet there are far greater things to come! 'Ayn and Nate' opens in two weeks and with that that we become the stuff of legend!"

His players, well contented with their checks from a day's work, whooped and cheered and all was right with the rapidly passing world.

But forces other than the smell of the greasepaint and the roar of the crowd were conspiring against the little theatre company's happy idyll. The people who had hired Tootie Wookums to sue Edward Smith, upon learning that the show must go on, were convinced that radical measures were necessary. These fanatics had decided that laissez-faire applied to the law as well as the market and the show would be stopped by any means necessary.

With the money he'd received from the Retalitron contract, Smith was finally able to launch "Ayn and Nate" in a real theatre and he set about the staging like the old trooper he was.

"I'm terrified," he confided his fears to Sylvia, "just terrified. I envy those film people who can just stop the action anytime they want. There isn't that kind of luxury when you're live."

"Stop whining," she scolded. "It's been rehearsed to death. Everything's going to be just fine. Thanks to Studs we already sold out opening night."

"That's what worries me. All the critics will be there. It's got to be perfect."

"Slip the publicist another five thousand and it's a hit."

"Do you mean..?"

"What's wrong with a little bribery?"

"I don't know," said Edward dubiously. "I'd really rather be judged on my merits."

"Oh, shut up," she scoffed.

"Well I would!" he protested.

And Smith wasn't the only one in a tizzy. Anna Bunch, confronted with her own possible stardom, was driving Gershem mildly crazy by refusing to come out of character. "To play Ayn Rand, I must be Ayn Rand," she was her bottled in bond reply to his request for her to stop using that voice all the time.

"I didn't know you were method," he needled her.

"But I am," she said. "Strasberg knew what it is to act. All encompassing, all embracing, all consuming. You live through the character and the character is brought to life in you. More opium if you please."

The two of them, without really noticing it, were becoming habituated to rectally popping a ball of opium whenever their bowels moved them, which was more and more frequently. Gershem obliged her with, "Only if you ask me in your real voice. I think I'll have one myself."

And speaking of illegal medications, Studs and Deirdre were showing more interest in the lines of cocaine on his glass-topped coffee table than the lines in their scripts.

"I can't do the weather without a little blow," he confided to her.

"Really? Aren't you worry you'll get caught?"

"Are you kidding? Everybody you see on the screen does it. Why do you think they look so peppy, so full of verve?"

"Full of what?"

"Verve. You know, enthusiastic, positive, forward looking, insane. They're all jacked up on vitamin C."

He vacuumed up another line and handed her his little silver tube. As she dealt with another line he started excitedly expostulating, as coke heads often do, on the possibilities that might open up for both of them if "Ayn and Nate" were a boffo hit.

"Just think. After the show opens we can write our own ticket! The Hollywood agents will be lined up at the stage door trying to sign us. And we'll be busy signing autographs, so many autographs. Have you ever seen my signature? It's really suave. Just like me."

"You want to sign my tittie?" said Deirdre.

Have I mentioned they were both naked, stoking up for another bout in the sack?

"Why not?" said Zenith, grabbing a felt pen and signing her left breast with John Hancock flourish.

"Wow," she said, "that even looks cool upside down and backwards."

"You're the one who looks cool upside down and backwards, baby," said Studs with a leer and snorted up another line.

The Happy Shadow was not going over his lines because he didn't have any. But he did want to be on stage, to get in on the action, if only in a very minor role. He just had to create a part for himself. And he would, he would, he thought as he rubbed himself off and ejaculated all over the big time lady wrestlers on his TV screen.

❖

28

Arm twisting Rhoda Memberman had full nelsoned reluctant Hyman Ryman into taking her downtown for brunch to a chic new eatery on 23rd Street that featured nouvelle Kosher cuisine, which she'd read about in Time Out magazine. Goldflugel's, owned by the eponymous celebrated artist Alan, served both dairy and meat, neatly separating the two with a scaled down copy of the West Bank barrier wall with checkpoints through which the patrons were free to pass with the proper credentials, Goldflugel drink vouchers.

"Isn't this so clever," Rhoda enthused to Ryman as they chose initial seating on the dairy side because she wanted to start with the blinis and caviar. Ryman was so visibly shaken by the prices that Rhoda had to admonish him, "don't Jew out on me, Hyman, We're here to have fun." And she not so gently reminded him, "Think of me as a loan from the sperm bank. You've got to pay interest, lover."

Ryman certainly understood the mercantile sensibility and the concept of fair value, but he was so pathologically cheap that the delicious blinis were ashes in his mouth, the residue of burning dollar bills. The only bright spot in this preliminary to the main event was a pleasing tingle from the Dewar's and soda she made him drink.

"Yummy, so good," said Rhoda chewing with her mouth open. "Tell me what you've been doing at work."

"You know I can't do that, Rhoda," he whined.

"Yes you can. Come on, Just a few tidbits." Her tone was somewhere between wheedling and giving orders. Since Ryman was no match for her in mano a mano combat, he had concocted a simple defense strategy, which, for want of a better description, was, "Just lie."

"Let's see," he said. "Today we discussed the rise in cynicism among young people and how to counter it."

"Well, how do you counter it?"

"That's the part I can't tell you. The plan is classified. Let's just say it involves a proactive shift in the paradigm."

"I see," Rhoda mocked him with eyes wide. "Well, I'm going to get proactive on your paradigm. I want a pastrami sandwich. We have to go to the other side of the wall with the Palestinians. For a few more dollars, we can sit at a table called a settlement."

"I don't know why you think that's funny," said Ryman. "I mean, God gave that land to us."

"And here I thought it was the British. Do you have your drink tickets? Let's go."

At the border wall, the handsome guards randomly frisked the lady patrons to keep the party going. Sort of like Club Med, where Rhoda liked to go when she was younger and get laid by the hunky gentils organisateurs. They found a table in the meat room and Rhoda ordered pastrami on rye. Ryman opted for a single Kosher frank.

"You know why young people are so cynical?" said Rhoda.

"Well, we've done some extensive studies on the subject and come to some conclusions that I'm not at liberty to discuss," Ryman sloughed her off.

"It's just my opinion, Hyman, and I'm free to say anything I want,"

Here it comes, he thought. Whatever she was about to say had to be in the nature of a personal attack.

"I think young people are cynical because of people like you, the manipulators, the hidden persuaders."

The An Idea Grows in America Institute's current area of inquiry had nothing to do with youthful cynicism so Ryman could now sit back comfortably and let her jabber. It was a small price to pay for the shagging he'd give her later. Frankly, he was more concerned with the tab for this feed than her opinions.

Rhoda only stopped her verbal assault when the huge pastrami sandwich on rye, which they'd agreed to split, arrived at the table in all its shining glory. The two halves looked like a pair of gaping vaginas accompanied by phallic half sour pickles.

"Oh my," said Rhoda, "this is what I call a real nosh. Even half is a bit much, don't you think?"

"Don't worry. I brought along a bottle of Pepto-Bismol," he teased her.

"I bet you did," she teased him right back and they got down to the business of consumption. Neither of them could wrap their mouths around these piles of sliced brisket and wound up resorting to forks.

"How can I count the ways I'm going to regret this?" Rhoda wondered. "It's just too delicious." And they both had another drink coming.

"So, what's new at your abnormal psych seminar? Making any progress?" Ryman asked nonchalantly.

"Are you making fun of me?" she demanded. "I can't tell you anyway. It's classified," she said peevishly. Then," My professor was on TV. He was at the Enoch Santina lecture."

"You just said that was all secret."

"Didn't you hear me? It was on TV. Everybody saw it."

"Not me. Who's Enoch Santina?"

Actually, Santina was one of the prime targets of the Institute's snooping. Ryman wondered if Rhoda knew any more than he did.

"You don't know?" she said as if he'd just crawled out from under a rock. "He's a famous conspiracy theory rabble rouser. Almost as famous as Alex Jones."

"Who?"

"You really are living in a bubble at that Institute of yours," she scoffed.

"I don't watch TV. I have to rely on you to keep me up to date. Tell me more."

"Well. Enoch Santina is a sort of paranoid anarchist calling for a violent revolution. He thinks if we just bump off all the rich people, things will work themselves out."

"Sort of a French revolution guy."

"Exactly."

"And your professor's a fan?"

"Of course not. It's just part of the study. It's abnormal psychology. Wackos"

"Did you know your professor's theatre company is putting on a play somewhere in the thirties next month? I read an ad in the paper."

Rhoda was surprised. "Really? I wonder if he's in it."

"Maybe we should go," Ryman suggested.

"I'll ask him about it."

Rino Matsui and Barry Breen were not eating at an overpriced restaurant in Chelsea but rather at a diner on Broadway near 86th Street before their appointment with renowned vlog hostess Mindy Manners, a real live certified witch. Over indifferent grilled cheese sandwiches, they worked on a list of questions that would theoretically keep the interview within the parameters of sanity.

"She's a Wiccan," said Rino. "I looked them up but they don't seem to have any sort of set dogma. It's sort of do your own thing witchcraft."

Breen looked at his watch and called for the check. "We're going to be late if we don't get out of here."

So they walked down Broadway to 83rd Street and were soon standing in front of an imposing brownstone with unkempt shrubbery threatening to overwhelm the lower floors. At the door they were greeted by Mindy Manners, a wild-haired woman wearing a robe whom they'd already viewed on her vlog. The robe was patterned silk with vividly stylized goldfish swimming through a dark blue background.

"Well, hello there. You must be Rino and Barry. Come in, come in."

She led them down a short hallway decorated with all sorts of bric-a-brac into a room with a red circle painted on the floor. It looked something like a Japanese flag. Plush cushions ringed this circumscribed space that Mindy prevented them from stepping into until they fulfilled one requirement. She doffed her own robe, revealing her drooping tits, belly and cellulite pocked thighs. "Take off your clothes. Don't be shy. We must all be naked before the spirits in the Magick Circle."

Rino and Barry looked at each other apprehensively, shrugged, and did as they were told.

"Uhm," said Mindy laying back on a pile of cushions like a Titian nude and beckoning her guests to do likewise. "Taut young bodies are so pleasing to the eye." She pointed to Barry's penis. "Nice one. I bet it looks really nice when, you know, when it gets excited."

Rino was not going to take that lying down. "What do you think you're..?"

"Calm down, sweetie, I'm harmless. You're a lucky girl. Now what would you like to ask me. Go ahead. Anything you like."

"Why don't you tell us a little bit about Wicca first," said Barry.

"We'll we're pagan. We worship the spirits of the forest, the water, the sky. Wicca predates any organized religion and we're not even organized. Every coven is free to pursue its own interests. My fellow witches and I are principally interested in breaking down taboos, restrictions on free thinking, that sort of thing."

"Do the Wiccans have any take on good and evil?"

"Are you kidding?" Mindy snorted. "What would you think about people who tortured your colleagues, burned them at the stake, hanged them from trees, cut off their heads, all in public as a warning to others to not pursue the true path. Any religion that persecutes us must be evil. What did we ever do to them?"

"They think you challenge their authority," Barry guessed.

"That's not true. Those people can believe whatever silly nonsense they like. Just leave us alone."

"So, organized religion is evil."

"Well, what do you think? Just look at the world around you.

One thing I'll say for the Jews and Muslims is they aren't hypocrites. They're all for war and killing. Just look at the Old Testament. Just look at the Koran. But it's the Christians who are the worst, supposedly worshiping the Prince of Peace while they slaughter millions and millions around the world. And look at their pictures of this prince, a Levantine Jew who looks like a Norwegian hippy. Really!" she drawled.

"How about the Buddhists?" Rino challenged her.

"What about the Buddhists? Just look at Burma, Thailand, what have you. And, of course, that CIA agent Tibetan lama. Mass organizations always devolve into lynch mobs. That's why Wiccans are skeptical of any centralized authority. But enough about the obvious, the tedious mundane. How about the hidden, secret world? Would you like to do a little magick?" (Just spelling "magic" the way the Wiccans do to distance themselves from worldly prestidigitators.)

Rino and Barry looked at each other. Why not?

"You have to stand up and join hands with me," said Mindy.

They did as they were told and Mindy went into some sort of incantation, which sounded suspiciously like the usual magic act gibberish. At least she didn't say, "Abracadabra!" or "Presto!"

"I am invoking Pan, god of the wild woodlands," she explained. "He will soon manifest himself through us. Arise, oh Pan! Make your presence known!"

And something did begin to rise. Barry's penis, that is.

"Pan is here with us!" Mindy said excitedly. "Get on your knees, Rino! Pay homage to Pan!

Rino was horrified. Well, sort of horrified. "Barry!"

"I can't help it!" he defended himself.

"It's the Oreades, the forest nymphs," Mindy explained to Rino. "They can be very provocative."

"You tell those nymphs to get their hands off my boyfriend," said Rino angrily.

Mindy looked surprised. "I can't tell goddesses what to do. If you want to join in, I don't think they'd mind."

"Join in?!" Rino hissed. "Stop that, Barry!" Little horns seemed to be sprouting from his head.

"I can't stop now," he growled in a voice not his own.

"Aibell! Show this nubile young woman the path!" Mindy roared, and Rino was quite suddenly overcome with the languor often associated with carnal desire. She looked at Barry, who had turned into a satyr, and gave into her mad desire. Barry howled as he mounted her billy goat style and huffed and puffed his way into an orgasmic frenzy. When he pulled out, he continued to spurt all over the place covering Mindy Manners with sticky streamers of jism.

"That's the sweet essence!" she gurgled. "How did you like that, Rino?"

"More, I want more," Rino gasped. "Fuck me more, Barry."

And so the priapic monster within did as bid until the two of them lay spent in the magick circle.

"Now wasn't that nice?" said Mindy. "Just delightful. That's what Wiccans are all about so we can't be all bad, can we?"

After the intrepid interviewers had recovered from their exertions, Mindy saw them to the door and gave them each a rabbit's foot. "They're not real rabbits' feet, they're Dynel," she explained. "I'm a vegan."

As Rino and Barry walked down the street arm in arm, neither of them remembered much of anything. It was like watching a ship disappear into the fog.

"Did we really do that?" Rino wondered.

"Do what?" puzzled Barry asked.

At that very moment, decidedly unpuzzled Ted Gershem was going over the short piece that Alvin Spurtz had requested for submission to the Spuyten Duyvil people. "Just a little progress report to let them know we haven't completely forgotten them," as Spurtz had put it.

"You mean to make sure they haven't forgotten us," Gershem rejoined.

"Yes, exactly."

Writing this sort of pap was second nature to Ted, He'd been doing it his whole professional life. He could play the audience with his encomiums like a bass viola if they would just read the stuff, which they wouldn't. But pro forma was pro forma and Ted's humbly laudatory words soothed him if nobody else. "Progress" leading to "an expanding area of inquiry" that could possibly result in "a whole new paradigm" in the analysis "of questions we've been asking since time immemorial." Blah, blah, blah. Actually, he liked writing this sort of thing because he didn't have to think at all. He also had more pressing issues on his mind.

"Hey there, Bob, this is Ted," he made himself known when Applewhite answered the phone. "Listen, I was wondering if I could get some more of that service you performed the last time you were in town."

"Sure. That was free though. The first one always is. I'm afraid you'll have to pay a nominal fee this time."

"Of course. I expect to."

"Marta's going into the city tomorrow morning. She'll drop by."

"Great."

After he hung up, Gershem realized that, if Applewhite's phone was tapped, it must have sounded like a call to an escort service. Maybe Bob would get busted for pimping rather than dealing dope. The truth of the matter, though he didn't realize it yet, was that he and Anna were gradually, almost imperceptibly, getting strung out, but their rude awakening to this unfortunate condition was still sometime in the future.

He finished the Spuyten Duyvil piece and turned his attention to his Old Nate part. He wasn't certain whether or not he would appear on stage after the opening scene until the last scene. If that were the case, they might as well tape record his narration and play it with a booming deus ex machina voice while he went out and had a drink. He'd miss all the fun, of course, but the repetition involved in theatrical work was simply tedious and he wouldn't mind missing most of the whole run of the show after the opening. For the productions that followed, he would simply do his lead-in and adjourn to the most salutary gin mill in the neighborhood until he was due back for his short swan song. But Edward Smith had other ideas. When Gershem called him to suggest his view of the part, Smith was quite insistent that Old Nate sit in an easy chair as an onlooker on one side of the stage and deliver his voice-overs in person. Gershem was not happy with this tasking, but then who was he to interfere with the writer/director's vision?

"Edward's right," Anna agreed later. "Everyone wants to see your handsome self in person. Besides, I need you there for moral support. I need you there to settle my nerves."

"You have stage fright?" Gershem scoffed. "You need me there to stop you from chewing up the scenery."

"Well, that too," Anna allowed. "I am a bit of a ham, you know."

Ted had no rejoinder for the glaringly obvious. "Marta Applewhite's coming by tomorrow with some more candy," he told her.

She was initially puzzled. "Marta… Oh yes! Great. I'd love to meet her but I'll be at work. You're inviting them to the play, aren't you?"

"They told me they wouldn't miss it for the world," which was pretty much true.

"How sweet. Let's put on our tin hats and go over to the Stay Put Club."

"You're joking."

"I am indeed."

Actually, they hadn't been to the Stay Put Club in the evening since they'd gotten together in a carnal sort of way.

"But we could just put on our tin hats and watch TV or something," she suggested.

"That sounds good except for the TV part."

"Feeling frisky, Teddums? You want to do me in my tin hat? You wear yours too. We've never tried that before."

So they put on their hats and went to at it. Later, as they lay in bed, Gershem, completely unaware of the storm clouds gathering on the horizon, found himself happily humming, "Whistle While You Work".

❖

29

Edward and Sylvia Smith were taping marks on the stage when Tootie Wookums walked into the theatre.

"I'm watching you!" he called from the cheap seats.

"Who's there?" Edward demanded, squinting into the darkness.

"Tootie Wookums, attorney at law."

"Get out of here, you shyster!" Smith roared. "You're trespassing!"

"It is you people who are trespassing on the legacy of Ayn Rand!"

"You don't even know who Ayn Rand is!"

"That's not the point!"

"Mr. Wookums, if you do not leave immediately I shall have you caned!" Edward hollered. "Sylvia?"

"My pleasure," she purred, picking up a fireplace poker from the set.

Wookums did not stay his leaving and fled the theatre.

"Coward!" Sylvia called after him.

"I think we need a real lawyer," said Edward sourly. "That sonuvabitch is going to try to get an injunction."

"Let him," said Sylvia. "It will land us on the front page of all the papers. It's as if these fools are working for us. Do you think he recognized me from court?"

"I didn't even recognize you in court. That was quite a show you put on."

"Why thank you, Edward," Sylvia simpered.

Smith hadn't told Sylvia or anyone else about the resurrection of Calvin Card but he thought it might be prudent to contact him and ask his advice on how to deal with the Rand people. If it took busting a few heads, well, c'est la vie.

The Happy Shadow, loyal to the show by default, had followed Tootie Wookums from the theatre back to the Woolworth Building and taken a seat in the waiting room where Wookums' gum chewing secretary failed to notice him. She was not an attractive woman, but the Happy Shadow decided to try and have his way with her nonetheless. To this end, he pulled down his pants and started masturbating so he would be prepared to act quickly should the opportunity present itself. And, lo, it came to pass that Mrs. Lepich, for that was the secretary's name, got up from her desk and bent over the bottom drawer of a filing cabinet. The Happy Shadow was there in a flash, inserting his Uncle Willy at lightning speed, very briefly pumping away, and ejaculating with a stifled grunt. It was all over before Mrs. Lepich even realized her pussy was wet. Of course, she didn't notice the Happy Shadow quietly slip out into the corridor. Well pleased with himself, he decided to spend the late morning shoplifting. Since nobody ever noticed him it was almost too easy.

Ted Gershem, eagerly anticipating the arrival of Marta Applewhite, was once again going over his lines from the play. In this particular scene, his tone had to be bitter and petulant but he could barely control his laughter.

"They were all there, the people I'd considered my closest friends, the people who had turned on me and cast me out into the wilderness. Alan Greenspan – the Undertaker we called him – come to pay his respects to the woman who had created him out of whole cloth, a court eunuch who had ridden Ayn's coat tails to lofty positions in finance and government…"

He was interrupted by the ringing doorbell. It was Marta. A few minutes later, he greeted her at the door and she immediately latched onto his arm.

"Ted! I just love seeing you so much," she gushed.

"Likewise," said Gershem. He ushered her into the living room and gently admonished, "Marta. You've got to let go of my arm if I'm going to make you a cup of tea."

"I'm not letting go, Ted. Not this time. You want something and I want something."

Gershem was bewildered. "I don't understand…"

Kevin Bartelme

"Yes you do. You want opium and I want to go to bed with you. Bobby never makes love to me anymore."

"But, Marta, I'm living with a woman," he tried to explain. "And you're married."

"I don't care. I'm a free spirit. I do as I like. Do you want the opium or not?"

Gershem was tempted to show her out, but only briefly tempted. He tried to negotiate. "But what if Bobby finds out?"

"He won't. Now let's see your bedroom." She dragged him more or less against his will down the hall.

"I can smell another woman in here. You haven't been faithful to me, Ted," she giggled. With surprising strength for a woman her size, she threw him on the bed with an esoteric wrestling hold and pinned him there for the duration of their coupling. Not that Ted was complaining or resisting in any way. But visions of Anna walking in unexpectedly prodded him to finish up as quickly as possible and get everything back on a lust free footing.

"Oooh myyy, that was sooo goood," Marta crooned as she released Gershem from her hold and allowed him to get up.

"Yes it was. Really," he agreed. "Let's do it again sometime. Now, about that opium…"

"Coming right up!" she said, twirling her finger like a cartoon character. She pulled a plastic bag of little opium pellets out of her knapsack and handed it over. "That will be one hundred dollars."

Given the cost of marijuana, the price seemed cheap, a real bargain in fact.

"Now I've got to go see Edward," she said.

"Please don't tell him you saw me."

"I wouldn't do that. I can be very discreet when I feel like it." And off she went out the door.

Discreet when she felt like it, Gershem mused. He hoped she understood how much blackmail material he had on her. Of course she did. What was he thinking? He inserted a ball of opium up his ass and his paranoia slowly dissolved into placid equanimity. He felt just fine and put any worrisome suspicions out of his mind.

Rino and Barry had decided to take the day off from their

investigations and go shopping. Or should I say, the decision to go buy stuff was all Rino's because she had determined that Barry needed new clothes. For his own part, Barry loathed shopping and freely acknowledged that if everyone were like him the consumer economy would collapse overnight. However, if it made her happy to dress him, he was willing to swallow his bile for one afternoon and go along for the ride. And that's how they wound up downtown on lower Broadway. Was it simply kismet that no sooner had they emerged from the Prince Street subway station, that they ran smack into grad school colleague Rhoda Memberman on a similar shopping expedition with her very own reluctant swain, Hyman Ryman?

"Well, hello there, you two," said Rhoda who was very proud indeed to be seen in public with her new boyfriend. "Hyman, this is Rino and Barry from my abnormal seminar."

Ryman nodded nervously and extended his hand. "Pleased to meet you."

"Hyman and I are going clothes shopping," Rhoda explained. "For him. He would never do it on his own."

That certainly struck a note with Rino. "Barry's just the same. That's why we're here."

"Well, let's go shopping together," said Rhoda. "What fun!"

Barry and Hyman not only didn't mind; they seemed to be relieved by this sharing of their irresponsibility. Rhoda and Rino quickly agreed on an itinerary and they were off, the first stop being right across the street, a cavernous emporium of moderately priced apparel called Rag Picker's. As they navigated through the racks, stopping here and there to examine the merchandise, the Rag Picker "look" became apparent – loud primary colors. Talking their menfolk into wearing this brash sort of thing was going to be a daunting task, so the ladies did the wise thing; they simply gave up and moved on to the next store down the block, *Playa La Ropa*. Similar to the other store in layout, the wide open interior yielded a more subdued color scheme in its wares that Barry and Hyman might be talked into purchasing without an inordinate amount of nagging. This hunting expedition did not go unnoticed by an interested party in the store, namely the Happy Shadow who was there to do a little shopping of his own minus bothering with the cashier. He of course recognized Rino and Barry but as he set eyes on Rhoda Memberman his heart skipped a beat. She was everything he'd ever dreamed of, his Venus of Willendorf, his Sarafina, his perfect woman! God, what he would do to get into that pussy!

So, as our foursome proceeded to pick out shirts and pants and sweaters, they were closely followed by a very Happy Shadow eagerly anticipating a possible opening in one of the changing rooms.

"Hyman, you must try on this jumper," Rhoda ordered. "It's just the thing this season."

"It's a sweater, Rhoda," Hyman whined.

"Sweaters were last year. Now it's jumpers. Come on, try it on."

"You know," said cynic Barry Breen, "fashion is just a way to get people to buy new stuff before they get any wear out of their old stuff. It's a conspiracy to advance never-ending consumption."

"Yeah, just like food. What do you know about fashion?" Rhoda scoffed. "Fashion is fun! Oh, look at this little dress. It would look so cute on you, Rino. Try it on."

In her T-shirt and shorts, Rino didn't have to go to the changing room. She simply pulled the bright floral print over her head and did a little turn around the sales floor.

"That is just so cunning," said Rhoda. "I wish I could fit into things like that."

Hyman Ryman, however, who was much attached to Rhoda's big tits and ass, was glad she couldn't.

"Did you know that Professor Gershem's theatre company is putting on a play?" Rhoda informed Barry and Rino. "Hyman saw an ad for it in the newspaper."

"Really?" said Barry. "Is he in it?" Now, that was a lapse in discretion. How did Rhoda even know Gershem was involved with the theatre? It would have surprised him to learn that it was Rino who had let that slip.

"I don't know, but I'm sure going to find out," said Rhoda. "You're going to go, aren't you?"

"Of course," said Rino.

"Just don't tell David Kogan," Rhoda warned.

"Who's David Kogan?" Hyman wanted to know.

"Just someone from class. He has a very disruptive personality."

"And I thought you two were an item," Barry teased her.

"Fat chance!" Rhoda harrumphed.

Ryman didn't know what to say. Did he have a rival? Was Rhoda using him as a pawn to make this David Kogan jealous? So were the thoughts engendered by freshly turned lust. But it was not David Kogan Hyman had to worry about. The Happy Shadow was circling Rhoda Memberman like a feral dog, sniffing the air, just waiting to pounce. The chance came when Rhoda picked out a pair of pants and adjourned to a changing room. He had to hurry. His window of opportunity was the short time between her taking off the pants she was wearing and putting the new ones on. He did manage to slide in from behind as she dropped trou but then something unexpected happened. Her vagina clamped onto his penis like a bitch in heat. When she tried to shimmy into the new pants his engorged member blocked the way.

"God," she muttered, "I really have to lose some weight."

Meanwhile, the Happy Shadow was trying as hard as he could to disengage without someone dowsing them with a bucket of water. After a few seconds of Herculean effort, his sore penis popped out with a sound akin to a champagne cork on New Years Eve. If Rhoda noticed this audio enhancement, she didn't show it and finally managed to squeeze herself into the pants.

"So, what do you think?" said Rhoda as she modeled her new look. "A little tight maybe?"

"You're telling me," the Happy Shadow grumbled as he skittered off unnoticed into the racks.

Anna Bunch was surprised by the strange odor in Gershem's apartment when she arrived in the late afternoon with a bag of groceries.

"What is that smell?" she wondered

"What smell?" said innocent Ted.

"It's patchouli oil!"

"Oh, that must be Marta. She was here earlier with the goodies."

"Is she a hippie?"

"Senior division. Would you like some candy?" he said, holding out an opium ball.

"I think I'd like that very much." Much to Gershem's relief, Marta was forgotten as Anna inserted the brown pellet. "Have you heard anything from Edward?"

"I imagine he's pretty busy with the theatre and all, Why would he call us?"

"Well, I am the leading lady, you know. And you're the leading man. Sort of."

"Sort of, "Gershem chuckled. "Let's go to King Wok and get something to eat."

And so they did, where he had his usual moo goo gai pan and she opted for shrimp chow fun. When they'd finished and the waiter brought their fortune cookies and she read hers first.

"'You are about to experience the worst disaster of your whole life.' Well, that certainly is cheery. Someone must have gotten out of the wrong side of bed at the fortune cookie factory."

"Do they have beds at the fortune cookie factory?" Then Gershem read his own future. "'You have experienced much pain in your life but nothing like what's about to happen.' Now wait a minute. Is this a joke? Wo Chung!" he called out and the waiter came rushing over.

"Yes sir, Mr. Gershem," he practically bowed and scraped.

"These fortunes. Well, they're very unusual." He handed the two of them to Wo Chung who studied them carefully.

"Into each life little rain must fall," he said sagely.

"That's not what it says. And what's that supposed to mean anyway?" Gershem demanded.

"I don't make cookie," Wo Chung protested and shrugged. "Japanese devils invent fortune cookie."

"I had no idea you were so superstitious, Ted," Anna teased him. "Just like a real actor."

Slightly chastened Gershem tried to slough it off. "You're right. Sorry for being silly." But that didn't immediately allay his sense of unease. He had to wait for the opium to do that.

As they walked down the street after leaving the restaurant, Gershem mused, "This school project is getting to me. I'm beginning to take all sorts of nonsense seriously."

"Don't worry, sweetie," Anna comforted him. "The world is nothing but a conspiracy to drive us all crazy. Let's just go home and put on our tin hats and watch TV."

"From one source of paranoia to another. Sounds good to me," he agreed.

Edward Smith was still at the theatre supervising two recently acquired interns from Juilliard who were moving around the furniture in Ayn Rand's apartment set when who should walk in but Calvin Card, still in his Santa Claus beard.

"I got your message," said Card. "What's this all about?"

Smith ushered Calvin to a seat out of hearing distance of the stage.

"Well, as you can see, we're mounting a play and certain highly unreasonable individuals are trying to stop us."

"Why?"

"They have their reasons. My problem is that these people are fanatics and seem to be willing to do anything to disrupt the production."

"What do you mean, 'fanatics'? Are they Arabs or something?"

"No, no, nothing like that."

"So what's this play about?"

"Ayn Rand."

Card lit up. "Really? She's my hero."

"Mine too," Smith agreed with a tight smile.

"So these people," said Card. "Are they Communists or something?"

"Oh my no. It's the Objectivist Institute. They think they own Ayn Rand."

"They don't?"

"Of course not, Calvin. No one owns Ayn Rand. She's a gift to the whole world."

"She was certainly a gift to me," Calvin rhapsodized. "The first time I read '*The Fountainhead*' I got so excited, well, I discovered just what my mind and body could do together. I had this vision of very juicy Dominique Francon that really, really got my motor running, if you can guess where that's going," he said with a wink. "Or should I say coming? Heh, heh."

"Calvin! I had no idea you were so well read," said Smith. "So you see what I mean. Ayn Rand was a gift to you and a gift to me. We can't allow some nuts to steal her away from us."

"I'll do what I can, Edward," Card promised. "I'll do what I can,"

On the misplaced assumption that the matter was taken care of, Smith went back to work, happily unaware that Studs Zenith was busy abusing his wife in the dungeon. Well, not exactly abusing. They had finished up with their fun and games and gotten down to the serious work of rehearsing Studs for the play.

> AYN
>
> Am I making a fool of myself? Have I made a mistake in believing your feelings were the same as my own? Do you love me as much as I love you?

> NATE
>
> Of course I love you.

> AYN
>
> Kiss me, Nathaniel. Kiss me, you fool! Then fuck me, fuck me till my guts fall out!.

> NATE
>
> But what about Frank?

> AYN
>
> Don't worry, my pet, he's out of town on business. Now take me, Nathaniel, take me to the glorious heights where the air is clear and we can see for miles and miles standing strong in each

others arms – together. We must tell Barbara and Frank immediately.

NATE

What?

AYN

To conduct a back alley affair would be intellectually dishonest, my darling. We must proudly proclaim our love for each other and let the chips fall where they may.

NATE

I'm sorry, Ayn, but I don't see any reason to cause them that kind of pain. Can't we just -

AYN

Just what? Sneak around behind their backs stealing kisses in the shadows? No, Nathaniel, we must have the courage of our convictions and present them with the truth, the whole truth, and nothing but the truth. It's what they deserve.

NATE

Excuse me?

AYN

I didn't mean they've done anything wrong, Nathaniel.

NATE

What did you mean? What exactly is it they deserve?

AYN

To be treated with consideration and
respect. Deceiving them would be
insulting. We shall all meet tomorrow
and discuss the matter. I'm sure Frank
and Barbara will understand.

NATE

I don't want to lose Barbara, Ayn.

AYN

You won't. You'll see.

"That was really very good, Studs," Sylvia congratulated him.
"Just the proper balance between lust and confusion."

"You sure didn't sound confused," Studs noted.

"I'm not supposed to be confused. Ever. I'm Ayn Rand."

"Well, I just hope I don't blow it on stage. I'm a little nervous
actually. Go figure. I perform on TV every day, no problem, and now
I suddenly get stage fright."

"It's good for you, Studdles. It will concentrate your mind."

"I thought it was the fear of death that concentrates the mind."

"Same thing. If you don't get over on the people out there in
the dark, you might as well be dead."

❖

30

Rino and Barry, their curiosities sorely piqued by Rhoda Memberman's news about the theatre company, had mulled over the idea of contacting the St. Mark's 9/11 coordinator Baxter Allen, decided against it, and then given in to their less than better instincts and made the call. They mentioned Columbia, of course, but not Professor Gershem, and Allen was only too glad to see them. Hearing Rino's last name, he asked if she could recommend a good Japanese restaurant in the East Village. She could and they agreed to meet at a little hole-in-the-wall udon place on Sixth Street. At three in the afternoon, the place was not crowded.

"Hello there," said Allen who was a little late. "It's so nice to find someone who even pays any attention to us anymore. What can I do for you?"

"The project we're working on," Breen began, "is an investigation into perceptions of good and evil…"

Allen held up his hands. "Hey, hold on. Just because we meet in a church basement doesn't make us dogmatic on the subject. "I've always been ambivalent about so-called good and evil."

"But you do believe there was a conspiracy…"

"I don't believe it. I know it. Even the government's absurd hypothesis is a conspiracy theory. They think it was a bunch of Arabs. I beg to differ."

"But whoever did it must have been bad people."

"I'm sorry, I don't think I made myself clear. I'm not interested in good guys or bad guys. I'm interested in historical truth, not relative values."

"So you think perceptions of good and evil are relative?"

"Of course they are. Look, just let me tell you what I think and take what you want from it."

"Sure," said Rino. "Shall we order first?"

"You order for me," said Allen. "You're the reason I wanted to meet here. I don't know anything about Japanese food."

"You say you're interested in perceptions," Allen continued after Rino chose three tempura udons from the menu. "Let me tell you my take on 9/11. It wasn't an attack on the buildings, it wasn't an attack on the United States, and it wasn't even the work of fanatics. It was a calculated, cold-blooded attack on reason itself. We are asked to accept the physically impossible as not only possible but as a fait accompli. You see, the buildings collapsed! Isn't it obvious it was the planes? That isn't logic. That's religion. By the way, I don't even think there were any planes."

"But people saw them," Rino objected. "They're on film."

"Are they? The videos I've seen show these so-called planes cutting cleanly through steel and reinforced concrete and even coming out of the other side of the building. Do you know what the nose of a plane is made out of? Plastic. I'm not preaching, mind you, but as far as I'm concerned, if even one thing is impossible, then it's all impossible. Those responsible for this event are trying to create false history, just like any other totalitarian government. It's our job to make sure they don't get away with it. Mmm, this is really delicious," Allen commented on the udon, "but I think I need a bib. I'm getting it all over my shirt."

Rino affixed a napkin to his collar.

"But these people who you don't want to get away with it, surely you must think they're evil," said Barry.

"I have no idea what their motives are, but trying to create truth out of a blatant lie is - how shall I say? – unwise. Unless they can get away with discarding science altogether, which already has a lot of support from reactionary religious kooks."

When they finished, Baxter Allen insisted on picking up the check. "I used to be a big honcho in the ad business, a hired liar. Paying for lunch is my way of doing penance."

And then, well, Rino just couldn't help herself. "Do you know Ted Gershem?"

"Yeah, sure. He hasn't been around lately. I heard he got absorbed into that theatre crowd. Why? Do you know him?"

"He's our graduate advisor in abnormal psychology."

"Really? Abnormal psychology," Allen seemed puzzled. "Did he set this up? What did he say? Go check out this bunch of nuts?"

"No, no. He doesn't even know we're here."

Allen laughed. "Well, I hope I haven't disappointed." He spun a finger around his ear and made a loony face.

"Actually," said Barry, "you're the sanest person we've interviewed so far."

"Should I take that as a compliment? Where else have you been? Bellevue?"

"Not yet, but it's on the list."

"Well, give my regards to Ted," Allen waved and walked off.

"He seems like a nice man," said Rino, "but does he really think there were no planes?"

"He's right about the science. It's a real conundrum."

"I'm sorry. A what?"

"A riddle. For every action there is an equal and opposite reaction. That's what should have happened."

"I don't know what you're talking about."

"I believe that was his whole point."

Edward Smith, who did know what he was talking about, was having his own problems in a world where Newton's laws still applied. The set transformation from ersatz Los Angeles mission modern to New York lower Fifth Avenue egghead chic was proving to be a daunting logistical task and his patience with his set designer wife was wearing thin.

"How do you expect to move all this junk around the stage in two minutes?" he complained about the abundance of props she'd collected.

"The look is important," Sylvia countered. "Ayn Rand was a woman. The look was certainly important to her."

"What has that got to do with scene changes?" exasperated Edward sputtered.

"Men!" said Sylvia. "Maybe we should just get all Beckett and put everybody on a bus bench like Waiting for Godot."

"Really, Sylvia, there must be some sort of middle ground."

"Middle brow Edward," she taunted him, "middling along with all the class he can muster. Middle class, that is."

"Stop being personal," he snapped. "Changing sets is a real problem that requires a real solution."

They might have nattered on indefinitely but for the arrival of their newly hired publicist, Junius Flatmeat, an enormously fat young man who was said to be a wizard in public relations.

"Junius Flatmeat!" he called out as he waddled down the aisle. "You must be the Smiths."

Edward smiled cordially and said, "Mr. Flatmeat, your reputation precedes you."

"Just call me Junius and nothing precedes me but my stomach!" the publicist guffawed, vigorously pumping Smith's hand.

"And this must be Sylvia, you lucky guy, you."

"Thank you, Mr. Flatmeat," said Sylvia, batting her eyes.

"Junius," he corrected her. "Now let's see. You've got Studs Zenith as the lead. Is he a fag?"

"I should say not," said Sylvia.

"That's good," said Junius, "unusual, but very good. I'll get one of the broads at the station where he works to claim he flashed her. We get the Post front page, just like that."

"I don't know if he'd appreciate that," said dubious Edward.

"Are you kidding? With a name like Studs? It's a natural! And this what's-her-name, Anna Bunch, do you have any dirt on her?"

"Now see here, Junius," Smith waxed indignant. "We're not trying to destroy these peoples' careers."

"Oh, I get it. You're an old-fashioned kind of guy, double-breasted suit with the carnation, Algonquin roundtable, the works. Well, let me tell you something, Eddy. Times have changed. You know, I actually read your play. I don't usually do that. I like to work with a clean slate, but let me tell you something. There are a lot of people out there who worship Ayn Rand — mostly morons and teenage girls and what's the difference anyway? — but these people might make trouble."

"They've already threatened us," said Edward. "They tried to get an injunction against us."

"Really?! That is like good booking awesome! That's the best news I heard all day! Talk about making my job easier! Are they violent?"

"I don't know."

"God, I hope they are! We've got to poke 'em, rile 'em up!"

"You want to incite them?"

"Fucking A! I want them to kill someone on stage! I mean, you can always get new actors! They're a dime a dozen in this town!" Suddenly realizing he was getting ahead of himself, especially with these new clients, Flatmeat pulled himself up short. "Sorry about that. Sometimes I get carried away, but you can imagine the publicity, can't you?" He looked at his gaudy gold watch. "I got to run. Just don't get too nervous from the service. I'll be in touch." With that he quickly waddled out of the theatre, leaving Edward scratching his head.

"I don't know about this guy," he said dubiously. He couldn't tell her that Calvin Card had recommended him.

"He's supposed to be the best in the business," said Sylvia. "Everybody swears by him."

"Well, he's already got our money. We'll see what comes out of this."

And they shortly would because Junius was just about to outdo himself. Unknown to the Smiths, Flatmeat was also a producer of crisis acted dramas and was about to put on a show for the ages.

The abnormal psychology seminar had convened once again and Akisha Lumumba was explaining her grandmother's cosmogony.

"She says that the lizard gods have sent their minions to earth to prepare for their arrival. Once they have control of the military, the media, banking, and government they will take their masks off and reveal themselves as the vicious, repulsive creatures they are, come to enslave and eat us."

"They're not doing a very good job of hiding it with their masks on," David Kogan observed.

"She says the last days are upon us, "Akisha continued, " and that we must stand up to the lizards before they close off the road to Blue Heaven."

"Excuse me, the road to what?" Rhoda wondered.

"Blue Heaven. It's a black folks' thing. You wouldn't understand."

"Only black people can go there?"

"The last I heard it wasn't integrated," Akisha chuckled. "That's what my grandmother thinks anyway."

"Tell her they should let white people into Blue Heaven," said David Kogan, "but only as slaves."

"Well, what next?" said moderator Professor Gershem. "Anyone else got anything to report?"

Rhoda, Rino, and Barry all looked at each other but none of them said anything.

"Well, then let's plan to meet again this Thursday," Gershem continued. 'In the meantime, try to avoid lizard people and stay on the road to Blue Heaven as best you can."

"They won't let anyone in but Akisha anyway," Kogan pointed out.

"Quite right, but remember what Groucho Marx said. He wouldn't want to join a club that actually would let him in."

Rhoda was sorely tempted to corner Gershem in the hall, tell him how handsome he was, and then ask him if he'd ever considered acting on stage, but she restrained herself. After all, he would probably think she was coming on to him.

Rino and Barry were not tempted to do anything of the sort and thought it better to let the whole matter slide, though they had decided to see the play if the tickets weren't too expensive.

Happily unaware of his students' quandary, Gershem went home to Anna to supposit some more opium and rehearse. Opening night was coming at them like an execution date. There would be no last minute reprieve. The show would go on and they would be exposed in the footlights as they had never been before, so they practiced their lines with a real sense of urgency, the way the condemned try to put their affairs in order and their mind at rest before their final appointment in Samarra when the curtain parts and the prurient critics out there in the dark search for vital signs. Talk about working a metaphor to death, but that's the way they felt.

"There a dress rehearsal on Friday," said Anna. "We really have to get ready. Before it was just fun. Now it's real."

"Don't get frantic. We've been over this so many times you could do it in your sleep," Gershem reassured her.

"A true artiste never gets frantic," said Anna in her Ayn voice. "She simply ascends to a higher plane where she can see for miles and miles and miles."

"You see? You almost are Ayn Rand."

"I hope you mean that as a compliment."

Gershem didn't bother to respond. "Who's doing wardrobe?"

"No idea. Probably the Salvation Army or someone raiding her grandmother's closet. I wonder how they're going to dress you as swinging sixties, L.A. pop psychologist? Love beads and long hair?"

"Old Nate was too square for that. How about a polyester leisure suit?"

"Perfect. I hope I get to wear long gloves and a pillbox hat."

"And nothing else. The first intellectual Playboy centerfield, the very first nude interview. Ayn Rand on the sexual revolution. Don't you think you should have a cigarette holder as well?"

"But of course, dahlink. Do I get to show my little puss puss in the magazine?"

"Not in 1953, baby," Gershem growled, "not in 1953. Just tits and ass. And lose the pillbox. It's tin hat time for the world of the future."

Who knows how long they would have gone on with this sort nonsense had they not been interrupted by the phone?

"Ted, it's Edward. We just hired this wonderful publicist, Junius Flatmeat. He's really going to put us on the map."

"Junius Flatmeat? Isn't he the guy who all those actresses and models claim raped them?"

"The very same, although I don't know how he did it. He's so fat I don't think he's seen his penis in years. I just hope he makes us as famous as he is. But that's not why I called anyway. We want to hold a little pre-show press conference with Anna and Studs. Do you think she's up for that?"

"Ask her yourself," said Gershem handing Anna the phone.

She heard Smith out and was more than agreeable. "I'd love to!" she gushed.

"Just don't do it in character," said Smith. "Save that for the show."

"I wouldn't dream of giving away the surprise," she did her best Ayn Rand drawl.

"That's wonderful. I'll set it up and get back to you with the particulars. This is so exciting."

"It is, isn't it." Anna agreed. After Smith hung up she turned to Gershem. "I'm going to be on TV again."

Gershem was not so sure. "A press conference doesn't mean television coverage."

"But Studs is going to be there. How can they resist?"

"You may have a point."

"Well, I can just cover that with my tin hat, can't I?"

At that very moment, Studs Zenith was also rehearsing with Deirdre as Barbara Branden.

> NATE
>
> You should have seen the way he treated us.
>
> BARBARA
>
> Nathan, I think I'm going insane.
>
> NATE
>
> He brushed me aside as if he were speaking to a retarded child.
>
> BARBARA
>
> Nathan, did you hear me? I think I'm going insane.
>
> NATE
>
> Insane? What are you talking about? You're a rationalist, an Objectivist. You can't go insane.

BARBARA

I had such a panic attack today that I tried to call you at Ayn's. She yelled at me on the phone, Nathan. She said I was invading her context, she said I would always be unhappy until I faced reality.

NATE

She shouldn't speak that way to you. I'll have a word with her tomorrow.

BARBARA

The problem is I think she might be right.

NATE

Don't worry, sweetie, you've just been under a lot of pressure lately. We both have. But everything's going to be alright. Trust me.

BARBARA

I do, Nathan

NATE

Besides, as the head of the Nathaniel Branden Institute and the Objectivist Newsletter I can't have my wife going bonkers.

BARBARA

I don't suppose that would do at all.

NATE

Good girl. Now what say we send out

for Chinese? Moo goo gai pan. You like
that, don't you?

BARBARA
You know I do, Nathan.

They embraced. "That was really good, Deirdre," said Studs
without breaking from their clinch.

"It gets better," she purred and led him off to the bedroom for
some more sexual gymnastics.

These doings were of no concern to the Happy Shadow who
had already staked out his box for opening night. It was in the far left
balcony, practically right over the stage. The reason that the Happy
Shadow was assured of this seat is that there was no seat. The balcony
was closed off and he would have to bring his own folding chair. But
he was happy to be above the fray rather than being immersed in a tale
told by an idiot, full of sound and fury, signifying nothing, as some
theatrically inclined bard might put it. He had a feeling that the opening was going to be a night to remember and he wanted a deck chair
view.

❖

31

Anna Bunch arrived at Junius Flatmeat's office in the Brill Building for her interview appointment a little early and was greeted
effusively by the morbidly obese publicist.

"Anna, Anna, it's so good to meet you. Studs ought to be along
any minute now," he said looking at his watch. "You know I have this
reputation for trying to put the make on actresses and I try to live up
to it, but, you know, you're kind of old for me."

"Pity," she said. "I could teach you some new tricks if I could
find your penis under all that flab."

"I can't find it myself," he guffawed. "Haven't been able to in years. I can see you're a woman with a sense of humor. Ah, here's Studs."

The weatherman walked into the office like the mighty Kong entering the village, exchanged greetings with Anna, and vigorously shook Flatmeat's hand. Junius was curious.

"How do they make you look like that? You look like you were extruded in a plastics factory."

"Trade secret," said Studs with a twinkle in his eye.

"Well. I won't pry. The press conference is at the Marriott in fifteen minutes so we better run along."

Flatmeat had borrowed a small conference room at the hotel from a friend in the rag trade who was going to use it for her own fashion week presentation later in the afternoon. The backdrop that Anna and Studs would stand in front of was plastered with a checkerboard of *Playa La Ropa* logos.

"Just look at this place," Flatmeat enthused. "It looks like the Academy Awards or something."

"Where's Edward?" Anna wanted to know.

"I told him to lay low," said Junius. "No one wants to see writers and directors. They might say something intelligent. No, they want to see stars. Now, I don't want to get too personal but have you two ever, you know...?"

"Not that I recall," said Anna.

"Believe me," said Studs with a broad wink, "she'd remember. She'd remember for the rest of her life."

"So, no woosome twosome here?" said Flatmeat. "Too bad. People like that. So I'm going to let the reporters in. Why don't you two stand right over there in front of that backdrop? Just make sure that there are plenty of logos visible."

The two actors took their positions and Junius admitted the scant press corps waiting outside. There was one television crew (not from Studs' station) and a few photographers and print people.

"Hey, where is everybody?" Flatmeat comically demanded. "Well, no loss. They'll sure be sorry after this show opens. Let me introduce you to Miss Anna Bunch and Mr. Studs Zenith who some of you may already know."

Anna and Studs waved to the small group.

"I'm not going to give away the plot but let's just say that 'Ayn and Nate' is a moving romance about an older married woman and her younger also married loverboy. Any questions for our stars?"

A mousy woman with a small tape recorder asked: "Miss Bunch, how are you playing a controversial character like Ayn Rand?"

Before Anna could get a word out of her mouth, Flatmeat answered for her. "With intelligence and style, of course. Who's next?"

The questioning, if you can call it that, went on in this vein until Junius got tired of answering questions and decided to wrap it up. "That's all, folks. These two are due for lunch with the President in fifteen minutes and we have to run along."

"The who?" someone demanded.

"The President. Don't you know he's a big fan of Ayn Rand?"

"Fuck you, Junius."

"Don't go away mad," Flatmeat singsonged, "just go away."

"So," said Studs after the press had departed, "I'm ready. Let's go meet the President." Big pause. "Just kidding, Junius, just kidding."

Rino and Barry just happened to be in the vicinity of the Times Square Marriott, when Junius, Anna, and Studs passed them on the street.

"God," said Rino, "that's the fattest man I ever saw."

"That other guy with him, he looked familiar," Barry noted but he couldn't quite pick him out of the line-up. "Some politician maybe."

The two of them were on the way to a meeting at the Dimitri Bobokoff acting studio to meet the eponymous owner who had contacted them rather than the other way around. Bobokoff was a well known acting coach whose specialty was teaching up and coming young authors, entrepreneurs, chefs, and so on the finer points of presenting themselves in public. He'd left exactly why he wanted to speak to the two researchers in the land of a vague, "I think you'll find it very interesting." Maybe, maybe not, but at least he was a respectable acting teacher with a school right in the middle of the theatre district.

The elevator opened into a bright, sunlit loft space where six or seven people going through spastic motions and making animal sounds, growling, squawking, barking, roaring, what have you. Presiding over this menagerie was Dimitri Bobokoff, a portly man in a caftan. He turned to Rino and Barry and snapped, "You're late!"

Barry looked at his watch. "No we're not. In fact, we're a little early."

Bobokoff slapped his cheeks. "Oh my, I'm so sorry. You must be Barry and Rino. I thought you were students. Silly me. The two of you do look like stars, you know. Please, come with me to my office," he said with a sweeping gesture and, leaving his class with the admonition to continue to do whatever they were doing, led the two of them off down a hallway in back to a small room plastered with eight by ten glossies. "Welcome to the whorehouse parlor. Please. Sit. I guess you're wondering why I contacted you."

"We're all ears," Barry shrugged.

"A friend of mine — no names — told me about your project and I said to myself there are a few things I know that I've never shared with anyone else."

"What sort of things?" said Barry.

"Things about actors. You see, there are thousands and thousands of actors out there but very few who actually get to perform on any kind of regular basis. Even the lucky ones only get a commercial or a bit part in a film every now and then. My studio is full of these people with a burning desire to be stars but who are, in fact, going absolutely nowhere. That's just the dreary lot of most actors. Most of them give up at some point, but there are others who will do absolutely anything to get in the limelight."

"Are you talking about porn?" Rino interrupted him.

"Well, some of the luckier ones, but most of them don't physically fit the bill, if you know what I mean," Dmitri simpered and leered, then snapped back to lecture mode. "No, I'm talking about the ones who will do anything to get "work" as they call it. There are certain agencies, not the reputable ones like William Morris or ICM mind you, that specialize in supplying talent to anyone who requires people with even moderate acting ability. I first became aware of these organizations when some of my former students, working under false names, started popping up on television news broadcasts of various disasters, anything from tornados to terrorist attacks, playing supposed victims, witnesses, what have you. I was, of course, curious and decided to track down these former students and find out what was what. I learned one thing in a hurry. Don't ask questions about these people. Two goons from the private security company Retalitron made it quite clear to me what the consequences of curiosity could be."

"How did they do that?" Barry asked. "Did they threaten you?"

"Threaten me? You're not going to believe this, but they snatched me off the street and waterboarded me in some basement dungeon."

"Dungeon? What do you mean?"

"I mean it had all these torture instruments, this big wheel and chains, all that kind of stuff. It put such a fright into me I haven't been able to talk about it with anyone, not even my shrink."

"Then why are you talking to us?" Rino wondered. "You might be putting us in danger too."

"I'm sorry about that, but I had to talk to someone. Just don't mention my name and I think we'll be alright."

Barry, who'd been processed by enough borderline nuts in their survey already, was skeptical. "You're sure this is for real? You're not just making this up for whatever reason people make stuff up?"

"I wish I were making it up. I really do," said Bobokoff sadly. "I'd look into this Retalitron if I were you. Just be careful. For all I know, they're holding my former students in cages and trotting them out like dancing bears when they need them."

"We'll look into it," said Barry with such a lack of commitment that anyone listening would understand he had no intention of doing so.

Rino, however, was a different mind. After they'd left the studio she said: "I'm going to find out about this Retalitron."

"Be my guest. This whole thing doesn't really fit into the project parameters, you know. And you might wind up in a cage like a dancing bear."

"If I did would you try and rescue me?"

"I might consider it. On the other hand…"

"God, Barry, you sound like David Kogan."

"Ouch! A low blow that."

But Rino, pretending to be an actress, did call Retalitron and was referred to something called Player Station, which, as it turned out, had no listed phone number, no website, no email and no street address.

Ted Gershem, sick of going over his lines and with nothing else in particular to do, decided to take a walk down Broadway and go book browsing at Barnes and Noble. He did it less out of actually wanting to buy a book than an obligation he felt to support the dwindling number of booksellers in New York with his physical presence. Maybe he could find something for Anna who favored mysteries.

When he arrived at the store, he noted that something unusual was going on. There was a reading and book signing in the middle of the afternoon. These events were almost always staged in the evening. The book in question was called "Sounding the Alarm" and it was about "Paul Revere's relevance to modern America" whatever that meant. It only made Gershem wonder what had ever happened to rock group Paul Revere and the Raiders. Maybe that's what the book was about. The author, one Ira Windsock, was scheduled to go on in five minutes so Ted decided to get a cup of tea at the café and take a folding chair well away from the podium. There were already a few older women awaiting Mr. Windsock's arrival who smiled coyly at Gershem and made him slightly uncomfortable. He wasn't that old, was he? He imagined himself on a Caribbean cruise liner playing mahjong with these biddies except he didn't know how to play mahjong. This idle comic projection was interrupted by the arrival of the author, a short man with wild grey Einstein hair and a thermos bottle, which he set on the podium.

"Welcome to all of you," he waved to the small audience. "I hate reading and I hate being read to so you'll just have to buy the book without a free sample. What I'd like to do today is just sit here and look at you until my allotted time is up and I can leave. I am, however, obliged to take your questions if you have any." He looked around expectantly.

One of the ladies raised her hand and asked him, "Can you at least tell us what the book is about?"

"Of course I can. I wrote it, didn't I?" He said no more, creating confused consternation in his small audience.

Amused pedagogue Gershem called out, "I think she means would you tell us what the book is about."

"Now that's another question entirely," said Windsock. "It calls for a preference. Would I prefer to tell you what the book is about or not? This seemingly simple question is rife with complicated unknowns. Will you still buy the book afterwards or leave me in the lurch, unable to even buy a decent lunch with the paltry expense money my publisher provides?"

"I'll buy the book right now," one of the ladies volunteered.

"Now we're talking," said Windsock. "Step right up."

And they did, even Gershem, whose book the author signed with a flourish and sotto voce, "Thanks for setting these people straight, buddy."

"My pleasure," said Ted.

Having dispensed with the last paying customer, Windsock stood up. "All right, let's get on with it. The premise of "Sounding the Alarm" is simple. People listened to Paul Revere when he warned them about the approach of the British and they responded in force and unity. Today, we have thousands of Paul Reveres galloping around warning us about everything from climate collapse to the coming of the Rapture. We can't possibly pay attention to all of them. We have to pick and choose. Or not pay any attention at all. I think more and more people are opting for the latter choice and that is not a good thing. Some of these Paul Reveres are right and we have to learn how to sort them out from the loonies, the agent provocateurs, and the false flags with actors pretending to be people they're not. Towards educating people, I've developed a simple culling method. If even one thing is fishy about a theory or hypothesis, it's all fishy. Lies and facts simply don't mix."

Recalling his own participation in the post hurricane telecast made Ted uncomfortable. It was for a good cause, the relief of storm victims, but it was nevertheless staged and might have been revealed as such, casting a pall on the very charities it was supposed to benefit. It was, however, a little late to worry about it now. What's done was done.

"For example," Windsock went on, "if a man gets his legs blown off in the Boston bombing and is wheeled away by non-medical personnel with no apparent bleeding and shows up cheering at a hockey game two weeks later yelling, 'Boston Strong!' we can reasonably assume that this obvious fakery indicates the whole thing was a put up job."

"But that's conspiracy theory," one of the women objected.

"It is indeed," said Windsock. "Just as the British conspired to take the American revolutionaries by surprise and were thwarted by Paul Revere. As soon as the establishment slaps the pejorative 'conspiracy theorist' on anyone who doesn't go along with their official story you know there's probably something to what that person is saying."

As far as Gershem was concerned, that was a non sequitur, but Windsock did have a point about demonizing the term "conspiracy theory." As if the official 9/11 report weren't a conspiracy theory as well.

But enough. It was time to look for a mystery for Anna. She didn't like the prim and proper Agatha Christie sort of whodunit but rather the antic cynicism of Patricia Highsmith where you could bet on the bad guy and have a chance of winning. He didn't know anything about contemporary mystery writers so he sought out one of the clerks for a recommendation.

"How about Pandora Stanford?" the neurasthenic Barnes and Noble girl suggested. "She writes international intrigue stuff with high society and dope dealers and lots of murders."

"That sounds like Hollywood."

"I don't think any of them are set in Los Angeles," the young woman said dubiously.

"No, I mean it sounds like a typical movie. I'm looking for something more twisted."

"Ahh, I understand. How about Medusa Wyatt?"

"What about Medusa Wyatt?"

"I'm sorry, I really can't describe her stuff without blushing," said the young woman with a mischievous grin who wasn't even slightly red in the face.

"Anything else?"

"Let's see. There's a new Kevin Bartelme out called 'The Tin Hat'. I heard it's kind of creepy."

"I think I'll try the what's-her-name, the Medusa Wyatt," said Ted and the deal was done. The book was called "Taking Stock" and apparently got all kinky on Wall Street.

❖

32

The dress rehearsal at the theatre, which the rental agents had graciously allowed Edward Smith to rechristen The Mason, though Sylvia thought the original Herpetarium had more cachet, rolled around neither sooner nor later than anyone anticipated. They were all prepared and they all needed more time. They were not going to get more time and whatever preparation they'd done would have to suffice.

The players straggled in around seven in the evening fully prepared to go all night if necessary and donned their various 1950's wear, mostly simple suits for the men and flouncy dresses with petticoats a la Doris Day for the woman with Sylvia supervising. Studs Zenith complained that suits made it look like they were going to a funeral.

"Remember, these people were complete squares," Sylvia chided him. "They didn't call Alan Greenspan the Undertaker for nothing."

The women were much happier with their costumes, twirling

around in their fulsome skirts and trying on different hats.

"I'm wearing this one," said Deirdre holding up a velvet beret with a veil. "I can't believe people actually wore this stuff. It's like Halloween."

"You were just a gleam in your grandfather's eye when the ladies dressed like that," Argyle waxed nostalgic. For some reason, Sylvia had dressed him as a cowboy with a string tie and Tony Lama boots. After all, Frank O'Conner had played bit parts in Westerns in his Hollywood salad days. "Getting through all those petticoats and garter belts was quite a challenge for the young men of the time. Even a very dexterous fellow like myself had to struggle."

"You're not that old, Argyle," Smith pointed out. "You were a baby in the fifties."

"Haven't you heard of infantile sexuality and the polymorphous perverse?" Argyle defended himself.

"The perverse part I can see," Smith allowed. "The rest is just Freudian quackery."

"You're in denial, Edward," Argyle sighed. "A session or two on the couch would do you a world of good."

"I hope you don't mean the casting couch," Sylvia scolded.

"No comment. Not one more word out of me," said cowboy Argyle.

Anna, who had already put on her Ayn Rand costume, a black pencil dress and a cigarette holder, was reading Ted's present, which she'd started on the subway. The story was about a kleptomaniac female Wall Street broker who gets her jollies stealing exactly one cent from every trade, which nobody ever notices. That is until she gets a threatening phone call from an anonymous woman who wants to meet for lunch and that was as much as Anna had read before Gershem interrupted her.

"Don't you think you should be going over your lines with Studs?" he asked.

"Why bother? I know mine. Do I have to give him an acting lesson?"

"How's the book?"

"I'm not sure yet. I've only just started. God, you look silly."

Gershem, in his canary yellow leisure suit with a maroon paisley scarf, took her opinion as a compliment. "I do, don't I? But it feels right, like I want to do the Frug."

"Whatever on earth that was. Weren't the Nixon girls always frugging?"

"Yes indeed. I believe one of them even tried to frug with Bonnie Prince Charles."

"Stop talking dirty."

It was soon time for Gershem's initial start turn where he and his new wife Amalia are interviewed by reporter Deirdre and the three of them acquitted themselves without any obvious hitches.

"Well done," said applauding Edward. "An opening for the rest of you to live up to."

And then it was on to the real red meat of the matter with Studs and Anna strutting their stuff. It was no exaggeration to say that she blew the weatherman right off the proscenium. Anyone who wasn't on stage was dazzled by her performance and the actors playing opposite were obliged to step up their games in determined, but more often than not, futile efforts to keep up with her.

"Wow!" was all that Smith could manage as one jaw dropping scene followed another to the bang-up climax and Gershem's epilogue, which he pulled off with properly ridiculous aplomb. "Gosh, you guys, I hope you didn't leave it all here in rehearsal," he gushed. "Do it like that again and we've got a hit!" And they all had to agree.

In this warm atmosphere of self-congratulation, even the Happy Shadow, up in his lone perch in the balcony, had to admit that the whole thing had been a very enjoyable theatre experience. Not that anyone was asking his opinion.

Ted and Anna took a cab back up the west side and he sang her praises the whole way. "You have no idea how good you were. You carried the whole thing,"

Summoning up as much modesty as decency allowed, she conceded, "I did, didn't I? I told you those people are a bunch of amateurs. Except you, of course. I just hope they don't make me look bad opening night."

"Don't worry. Once the audience gets a load of you, nobody will be paying any attention to the other actors. You own it, baby."

"Oh, Ted, you're such a sweetie," she shnuzzled up to him. "Can baby have some candy when we get home?"

"Baby can have anything she wants."

When the Smiths left the theatre after all the others, Edward was exultant. Sylvia not so much, but then she had all that jealousy to overcome. Anna Bunch was obviously a much better actress than she was, but she tried not to let her envy show and agreed with her husband that they might very well have a hit on their hands.

"I don't understand why Junius didn't show up," said Edward. "I said he wanted to see the rehearsal."

"Publicists will say anything their clients want to hear. It's their job. Besides, he's probably busy."

Then from out of the shadows stepped Gunner Black. "Mistress, I know I'm here without your permission but I have to talk with you," he whined.

"You worm!" she snarled. "How dare you approach me outside of business hours?! What is it?"

Black timorously waved her over out of Edward's earshot and whispered, "I have to use the facilities again."

"You have the key," she said quietly. "Just let me know." Then she barked, "You vermin! You filth! Get out of my sight before I throttle you!"

The hulking mercenary skittered off like a shamed child and disappeared around the corner.

Ordinarily, Edward wouldn't have been particularly curious, but the Calvin Card connection was too obvious to ignore. He hadn't mentioned Card to his wife and didn't intend to but Black's appearance complicated things.

"What did he want?" he asked.

"What he always wants," she said without missing a beat, "To be chastised and humiliated."

"For free?"

"He made an appointment." Which was more or less true, but it didn't do much to allay Smith's uneasiness.

"Charge him double for bothering us on the street," he snorted. "And how did he know you were here anyway?"

"No idea."

They got a cab and no more was said about Gunner Black. Rather they discussed the production. They were both reasonably confident that their cast could pull it off but the live show is unforgiving. There are no second chances once the curtain goes up. A bad movie actor might go through dozens of takes before there is some semblance of a convincing performance, but the stage director can't yell, "Cut! Do it again!" in the middle of a performance and that's why so many theatre directors don't even go to their own productions. The temptation to stop the whole thing in its tracks might overwhelm them.

Before we go any further, perhaps it would be a good time to examine the whole murky history and practice of the dramatic arts. In the theatre, we are not merely asked but permitted to accept an obvious sham as real, just as the actors are given license to pretend that they are someone other than they actually are. The more convincing their performance, that is, the more effective they are in making the audience suspend its disbelief, the more they are admired and acclaimed. This peculiar art of dissembling has its roots in ancient ritual and has been legitimized in every culture where it has flourished as an acceptable form of deception. Not that it has always been socially approved; Shakespeare's Globe Theatre had to be located outside of London because the law forbade any theatrical performance within the city limits. Furthermore, when the Puritans came to power some years later, they closed it down completely. Stage acting was looked upon with great suspicion by the authorities, both secular and religious, precisely because it was deceitful and actors were viewed as a generally disreputable lot, treading a very thin line between providing mere distraction for the mob and promoting blasphemy and sedition.

Our own age, however, holds no such qualms and has elevated theatrical performance to dizzying, unparalleled heights. When a movie actor or game show host can be elected to the highest office in the land, all the world has indeed become a stage and we are all of us encouraged to respect and emulate the great dissemblers of our time. Presentation is everything and it must appear as sincere and genuine as a movie actor's tears. Politicians, salesmen, television journalists, talk show hosts, stock market touts, even robber barons must cultivate an image and manner that, in con man parlance, "gets over" on their credulous audience. When the entire elite of the society is required to behave as if they were putting on a raree show, the public they are pitching must be excused if they begin to regard play acting as perfectly normal and conduct their daily business in an environment where nobody believes anybody and it's strictly every con man for himself. If the President is a liar, so what? Who isn't?

Is the cynicism this ethos of deception engenders harmless or highly dangerous? Nobody knows because there's never been a historical precedent, but we're about to find out. That's for sure.

❖

33

When Barry Breen woke up in Rino Matsui's bed, which he usually did lately, she handed him a cup of green tea and informed him, "Professor Gershem called and cancelled tomorrow's seminar. I guess we know why."

"We do?" asked puzzled, still half asleep Breen.

"The play's tomorrow night and we're going. I already bought the tickets."

"But we don't even know he's in it."

"If he's not, at least we get to do something else besides interview nuts or watch TV."

"You may or may not have a point there," Breen agreed with himself.

"I read up on this Ayn Rand. She's very popular. Have you read her books?"

"Uh, no. I don't really know anything about her. There was this girl I knew in high school who thought "*The Fountainhead*" was really cool but she was sort of a dork Junior Chamber of Commerce type."

"Ayn Rand was a major supporter of big business."

"Why does big business need support? Don't they have enough already? They own the government and everything else. They already charge us for water. Next it will be air."

"So you think big business is a conspiracy?" she teased him.

"It is, indeed, and a fucking evil one at that," he said grabbing her wrist and pulling her into bed. "But not as evil as me!"

What followed is best left to the imagination.

Barry Breen wasn't the only one wakened that morning with a question. "Mr. Smith? This is Serena Lepich from Tootie Wookums' office. You still have an outstanding bill for services rendered…"

"Listen, you silly twat!" grumpy Smith roared into the phone. "You tell Mr. Wookums to take that bill and shove it up his ass!"

Mrs. Lepich, who was accustomed to this sort of abuse from Wookums' legions of dissatisfied clients, responded coolly, "There's no need to get excited. Mr. Wookums is willing to settle for eighty percent of his usual fee. How about that?"

Smith slammed down the receiver. "The nerve! That fucking Tootie Wookums should be paying my legal costs for dragging me into court!"

"You're right," Sylvia agreed. "I'll send him a bill."

"No, no, don't do that. They'll find not you're not a lawyer."

"But I did have expenses – dry cleaning, makeup, new shoes."

"This isn't funny. I know he's going to pull something when the show opens."

"Let him. Have you spoken to Junius?"

"Yes I have. He wants fourteen seats for the bigwig critics he's bringing along. The strange thing is he wants them scattered all over the theatre."

"It's not strange at all. They probably all hate each other and he doesn't want them to be uncomfortable."

"Hmm, I hadn't thought of that. Maybe you're right."

Ted Gershem and Anna Bunch, having just supposited their morning opium, were sitting at his kitchen table in their tin hats discussing the Spuyten Duyvil Trust which Anna had just read in the paper was being investigated for certain financial irregularities. The always demure Times was maddeningly vague about just what these possible crimes might be and what had instigated the investigation in the first place. Something to do with channeling money to certain unnamed people in return for certain undisclosed services.

"I wonder if Alvin knows about this?" Ted mused as the phone rang.

"Ted, it's Alvin Spurtz. Have you seen the paper?"

"I was just looking at the article. Do you have any idea what's going on?"

"It seems the Trust had been funding some pretty shady characters. I don't have any details but we have to categorically deny that we know anything. We don't, do we?"

"I certainly don't."

"I'm not saying you do. Of course you don't. We have to put up a united front. The reputation of the department, the whole university is at stake!"

"Calm down, Alvin. If we lose the grant, well, that's just the way things go."

There was a pause at the other end. "Who said we were losing the grant?"

"Nobody. I thought that was what you were worried about."

"Well, I am. But it's much more than that. We can't be swept into some scandal that we don't know anything about!"

"Let's keep it that way. The less we know the better. You better call Alan and Conrad if you haven't already."

"Right. I'll get back to you if I hear anything more."

"Yes, do that, Alvin."

"What was that all about?" said Anna.

"That was my boss. He seemed very nervous," said Ted flatly

"Maybe you should give him some opium and a tin hat. It certainly works for me."

"Now there's an idea," he had to agree.

Rhoda Memberman, who was neither loaded on opium nor wearing a tin hat, was even more upset than Alvin Spurtz by the

Times article. "I think it's time we had a little talk about exactly what you're doing at the An Idea Grows in America Institute, Hyman. And don't give me any of your 'classified' bullshit," she growled.

Furtive Hyman Ryman, who eschewed not only the limelight but any sort of light at all being turned on his activities was in a state bordering on panic but seemed to the ignorant outside observer to be cool as a cucumber. "I assure you, Rhoda, that the Institute isn't involved in anything illegal." This was a blatant lie since almost everything he did involved ignoring several amendments to the Constitution as well as all sorts of state and local laws pertaining to privacy rights. "And what about your abnormal psychology seminar project?" he defended himself by deflecting. "Your program takes money from Spuyten Duyvil. Are you doing anything criminal?"

"Maybe. Maybe I'm an accessory to all the crimes you won't tell me about."

Misdirection was all he had left. "Okay, I'll tell you, but you have to promise to never repeat this to anyone."

"I won't," said Rhoda eagerly. "Tell me."

"The An Idea Grows in America Institute is a front for the biggest bookmaking operation in the country. We take bets from anywhere anytime on anything. It's my job to the crunch the numbers and make sure the house – that's the Institute – always wins."

"You are such a bad liar," Rhoda snorted. She didn't realize that what he had just told her was an almost perfect metaphor for what he really did in terms of information gathering and analysis.

"If you think I'm a liar, please don't ask me questions I can't answer anyway," he whined.

"You're upset," she pounced. "You're on the verge of a nervous breakdown, sweetie. It's obvious to a psychologist like me."

"An abnormal psychologist like you," he retorted. And the subject was dropped for the time being.

Actually, as it turned out, no one had anything to worry about. The only thing the Spuyten Duyvil Trust had done was provide a small grant to the Perestroika Foundation, an organization that favored a better relationship between the United States and Russia. That, of course, was enough to set the CIA/Mossad controlled media to

THE TIN HAT

frothing at the mouth about this imminent danger to right thinking, petrodollar supporting, full spectrum dominance imperialists across the nation – all twenty of them at the Project for the New American Century. This gale of bluster from the Ministry of Truth would blow over by the next morning when a bulbous, stinking drunk, southern senator took center stage with his proposal to rename *piroshki*s "Freedom Buns."

Coincidentally, the Happy Shadow just happened to be eating a *piroshki* at a Russian restaurant on 20th Street, happily unaware that his lunch was about to be relabeled. As he sat there surrounded by the incomprehensible chatter of the Russian emigres who frequented the place, his thoughts turned to the premiere of "Ayn and Nate" the next evening. Ayn was a Russian. Had she liked *piroshki*s? She'd lived in New York. Maybe she'd eaten a *piroshki* right here where he was sitting. Right in the same chair. He imagined he could smell her, touch her, and a few other things.

At the Mason Theatre, not very far uptown from where the Happy Shadow was eating, Edward and Sylvia Smith arrived early to get ready for the final cast and staff meeting scheduled that evening. There were a few blocking and set change problems to work out, but, all in all, they had every reason to be confident that things would run smoothly, which of course meant that they were thoroughly convinced that everything would go wrong and they had an impending disaster on their hands.

"I'm so nervous," Edward whined. "I hope it doesn't show. I don't want to give anyone else the jitters."

"You'll do fine. Just tell everyone how great they are and how they can't possibly go wrong," was Sylvia's advice. "Maybe we should cook up some sort of ritual, you know, where we all hold hands and shout, "Ganbatte!"

"What's that?"

"'Go for it' in Japanese."

"Why not just shout, 'Go for it'?"

"Ganbatte is more exotic. It's like our little secret."

"Yes, I see. That's a good idea."

When the cast and crew that Smith had hired were all

assembled, he took the stage and gave a little speech, a pep talk really. "We are gathered here today to mourn the departed... whoops, wrong speech!" He slapped his knee, got his laugh and continued. "If you're wondering why I asked you all here today, I can only say I don't really know myself. You've already done all the work and we have a show here that people will be talking about for a long time to come. We re going to be the toast of the town! The cat's pajamas! The bee's knees! All of our lives are going to change. We won't be the little amateur theatre group anymore. We'll be the cream in your coffee, the fruit in your mellow Jello, the talk of the Great White Way!"

"This isn't Broadway," Arthur Sachs pointed out.

"Don't be so literal minded, Arthur. It's New York! The center of the universe! With our names in lights!"

Which made grain-of-salt taking Ted Gershem remember an old tune that went, "There's a broken heart for every light on Broadway." He might have hummed it out loud but he kept quiet for fear that someone would get the joke.

"We are in the vanguard of players bringing serious drama back to the big stage! The audience is fed up with banal, saccharine schmaltz! They want real meat and we're going to give it to them! Right up the old..." Edward caught himself. "Sorry, sometimes I get carried away. But I'm excited! Aren't you?!"

They all laughed and cheered.

"Now I want all of you to come up here on stage and form a circle."

They all did so without complaint.

"Now I want you to all hold hands and repeat after me. Are you ready?"

"We're ready!" Studs Zenith whooped.

"Okay, let's do it!" Smith yelled. "GANBATTE!!"

"GANBATTE!! GANBATTE!!" his congregation sent up a clamor that echoed off every surface in the theatre, a rolling wave of infectious enthusiasm that set the air atingle.

"All right!" Smith applauded them. " Big day tomorrow! Let's all go home and get some sleep!"

Ted and Anna had other ideas. Since they were in the neighborhood they had decided to do something that neither of them, typical native New Yorkers that they were, had ever done before – go to the top of the Empire State Building.

"Edward's so nervous," said Anna as they walked down Fifth Avenue.

"With me opening the show he should be."

"Don't be silly. You're a natural. You are a psychoanalyst after all."

"That's what's wrong about the part. Analysts don't talk. They listen."

When they boarded the elevator to the observation deck with a bunch of real tourists, they were surprised at how old fashioned it was, an elevator from an old Hollywood movie. The tourists were all giddy about the possibility of the cable snapping, which the operator explained is exactly what happened in the aftermath of a plane crashing into the building in 1945. But not to worry. The woman in the elevator actually survived plunging seventy-five floors. Gershem wondered if this sort of grand guignol storytelling was part of every elevator operator's script or if this guy was just particularly morbid.

The observation deck was also pleasantly old fashioned with exposed wiring and those antique mounted binoculars.

"This is so cool," said Anna. "It makes me feel like you're Cary Grant in - what was that movie called?"

"'An Affair to Remember.' That would make you Deborah Kerr."

"How very elegant. She was English you know," said Anna apropos to nothing. "You know, views don't do anything for me anymore. And I'm afraid of heights."

"Well, aren't we romantic," Gershem teased her. "What would Cary and Deborah say?"

"You want to do a little improv?"

"Okay."

"Cary, I want you to take me, take me right here at the apex of the Manhattan skyline!" Anna demanded in the poshest of British accents,

"Hey there, old girl, what exactly do you mean by that?"

Gershem played the foil.

"Fuck me, Cary! Fuck me right her in front of everybody! I want the whole world to remember this affair!"

Anna was no shrinking violet and had failed to modulate her demands enough so that the other observers didn't hear every word she was saying.

"Hey there, it's not the mile high club, but go for it," one of the tourists wisecracked and Anna was ready for them.

"If you want to see more," she pulled out a stack of fliers from her purse, "you can come by and see me tomorrow night at the Mason Theatre right up the street. I promise you it will be fun for the whole family!"

The curious tourists were glad to take the fliers and the presence of real live theatre actors in their midst set them all abuzz. Two women even asked for autographs. For Anna the elevator descent was all feigned modesty and pushy promotion.

"I'll see you all tomorrow night!" she waved to her new fans as she and Ted hurried away to the west.

"Don't you think you're pushing this thing a bit far?" he took her to task.

"What's the matter with creating a little buzz?" Anna shot back. "You're such an introvert."

"Is that some sort of insult? It's the extraverts who make all the trouble in this world."

"What's with this 'vert' business anyway?" Anna wanted to know. "Is it all derived from pervert?"

"Hmm, it's from the Greek and they were all sissies and catamites," was Gershem's final word.

In an expansive mood, they decided to cab back uptown rather than take the train.

❖

34

The next morning was so full of alarming omens, it might have driven any soothsayer to distraction trying to decipher them. The stock market took a tumble, the President cancelled a golf date, a pop tart entered a convent, an oil pipeline burst in Pennsylvania, the temperature was 118 degrees in Phoenix, Arizona where a fleet of flying saucers had been spotted at dawn, a late night talk show host was arrested for public urination, the list went on and on. Aside from Akisha Lumumba's clairvoyant grandmother, no one paid much attention to these signs of impending disruption and despair and the late morning found Gershem and Anna at a coffee shop on Broadway going over their lines. Since they were never in the play together, they each had to take different parts to play off. Ted was playing Frank O'Conner in the scene they were doing when his bran muffin arrived at the table.

"Did my passion for Nathaniel come as a surprise for you, Cubbyhole?" Anna started off.

"It sure did, Fluff. But then you're full of surprises."

"I suppose that's my charm. Imagine a man half my age falling head over heels in love with me. Don't you think it's flattering?"

"Well, I guess it is. Could I ask you a favor, Fluff?"

"Of course, my darling."

"When you two do it, would it be okay if I watched?"

"Really, Frank, I think that would be most improper."

"Well, if that's the way you feel about it – "

"I never realized you were such a pervert, Frank. It actually makes you more interesting."

"You think so?"

"Oh my little Cubby Wubbyhole, I think you're jealous. Don't worry. I do love you, you know."

"Well, at least you're not throwing me out."

"I wouldn't dream of it, Frank. Who else would I have to humiliate? Now clean up the kitchen. We have guests coming."

Anna could not contain herself any longer and was first off the line as they both broke into raucous laughter, which attracted the attention of their fellow diners, the grey, hollowed out denizens of the coffee shop who appeared to be stuck in a George Tooker painting. These faded souls scowled at the two of them suspiciously as if good cheer were best not displayed in public. But who cared what they thought? They didn't even care what they thought.

Argyle, who actually was playing Frank O'Conner, was hunkered down in his east village hovel trying to forget his lines. As far as he was concerned, the way O'Conner was written was pure wuss, not a trace of bitterness or anger when Ayn shits all over him. Argyle himself wouldn't behave that way. He'd knock that bitch's block off, which was one of the several reasons there never had been a woman in his life. His own terministic screen did not include cohabitation with the female of the species or much other contact for that matter. Argyle liked to think that this aversion was his own choice but the fact was he simply had no game. Never had, and certainly never would at this late date. At his age, that was all water under the bridge. What he planned to do now was simply ad lib when the Anna woman spoke to him, catch her by surprise and see how she reacted. For example, when Ayn announces that she and Nate are having an affair, he was going to say, "If I ever catch you two in bed together, I'll kill you both." Now wouldn't that set her on her heels? What could she say? "Then we better kill you first." Of course, he was just fantasizing and would play the cuckold just as Edward wanted. After all, Smith certainly understood the part better than he did with Sylvia screwing everybody in town and all.

Deirdre, who was doubling up as the news reporter and Barbara in two different wigs, was studying her lines and wondering what she would do if her husband was having an affair with an older woman. The affair thing didn't bother her so much as the idea that he could find some old bag so attractive. What did that say about her? So she could understand her character's resentment, but hadn't Barbara two-timed Nate with Alan Greenspan? It was like stepping out on Studs Zenith for Arthur Sachs. Except Studs Zenith wasn't her cheating husband. He was more like a summer fling that would be over after the show closed, which of course might be right after it opened, which was that very evening. Studs called her his "sweetest little coke whore" when they made love. She wondered if he'd feel the same way if the show bombed.

These idle musings were interrupted by a call from her friend Amalia.

"Aren't you nervous? I sure am."

"Calm down, girl. It's not like you have a reputation to ruin," Deidre pointed out. "The only casting problems are Argyle and Arthur. Argyle plays a drunk so it doesn't matter if he fucks up and Arthur plays the nebbish he is. What could possibly go wrong?"

"I don't know. I've just got this feeling."

"Do your yoga. Calm down. Everything's going to be alright. Look on the bright side. After this we might actually be working actors."

"Which is more than most people we know," Amalia had to agree. "I've just got opening night jitters. I think I'll have a drink."

"Just one. Argyle is one drunk too many."

"So, how are things working out with Studs? You know I'm jealous."

"Well, I'm not. If you want to fuck him you better do it soon. I think he's going to dump the whole Downtown Illuminati right after the show."

"Really? It's okay with you?"

"Go ahead. Maybe he'll want to do both of us at once."

"Oh my. Does he have two dicks?"

They both laughed with the nervous glee of bad little girls realizing they weren't getting any younger.

Arthur Sachs, who couldn't get anyone to rehearse with him, had pinned up an official Federal Reserve portrait of Alan Greenspan next to his mirror to help him get into character and was making every effort to look as portentous as the worthy former Rand acolyte. He had never understood the irony in the script of the young Greenspan denouncing the whole Federal Reserve system and advocating that it be abolished. Arthur did not get the joke, which made him absurdly perfect for the part. He didn't have to work to maintain a straight face and his pompous line reading was bound to be one of the comic highlights of the show, though he himself would be surprised by the laughter and almost certainly take it the wrong way. Taking things the wrong way was what Arthur Sachs did and had been doing all his life and that was not about to change. So he stood before the mirror and spoke his lines from memory while he recorded the little soliloquy on his phone.

"If we accept that government intervention in monetary policy will always lead to disaster, we must be vigilant and make sure that no cabal within the Federal government ever attempts to dictate the value of currency and credit. Only the invisible hand of the free market can do that. Thank you."

He played it back and wrung his hands in despair. He sounded so wimpy! Nothing like the masterful Greenspan. He didn't know it, but he sounded just perfect.

"Do it again, do it again until you get it perfect," he mumbled to himself and kept at it for the better part of an hour. The result could hardly be improved upon.

Edward and Sylvia Smith were at the Mason going over the final plans for the premiere with Junius Flatmeat whose bubbly enthusiasm was contagious.

"We're going to knock 'em dead!" he enthused. "Dead, dead, dead! You know what I mean?"

"Well, I hope a few critics survive to give us rave reviews," said Sylvia., whose initial impression of Junius as a perfect dungeon candidate had been scotched when she'd subtly broached the punishing aspects of a career in the theatre.

"Whaddaya mean?" Junius had napped back. "You're not a masochist or something, are you? Those people are sick."

But back to the present where Edward was pontificating. "Players and the painted stage took all my love, and not those things they were emblems of. Willy Yeats wrote that."

"Who the fuck is Willy Yeats?" Junius demanded. "Never heard of him."

"No, I don't suppose you have," said Edward drily. "Now where were we? The red carpet."

"Right," said Junius, "I made a deal with this cousin of mine who owns a limo company in Queens. He's providing the carpet, which I brought along with me, and six limos to make it look like the real swells are showing up. For a nominal fee, of course."

Smith was getting used to Flatmeat's "nominal fees" or "cake icing" as Junius called these extras, but his counting house wife was not pleased by the tab Junius was running up above and beyond the contract.

"What does that fatso think?" Sylvia complained. "We're made of money?"

So, as a small herd of interns from the NYU theatre program installed a moth-eaten red rug outside the entrance to the Mason and attended to all the last minute details of the production, the sun shone down on a job well done and all seemed right with the world.

Edward put his arm around Sylvia's shoulder as they stood in the glare of a spotlight being tested, and murmured: "We did it, baby. We did it." They looked much as Ayn Rand might have appeared standing by her own man on a mountaintop where they could see for miles and miles and miles.

"We did, didn't we," Sylvia agreed, proudly shnuzzling up to her husband.

Junius Flatmeat watched them from the cheap seats in back and contemplated the surprise he had in store, the move that would really put the show over the top. The public would never know, but Junius was about to become legendary in P.R. circles. Well, quietly legendary, honor among thieves and all that, but the people in the know would be lined up to contract for his services after this all-or-nothing, make-or-break premiere. He was damn sure of that.

❖

35

In a show of sisterly solidarity, Rhoda Memberman had called Rino Matsui and asked if she and Barry would like to share a cab downtown to "Ayn and Nate". Rino was not keen on the idea but what could she say?

"Next they'll be inviting us over for dinner," said Barry when he heard this unwelcome news. "I just want to let you know that being all buddy-buddy with Hyman Ryman is out of the question. The guy gives me the creeps."

"Just be polite," Rino admonished him. "It's only for this one evening,"

"Famous last words," Breen groused.

So, promptly at seven, they all met up in front of the university and hailed a cab, Hyman Ryman took the seat next to the driver, a bald man with a fake "New Yawk" accent, the kind you hear in old movies. They told him where they were going and the cab suddenly light up with flashing lights and the driver announced, "Hey there! I'm Ben Bailey and you're in the Cash Cab!"

"Oh, my gawd!" Rhoda squealed. "I love your show, Mr. Bailey!"

"Well, let's see if I can make you love it even more! Are you ready to play?"

Hyman Ryman answered every single trivia question that Bailey put to them on the drive downtown and they got out of the cab four hundred dollars richer.

Ted and Anna, who had not been so lucky in their choice of cabs, were getting their makeup done backstage at the Mason, when Sylvia walked into the dressing room. She took one look at Gershem in his leisure suit and marveled.

"Oh my, so Hollywood. That scarf is just perfect. And look at you," she turned to Anna. "You really are Ayn Rand."

"Of course I am," said Anna in her thickest Ayn accent. "Who else would I be?"

They all laughed and Sylvia got down to business. "You're on first, Ted, with Deirdre and Amalia so try to open big."

"What do you mean, 'big'?" Gershem wanted to know.

"Pompous, grandiose, puffed up."

"Just pretend you're lecturing one of your classes," was Anna's deadpan suggestion.

Outside the theatre, Junius Flatmeat was directing traffic as the limos arrived and disgorged formally dressed actors from another Retalitron booking agency and the paparazzi clicked away.

"Wow," said Rhoda Memberman as the Cash Cab pulled up in front of the theatre. "Look at all these people." And they themselves were among the privileged ticket holders to stroll into the Mason on red carpet and be ushered to their seats, the cheap seats in back in their case.

Edward Smith, no authoritative Grand Poobah tonight and unable to stand the tension of the dressing room, had left his wife to act as stage manager and taken up a position in the balcony from whence cries of "Author! Author!" after the performance could be acknowledged graciously or he could go entirely unnoticed if the response were a chorus of boos and catcalls. He did not notice the other occupant of the balcony, but the Happy Shadow certainly noticed this intrusion into his dark space and was none too happy about it. But what could he do? Push Smith over the railing into the orchestra? That's what he felt like doing but he couldn't quite bring himself to act on the impulse.

Below them, the members of the audience were buzzing with anticipation because their employer Junius Flatmeat had told them to buzz and it sounded something like a beehive. Gershem's students were puzzled by this behavior.

"Why is everybody making that sound?" Rhoda wondered. "Is that some sort of theatre crowd thing I don't know about?" She tapped on the man's shoulder in front of her. "Excuse me..."

"Zzzzzzzzzzzz," he replied, and the evening was still young!

There was no curtain so the Mason's stage was blacked out prior to the opening where Gershem and the two young women were already ensconced in the Old Nate Los Angeles apartment set in the left corner. This is where he'd do his voice-overs for the duration after his opening scene.

"Jesus," Deirdre whispered. "The place is sold out. I didn't expect that."

"Does it scare you?" Ted asked.

"A little."

"Just wait till the lights go up and you can't see them," he advised. "Then it's just another rehearsal." For all his reassurance, Gershem was pretty flustered himself.

Anna, on the other hand, was ecstatic. "Look at all those people!" she gushed sotto voce from her spot in the wings. "All for little me!"

"They're here to see me," Studs reminded her. "I'm the only real star here."

"We'll see about that, sonny, after the encores."

The house lights dimmed and the stage light suddenly went up with the spotlight on Gershem, with Amalia playing the reporter and Deirdre doing his wife Devers.

"My God!" Rhoda gasped. "It's Professor Gershem!"

"Of course," Gershem began, "as the twentieth century's foremost intellectual, Ayn Rand's legacy will live on in the universities and think tanks where other great minds who were influenced by her philosophy will carry on with the core of her teachings."

"How would you summarize those teachings, Mr. Branden?" Amalia prompted him.

"Well, it's a bit complicated to attempt in a sound bite, but the short answer would have to the supremacy of reason, meritocracy, and free market economics."

And so the play rolled on without any egregious mishaps. Anna, of course, stole the show with her inspired comic performance and things were cruising along to a highly satisfactory conclusion when something unexpected happened. Right at the end of Ayn's impassioned curse on Nathaniel, when she hopes his balls shrivel up and his cock falls off, a man in the audience stood up, shouted, "I hope your titties get caught in a wringer, you bitch!" and threw a tomato.

"She's making fun of Ayn Rand!" someone else shouted. "Kill her!" These outbursts were immediately followed by a barrage of overripe fruit and vegetables directed at the players on stage who quickly fled to the safety of the wings. The provocateurs in the audience precipitated a melee with people punching each other and generally behaving in a most disgraceful manner that had Edward Smith wringing his hands and shouting to the heavens, 'Bacchus! Why have you forsaken me!!" from the balcony.

Eventually, the "police", more of Flatmeat's actor hirelings, rushed in and set on the audience with billy clubs and rubber truncheons.

Our three students and one think tank swain, who had taken advantage of their rear seats in the theatre to quickly flee from the mob without injury, stood outside in wide-eyed wonder as frantic television crews rushed in from all sides to cover the spectacle. Right in front of them, a middle-aged man with a walking stick was using it to beat a younger man in a blue suit lying on the sidewalk.

"I'LL KILL YOU!! I'LL KILL YOU!!" the man with the stick howled as he flailed away.

"I didn't do anything! I just came to serve you a subpoena!" the younger man protested. "I even bought a ticket!"

Rino Matsui thought the man with the stick bore a striking resemblance to the Magus of the Tabernacle of Lucifer and indeed he did. Real police had to drag enraged Edward Smith off whining, cowering Tootie Wookums who cried out in terror: "Stop him! I have very expensive dental work!"

Backstage, the players were doing the best they could to keep calm, but the pandemonium reigning in the orchestra seating was certainly exciting in a morbid sort of way.

"God," said Anna, "it's like we're in Paris in the twenties when the avant-garde had to go through this sort of abuse all the time."

Gershem, whose leisure suit was spattered with tomato juice, waxed equally philosophical. "I take this tomato as a compliment. I had no idea we were that provocative."

"That wasn't any kind of spontaneous reaction," said Sylvia. "It was a set-up. We've been getting threats for weeks."

"Why didn't you tell us that?" Studs Zenith demanded.

"We didn't take them seriously."

Just at that moment, Junius Flatmeat bustled in. "Is anybody hurt?"

"No, everybody's fine," said Sylvia.

"Really? That's too bad. I didn't mean that. Don't listen to me. Now listen to me. The press is all over the place. They're going to want to talk to you. They're probably going to want you to go on the morning shows."

It began to dawn on Sylvia that it wasn't the Ayn Rand freaks who had disrupted the show. It was Junius Flatmeat. She should have been angry but she wasn't that dense. The fat fuck had guaranteed a sold out show for months!

"Hey there, Ted," Bob Applewhite poked his head into the dressing room. "Tough crowd."

"Hey there, yourselves! What are you doing here?" Gershem greeted Bob and Marta as if they were the only people in the world he wanted to see. And they were.

"We came down to see you," said Bob, "and it was certainly worth the price of the tickets."

Marta clamped onto Gershem's arm and spoke to Anna. "You must be Ted's lady friend. I think you were just fabulous on stage."

"Well, thank you very much. And you're the ones who bring us candy."

"That's us," Marta simpered. "Bob and Marta."

"Well, what say we go for a drink?" Gershem suggested.

Junius was not happy about Ayn Rand disappearing. "Hey, Anna, you've got to meet the press."

"Don't worry. I'll run the gauntlet right now. Set up the morning show thing and call me. I'll be there."

This suddenly highly professional Anna was all right with Junius. "Aces, sweetie. You'll hear from me. By the way, you really were great."

"Thank you, Junius, but I bet you say that to all the girls," said Anna in her Ayn Rand voice and everybody laughed.

Junius wasn't the only one who had thoroughly enjoyed this grand debacle. From his perch in the balcony, the Happy Shadow had watched the whole thing unfold into chaos with the greatest enthusiasm and his close-up view of Edwards Smith's wretched despair had only served to further enhance his theatre experience. He finally understood what the twin gods of comedy and tragedy were all about! It should be noted that the Happy Shadow was not a Broadway aficionado or a fan of performing exhibitions of any kind, but if they were all like what he had just witnessed at the Mason, he would gladly sneak into every show in town.

Ranting Edward Smith, who had been briefly taken into custody, was allowed to leave in the company of his wife who had a business relationship with one of the detectives on the scene.

"Let that man go," she had commanded and the detective had immediately taken her order.

"Are we still on for Thursday, mistress?" he whispered.

"We'll see about that, you worm," she purred. "Edward! Come with me! And behave yourself!"

"I really gave that Tootie Wookums the old what for!" said Smith proudly. "He can take his subpoena and shove it up his ass! After what his people did tonight, I'm going to sue that sonuvabitch – "

"Edward! Just calm down and listen to me," she demanded as she pushed him into a cab.

"Why are you taking this so lightly?" Smith whined. "He just ruined my only shot at the big time! My name in lights! My Tony award! All down the drain!" he wailed.

"Would you kindly shut up?" said exasperated Sylvia. "It's not as bad as you think." Then she patiently explained what had really happened. "We'll be sold out for months and you'll win the Tony on a sympathy vote. 'Brave director stands up to mob! Refuses to compromise artistic integrity!' That's what they'll all be saying."

"Hmm, you might be right," Smith conceded. "And you think Junius set this all up."

"I'm pretty sure he did. You should have seen him in the dressing room after the show. He practically took a bow."

"What about Tootie Wookums? He slapped me with a

subpoena."

"Really? That's even better. You can threaten to have him arrested for incitement to riot."

The night was just beginning for Junius Flatmeat. He'd already booked Studs Zenith on Good Morning America and he was working on the Today show for Anna Bunch. The Post had given him the front page and one of their opinion hacks was going to write a ringing defense of Ayn Rand while at the same time deploring mob violence, even though there were some "very fine people" in the mob. Junius had set the carnival in motion and it was going to be a smooth ride to the top. He'd have the show booked on Broadway in less than a month.

❖

36

Ted Gershem had sent Anna off at five o'clock in the morning to the television studio where she was booked to appear for an interview with a congenial young blonde woman wearing one of those weird dresses seen only on female television personalities. Ted did not know that yet since Anna was still in make-up when he turned on the TV to catch her act. He, of course, had not been invited to be on television and wouldn't have accepted the invitation if he had.

"Is she on yet?" Marta called out from the kitchen where she was making coffee. The Applewhites had stayed over after a long late evening of opium and champagne and no one was feeling any pain.

"Any minute! Right after the weather!" Gershem answered.

Bob Applewhite joined him in front of the television. "Wow. Old Edward really hit the jackpot. He probably won't be dealing any more weed."

Marta came in with the coffee on a tray and they all focused on the flickering screen that was just about to deliver a fair approximation of Anna. "She must be nervous," said Marta.

"She doesn't get nervous," said Ted. "She loves the limelight."

A commercial ended and it was on to, "Dawn deVere, talking this morning with Anna Bunch, star of the new play 'Ayn and Nate'. So, Anna, welcome to the Today show."

"Thank you for having me, Dawn," said Anna, who was wearing a demure skirt and blouse ensemble. They were seated facing each other on dining table chairs.

"Your opening last night is the talk of the town…"

"Not for the reasons I expected," said Anna.

"No, I guess not. From what I heard the audience went wild in all the wrong ways. What was that like? It must have been humiliating."

"Humiliating? Are you joking? Honestly, I was flattered. The play is meant to provoke and it certainly delivered."

Miss deVere, whose not so subtle put-down had fallen flat, instantly went on the defensive. "You mean you expected trouble?"

"People have been threatening the production since it was publicly announced. I really had no idea how crazy these Ayn Rand fans are. I have no idea what they were so excited about."

DeVere was startled. "But you're playing Ayn Rand…"

"Quite faithfully, I hope. Come see the show."

"I think I will." Dawn turned to the camera. "That's 'Ayn and Nate' playing at the Mason right now." Then back to Anna. "I know what happened last night must have been very trying, so a double thank you for joining us here this morning, Anna."

"It was my pleasure."

Junius was waiting as she walked off the set. "You were great, Anna. That bitch tried to high side you and got smacked right upside the wig. You've really got what it takes! I'm hungry. Let's have breakfast on Edward's dime."

"What about Studs? Don't you have to check how he's doing over at ABC?"

"He's a pro, he's doing fine. Besides, he's just a weatherman.

You're a star!"

Back at Ted's apartment, Marta and Bob gave Anna a round of applause.

"She was so good! 'Humiliating? I was flattered,'" Marta vamped.

"I'm sure it will go to her head and she'll leave me for Hollywood," Gershem chuckled.

"What's so funny?" said Marta. "She might, you know."

Bob laughed. "Yeah, it might get all tragic like Arthur Miller and Marilyn Monroe, the egghead and the showgirl."

"Are you going on tonight?" Marta asked Ted.

"I guess so. Nobody's called to say it's been cancelled."

"Can you get us in?"

"I'm sure I can arrange something. You can even watch from the wings if you like."

Which is exactly what they'd have to like. Junius was right about one thing. There is no such thing as bad publicity and the show was now booked solid for its entire one month run.

As a professional courtesy, Studs Zenith had been allowed to bring Deirdre along to the ABC show and be interviewed together, though she could only speak when spoken to. Sort of like Old Nate and Devers. Studs was the big name on the marquee, after all, and the producers didn't want to waste time on some nobody ingénue. Deirdre was nevertheless thrilled to be on TV, if only in a supporting role.

Since Studs didn't actually "get" the Nate part he was playing, since he thought Sylvia's "Ayn Rand freaks" were people who didn't like Ayn Rand, he blandly assured the interviewer that the rioters must have been "violent free market opponents". Starstruck Deirdre did not bother to contradict him and this interview worked even better than Anna's because it drew in all the Rand proponents. Even the real Alan Greenspan and his wife bought tickets, along with nitwit congressional twins Rand Paul and Paul Ryan. Junius was, of course, all agog. Important men, men of substance were going to the show! Just imagine the publicity!

And the Smiths, flush with seeing their name on the covers of all three New York dailies, were practically ecstatic.

"I can't believe it!" Edward exulted. "I can't be true. It must be a dream! Pinch me! Wake me up! Better still, take me down to the dungeon and beat me!"

"Really, Edward," Sylvia scolded. "We've got a show tonight."

The Happy Shadow hadn't been invited to do any interviews, even though he'd had the best seat in the house to watch the whole thing unfold. But then, if someone had asked him to comment, he probably wouldn't have shown up on video anyway.

❖

37

By noon that day, Rhoda Memberman and Hyman Ryman had finished their mit Schlags at Kaffeeklatch and were walking Petunia along the Hudson River.

"I really don't know what to say to Professor Gershem. It was a small part, but I thought he was very good."

"You don't have to say anything. He doesn't even know you were there."

"I heard that woman friend of his who played Ayn Rand was on television this morning."

"You heard? You were watching it with me."

"But I was otherwise occupied," Rhoda leered and batted her eyelashes. "I'm going to have to say something to Professor Gershem. Rino and Barry are bound to let the cat out of the bag."

Rino and Barry were not bound to let the cat out of the bag and were discussing the situation at that very moment.

"I don't think we should bring it up," was Barry's opinion.

"But that blabbermouth Rhoda is bound to say something,"

Rino pointed out.

"Well, let her go first. You can just blame your reticence on Japanese reserve."

"How about you?"

"Under your influence, I have absorbed the natural quiet good manners of the mysterious east."

Arthur Sachs didn't know what to think about all this brouhaha. His only concern was that old Alan Greenspan was going to watch him perform young Alan Greenspan. Arthur wasn't old so he had to imagine what it would be like to watch someone play him at the age of twelve. What would he think of that? Not much probably. He didn't like child actors anyway.

All of this was of no interest to the principals in the unfolding public relation melodrama. Junius Flatmeat, who had very little patience for improvisation, had already arranged for real security guards at the evening performance just to make sure no one tried to tamper with his script. The show would go on, every critic in town would be there, and they had all been sufficiently greased to be very kind indeed.

However, he who plans too far ahead is bound to be confounded by events beyond his foresight or control and the headlines were just about to be stolen by an addled adolescent who didn't actually exist who was just at that moment shooting up the Hook's Roost Elementary school, leaving a grisly trail of eighteen equally nonexistent dead children and three teachers before committing suicide. Anderson Cooper was already not on his way to interview school principal Anna Bunch and County Coroner Ted Gershem was preparing to meet the press in a video replay.

Happily unaware of the drama that was about to unfold, the Smiths were concentrating on their own theatre piece and planning for the triumphant evening ahead.

"Don't hide in the balcony tonight," said Sylvia. "You have to appear with the actors for the curtain call and standing ovation."

"Don't jump to conclusions," said Edward.

"Don't be a sourpuss. Modesty doesn't become you."

"You have a point. I am the greatest director the theatre has ever seen," he mocked her. The phone rang. It was Amalia.

"Have you seen the news?"

"Not in the last half hour," said Sylvia. "One does have to take a little time off to eat, do your nails and so on."

"You better turn on the television," said Amalia and hung up.

Now just imagine the Smiths' reaction when they turned on the news, and rather than seeing a blurb for "Ayn and Nate", were confronted with another production in which they'd been very much involved. You might have thought they'd be deliriously happy, as if they'd swept a doubleheader, but no. As they sat there in horror, as implication after implication began to pile up until all the ramifications were putting pressure on the ceiling, Edward could only sputter, "WHAT THE FUCK IS THIS?!"

And there was Sylvia, albeit in lady broadcaster mufti, right there on the screen interviewing Deirdre the distraught school teacher massacre survivor.

"I made all the children get inside the utility closet. We were packed in the there like sardines. Then I heard him come into the room. It's a miracle he didn't open that closet door," crestfallen Deirdre managed.

"OMIGOD!" aghast Sylvia shrieked.

The phone rang again and Sylvia answered it with some trepidation.

"Put Edward on," a muffled voice demanded and Sylvia handed her husband the phone.

"Hello, Edward, it's Calvin. "

"Listen here, you…"

"No, you listen here. Are you familiar with the phrase, 'terminate with extreme prejudice'? It's the unspoken part of your contract. Capiche?"

Smith was too stunned to answer.

"Your people did a great job, by the way, and there are plenty more roles where that one came from. Remember, if you try anything foolish, no one's going to believe you anyway. Another thing. GoFundMe accounts have been set up for all the participants and they're filling up very quickly. As for your theatre piece, the show must go off. You're stepping on some very important toes when you fuck with Ayn Rand. Ciao, baby."

When he put down the phone, Smith looked as if he'd just been run over by a truck but left miraculously intact.

"What's wrong?" Sylvia demanded. "Who was that?"

"Retalitron. We've got to cancel the show for tonight and keep our mouths shut."

"What are you talking about? We've got to go public with this!"

"I don't think that's a good idea."

"What do you mean? They used us! This shooting business is all a sham!"

"Yeah, well they just threatened to kill us if we say anything."

"Can they do that? Do they think they can get away with this?"

"Do you want to find out?"

Smith spent the next few hours watching the news and ascertained that out of all the Player Station actors, only Ted Gershem and Arthur Sachs were even recognizable as themselves. The woman all wore wigs and could not be easily identified as anyone other than who they claimed to be. Studs Zenith had not participated so he was no problem, Sylvia wasn't in the play, and he himself could take over the Old Nate part. Who would pay any attention to the minor role of Alan Greenspan anyway? He had to call Calvin Card back and present his case for "the show must go on!"

Strangely enough, Card readily agreed that closing the performance down might attract more unwanted attention and told Smith he'd get back to him within the hour. What Edward must immediately do is call Ted Gershem and explain the situation.

Edward," Gershem acidly greeted him on the phone, "Anna and I have been trying to get a hold of you for hours."

"Listen, Ted, you have to understand that I had nothing to do with this. They bamboozled all of us, but we have to forge on as best we can."

"You've got to be joking. Have you caught my coroner act on the tube."

"That's my point. We just have to forge on without you. You, not Anna. She's not recognizable on the television coverage and neither is anyone else."

"Do you realize what you're asking, Edward?"

"Yes I do, Ted. Unfortunately, going public is not an option."

"I thought that might be the case," said Gershem dejectedly. "Are we in any immediate danger?"

"Not if we play ball, Ted, not if we play ball. By the way, the compensation for our silence is rather handsome."

"It better be," Gershem muttered.

Right after that, Calvin Card called back and gave Smith permission to go ahead. In fact, his superiors at Retalitron had never ordered a cancellation and Card's own unilateral display of his nonexistent power, was easy and quite enjoyable to rescind. I mean, Smith practically groveled in gratitude. Edward and Sylvia got on the phones and found that convincing their actors to go ahead with the show was much easier than they'd expected. In fact, watching themselves on television had given the cast members more confidence in their abilities. Studs Zenith even offered to provide an alibi for all of them to keep the production alive. After all, he could prove he'd been in town all day and his ride to Hollywood stardom wasn't going to be held up by a little hiccough along the road. Junius Flatmeat, whose recognition factor was confined to women's rear ends, was none the wiser and didn't have to be told anything.

The attitude in the Gershem/Bunch love-nest was not quite so sanguine and hadn't improved after a call from Alvin Spurtz.

"Ted, have you seen the news? You look just like the coroner at the Hook's Roost shooting."

"You think I look like a mortician, Alvin? I don't know how to take that."

"Just kidding, Ted, just kidding, but there is resemblance. Just turn on cable and see for yourself."

"I don't have cable, Alvin."

After he'd got rid of Spurtz, it was time to take on Anna.

"What are you going to do about this?" he asked her.

"I'm going to go on. If people recognize me as Ayn Rand, accent and all, they won't make any connection. It's a shame about you, but what can we do?"

"We could refuse to have anything to do with Edward Smith anymore."

"What good would that do? And don't get all moralistic on me.

What's done is done."

"That's easy for you to say, but I'm the one who's been compromised. I could lose my job. Not to mention the larger scandal of helping perpetrate this sham."

"But you're for keeping guns out of the hands of lunatics, Ted. Just think of it as working for a good cause."

"Keeping guns out of hands of fake lunatics by staging fake events is what we worked on. It's called propaganda, Anna."

"Oh really, Ted, it's just an actor's job. There are plenty of hard up actors who would jump at the chance to do an N.R.A. commercial."

"So you think it's okay to snow the public if you believe in the cause. The ends justify the means."

"Don't get all bent out of shape about it, darling. Have some candy and relax."

Which is exactly what Gershem was thinking of doing anyway and it did make him feel better.

The only member of the cast who did not feel better was Arthur Sachs. Edward had called him and told him he could still play Alan Greenspan because nobody noticed him anyway. "You're a sort of black hole, Arthur," Smith had explained. "You simply don't shine."

That's certainly not what Arthur thought. He was convinced his performance on television as the grieving school neighbor was one of the highlights of the news broadcast. "I thought I did pretty well in the shooting thing," he groused.

"Of course you did, Arthur, of course you did, but we don't really want to bring that up in polite company, do we?"

"I guess not," said Arthur meekly, but inside he was boiling with rage. Something he'd done well, and Lord knows there weren't many of those, was being disparaged and relegated to the ash heap by Edward Smith, who added insult to injury by patronizing him!

"Well, see you at the theatre," said Smith.

"You sure will," said Arthur.

Coincidentally, just at that moment Rhoda Memberman was watching Sachs play good neighbor Eugene Pollack on the news and she recognized him.

"Isn't that the guy in the play?" she said to Hyman Ryman.

"The one who played Alan Greenspan?"

"I don't know. He looks sort of like him I guess."

"And that coroner we saw before. That's Professor Gershem for sure."

"Whatever you say. I think you're seeing things. Lots of people resemble someone else. People tell me I look just like Don Knotts."

"Who?"

"An old television actor."

"Who do you think I look like?"

"I don't know. Golda Meir."

For that, he got a good pillow bashing and the subject was dropped. Besides, she'd actually seen Gershem on the street that morning buying a newspaper when she was out walking Petunia. He couldn't be in two places at the same time, could he? She'd tried to catch up with him to ask about the play but constipated Petunia was taking some time doing her business and couldn't be interrupted.

Bob and Marta Applewhite, who had gone out that morning to make deliveries, were completely unaware of the Hook's Roost school shooting, and were looking forward to the evening performance at the Mason when they returned to Gershem's apartment in the late afternoon.

"So Ted," said Bob, "are you ready for another big night in the limelight?"

"Didn't you know? I was just Edward Smith's understudy. He's going on tonight." Gershem informed them. Apparently, they hadn't seen the news and maybe they wouldn't notice his appearance in another venue entirely.

"What about Anna?" asked dismayed Marta.

"Oh, she's going on," Gershem reassured. "We're all going to watch her, aren't we? From backstage."

"Well, yeah," said Bob. "That was the idea."

"Good. Anna's already at the theatre. What say we go out and get some Chinese before the show."

"Sounds good to me." said Marta brightly.

And off they went to King Wok where Wo Chung greeted them

in something like awe. "I saw you on TV, Mr. Ted. Terrible thing."

"Really?" Gershem cut him off. "I didn't know I was in any footage from the show. Don't worry yourself about it, Wo Chung. Everything's fine now."

"Okay, I don't worry. So sad."

After Wo Chung took their orders, Bob was curious about the waiter's distress. "How well do you know this guy? He seemed genuinely upset."

"I come here twice a week," Gershem explained. "For years."

"I see."

But that was not the end of it. When they were finished and asked for the check, Wo Chung's boss, Mrs. Lin, came to the table with a small charcoal brazier and some so-called Hell notes, the bogus currency used at Chinese funerals. These she burned, "For the children."

"Thank you, Mrs. Lin," Gershem squirmed. "It's over now. Better to forget." Then he quickly hustled the confused Applewhites out of the restaurant.

"What was that all about?" Marta wondered.

"Beats me," Ted shrugged. "The Chinese really are inscrutable, aren't they? Shall we head downtown?"

"Let's go back to your place and have some candy first," Bob suggested.

"Of course," Gershem agreed. "I've got to bring some along for Anna or she'll get cranky."

The Happy Shadow had once again secured his seat in the Mason's balcony and was hunkered down with a thermos of grape Kool-Aid laced with cyanide which he would drink very slowly during the course of the performance so as not to poison himself to death. He appreciated the breathless feeling of mild cyanosis but he was very careful not to pig out. He also liked the blue pallor it lent his skin, which may have had something to do with his invisibility. Anyway, he was eagerly anticipating this second version of opening night and wondering if it could challenge the first in sheer entertainment value. He was there to find out and so he would.

Anna was backstage going over her lines when Ted and the

Applewhites arrived with a large bouquet of yellow roses and calla lilies.

"And I brought something else too," Ted whispered and handed her a cellophane wrapped ball of opium.

"Flowers and candy," she purred. "What more could a girl want?"

"I know you're going to be just fabulous tonight, Anna," Marta gushed.

"Lord, I hope so, but save the accolades for cocktails after the show. We'll all go out and celebrate."

Junius Flatmeat, who'd been listening in, immediately put the kibosh on that idea. "Sorry, folks, but Anna and Studs have a date at the Tratt dell'Arte at ten thirty. You can have her after that."

"Don't you think you should tell me these things, Junius?" said Anna acidly.

"Sorry. I want you to think about the play, not your schedule."

"Well," said Anna to Ted and the Applewhites, "we could all get together at the Stay Put Club later."

"We haven't been there in a while," said Gershem dubiously.

"It's where Ted and I first hooked up," Anna confided to Marta.

"Really? How romantic! We have to go."

"Let's see the show first," her husband suggested.

They were joined by Edward Smith in his Old Nate leisure suit. "Sorry about this mix-up, Ted. I just hope I can do you credit."

"Just do a little Aztec brain breathing before you go on," said deadpan Gershem. "Does wonders, I hear."

"Maybe I'll try that," Edward chuckled. "Clears the sinuses and the synapses all at once."

Bob looked at his watch and pointed out, "There's still forty minutes before the show. Why don't we go get a drink?"

So the three of them left the players to their last minute make-up and wardrobe adjustments and headed off to the local tavern just across the street from the Mason.

"Use the stage door when you come back!" Smith called after them. "And don't let anybody see you!"

Sitting at the bar in The Pearl of Erin, a garment center truck driver joint during the day, was like being instantly swirled back to the fifties when the rag trade sweat shops were actually located in the neighborhood rather than China and points east. There was a little stand of hard boiled eggs on the bar and Marta picked one up after they ordered drinks.

"I knew this guy who could balance a hardboiled egg on one end. Nobody else could. Not me anyway," she said trying and failing as the egg fell over.

"You can only do that twice a year for a few minutes on the equinoxes," said knowledgeable Ted. "It's an old barroom trick."

Bob tried it and the egg fell over again. "Humpty Dumpty had a great fall," he said.

"Why do people think that Humpty Dumpty is an egg?" Marta wanted to know. "It's not in the rhyme."

"Lewis Carroll." Said Bob. "He made Humpty Dumpty an egg in 'Alice in Wonderland',"

"There's another reason on the symbolic level," said knowledgeable Ted. "Eggs are fragile and shatter easily. So are government promoted belief systems, otherwise known as propaganda. When the propaganda fails the individual's cognitive imperative shatters and the government, 'all the King's horses and all the King's men' can't reassemble it. Another empire bites the dust."

"Right,' said Bob, "Look on my works ye mighty and despair and all that."

And with all that, Marta, who was not on the symbolic level, cracked the shell, peeled it off, and ate the hardboiled egg.

By the time they made it back to the theatre side entrance, it was almost show time and the house was packed. Our threesome commandeered folding chairs in the wings and watched Edward Smith open as Old Nate.

"God, he's such a ham!" said Marta. "You were much better than him."

"Shh," Gershem shushed her.

When Anna came on, the audience came alive. You could actually feel the electricity as she put everything she had into her performance. No one knew whether to cheer or laugh. Anna's Ayn was so imposing it was impossible to react with anything but awe.

"She's fantastic!" Marta had to squelch her squeal.

The show was well on its way to theatre transcendence and everyone could feel it. They were there! It was like watching Sarah Bernhardt commandeer the stage in a performance for the ages! It was like being present at the Resurrection! Or when Moses parted the Red Sea! It was epic!

And then Arthur Sachs made his presence known. In the short scene where Nate and Patrecia are making out in the Objectivist office, Alan Greenspan catches them in the act and blandly informs:

"Well, hello there, you two. I understand that Ayn has reinstated Leonard."

"That's wonderful, Alan, just wonderful," Studs responded.

"I also heard that you and Ayn got in a tiff. Is everything all right?"

"I don't really think that's any of your business, Alan."

"Well, let's make it my business, Studs."

Zenith didn't quite know what to do. The Studs thing worked with the action. "It's Nate, Alan, Nate."

"Who do you think you're kidding?" Sachs snorted as he emerged in all his resentful, incoherent glory like a butterfly from his cocoon. He turned to the audience and began to strut back and forth across the stage. "In case you don't know already, this whole thing is a sham! That's right! A sham!" He pointed at Zenith. "He's not even an actor. He's TV weatherman Studs Zenith! I, however, am the real deal! You probably caught my act playing good neighbor Eugene Braddock in the Hook's Roost school shooting today! Now that was acting! I think I did a damn good job of it too, a damn good job! But do I get any credit? No! I don't get shit! I get bupkis! Nada!" He wrung his hands and looked on the verge of tears.

Edward Smith watched in horror from his chair at the side of the stage, too surprised to immediately intervene. It was Sylvia who had to rush out and try to corral Sachs.

"Look who it is!" Arthur brayed. "The Hook's Roost network lady!"

Sylvia immediately froze, turned to Edward, and hissed, "Do something!" Then she quickly disappeared back into the wings. But Junius was way ahead of her. He'd already ordered security to grab

Sachs and get him off stage.

"Get away from me, you goons!" Arthur wailed as two burly guards grabbed him and frog-marched him out of view. "You have no right! This is America! Ooof!" Then there silence.

Thinking as fast as he could under the circumstances, Edward took his spot in the limelight and explained. "I am truly, truly sorry for this unfortunate interruption but Eugene just hasn't been himself today and I really can't blame him. In fact, I'm amazed he's here at all tonight. You see, Eugene lives in Hook's Roost and he was there today for the whole horrible thing. All our sympathies are with him and I'm sure he'd want us to carry on…"

But the magic moment had passed in a blur and from the stage, Smith could make out the audience storming the exits in flight from this debased and humiliating exhibition of degradation and despair.

"Come back!" Smith bawled after them. "The show's not over!"

But it was. Smith rushed backstage to beat Arthur Sachs to death but he'd already been escorted from the theatre by Flatmeat's thugs and turned over to none other than Calvin Card.

Diva Anna was as livid with rage as Smith and had to be taken in hand by Gershem and the Applewhites.

"How could he?! How could he?!" she seethed. "With only a few minutes to go! He didn't even have the decency to let me take a curtain call!"

"It's going to be all right," Marta soothed. "I thought you were fabulous."

"Don't you see?' said Anna despondently. "That's just it! I gave the performance of my life! For nothing! Nothing!"

"Hey, put a cork in it," irritable Studs Zenith horned in. "How do you think I feel? I was doing a pretty good job myself."

"Oh, please," said Anna scornfully. "I was blowing you off the stage and you know it!"

"Hey there!" he shot right back. "I'm Studs Zenith, I'm the reason the place was packed."

"Would you two shut up!" Sylvia came very close to screeching. "Don't you see what's going on?! The only audience we're going to have from now on is people buying tickets to a freak show!"

"Well, that's so bad about that?" Gershem put in his two cents.

"Look how popular all those Real Housewives shows are."

"What on earth..?!" Anna's claws came out.

"I didn't mean it like that," Ted quickly retreated. "All I meant is a packed house is a packed house."

Of course, he was right, but being right wasn't necessarily being as realistic as a real housewife. The powers-that-be at Retalitron would not take kindly to this kind of publicity and Sachs had violated his confidentiality agreement for which there was a price. Not to go into all the grisly details, but he was not seen again until the Happy Shadow, who had made it his business to find out what Calvin Card had done with Arthur, staged a one man raid on the private prison where the poor man had been confined and set an addled, amnesiac, torture victim free to tell the world- nothing. But that was months away and this was now. Card called Smith and told him the show was cancelled. Junius Flatmeat got all apoplectic when he heard this most unwelcome news and immediately sued for breach of contract. Retalitron would respond to the problem by making Smith sign over permission for Junius to produce "Ayn and Nate" himself with a whole new cast, something he would never get around to.

❖

38

The next abnormal psychology graduate seminar was a rather stilted affair. There was a tension in the air that Akisha Lumumba and David Kogan could feel without having a clue where it originated. They were not kept in the dark for long.

"Professor Gershem," Rhoda Memberman jumped right in. "I just wanted you to know how much I enjoyed your performance downtown."

"You went to the show?" incredulous Gershem asked her.

"My boyfriend and I…"

She was immediately set upon by Kogan. "Are you trying to prove you have a boyfriend again? What are you talking about?"

"I was in a play, a minor part – "Gershem started to explain.

"Not that thing that police raided," Kogan guessed correctly.

"Well, it wasn't exactly a raid. A few members of the audience got unruly and the police had to intervene."

"Professor Gershem got hit by a tomato," Rhoda helpfully volunteered.

"Cool," said Kogan. "What was the play about?"

"Ayn Rand."

"You're into Ayn Rand?" said startled Akisha. "Me too. She was all about sticking it to the man."

"She'd have put you in a concentration camp," said Barry.

"Look, the play is comedy," said Gershem. "And no, I'm not into Ayn Rand. What I do outside of this classroom is my own business and that's not what we're here to discuss."

Quite unexpectedly, Rino Matsui piped up and countered, "But Ayn Rand fits right into both conspiracy theory and the concept of good and evil."

"Have you ever read Ayn Rand?" Gershem asked. "I haven't. Has anyone here?"

There was an awkward silence.

"Yeah, but everyone knows what she stood for – elitism, libertarian economics, atheism," said Kogan.

"She was a Jew," said Rhoda.

"So are you," Kogan retorted. "I haven't seen you at synagogue lately but that's probably because I'm not there either. So why did these people disrupt the show?" he asked Gershem.

"I think they thought we were showing a certain lack of respect for Rand."

"Were you?"

"The show is satire. It makes fun of a couple things you just mentioned – elitism and laissez faire capitalism. I don't think it's offensive enough to get violent about. But these Ayn Rand people are like a cult. She's a god to them."

"So they are religious," said Kogan. "They just replaced God with Ayn Rand."

"At least she's a woman," said Rhoda. "I guess that's some sort of progress."

"I think we're going off the tracks here," said Gershem. "If you want to talk about conspiracy and the good and evil thing, these people did indeed conspire to attack something they thought was evil, namely me and the rest of the cast."

"That's so cool," said Akisha. "You're a star. I want your autograph. I want to see the show."

"I'm afraid it's been cancelled," said Gershem. "Insurance reasons."

"But that's caving in to mob censorship," said Breen.

"Not my call. What say we move on to something we do know about. Like reptile people."

Even Akisha had to laugh.

Things did not go so smoothly at home. Having received two death threats on her home answering machine, Anna was torn between fear and righteous indignation.

"Well, at least they don't know you're staying here," Ted pointed out.

"I don't care what they know. I'm not afraid of them." This proclamation was not entirely convincing.

"Maybe it's a good thing the show closed."

"How can you say that?" she sputtered. "This was my opportunity, my opportunity of a lifetime. I can't pretend I don't care like you." There were tears in her eyes and Gershem took her in his arms.

"Everything's going to be alright," he soothed.

"We should have worn our tin hats more," she sobbed. "We let in too many bad rays."

This novel appraisal of their misfortune piqued Gershem's curiosity.

"Well, then all we have to do is put them back on. What say

we take a drive upstate and wear our tin hats for two weeks straight."

"You're making fun of me," she snarfled.

"I'm not. Marta invited us up. We can go anytime we want."

She stopped puling. "Well, that sounds nice. We should go."

What went unspoken was the easy access to a certain favored substance where an imperceptible dependence was creeping into the picture, at least if they chose to ignore it, which they did.

"Let's. I'd like to be out of town when this whole Retalitron business blows up in Edward Smith's face," said Gershem.

But that was not to be. Both the theatre fiasco and Hook's Roost were completely forgotten that very afternoon, replaced by a new, much sexier story. Ted and Anna were driving up to the Catskills in his old Volvo when North Korea accidentally blew off the top of a mountain with an underground nuclear blast, releasing a radioactive cloud that made Fukushima look like small potatoes. That, however, did not stop a state trooper from pulling them over on the thruway.

He approached the driver's side window with his hand on his holstered Glock and demanded to know, "What's with the hats?"

Anna had every right to be indignant. "That's what you pulled us over for?"

"If you were me, wouldn't you?" said the trooper as if that settled it. "They're too reflective. You don't want to blind oncoming traffic, do you?"

"I guess you have a point, officer," Ted agreed and took off his hat. Anna quickly followed suit. "Is that all, officer?"

"That's it. Have a nice day," said the trooper and off they went. Ted hummed "It's Only Make Believe" until Anna told him to shut up and they only put their tin hats back on when they turned into the Applewhite's driveway where the lady of the house was pulling weeds. As soon as she saw them she hurried back inside and emerged in her very own tin hat.

"Welcome!" she squealed, embracing Anna then clamping onto Ted and not letting go. "Look what Bobby had made for me by the air conditioner guy down the road!" The two dogs shimmied and leaped around the new arrivals with unbounded enthusiasm.

"Marta, let go of me," Gershem said firmly.

She did so instantly. "Oh, right. Not in front of Anna, What was I thinking?"

Bob, also sporting a tin hat, came out of the house with his shotgun and joined them. "Well, hello there, you two. Glad you could make it. Marta's got the guest room all fixed up and" – he looked at his watch - "it's Happy Hour! What can I get you?"

"What are you doing with that gun?" Anna wanted to know.

"Demonstrating my rights under the Second Amendment," said Bob. "Just kidding, but you never know when you'll run into a gang of raccoons. And these chickenshit dogs are useless. So what'll it be? Wine, beer, whiskey?"

Rino and Barry had one last appointment they'd set up with YouTube vlog host Wolodymyr Piatkowski who provided a platform for exponents of just about any conspiracy theory you could think of. Claiming to be a neutral open forum, his show had been denounced as a CIA front, a Blood and Soil launching pad, a coded pedophile meet-up site, and a veritable herpetarium of secret Reptilians. These aspersions were probably the result of his striking resemblance to Peter Lorre as Mr. Moto with his accent and round glasses and he didn't seem to mind puckishly denying all these damning allegations with a knowing wink. Rino and Barry had agreed to meet him at the very same Russian restaurant in the twenties favored by the Happy Shadow and they were there promptly at six. Piatkowski was not hard to spot.

"Ah," he looked up from his borscht, "you must be the two students," His accent wasn't immediately identifiable but it seemed to be more Jersey mook than Slavic growl. "Please, have a seat."

They thanked him and sat down.

"You're probably wondering why I even agreed to meet with you," he said. "I'm a busy man and I don't usually give interviews but I was curious. Tell me something, Miss Matsui; is it true that Far Eastern women…?

"You creep!" Rino huffed and stood up.

"I'm sorry," Piatkowski apologized. "What did I say? I was going to ask you about passive aggression, but I can see that's not true. Please, I meant no offense. I've been misinformed. Perhaps you should ask the questions."

Ruffled Rino sat back down and Barry agreed that was probably a good idea.

"Fine," said Piatkowski. "But there's one more thing you should know. I know everything about you. I know even more about your professor. I know all about the Spuyten Duyvil Trust. Just so you know."

Barry immediately sensed they were on to something and pressed Piatkowski. "You seem to know a lot more than we do. What else?"

"I hope you have some time. This might take longer than you thought. I recommend the tea and *piroshki*s. Settles the stomach and the mind."

They ordered and got down to business.

"What is the Spuyten Duyvil Trust?" Barry asked.

"It's a deep state front. They give money to everybody. Even me."

"Why you?"

"Ask them."

"You just said you knew all about the Spuyten Duyvil Trust. Why don't you just tell us?"

"I'm sorry. If I sound paranoid, it's because I am. Sometimes I think that everyone is after me and sometimes I think I'm right about that. But you really are a couple of whizzed out college students. I know that. I checked you out. But the people you've seen so far - and this is probably only a partial list - read like a who's who of the alternative reality set."

"That's our course assignment, Mr. Piatkowski" annoyed Rino pointed out.

"Assignment. That's an interesting word. So many different connotations. Like appointment. Have you ever read 'Appointment in Samarra'? John O'Hara? A contemporary of Ayn Rand. Are you beginning to see the picture now?"

Breen shot a glance at Rino, which translated into, "Okay, he's nuts, but aren't they all?"

"No, I'm sorry, I haven't read it," Rino admitted to Piatkowski.

"I can see that. A whole generation of illiterates. You're probably really working for an MBA or something. Pathetic."

"No, I'm not working for an MBA," said Rino. "Tell us about

'Appointment in Samarra'."

"Well, Samarra's in Iraq. Does that ring a bell? Iraq? So Death was stalking this Iraqi and the Iraqi found out. So he fled to Samarra. When a friend of Death asked him if they were all getting together to play cards that evening, Death begged off, "No, I'm sorry I'd love to be there, but I have an appointment in Samarra."

The college students were completely befuddled.

"Don't you see? The Iraq is Saddam Hussein. And John O'Hara wrote that ninety years before it actually happened."

The *piroshki* arrived with hot tea in glasses. The waitress, who apparently did not speak English, held up a jar of raspberry jam and asked them a question in Russian.

"She wants to know if you want jelly in your tea. Just say yes," which they did.

"Okay," said Barry, "how could John O'Hara have known about Saddam Hussein?"

"That's the question, isn't it?" said Piatkowski, a bit triumphantly. "But he did. That's obvious."

Here we go again, thought Barry. Why did all these conspiracy freaks think their theories were "obvious"? "I think we're getting a little off track," he said. "Tell us more about the Spuyten Duyvil Trust."

"Okay. Do you even know what Spuyten Duyvil means?" Piatkowski challenged him. "It means the spouting devil or, as some more pornographically minded linguists have suggested, the spurting devil. What do you think of that? Puts a whole new perspective on things, doesn't it?"

Rino tried to intervene. "Mr. Piatkowski, we contacted you because we understood your show featured a lot of conspiracy theories…"

"Stop right there. Those words are meaningless. That is, they approach meaning zero. That's Wittgenstein for you. Right to the point. The official 9/11 report is a conspiracy theory, but anyone who points that out is called a conspiracy theorist. How weird is that? I prefer the description alternative points of view."

"Like alternative facts," Breen all but scoffed.

"There is no such thing as an alternative fact. There are only facts and nonsense. You have to sift out the nonsense in order to glean the facts."

"I'm sorry," said Rino. "Glean?"

"Separate the wheat from the chaff. That's what gleaners did back in the old days when people still ate gluten. There's a famous painting by Millet. Poor devils."

"So you think devils have something to do with gleaning?" Barry pounced.

Piatkowski was astonished by the question. "What are you? A complete idiot? You should quit school and get out in the world. Or maybe you think spouting devils have something to do with harvesting wheat."

Rino, who had started this whole brouhaha and knew it, quickly stepped in. "I don't think we're here to talk about wheat, are we?"

"No we're not," Piatkowski backed off. "Have you ever heard of the Uptown Manhattan Illuminati? Not the Downtown Manhattan Illuminati. That's your professor's gang. The uptown branch. Everybody who's anybody."

Rino looked at Barry who shrugged his shoulders.

"Well, if you're doing conspiracy research, I can see you've been distracted. Probably by each other I'm guessing. This whole academic thing is just an excuse for you two to get together and go at it like rutting beasts, isn't it? Hot and heavy! Sperm and pussy juice flying all over the place! Am I right?"

"Look, Mr. Piatkowski…" Breen started out angrily.

The talk show host held up his hand. "I didn't mean anything personal. It's just that all you young people can think of is sex, sex, sex. When you get to be my age, you'll worry about taking a shit. That's assuming you live that long."

"Okay, right," said Barry. "Now what about this uptown whatever it is?"

"So, I have to do all the work for you? Some researchers you are," Piatkowski discounted them. "The Uptowners, as I call them, are the swells, the ones in charge. For them the whole world is just a playground to pull practical jokes. The whole thing is just a rich man's trick. You see?"

Barry and Rino did not see, not exactly, but they kept quiet.

"Let me give you an example," Piatkowski continued. "The International Space Station. You probably think the ISS is up there in the sky. Actually, it's in Los Angeles and Russia, Los Angeles for the interiors and Russia for the so-called space walks. Boy, do they have a lot of fun with that one. All they need is a crummy set, a swimming pool and a green screen. The cash rolls in like a never ending tsunami. What television series did you ever see that made billions of dollars? And they don't even worry about ratings. They don't care if nobody watches at all. That's the artistry of the thing. Art for art's sake. Complete freedom from all the corrosive pressures of the Philistine market. How I envy them," said Piatkowski dreamily, then snapped back to attention. 'I'm sorry, my mind tends to wander sometimes."

"Okay," said Barry, "just for the sake of argument we assume the space station is fake. What's that got to do with the Uptowners?"

"How dense can you get?" Piatkowski scolded. "It's their concept! It's their great work of fiction, their very own Star Wars franchise. Don't you see? Instead of paying Harrison Ford twenty million dollars, they pay some nobody ten thousand and pocket the difference. And even that's chicken feed. It's pure genius. Everyone thinks these people sit around in their private clubs playing three dimensional chess all day. Nonsense. They're out playing in the backyard, which for them is the whole world. They're more like bored children than insidious connivers. I just wish they'd let me play with them. I've got all sorts of good ideas. Great ideas. Especially for wars and disasters, but they just shut me out. These people are so cliquish. But this is all on my TED talks, which I assume you've seen."

With all this food for thought, Rino and Barry were fresh out of questions, but Piatkowski was by no means finished with his answers. Not by a long shot. He rambled on for the better part of an hour, like a free associating learning machine going off on tangent after tangent, until a flow chart of the whole mess would have resembled the fevered doodling of a methamphetamine freak. When the two researchers finally cut him off, he continued to jabber even as they got up and left.

"Did you get all that?" Barry asked Rino.

"Every word," she assured him and they both cracked up.

"How did you find out about this guy?" Barry asked her.

"I didn't. He called me up."

They looked at each other and stopped laughing.

"Well, people do talk," said Rino.

Edward Smith was in no laughing mood either. He'd just got off the phone with Calvin Card who had made things more than clear.

"Listen, Edward, I just want you to remember that you're the one who brought all those poor dead children to Hook's Roost. Wouldn't look good at all if that were revealed, would it?"

"Are you threatening me? Those dead children aren't dead and what are you going to do if that comes out? Blame me? Are you trying to make me out as some kind of child molester?"

"Take it anyway you want it. By the way, the bonus for the job, which is very substantial, will be paid through a GoFundMe account that we've established. I don't think you'll be disappointed."

"How about the play? Is Junius really going to produce it?"

"Probably not, but then what do you have against Ayn Rand anyway? I used to watch my sister masturbate when she read 'The Fountainhead'. Very juicy."

"And you're trying to set me up as the pervert. Go fuck yourself, Calvin."

"Hey, relax, let bygones be bygones. There's plenty more steady work for you and plenty more Retalitron cash just waiting to be transferred to your account. Take my advice and play ball, Edward."

Sylvia was less concerned about shutting down the play than her husband was. Actually, there was a part of her reveling, almost gloating in the demotion of Anna Bunch from up and coming star to yesterday's news, though she kept this spiteful glee well hidden behind the façade of a concern troll.

"Oh, poor Edward," she consoled him. "I know how much this play meant to you but at least you'll have steady work as a casting director now. And you won't have to be bothered with the press or Tootie Wookums."

"I win the booby prize and you think I should just suck it up," he said bitterly.

"You said it yourself. We have no choice. We're just as much victims as those poor nonexistent school children,"

"Are you joking? We're real. Not someone's sick fantasy. We're the ones who really died."

"But don't you feel privileged to be on the inside. We've been on the outside for so long. Maybe this was just your initiation into the Uptown Illuminati, a sort of ritual hazing. They want to see if you can take a little humiliation. I understand it. I humiliate people all the time." She looked at her watch. "Which reminds me I have a session with that detective who let you off for beating up Tootie Wookums. I'm certainly not going to let him off. Would you like to film it?"

"Oh, why not? Actually it would be my pleasure."

After he broke Arthur Sachs out of the shady sanitarium where he was being tortured, the Happy Shadow decided to join Ted and Anna in the country, and then move in with the Applewhites for good. Nobody noticed him, of course, and he now fucks Marta all the time, which she seems to very much enjoy. She attributes that thrilling tingle in her loins to her tantric yoga exercise program.

When Ted and Anna got back to the city, Professor Gershem gave all the seminar students A's and they were relieved of their research duties which would be taken up by the next batch of grad students. Edward called up Anna and asked if she and Ted would like to do a Carnival Cruise to Nowhere hijacking by Al Qaeda, but she begged off. The truth was the happy couple didn't want to be separated from their opium supply, a bad habit which would catch up with them sometime in the future. But this was now and now was sublime enough to set Gershem humming, "It's a Wonderful World."

❖ ❖

THE AUTHOR
As an admirer of Marcel Proust,
Kevin Bartelme has spent the last few
years in a cork lined room fasting and meditating
on his numerous previous sins which, if revealed,
would fill another book or two.

The author, somewhere south of the border taking a break.

THE TIN HAT